The Carnforth Double

The Fourth Catrin Sayer Mystery

ALLAN JONES

ISBN: 978-1-9993813-1-8

Cover: The Petronas Towers, Kuala Lumpur (author photograph)

THE CATRIN SAYER MYSTERIES

The Chinese Sailor
The Scottish Colourist
The Falmouth Model
The Carnforth Double
The Powys Deacon
The Stratford Hunter

This book is a Kindle Direct Publishing paperback.
The series is also available as e-books from
Amazon Kindle eBooks and other suppliers.

CONTENTS

From Book 3 (The Falmouth Model)

Prologue 1

PART 1: AFTERMATH

1 Mrs. Rosalind Heaton 5

2 Kuala Lumpur 9

3 Emma 18

4 Triad 21

5 Rome 30

6 Guanxi 36

7 Spitalfields 47

8 The Houghton Bank 56

9 Hodson 65

10 Herrington 69

11 Pralla 75

PART 2: SET-UP

12 Mrs. Rosalind Heaton 82

13 Assignments 85

14 The Queen of Heaven 96

15 Hong Kong 109

16 Borghese 114

17 Persuasion 118

18 Proposal 123

19 The White Moon 129

20 Sophie 136

21 Covent Garden 143

PART 3: TRAP

22 Cronin 152

23 Hamlet 161

24 Pentimento 170

25 Tracking 179

26 Bloomsbury 186

27 Interview 193

28 Better late than … 198

29 Denial 205

30 Dartmouth 213

31 The Light of the World 223

32 Malta 229

33 Arrests 232

34	Mrs. Rosalind Heaton	242
35	Decision	245
36	Brixton	256
37	The Heavens	272
38	Transition	281
39	Valetta	287
	Epilogue	298
	Notes	311
	About the author	313
	The Powys Deacon (excerpt)	315

Pentimento. A pentimento (plural pentimenti) is an alteration in a painting, evidenced by traces of previous work, showing that the artist has changed his or her mind as to the composition during the process of painting. The word is Italian for repentance (Wikipaedia).

'I must never cause harm or bring trouble to my sworn brothers or Incense Master. If I do so I will be killed by myriads of swords.'

One of the thirty-six oaths of membership of triad groups.

The Carnforth Double

FROM BOOK THREE (THE FALMOUTH MODEL)

Catrin heard the first shot and saw the red hole appear in Sergeant Farra's left shoulder, through the scapula; a deep red stain appearing on the back of his suit jacket. She noticed uncomprehendingly both bone fragments and blood spurting from the exit wound, some hitting the vehicle. She threw open her door instinctively and got out herself, crouching down behind both the door and the man. She said later that it was a fear of being trapped in the vehicle as the gunman approached, claiming she had not thought about how she could aid Farra at that moment.

The Malaysian officer spun round, his service weapon in hand, as the second bullet hit him somewhere in the back. She heard it hit. Looking at Catrin, he passed over the Sig Sauer automatic, holding it out to her crouched body as if he were offering pennies to a street beggar. He said nothing but his eyes were clearly indicating she needed to use it.

The windshield shattered near the driver and Catrin heard Turner-Jones scream, "Oh my God…"

She didn't think about it or hesitate. Somehow the training from the firearms course at Milton years ago automatically kicked in, the way it was meant to. She stood upright, took one step to the side, arms outstretched with the left hand supporting the gun hand. As she moved from behind Farra's bodyline into view of the assailant the policeman crumpled; his legs folded beneath him.

Catrin saw the young Chinese man, his gun pointed one-handed and aimed slightly to the left, towards Constable Ashland still at the wheel. He immediately saw Catrin and swung his arm back towards her, but he was too late. She had fired twice rapidly, hitting his body in the stomach and lower chest. His gun arm stayed up and she automatically fired two more rounds, adjusting her aim slightly higher. These shots hit as well, both in the centre upper chest. He went down face forward, his momentum proving greater than any arresting impact of the bullets.

Catrin kept the gun trained on him as he fell. She heard car tires squeal and caught in her peripheral vision a glance of the Mercedes leaving, but her eyes were locked on the man prone on the ground. His left leg moved, shook once; then he was still.

PROLOGUE

Essendon, Hertfordshire.

Two cars, a BMW Tourer and a smaller Audi, drew up at the house on the country road, switching off their lights and engines in unison. Four men dressed in black and wearing balaclava-type masks and gloves exited quietly leaving the driver of the BMW to keep watch. They moved quickly to the front door and entered the home. The watcher stayed on alert; there were no neighbours nearby but there were other homes along this stretch of road.

By the time the family sleeping inside realised there were noises of movement in the house, bedroom lights were being switched on and they were being manhandled forcefully downstairs. Once they were sufficiently awake it was made clear what was happening; the man would dress in his work uniform and accompany some of the intruders. The woman and daughter would wait here with two of the men.

It was the leader's voice which conveyed the menace, even though he was speaking quietly, precisely. Any problems from the man; his family would pay the price. Any problems from the wife and daughter, he would similarly do so, even if he co-operated with them fully. The family's eyes were on the FNP-9 handgun he had placed on the table, emphasizing his point. They saw that two other intruders were also armed. The wife and daughter had never seen a real weapon like this before; the sight of it was as chilling as the man's voice in their ears.

They understood the price being referred to; their survival as a family, their survival individually.

The leader finished with, "It's now 1.10 a.m. Do as we say and by 5.00 a.m. you will be a family again; if you don't, then some of you will be picking up the pieces. Your lives will never be the same again."

The leader had little understanding how, following their invasion and threats, the family's life would never be quite the same again anyway.

After a drive in the BMW into London, mainly in silence and in darkness for the kidnapped man, the wrap-around opaque glasses were removed from his eyes and he realised where he was. He assumed he would be taken here, to the bank where he worked.

He was led over to insert an access code at a panel beside a door. Once inside he similarly disarmed the entry alarm and several sets of wall sensors. Someone had inside information, he knew. He was one of only three people who carried in his head all the current codes needed by this gang. Others at the bank would need access to a physical log book kept in a safe to get these codes.

He had been told on the journey into London that afterwards he would be taken somewhere, locked in and left alone with his own mobile phone. He had his doubts, his terrors really, about that promise now that these men had what they wanted.

At 4.55 a.m. precisely, they said, he was to text a message to a telephone number now entered into his mobile by one of his captors; a three letter code that needed to be sent. They made him repeat it several times. At 5.00 a.m. exactly he could use his mobile to call his wife on their home phone, not before. No other contact with anyone, no deviation from that plan, would be tolerated.

He watched as the men removed three paintings from the walls of the rooms, three specifically selected from around a dozen potentially available. Then he was hustled downstairs and out to the BMW again, the glasses replaced, taking him back into darkness.

He had worked here a long time and knew the paintings being stolen by name. Two were near-priceless works by the artist George Stubbs; paintings of horses. 'Mr. Frederic Allenby of Hythe, mounted,' was the larger; 'Senator II', a black thoroughbred, was the second.

The third painting they removed had been acquired only recently by his employers. Mrs. Woodley had told him it was called 'Mrs. Rosalind Heaton of Carnforth', painted by an artist he hadn't heard of, a man called Hamlet Winstanley. Despite his plight, the man wondered why they had chosen this one rather than other, more famous works that were there for the taking.

PART 1

AFTERMATH

1 MRS. ROSALIND EATON

Carnforth, Lancashire, 1742.

Rosalind Heaton looked carefully at her husband John dressed in his best black suit normally reserved for Sunday, taking in his discomfort and foot-dragging. Their oldest daughter, Sarah, was standing to one side of the doorway marshalling the smaller children to admire their parents in their fine attire before departure. In a moment they would leave for the short ride from Longfield Farm into Carnforth. It was fine weather, but it would not do to walk and get dusty or muddy today.

"We had better be moving, John, my dear," Rosalind said, more as a suggestion than anything stronger, something that might inflame her husband into contrariness. He was still uneasy with the decision; moreso now its implementation was imminent.

She added, "Our appointment is on Mr. Winstanley's last day here. We cannot afford to miss it or be late for the session. He is doing the drawing with the Moore's daughter this afternoon, Mrs. Moore told me after the bible group meeting on Tuesday afternoon."

John Heaton had heard this point several times this week.

"Mrs. Heaton, I would rather buy a new plough or give the

money to the church than pay to have my face recorded in paint; you know that."

She knew this issue was coming to a head. His formality with her was an indicator of the impasse they had reached. Each time they had discussed having their portraits painted in the manner of the gentry he had objected; the man of the house had made his decision.

Last month she had caught him in a good mood when the annual visit of the artist Hamlet Winstanley to the Carnforth area was announced, a Warrington man made good. Hamlet was wealthy, based further south in his home town, but he was also a London-trained portrait artist with business ties and friendships within the aristocracy. Here he was in Carnforth for two days, offering his fine artistic services to all. With his two apprentices, he would be staying and receiving clients at the 'Crossed Keys', it had been announced by his agent. Mr. Winstanley would then move on a little north, for a two-week visit to the Strickland estate at Sizergh Castle, where he would draw and paint the family and guests.

"A fine opportunity for the good people of Carnforth to have portraits as handsome as those that will adorn the walls of the castle itself," the agent had said, checking the eyes to see who would be interested enough to enquire about the price.

Today was the fruit of that discussion with the agent, at which John Heaton had relented.

Rosalind said, "John, we have been through it too many times. It is settled. We agreed."

She knew he was a man who did not go back on his word, and he had made the firm booking with the agent. She looked at him again, taking the measure of her husband then adding reinforcement to her argument.

"The donation to the new altar screen three years ago; we gave twice that of either the Lees or the Crankshaws. It was praised for a day at the time but what now? It is forgotten. Why, even Reverend Aspinall had his portrait painted last year during Mr. Winstanley's visit.

"It's not the portraits, John, although they will be nice to look at and show to people. It is that we are having the portraits painted. It says something. Longfield Farm is prosperous and well managed, it says. We are a good, hard-working family with taste, it says. It is about us in this community; our standing. We have Sarah to think of."

Their oldest daughter would, in a couple of years, be of marriageable age. Rosalind was looking ahead, thinking of families she knew, social circles she would like to be part of that would perhaps lead to a suitor.

John softened his response.

"I have no problem with your portrait being painted, Rosalind. It will be a pleasure to give it to you and to enjoy it. But my own; I am uneasy with it. You know that."

Sarah watched her parents bicker gently all the way to the two-wheeler. She had brushed off its seat herself, to help keep their clothes clean. Their voices carried more faintly as they set off down the path, still on the same topic.

She knew that in the end they would both get their way; mother would be painted, father would not. She was not sure when this would happen, though. She had heard from other girls she knew that their parents had booked sittings with Mr. Winstanley, some yesterday, some today. She was not sure how long it took an artist to do a portrait drawing but the thought of the lambing season crossed her mind; each year there was the wait and then everything seemed to happen at the same time. She thought it would be like that, somehow.

Two months later, when the family gathered around to examine the painting delivered from Warrington by Mr. Greenhalgh, the haulier, they were all truly impressed. Rosalind Heaton's portrait showed her looking confident, serene; a woman at ease with her role in life. The artist had caught her expression well, Sarah thought.

She came to the conclusion that it didn't take that long to

do a first drawing for an oil painting, after all, if you were an artist of the calibre of Mr. Hamlet Winstanley. The girl secretly hoped that next year, if a portrait painter visited the area, she might also be painted in this manner.

2 KUALA LUMPUR

As Catrin awoke she saw the pale, blue-white columns of light outside the hotel room window. Then she remembered her decision not to close the blind before climbing exhausted into bed. As her eyes focused, the intricacy of the illuminated structure of the Petronas Twin Towers was revealed and she realised that her waking thought, that she was still at the hospital, was part of her dream. She was actually back at the Hilton Doubletree hotel in Ampang, but not in the room she had stayed in last night, the night of her arrival in the city.

The light of the desk lamp in the adjoining living room was the only internal illumination. Both rooms were bathed in the low light of the towers, occasionally tinted with the colours from neon signs on neighbouring buildings. Through her bedroom doorway she could see Li's profile; her friend was in a hotel robe sitting in an easy chair by the window, sipping tea and looking out at the view.

She lay still a moment, thinking. Two days ago I was flying here hoping Madeleine Turner-Jones wouldn't bore me to tears on the long flight and wanting to see Li, have some holiday, then go home and see Chris. And now this fiasco; yesterday I killed a man. It happened, but I can't believe that I actually ended the life of another human being. But I did, I had to.

On the previous day, the Twin Towers had been the scene of bloodshed and death, not spectacle. Sergeant Jared Farra and Constable Jamilah Ashland, the driver, both with the Royal Malaysian Police, had turned up at the Doubletree Hotel to collect Detective Sergeant Catrin Sayer and her colleague, Madeleine Turner-Jones, from the Foreign & Commonwealth Office.

Turner-Jones was an older, officious bureaucrat. Catrin had been asked to accompany the woman to Kuala Lumpur, to make her own three-minute speech on the police role in the recovery of a stolen ceremonial knife and a painting. The hand-over ceremony of the kris, the knife, had taken place at the National Museum. The items belonged to the family of a Malaysian dignitary, the Datuk Jerome Allam, and they had been stolen during the era of British colonial rule in what was then called Malaya. Ironically, it was a case in which Catrin had only peripheral involvement.

That ceremony had taken place on Thursday afternoon; it was now the early hours of Saturday morning. The Friday morning rendezvous with Farra and Ashland was meant to be an informal sight-seeing tour provided by the Royal Malaysian Police; an impromptu arrangement after the more formal events of the previous day.

The tour had ended as soon as it began after a chance encounter with three men at the Towers, where one sent another to shoot Sergeant Farra. After the Malaysian officer had been wounded, Catrin had drawn on training received earlier in her career, taking up Farra's weapon to shoot and kill the assailant. She had then gone into shock and had been taken to hospital where she was monitored for several hours.

As she looked out of the bedroom window she thought about the incident; that it happened only yards away, at the base of the towers over there. Catrin's original plans for the remainder of Friday and the weekend had been to meet up with Jian Li who had flown in that morning from Hong Kong. The friends were going to be tourists for a weekend, a plan now completely out of the question, Catrin realised.

She remembered being brought from the hospital back to the hotel in Ampang, wanting to see Li. On arrival, she had been escorted to this suite rather than the standard room she had occupied the previous night. Jian Li was there, waiting with a police officer. With the assistance of the Malaysian police and the hotel, Li had commandeered the suite to replace their two rooms, she said. She had also arranged for the transfer of Catrin's belongings although there didn't appear much to move; a small carry-on case and clothes for a few days.

Li had said at one point, "I suspect you planned to go shopping for more clothes here, Catrin. I am not sure we are going to get the chance to do that now."

Jian Li Yeung knew nothing of this development until she found two police officers meeting her flight on arrival at KLIA. They escorted her to the hotel, saying that her friend was currently being checked at the hospital. There had been an incident, they explained. When she asked if she could go to the hospital the request had been rejected immediately.

Detective Sergeant Sayer would be brought to the hotel 'shortly', she was told; there were security aspects to consider. She had read the faces on these officers. This was the Royal Malaysian Police she was talking to and they weren't messing around; Li wouldn't get to see Catrin at the hospital, that was clear. All she knew was that Catrin wasn't injured but had gone into shock at the incident scene. An officer of the RMP with Sergeant Sayer had been badly injured by an assailant.

She found herself delivered to the Doubletree Hotel into the company of a pleasant female police officer who was waiting for her there. She, too, was no more informative, repeating only that 'Sergeant Sayer will be brought here as soon as possible'.

At the check-in desk Li asked if her room was adjacent to Miss Sayer's.

"No," said the young woman at reception, "you are on different floors and the hotel is rather full so…"

Jian Li placed her Platinum-level Amex card on the desk and said softly, "I want a suite, now; with two bedrooms. And I want my friend's belongings moved from her current room to one of them, with a female police officer supervising their transfer."

The agent, startled, was about to say something but the RMP officer spoke quietly to her in Malay. Instead, she said, "I will get the manager of Reception."

After a conversation between that gentleman and the police officer, in which the name 'Superintendent Baksh' was mentioned, the first time Li had heard the name, it was plain sailing. The hotel bent over backwards to accommodate Li's request.

'Shortly' turned out to be four interminable hours of waiting, during which Li received a call in the hotel suite from London, from Catrin's boss; Detective Chief Inspector Jane Worsley, the head of the Art Crime Unit of Serious Crime Command, Metropolitan Police.

She learned more from Jane Worsley in five minutes than she had learned so far from the RMP and not simply for general information. Worsley wanted her help, she was told.

So Catrin found herself in a strange, sumptuous bedroom, in a king-sized bed. The suite had a living room and two bedrooms, she knew. Then she recalled it also had a bathroom about the size of the main living area in her flat in Spitalfields.

Li turned as she heard Catrin stir.

"How are you feeling?" she asked.

"Alright, Li; I slept well, other than waking up thinking I was back at the hospital. It must have been the sleeping pill. What time is it? And why aren't you asleep in your room?"

"It's just after 5.00 a.m. Would you like some water or juice, or coffee or tea? We have it all here," said Li. "I don't think I am going back to sleep."

Catrin answered, "I'd love some orange juice and then some coffee, despite it being early. My body doesn't know what time it is anyway with the jet lag. I need to get up, get myself ready at some point. We won't be going sightseeing, that's for sure."

As Li went over to the side counter with the refrigerator and refreshment centre, she said, "We both need to get ready, but not just yet. We have a meeting with Superintendent Baksh and Mrs. Turner-Jones, your colleague from the Foreign Office. Baksh spoke to Jane, I know, and I am allowed to attend, apparently. She vouched for me and asked for my inclusion. Later we leave on the overnight flight to London. It departs just before midnight."

Superintendent Baksh was the senior officer who had led the meeting two days earlier at the Royal Malaysian Police Headquarters held prior to the handover ceremony at the museum.

"We?" said Catrin.

"I will come with you. And stay a day or so in London before heading back to Hong Kong. Besides, I want to meet Chris in person, so I can see who has charmed you despite your earlier claim about him being too quiet for you."

Catrin smiled at the thought of her boyfriend. She knew already he was going to be at Heathrow Airport, travelling up from Exeter. They had met at the beginning of her last big case, in Cornwall, where he worked as a civilian computer expert with the Devon & Cornwall Police. Catrin's efforts to tell Chris that his interest in her was futile, that a long-distance relationship wasn't really practical for her, had led to them falling for each other. Logic and practicality had been thrown out the window.

She had spoken to him yesterday evening, half-explaining in broken sentences the tumultuous events of the morning. He was only worried about her, it seemed; when would she get back? Did he need to come out?

No, she had said. It wasn't necessary. She was hoping to fly home even sooner than originally planned. Then finally they agreed he would be at Heathrow to meet her on her return, no matter when that was. It made her feel warm, reassured.

After she had closed the call with Chris, Li had said to

Catrin, "And now, your mother. Break it gently for her and your dad before the media gets it wrong. Given the time zone differences, who knows what will hit the news."

Catrin had looked at her and nodded; it was for the best to break it directly and reassure her parents she was safe. They lived in Pontypridd, where Catrin had grown up. Malaysia was an exotic place for them to take in to begin with, never mind the news of an incident involving firearms.

After hearing the news and calming down, her mother told her on the call they hadn't seen anything on the television news about a shooting in Malaysia, but they were relieved to hear her voice and were happy that she was safe and uninjured. She kept on asking how Catrin was doing.

"Absorbing it all, mum; that's all I can do. There are moments when it doesn't seem real yet. I really need to sleep."

They agreed to talk tomorrow, when Catrin could get the opportunity to call again.

On Malaysian television channels and the internet, Li said afterwards, there was a reference to the gunman being killed by a 'police officer accompanying a foreign visitor'. No more details had been revealed so far, she said, the focus was on the injured police officer. Catrin hoped it would stay that way.

Within half an hour together after the calls, despite the two friends not seeing each other in person for months, Li said, "Catrin, you look really worn out; go get some sleep. We can talk tomorrow and see what we need to do then."

She needed to tell her about Worsley's call, but now wasn't the time. Her friend didn't protest, just nodded, gave Li a hug and headed into her bedroom.

~~

Li said, "But first we go to RMP headquarters and they will fill the day, keeping us secure until our flight, I gather, and in various meetings. They will be needing a formal statement from you."

"Baksh spoke to Jane Worsley?" replied Catrin. "Now why

do I get the impression that you talked with my boss also?"

Jian Li smiled. "Well, yes I did. She called me here once she knew you were in the hospital, in shock. Aina had reminded her that I was flying in and staying at the same hotel."

Aina Jinnah, the civilian administrative and file officer with the Art Crime Unit, had organized the travel arrangements for Catrin.

"And...?" asked Catrin.

"That's why I am sitting in. She wants a separate, informal report on what happened if there are any complications and she said she is not going to be satisfied with feedback either from Mrs. Turner-Jones in her 'liaison role' or some FCO lawyer based here. She said she will breathe easier when you are on your way home."

Catrin nodded. "I will too. I have no idea yet why this mess happened but it smells to me of organized crime. The Malaysian police are taking no chances; that's the reason for the security, I think. I hope there won't be an enquiry that means I have to stay. I only packed for two business days and brought some casual clothes for the two days with you."

Jian Li replied, "Speaking of which, there is a new suit in your size, cream, a nice silk material hanging in the wardrobe, courtesy of the police department. It was delivered after you went to sleep. The cream-coloured pants you were wearing yesterday for the tour are history, I gather, not even worth cleaning. The hotel tried to do something with them but…"

Her clothing and Ashland's uniform had been splattered with blood, she knew, and her pants had torn as she landed heavily.

Catrin sighed. "They were new, too. Anyway, I need the bathroom and a shower and… thank you for being here, staying with me."

She wondered how Sergeant Farra was doing in hospital. Then she thought about Mrs. Turner-Jones. The incident had been frightening for the older woman, naturally. She had wailed about peeing herself, but she didn't seem to be injured.

Catrin felt a little guilty about not thinking to call her last night once she got back from the hospital.

As she got out of bed and moved, she winced as she moved towards the bathroom.

Jian Li said, "What hurts?"

Catrin answered, "Where I landed," pointing at her rear. "I went down like a pile of bricks falling over when the shock hit. It feels like the bricks landed first and I landed on them."

Jian Li smiled. "It could be worse."

"Yes, I know," said Catrin, as she shut the bathroom door. It came to her again that she could have been in a morgue by now if the assailant had shot her first.

When she returned to the living room she drank some juice and sipped her coffee, sitting across from her friend.

"Are you sure about coming to London, Li? I mean, the cost must be a lot… and the time."

"Catrin, the cost is immaterial for me now, you know that, and… I talked to Mr. Lin. I only told him a little more than what was in the news. He is talking to my boss and I can take the time I need."

Enlai Lin was a friend of her father and co-owner of the company, LinTan Shipping, Jian Li's employer. Li was now wealthy, owning stock in the company given to her by Enlai. How wealthy Catrin didn't know, but clearly it was no problem for her to change her travel plans and fly to London instead of back to Hong Kong.

Her friend was in some ways a different person from the hesitant student she had first met in Bangor during the investigation into her brother's disappearance, but in others she was still the same woman. She worked hard, was pragmatic and plain-spoken; a solid friend, despite the large geographic distance between them.

Jian Li looked at her. "You are out of shock, I mean, is that right, you are OK?"

Catrin said, "Out of shock, yes; but still a big thing; I killed a young man. I suddenly think of… well, I am going to get flashbacks, that sort of thing. It's natural."

Li looked at her. "One, they say, who would have killed the other police officer after shooting the sergeant and probably then would have killed the rest of you."

Catrin said, "I know I had to shoot him. It doesn't make the fact that I killed someone any less of a shock. Everyone is different. When I get back I will go to see Dr. Herrington and talk it through. He helped me last time."

Herrington was a psychologist who had worked with Catrin after an incident in Glasgow two years earlier. She had arrested a man, Colin Cheney, during a robbery at a church but in the process she had been injured. The legacy of that encounter was a two-inch scar on her left cheek.

Li nodded. They needed a lighter subject.

She said, "So, let's talk about Chris; he bowled you over and I am so happy for you. But I know so little…"

Catrin smiled. "I think we just fell for each other while I was in Falmouth. I was giving him the brush-off as he lived in Cornwall and I lived in London; too big a distance I thought. I was being practical and… it just happened."

Li said, "You told me that before. I want more; I am still looking myself, remember? I want to know how you knew it was right when you changed your mind about him, when you knew…"

As dawn came to the Petronas Twin Towers, the friends sitting in a corner of the large suite talked about normal things.

3 EMMA

The cry penetrated the silence. Wendy woke up as it registered through her dreams and as her husband stirred next to her. She looked at the illuminated dial of the clock. It was nearly 4.30 a.m. on Saturday morning.

She and Des waited a moment, as sometimes it was an isolated occurrence. Then a second cry was heard, followed by sobbing.

"I'll go," she said, "you have to be on the road in less than two hours. Get more sleep."

They lived south of Hatfield. Her husband worked in central London and had a drive, a train trip and an Underground connection as part of his regular commute. But the location suited Wendy's own work and it was a smaller rural community for them to live in. Wendy had grown up in the countryside; she felt it would be impossible to live in London or the suburbs and Des endured, generally cheerfully, the long commutes. The only time he became disgruntled about it was when the season train ticket prices increased. But they got by. Apart from the nightmares now, they and their daughter were happy here.

He didn't like working on Saturdays; the trains were always less reliable, for some reason, even if they were less crowded.

But it was a shift rotation; someone from security had to be in on a Saturday, even if the bank, as such, was closed. There were always members of staff or management in, for some reason or another.

Being only partly awake, Des murmured something indecipherable and turned over. Wendy put on her dressing gown and went into Emma's room, to find her daughter now curled up, crying softly as usual.

Wendy said, "It's alright, love, I am here."

She sat on the bed, putting her arm on the young teenager's shoulder. The girl reached out, wrapping her arm across her mother's knees, saying nothing but no longer crying.

Wendy knew that in a few minutes Emma would be fast asleep again. It was always this pattern now.

At first it had been multiple occurrences each night, which was understandable. They accepted the doctor's advice about a paediatric sedative and for a month or so they had their sleep unbroken by their daughter, just by their own nightmares. Two years ago they were all in therapy; now it was just Emma. She and Des had alternated their own sedation back then as they didn't want everyone in the house drugged up overnight. Something ordinary could have occurred.

Then the psychologist recommended that they should not use sedatives with Emma on a continuing basis.

"It will cycle, get less frequent; hopefully it will just diminish and disappear in time. Save the sedatives for the deepest part of the cycles; you will get to know when those occur."

They knew indeed. But the hope that the nightmares would disappear was still that; not a vain hope, Wendy thought, but one not yet fulfilled.

Emma was appearing to nod off when she suddenly looked at her mother.

"He's still out there, isn't he?"

It was an old question; one that had been answered many times in the same way; as truthfully as possible.

"Yes, he is; somewhere. But he has no reason to come back here. And we are keeping you safe."

She smiled at her reassuringly, she hoped. Her own physical injuries had healed. There was no scarring or signs at all externally from the beating she had received.

Her daughter lay back and closed her eyes. She was asleep in seconds.

Wendy sat there a while. She always said, "We are keeping you safe," and meant it, she thought.

As a girl her father had taught her a lot about gardening and country matters, treating her maturely about them, including the control of pests and vermin. In behind a plant-pot stand in the kitchen now was a small, screw-top jar with some of her dad's old strychnine supply, now banned. It should have been handed in years ago for safe disposal. She had kept it originally in the garden shed for the mole problem but had relented on using it for that purpose. After the invasion and the bank robbery, she had filled the small jar and brought it inside. She looked after all the plants; Des and Emma wouldn't bother with it, she knew.

She wouldn't hold back on using it if that man ever came back. It would go into his tea with the sugar this time.

4 TRIAD

Catrin had called Madeleine Turner-Jones' hotel room around 7.00 a.m. to find that she had already checked out. She then saw the email from the FCO staffer on her mobile, down among a list of fresh emails she had not yet opened. When Catrin reached Madeleine on her mobile number, she learned that she was in the nearby British High Commission building. Turner-Jones had been taken there directly from the hospital yesterday evening.

"I was going to call you around now, Catrin. The RMP were particularly insistent about looking after you and, as your friend is visiting also, we felt it best not to push it and bring you into the High Commission security area."

Catrin said she understood, secretly relieved. She needed Li's company rather than that of strangers.

The diplomat asked after Catrin and said she would see her at the RMP headquarters later. She sounded back to her old self, despite the trauma yesterday.

"I will be accompanied by Roderick Gibson, a local lawyer who works for the Commission here; a good man, he knows the ropes. Look to him if you feel anything getting awkward and, of course, I will be watching out myself.

"Catrin, you did a superb job, I don't know how to thank

you, really. It seems like a dream, a bad dream. The Foreign Office will be looking out for your interests here, be assured of that."

Catrin thought it was a good description; a bad dream.

~~

The car took Catrin and Li from the Doubletree hotel directly to the Royal Malaysian Police Headquarters in Bukit Aman where they were escorted to a meeting room. Several officers Catrin had not met before and Superintendent Baksh were there. So was the British contingent from the High Commission; they were standing around, talking informally. From the layout of the belongings around the table, it appeared that some sort of pre-meeting had already taken place.

Mrs. Turner-Jones came over as Catrin entered, taking her arm and steering her away to the side for a private moment, during which Jian Li found herself being introduced to other people.

Madeleine said quietly, "Everything is fine; we have had a preliminary discussion. There will not be any problem. It's just protocol now, so you will be on the plane tonight. And thank you, thank God you knew how to fire a gun and react so well. You saved all our lives."

She squeezed her arm; that was the extent of it. She turned, leading Catrin over to meet Gibson, the High Commission lawyer, as an inspector asked people to take seats at the table and Baksh returned to what was obviously the chairman's seat.

The RMP superintendent directed his comments to Catrin after formally opening the meeting.

"I understand from Chief Inspector Worsley that Miss Yeung has been requested by the Metropolitan Police to sit in during this briefing, DS Sayer. It's unusual but we have no objection if..."

Baksh was now looking at Mrs. Turner-Jones. She was sitting beside Roderick Gibson. Catrin was flanked by Gibson on one side, Jian Li the other.

Madeleine spoke up. "No objection here. I understand Miss Yeung is an accredited lawyer in Hong Kong and we will take it that information provided here is to be treated as confidential. Miss Yeung?"

Li said, "Yes, regarding confidentiality I will treat this meeting as if Detective Sergeant Sayer were my client."

Which she wasn't but, to all intents and purpose, that was why she was present. She and Jane Worsley had talked candidly.

"I don't rate the FCO woman highly," Worsley had said, "so I am going to ask you to sit in. I would send someone out from here but it would delay things. I don't know the people in KL but I want Catrin out of there as soon as possible. If that isn't going to happen, call me directly on my mobile at the earliest moment, even if you have to break out of the meeting to do it - and no matter what time it is in London."

Baksh continued. "Then let me begin with a status update on Sergeant Farra for you. He underwent surgery yesterday; the bullet still in him after the incident was removed successfully and the haemorrhaging controlled. He is stable, but seriously injured. However we are thankful that he is alive and holding his own, due to the actions not only of Sergeant Sayer - which was crucial, of course - but those who attended him promptly. The doctors say he is likely to pull through. It is early days, but we all must hope and pray for a steady recovery.

"And the fact we don't have more tragedy on that front is, of course, entirely due to you, Sergeant Sayer. For that, too, I sincerely thank you."

Catrin nodded, blushed and looked down at the table.

He continued, "When I saw you yesterday at the hospital you asked me if there would be a formal enquiry; would you be detained here or would you need a lawyer."

Catrin looked up, turning her head towards the top of the conference table where the senior officer was seated. From her face it was clear that she had no recall of the discussion. So much of yesterday immediately after the event was a blur to her despite the clarity of recall of the attack itself.

He continued, "It was almost the first thing you asked me. I realized you were still in shock but obviously that concerned you. From a discussion I had subsequently with Assistant Commissioner Hunt, I have a little understanding about your concern."

Catrin realised that Baksh had spoken with Worsley and others at higher levels at the Metropolitan Police. Hunt had obviously given him some of the Glasgow incident background.

"Sergeant Sayer, the review of your actions is mine; right now. I can say that unequivocally and have the support of the Attorney General's office on that matter. There will be no special investigation by any police commission of the incident; this is a criminal investigation only, not a question about the conduct of any officer present. Our focus now is to pursue and arrest the man who, it appears, ordered the assailant to shoot Sergeant Farra."

He paused and smiled.

"We owe you our immense gratitude, nothing else. I reassure you that you will be on an aircraft heading home this evening."

"Thank you, sir, it is a relief to know that," said Catrin.

Li was making notes.

He continued, "We will want a formal statement. The British Foreign and Commonwealth Office is providing you with legal representation and Miss Yeung can also sit in while you give it, as requested by DCI Worsley. You will understand well that we need it for evidence purposes as we pursue the case.

"After taking your statement, I would ask you to accompany me, if you would, to visit the hospital. After yesterday, no doubt, you would rather not be back there but Sergeant Farra's family is with him now. They have asked to thank you if they get the opportunity to do so. Would that be agreeable?"

Catrin nodded, finding she could say nothing, afraid that her voice wouldn't hold steady. There were tears in her eyes and she was wondering how she was going to get through all this activity today.

"Good," said the senior officer.

Baksh looked briefly at an agenda in front of him, reviewing the list of items he wanted to cover.

"Let us move on to the next steps. First you need the background. As you said to my officer in the ambulance, 'you were in the wrong place at the wrong time'."

Catrin remembered thinking that; she hadn't realised that she had vocalised it.

"Personally and selfishly speaking - and we have had our analysts going through this overnight as part of the investigation - you were in the right place at the wrong time for all of you. Your actions saved four lives, including your own, we suspect. Certainly it saved Sergeant Farra, the primary target. There is debate in our Triad Crime Unit whether the instruction to kill would have extended to you and Mrs. Turner-Jones or not; certainly it was focused on Sergeant Farra and a shot was fired at Constable Ashland."

Catrin said, "She was extraordinarily competent and did well, sir."

He nodded, "I agree, but thank you for your comment, we will note it."

Li said, evenly, "Triad Crime Unit, Superintendent?"

Baksh looked at her, seeing that his comment had not been lost on the young lawyer from Hong Kong.

"That is what I was coming to. There were three men with the Mercedes from which the assailant emerged; a driver, an older man and the gunman that DS Sayer brought down. The older man is a known triad gang member, part of a group known as Ten Dragons. His name is Nam Wu. We have had no sighting of him for some time but he was wanted before this event. Now, you can appreciate, we want him even more.

"We believe we know the motive for the attack. This man was present several years ago during a raid in Petaling Jaya by a police team, an incident in which another triad member was killed during an exchange of gunfire. Sergeant Farra was the officer who fired that shot. We think yesterday's attack was revenge; simply opportunistic, sudden revenge.

"From Sergeant Farra's comment to Ashland then, corroborated by Mrs. Turner-Jones, he was already responding, understanding what was happening. He had checked to see if there was an exit point and saw that your vehicle was blocked in, so he got out of the car to defend himself and you also."

He looked at Turner-Jones.

"I should add that your idiomatic Malay, ma'am, is excellent and your statement has provided very useful corroboration."

He addressed the room again.

"Farra is a seasoned, experienced officer. If he had spotted the wanted man first he would have ordered Ashland to drive on and call it in, not put visitors or the public at risk. We haven't been able to talk to him, but I am sure his decision was a result of limited options."

Catrin said, "Given that the first shot hit him before he had a chance to fire, the gunman was already moving; I saw how close he was as I took a firing stance."

Superintendent Baksh nodded. "Yes, but we should take this formally in your statement.

"But it now raises a possibility of future retributive action against you in the same manner as this attack on Sergeant Farra. The man you killed, Loh Ghee, was also member of Ten Dragons and possibly a distant relative of Wu; but we are not sure of that at present. But that is the reason for the security presence around you now.

"As you know, Sergeant Sayer, the Metropolitan Police also have triad expertise as part of your organized crime response structure. We have assigned one of our own experts on this case to liaise closely with his Metropolitan Police counterparts. Assistant Commissioner Hunt will be needing to decide what to do at your end, of course.

"We are sorry that this matter involved you at all; however, as it did, we are tremendously appreciative of your courage and your actions. Better words than these will be transmitted formally from higher levels of our government to yours, of course."

Catrin thought that Mrs. Turner-Jones looked like the cat that had licked the cream.

He stopped, looked at his watch and then at a member of his team, who nodded.

"But first, ladies, we have a meeting in ten minutes with the Commissioner. He wants to thank personally DS Sayer for her actions. Afterwards we will take your formal statement. So if you want to freshen up before we head to the top floor?"

"Yes, thank you," said Catrin.

She thought, it is all this 'thanking personally stuff' that got me into this in the first place; a visit all the way here just to satisfy FCO and a Malaysian dignitary. An email would have been just fine.

~~

"The appearance of Sergeant Sayer's friend from Hong Kong seemed to help her recovery a lot overnight, Assistant Commissioner. She also seemed much relieved once her fears about an enquiry were allayed, so she looked almost back to normal when she left for the trip to the airport," said Superintendent Baksh.

"Your officer was also particularly gracious with Mrs. Farra when we visited the hospital."

He was in conversation with Assistant Commissioner Sandra Hunt of the Metropolitan Police, who was at home. It was 11 p.m. Kuala Lumpur time and tea time in London. Catrin's flight was due in to Heathrow in just over fourteen hours and Hunt had requested a personal update from Baksh once Sayer was on her way home. Her concern was not only this officer but the howl in Whitehall about Turner-Jones, still in Kuala Lumpur, 'liaising on the incident'. Hunt had her own briefings to give outside the Met.

This was the second conversation between the two senior officers. During the first discussion giving her directly the news of the incident, Baksh had asked Hunt why Sayer was so anxious about an enquiry.

"She mentioned it to me at the hospital despite being. traumatized, still in shock."

Hunt said, "DS Sayer was subject to an official enquiry into her conduct in Scotland after a violent encounter arresting a member of a drug gang, Superintendent Baksh; a review by the police watchdog there, PIRC. It was unfounded and the allegations were dismissed but she is naturally sensitive to the situation."

Baksh had responded, "Well, there won't be anything like that here; I will make sure she understands that."

In the Saturday morning meeting he had lived up to that promise.

"Sayer made her statement and we have given a copy to your High Commission. Now we are focused on apprehending the others involved."

Hunt said, "Could you send her statement to me directly? Departmental…"

Baksh said, "Of course; we will do that with a blind copy of our own incident analysis. She will most probably be recognized formally for her act. And I have instructed our triad unit to liaise with your team as we learn anything, as you requested."

Hunt wanted to wind up the discussion. She said, "We have made arrangements to meet her on arrival. Thank you for your assistance and the continued support on this matter. We very much appreciate it."

Superintendent Baksh hesitated; he was nearly complete.

"There is one other thing, a personal observation, Assistant Commissioner Hunt. I think your officer was quite distressed to have killed this man but she is a 'natural' with a weapon when under fire. When I heard that DS Sayer had only a preliminary firearms course and no regular practice I was surprised, but thankful. You know the percentages, I am sure."

"Thank you, Superintendent Baksh, I do. And I appreciate the observation. We will be in touch as this develops. Please pass on to Sergeant Farra and his family the best wishes of the Metropolitan Police for his speedy recovery and thank you for your help in expediting DS Sayer's return home after this unfortunate incident. Goodnight."

"Good afternoon, Assistant Commissioner."

Rituals observed, the two senior officers closed the call.

Sandra Hunt filed away in her mind his last remark. It was true. The accuracy rate with sidearms by police officers dropped dramatically under fire compared with on the firing range. Somehow, when the target fires back it becomes a different matter. From what Baksh had told her on the first call, Sayer's aim was spot on, and with a make of firearm with which she had no prior training or familiarisation.

Fifteen minutes later Hunt sent an email to several people, calling for a briefing session at 10.00 a.m. the following morning in her office, despite it being Sunday. Included in the list was Inspector Terry Entwistle, part of the Organized Crime Command and the most experienced Met officer on triad gang activity in the UK.

She would change her plans for tomorrow; go to early communion at St. Paul's first, she decided, instead of attending her regular morning service.

5 ROME

If Catrin Sayer was looking forward to her flight home and spending time with her boyfriend, she probably would have been dismayed to find that her next case assignment had started already; on the day she flew to Kuala Lumpur, in fact. As the Malaysian Airlines jet was leaving London heading east, an Australian in Rome was contemplating his fate. He was not too happy with the result of his deliberations.

Edmond Cox had just been returned to his cell after another meeting with his defence counsel, a man called Rimini. It was a single cell he shared only with Giovanni Berti. The prognosis for his current situation did not look good. Cox was at least fortunate in terms of his accommodation, he mused; some single cells at the notorious Regina Coeli Prison housed three prisoners these days. It was the fact that Giovanni not only spoke English, he loved to practice it. Another inmate would be driven crazy at the constant 'language lesson' aspect of their conversation.

Edmond was past self-pity about his circumstances. He had chosen to work on a break-in in Rome and had been caught with two others, red-handed. Well, at least carrying paintings and rare manuscripts from the home.

The fact that he spoke no Italian was a problem, but it also had its benefits. He was a foreigner, but there were a lot of foreigners in Regina Coeli, mainly drug trade players. Not being involved in drugs, Edmond was outside the main power structure of Mafia control groups in the place. He was a tall, strong man and he wasn't good-looking, young or a first-timer in prison; he got by.

He thoroughly disliked his lawyer and knew from the meeting that Rimini would be unable to do more than steer him through to minimal sentencing, at best. Today the man didn't seem to be too confident about being able to achieve even that. Edmond needed some leverage, something to give him hope, a sense of making progress rather than sliding down further into the Italian sewers. And the only thing he could think of to improve his situation would result in another prison sentence, but at least one that would be in the UK, not Italy.

He knew the sentencing guidelines in the UK as well as some people know their catechism. In a sense, it had been a training manual. Like the lifeboat drill on a cruise ship, you needed it when things went wrong. Cox had done the calculations, including the potential benefits for reduced sentencing if he turned Queen's Evidence. He now needed his UK solicitor, Hathaway, so he could review the plan with him. But Hathaway was in another country.

Edmond read again the letter from his ex-wife. They were on neutral rather than good or bad terms and she respected his interest in the welfare of their daughter, Pam. It was only recently, in the year and a half before his 'Italian caper', as she put it, that his 'ex' allowed him to have Pam visit him for full days at the weekends. With his record, a custody and access fight would have been a 'no-brainer'. Now, she wrote, 'What do I tell her? How long can I continue to say you are in Europe for work?'

But she at least gave him updates on Pam, including the small stuff; school, latest interests, and her growing interest in boys. He could almost hear his daughter talking away. Both parents were fortunate in that their relationship with their daughter and the girl's good-natured disposition resulted in bonding rather than distancing now she was in her teens. He missed his days with Pam more than anything else, really.

Cox reached a decision. He was seeing Rimini again tomorrow, Thursday, and would tell him then; he wanted a message passed to Detective Chief Inspector Coltrane at New Scotland Yard. Neville Coltrane would be asked to come to see him - and Edmond thought he would do just that.

The message was going to be short, he decided, just a one-liner email. 'Stubbs; and bring someone from HSCC with you. Edmond Cox.'

He wasn't going to give more information to his Italian lawyer and he knew that until Coltrane had heard his offer himself, he would not get to Hathaway. But it should be sufficient.

The English painter George Stubbs was renowned for advancing the accuracy of equine painting and was also front rank in anyone's books in terms of artistic quality and market value. The request for a representative of Homicide and Serious Crime Command to accompany the art detective would clue Coltrane in. Edmond knew his name was already in play for the Houghton Bank robbery. He had even been interviewed at the time but his alibi had held solid.

Coltrane would be tripping over himself to get to Rome, he thought.

~~

On the Friday of the same week, DCI Neville Coltrane, head of the Art and Antiques Unit of the Metropolitan Police, looked again at the email just received from a lawyer in Rome. He picked up his phone and called Caldwell's extension, getting his voicemail.

Instead, he called his team member's mobile. "Where are you, Philip?"

"At the Old Bailey, the Geraghty trial, sir. I am the first witness when the morning session opens, so may have to break off."

Coltrane said, "I am forwarding you an email. Review it when you can and get back to me, please, but make it today."

DI Philip Caldwell walked into Coltrane's office the same afternoon.

"I checked the record and talked with Rayner. Cox's alibi seemed solid; it was his sister, visiting from Melbourne at the time, and she has no prior involvement with police - here or there, we did check. And it had detail, not the normal fabricated stuff, so it seemed credible to DC Rayner."

He could see the skepticism on Coltrane's face. There had been a cock-up, clearly. If Cox now wanted to talk about the Houghton Bank robbery he had been involved in it directly, particularly if he wanted to talk about a deal of some sort.

"Do you want me to go and talk to him?" Caldwell asked.

"No," said Coltrane, "I will go. And I will take DCI Worsley with me, if she is available."

As Caldwell's face registered his surprise, Coltrane added. "I will ask ACU to join in on the case, at least for the Hewitt family element. Probably given Cox's request for Serious Crimes to be present, we could lose that aspect of it anyway. And everyone here is busy; it is better for ACU to be involved than have someone else assigned from Serious Crime Command who knows nothing about art."

Caldwell stayed silent; the retort on the tip of his tongue was that DCI Worsley knew nothing about art anyway. It would not be welcome, he felt. Despite the origins of this second art crime team at the Met and the original friction between ACU and the Art and Antiques unit, Coltrane and Worsley seem to get along better these days.

Caldwell said instead, "The insurance groups are still actively working this file, Neville, and it's a high value case; two paintings by Stubbs."

The paintings are the main priority, he was saying.

Coltrane looked at him. "We will see if the ACU wants to be included on this one, first. You will still be on the investigation into the whereabouts of the paintings once we see where this is going."

He was telling Philip that the priority for him was the arrest of the men who had stayed at the Hewitt house. Caldwell knew the reason; he was close to Coltrane and had worked with him since his appointment as head of Art and Antiques. They got on well. He was also too experienced an officer and near enough to retirement to take the decision as a slight.

His concern, he knew, was a little petty. It was that Worsley would give the job to Inspector Keith Marshall. It still rankled him that Sergeant Marshall, as he was then, walked out of A&A for the upstart new art crime unit in Superintendent Jack Taylor's group. He still thought that art crime investigation should be the sole purview of Specialist Crime Command; they didn't need to be tripping over the ACU, part of the 'murder and mayhem mob', as he sometimes referred to HSCC.

When Caldwell left, Coltrane pulled up the file with the interview with Emma Hewitt. He knew exactly where it was, he could find it blindfolded. He re-read it and then he called Jane Worsley.

"A new development in an old case, Jane, one that could logically fall into your remit now, at least part of it; the Houghton Bank robbery. Remember it? Two Stubbs paintings were stolen from the bank, with the related kidnapping issue?"

Normally Jane Worsley would fire straight back at him, but she was silent for a moment, then she said, "Could we talk about this later, Neville, please? I am up to my eyes with… well, it will be out soon. Sayer is in Kuala Lumpur and there is a problem. I am standing by, waiting for more news."

Alerted, he said, "What's wrong?"

He had heard that Sayer was going to Malaysia, covering for her colleague DC John Obi, despite having just come back from the case in Cornwall.

"She's in hospital, in shock they say. She was with Madeleine Turner-Jones from the FCO and some Royal Malaysian Police officers. An officer was badly wounded in an incident there."

"Not Sayer?" said Coltrane.

He had come to like the young Welsh officer; he thought she was pretty good, in fact. Neville knew she had good head for art - and not only for this sort of criminal investigation work. His partner, Sylvie McNair, had commissioned several pieces of pottery from Sayer and her friend, the one who owned the pottery in Spitalfields Arts Market.

"No," said Jane, "Sayer shot the assailant with an RMP weapon; she killed him. I am waiting to hear more but that's about all I know at present. FCO have just been on to Sandra Hunt and I had a call from an RMP superintendent there, someone called Baksh."

He looked at his watch. It would be late-evening or nighttime in Asia, he thought.

"Why don't I come down and we can talk; I can wait with you and if any calls or emails come in… you can just kick me out?"

From his voice Jane could tell that Coltrane wasn't simply trying to push the agenda for the case he had mentioned; he, too, was concerned. After all, he had volunteered to help the last time Sayer had got into trouble.

"Thank you, Neville, I would appreciate that," she told him. Strangely enough, she found that she meant it.

Assistant Commissioner Hunt and Jane's boss, Superintendent Jack Taylor, had been in some other meeting together. They were now heading back to the Yard. She suspected that she and Taylor would be talking and probably meeting with the FCO or people at the Malaysian High Commission later.

But to have someone to talk to now would be a help.

6 GUANXI

On the Malaysian Airlines flight to London, Catrin found her business class seat upgraded to first class, across the aisle from Jian Li. Whether her friend had fixed this or the Malaysian authorities, she had no idea. But the quiet of the cabin and the space was welcome. Of the eight first class seats on the Airbus 380, only four were occupied, making it even more spacious, it seemed.

Her day had been overwhelming. Occasional waves of fear and flashbacks were tempered by the time spent dealing with events.

Somehow the analytical elements of the formal statement at RMP headquarters made it easier, not harder. It was familiar ground, an interview room. There was a sense from all present that they were on her side.

The visit to the hospital had been the hardest part, particularly meeting Sergeant Farra's wife and children, despite the warm welcome by the family. It was explained that it was pointless for her to go into the intensive care room to see the policeman. He was still heavily sedated after his surgery and they were reducing any risk of infection by limiting visitors. She saw Farra briefly through the glass panel in the door, lying there, now looking like a victim similar to others she had seen in hospitals over the years. Next to her, standing by the door, was a young uniformed RMP officer, on guard; they were taking no further chances with Farra.

Mrs. Farra left her children with their aunt for a few minutes while she spoke in private with Catrin in a borrowed office. She was controlled, eloquent and almost formal in her personal gratitude, for which Catrin was thankful. She felt on the edge of an emotional precipice herself.

It was later, during the build-up to her departure that Catrin felt the tension building. It peaked during the pre-boarding wait with Li in a private diplomatic lounge at the airport where they were accompanied by two High Commission staff and RMP representatives, several of which escorted them to the boarding gate.

As the push-back of the aircraft from the gate started she realised she was truly on her way home. Her spirits rose momentarily as they taxied and took off but in no time she was feeling exhausted again, nodding off to sleep as the aircraft rose into the sky seeking its initial cruising altitude.

In the sequence of emails she had received during the day, two concerning the recent Greaves case in Cornwall seemed almost alien to her for a moment.

There was a formal closeout and thank you from Inspector Stephen Hicks for her help, an email that he had copied quite broadly within Devon & Cornwall Police and to key people in New Scotland Yard.

Another from Worsley copied an email from Chief Superintendent Matheson of Specialist Crime Command to her boss, Superintendent Jack Taylor, thanking him for the strong co-operation on the Greaves case and particularly the agreement to the assignment of Sayer in Cornwall. Worsley's note attaching it simply said, "A little sunshine in the middle of a day in hell for you. We look forward to seeing you back home. Keith will meet you; I will be preparing for a meeting at the Yard."

Catrin's part in the investigation in Cornwall had concluded only days ago. It seemed another world away at present.

~~

Across the aisle Jian Li was awake, looking out the window. In the moonlight entering the cabin she occasionally glanced across to see her friend fast asleep, full length on the lie-flat bed. It had been quite a day, all things considered, she thought. She had accompanied Catrin through the meeting with the Commissioner, then the interview about the incident, the hospital visit and eventually they arrived at a private suite in the international airport.

Li was struck by the security arrangements; men and women around them whose eyes were always elsewhere. They reminded her of the security people she saw but never talked to during the drive south from Glasgow with Catrin and Jane Worsley over two years ago. She was affected also by the memory of Inspector Khan with the RMP, a nice man who had spent much of the day with them. He was Farra's superior officer and she could tell that he was carrying an unwarranted burden. He told her that he had conflicting personal arrangements for the Friday that prevented him looking after the visitors, so he had instructed Farra to make the offer to be the host that morning.

However, the reason Jian Li couldn't sleep, she realised, was not the stimulation from these events but the gnawing problem of guanxi; a bond of obligation between two people that went beyond friendship. Some would say it was separate from friendship entirely. Catrin Sayer had saved her life in Bangor and now she had almost lost her own in Kuala Lumpur. Linking the two events was the same word; triad. Jian Li was not involved in that world, but she knew someone who was.

She looked at her watch. Another two and a half hours remained of the long flight. They would be waking people soon, lights would start to go on and breakfast would be served before the descent into an early morning at Heathrow and the start of another strange day.

She flagged to the attendant quietly that she would like some tea, a period of calm while she watched the changing patterns of moonlight on the cloud base below. She was working out her plan of action for her return to Hong Kong.

First, she would buy her parents each a new smartphone, she thought. Her parents were at not at ease with computers or electronics; they relied on her to choose equipment, fix things and set up their phones and computers. It had been nearly two years since she had gone through the ritual of setting up their current phones, explaining the differences from the previous models and dealing in the weeks afterwards with the calls saying, "Li, how do I…"

In updating her father's phone she would have access to his contacts.

~~

Catrin and Li were met at the jet bridge at Heathrow, taken off the aircraft first then routed through a plain door and down some internal corridors away from the general traffic. An immigration officer quickly stamped Li's passport and waved them through. They found themselves in a room with Catrin's boyfriend, Chris Treneer, and Inspector Keith Marshall, Catrin's colleague.

Catrin hugged and kissed her boyfriend as Marshall and Li turned away, making a fuss of re-acquainting. The last time they had seen each other was in Colwyn Bay, at the North Wales Police Headquarters three years ago. At the time, Li had just finished participating in an interview with a female co-conspirator involved in the death of her brother.

Catrin asked, "Chris, how long are you up here for?"

She meant, on leave from the Devon & Cornwall Police.

He smiled, "As long as I need. We can talk later about that. How are you doing?"

"Still in a daze when I think about it, otherwise, I feel OK.

I am not sure what that means now."

He said, "It means you are home, that's what counts."

After a long, few seconds Catrin broke away from the embrace and introduced Chris to Li. They smiled at each other and shook hands.

"Nice to meet you," said Li.

Chris Treneer was taller than Catrin, bigger than she had registered from his photograph, dark-haired and fit.

"And for me too, but strange circumstances, though," said Chris.

Marshall was watching Sayer carefully. He said, "Catrin, there is a car to take you home and Worsley wants to see you later, of course, even though it is Sunday. Did you sleep on the plane?"

"Yes sir, quite well, actually; I went out like a light."

He said, "So let's go. Where is Jian Li going?"

"To my place," said Catrin. "There is a spare room."

"No," said Li, "I will ride with you to your flat but will go on to the Montcalm from there. You two need time together without a guest, I think, and I have already made arrangements. And then I am going to see Jean and Melanie."

The Montcalm, Catrin knew, was an upscale hotel on the other side of Liverpool Street Station from the Spitalfields Arts Market, but not that far away from Catrin's flat. Jean Hughes and Melanie Farrell were Catrin's friends, who also lived in Spitalfields, co-owners of a boutique pottery, the Cwmbran Kiln.

It was clear that Li was already well organized.

Marshall had been called at 9.00 p.m. last night by Worsley and asked to head to Heathrow to meet the flight, assess Sayer then give her feedback.

He told her, "Catrin, you are slotted to see Dr. Herrington as soon as you want; he will fit you in, his receptionist said. You are to call his home number, I gather. He says you should have it from last time."

Catrin nodded. "Thank you, sir, I do and I appreciate it

being set up so quickly. I will call him later."

No objections this time, not like after Scotland, Marshall noted. She knew the value of such therapy now.

"So we will have a car to collect you at 2.30 this afternoon from your flat and you will meet with Jane in her office at the Yard unless you are summonsed elsewhere. You did a good job; not one you would want to do, but one that needed doing."

Catrin looked at her senior colleague and remembered he had previously been a serving soldier, a lieutenant in the army. It was in his eyes, the understanding; the use of firearms in action. She recalled the same look from him years ago when she was a new member of the ACU, but not to her at the time.

In Bangor, she and Marshall had met briefly with a Superintendent Morgan of the North Wales Police. They had exchanged polite comments, then it emerged that Morgan and Marshall had met previously, both being Authorised Firearms Officers in the past. It was her intuition at the time, based on the looks exchanged, that both officers had used firearms in incidents. Now it was no longer intuition, it was experience.

She said, "Thank you, sir. Are you coming with us?"

"No. I have separate arrangements and other things to do; I just wanted to see you back safely, that you cleared 'Arrivals' here OK and to make sure all went smoothly. Worsley wanted no glitches. I will see you tomorrow. I won't be around later today in the meeting."

They were now standing in the doorway. An unmarked police car was sitting outside, its driver waiting for her. A case Keith is working on, Catrin thought, so he won't say any more now. It would also account for the second police car now drawing up behind as they spoke. If it was personal commitments, family stuff, he would have said something.

She said, "Thank you for taking the time; it was good to see you here to meet me."

He touched her shoulder and then walked to the other vehicle, pulling out his mobile. Catrin knew why he was really meeting her; he would be feeding his assessment of her status right back to DCI Jane Worsley or Superintendent Jack Taylor.

As they drove away Marshall phoned DCI Jane Worsley.

"Sayer looks and sounds OK but is clearly shaken up by it all. She is fine for coming into the Yard later and also with the Herrington appointment. It wasn't the time to talk about security; you will be doing that later, so I didn't mention to her that her place is being watched. Her boyfriend and Jian Li Yeung are with her now and Yeung will head to a nearby hotel."

Jane thanked him for the status update. She knew that Yeung had decided to travel back with Catrin; she had mentioned her decision when they talked earlier and Jane was glad the friend had chosen to do so.

"It will at least stop Madeleine sending an FCO flunky from the High Commission back to babysit, one who wants some unplanned leave in the UK," she had remarked.

The comment had reminded Li of the ride south from Glasgow after Catrin's injury. Her friend's boss could be openly candid at times, saying what she thought.

At 10.00 a.m. DCI Worsley would be in a meeting called by Assistant Commissioner Sandra Hunt, one that would have significant consequences for Catrin Sayer, one way or another.

~~

Hunt said, "Please, Inspector Entwistle, go ahead."

The middle-aged inspector in uniform had arrived with his sergeant, a younger ethnic Chinese officer who had said nothing so far in this group of senior staff.

Entwistle began, "Sergeant Hua and I have been working on triad crime issues in the UK for - he looked at his colleague - in total fifteen years between us. So we have experience; sufficient to realise that any predictions in this sort of situation can be way off the mark. You need to bear that in mind.

"From the Malaysian information, the man Sergeant Sayer shot was called Loh Ghee, a member of a triad gang called Ten Dragons. It is a medium-sized operation, largely focused on

Asian casino gambling operations where it controls some of the drug flow business; a somewhat specialized distribution market. They do that here also. If they got into broader distribution of narcotics they would have problems with others, so they are not that big in the UK.

"The injured police officer was previously involved in an incident with the same gang, so there is an existing vendetta issue between the man who ordered Ghee's attack, a man called Nam Wu, and this officer. We are told that this shooting was purely opportunistic; no-one other than Sergeant Farra and his driver really knew his timing or the itinerary for looking after the visitors that morning, so the presence of this wanted man, Nam Wu, and Farra together at the Twin Towers couldn't have been orchestrated.

"We don't know whether Wu instructed Ghee to kill only Farra or all persons in the vehicle. It would be really nice to know and we have asked our colleagues in KL to see if any noise on the street or from sources can shed light on that."

He paused to collect his thoughts and Superintendent Jack Taylor asked, "And why is that so important now?"

Entwistle seemed to be about to launch on his next point, but stopped. His sergeant jumped in.

Hua said, "It's a peculiarity. If the instruction was to kill only Sergeant Farra, then Sayer's response, stupid as it may seem given the speed of the incident, would be seen by some as intervening foolhardily; it was not her affair. Hence any attack on her would be seen as punishing someone who stuck her nose in… justified, in a sense."

Taylor intervened, "Fools deserve all they get… right?"

"Something along those lines, yes, sir. If Nam Wu's instruction was to kill Farra and all the witnesses, then her response would be seen to be simply self-defence, something quite understandable, honorable in fact. Others in the triad would see it as an action that went wildly wrong and they should cut the losses, move on. Any retributive action now could be seen as contrary to business interests."

Entwistle continued, "In any event Nam Wu is in deep

waters, I think. He will be having problems within his triad, perhaps a loss of standing or confidence in the man's abilities. He is a mid-level operations executive in Ten Dragons and this was a disaster of an operation; unplanned, with no business benefit at all, a spur-of-the-moment retaliation.

"Hua and I think that it is unlikely that the triad will go after Sayer. Given that the incident in Kuala Lumpur was unplanned, that Farra shot the gang member three years ago and no-one went after him sooner, we don't see a high probability of a revenge attack either. We think it is unlikely that Sayer will be at risk.

"As I said at the beginning, this is all guesswork at present. But we will continue to monitor triad-related intelligence here and the Malaysians will be doing the same. Anything that gives us a concern will be flagged immediately."

Superintendent Taylor asked, "What if this man Wu goes after Sayer privately, not a triad thing, just …revenge? He sent the young man to his death."

Entwistle said, "We don't rate that to be a high concern, sir. The man is wanted, he has been for some time; he will have too much on his plate."

Assistant Commissioner Hunt had been watching the discussion and said, "Sergeant Hua?"

She had seen the Chinese officer's expression change as his superior answered Taylor. Clearly, she thought, he was not so sure.

Hua said carefully, "As this is speculation… in a worst case scenario Nam Wu is very wealthy; he could hire anyone, including personnel from his triad based here in the UK on a private basis. If he did so as a private matter, however, he would want to take a personal interest, not simply contract with someone to kill Sayer."

Hunt responded, "Well, he isn't coming to the UK; the Malaysian police are looking for him and he wouldn't get here by any official means."

Hua sat stone-faced, sensing that his boss was not too

happy with this line of discussion, "He doesn't have to come here. He could send a family member to be present; it would be almost as satisfactory for him."

Hunt asked, "And what do we know about his family?"

"It's big."

"Wonderful," said Jack Taylor.

"So what security do we go with for Sergeant Sayer, other than the coverage now?"

Hunt asked the key question a few minutes later, her gaze moving around the room; it was the outcome decision she needed from this meeting.

She added, "After the Scottish incident Sayer had round-the-clock coverage for nearly three weeks. It's not just budget; it's the practicality of the thing longer term."

There was a silence, then Entwistle spoke up.

"It's not my officer, I know, but I hope this is taken in the light of all of us wanting to do the best for our fellow officers. There is no known threat, nothing in the intelligence networks. I don't see that security coverage is warranted, frankly."

He looked across at Worsley; it was her team member, after all.

"Jane, this is your background too, security coverage; what do you think?" asked Hunt.

Hunt was recognizing Jane Worsley's past experience. It was understood that she had no particular expertise or interest in art, despite nearly five years as the first team leader of the Art Crime Unit. For a longer period she had managed a significantly larger team in the Diplomatic Protection Branch, the group providing security coverage for foreign embassies, politicians and diplomats.

The ACU appointment had been Jack Taylor's choice after Worsley had made an arrest decision that was well-deserved, but one which ran afoul of a political and diplomatic dogfight. Taylor liked the fact that she had made the difficult choice on the arrest; it was what he wanted in the role of the leader of the newly-established Art Crime Unit.

Worsley said, "Intuitively it doesn't sit right, but logically I have to agree with Terry. However, if there is a whisper…"

Assistant Commissioner Hunt nodded; they had reached a conclusion.

She said, "Inspector Entwistle, please make this one a high priority. If you need to go to Kuala Lumpur to move this, let me know; you will have the authorisation."

"Yes ma'am," Entwistle said, failing to sound enthusiastic and drawing a sharp look from Taylor.

Entwistle had no wish to go to Malaysia; he found from experience that he hated high humidity in equatorial Asia. Sergeant Hua was looking far more enthusiastic about the idea.

Then Hunt said, "Jane, talk to Sayer, give her a week's leave outside her normal allowance to be taken away from her usual haunts and arrange some monitoring of her home environment for anything unusual. Then probably, if Herrington clears her, you should give her something meaty to work on. It will help her, I think; the way I read her, she is that sort of person.

"I thank all of you for coming in today to sort this out."

She stood up. The meeting was over.

7 SPITALFIELDS

Later, after Li had gone off to her hotel, after they had made love and Catrin had tried but failed to sleep more before her afternoon meeting at Scotland Yard, they sat in the kitchen talking.

Chris said, "I have been thinking."

"Oh dear," said Catrin, smiling.

"Do you think this place could hold the two of us?"

Catrin's flatmate had left over four months ago to move in with her boyfriend. Catrin had been on the verge of looking for a replacement as she started the case in Cornwall and had not had time to do anything about it since. She needed to split the costs of the flat with someone.

She looked at him and started to say something, then stopped.

He said, "If we are going to make it work as a couple we need to be together and… one of us will have to move some time or other. I talked with DI Steadman; they will look at fitting me in if a vacancy comes up; but I have to go through the formal interview and selection process, he said; it's no preferential shoe-in."

Steadman was in PCeU, the cybercrime unit at New Scotland Yard. It had been his discussion with Keith Marshall that had first led to Catrin being assigned to the case in Cornwall where she had met Chris.

His voice became anxious. "Is it too soon to ask? I have been thinking about it ever since the call from you in Kuala Lumpur. Well, before really, but now it seems more… immediate. And there is no rush to decide, I don't even have a job around here yet."

She looked at him; at his expression.

She said, "You must be mad. I just killed a man and, based on what Superintendent Baksh said, some character could come looking for me in revenge and you want to move east and get in the way. I should be moving west to lie low in Falmouth, hide behind the vat where Jen and Harry prepare the paper pulp."

Chris and his sister Jenifer owned a small business in Falmouth, 'Treneer Handmade Paper', managed by Jenifer who worked with an older, experienced employee.

Chris said, "But you won't will you? Move down to live in Exeter with me or to Falmouth, I mean? You won't give this up, will you?"

"No," she said simply. "If I move or change, it won't be to get away, to hide. I did nothing wrong."

He smiled, "So my moving here is not a sign of madness; it just means I am in love. Besides, you can't squat behind our vat. It's a workplace. There are health and safety regulations to follow. We wouldn't want to place you at any risk. You could be coated in wet paper pulp by accident, then catch a cold and sue us."

Catrin howled with laughter.

"You are mad after all! It will be lovely having you here, but I am still spending Saturdays working in the Kiln on my art. I don't want to let that go."

"I hope so," he said, "it's my cleaning and laundry day; I don't want you underfoot. And I will be joining a five-a-side team here if I move, hopefully one that plays on a Saturday, the same arrangement as my current team in Exeter. Saturdays are busy for both of us.

"And talking of that, you need to be getting ready for the car to the Yard. Clothes would help; a dressing gown and little else probably isn't going to cut it."

She said, "There's lots of time. I need to get to know the prospective new flatmate a little more, to see if he is a suitable character for this nice neighbourhood. It's my civic duty."

~~

"Did you get some rest, Catrin?" asked Worsley.

"Yes, ma'am, thank you."

She was in her boss's office. No one else was in the ACU area; Marshall was away today, she knew. Aina and DC John Obi, the two other ACU team members, wouldn't be working at the weekend unless there was a crisis, so she didn't expect them to be in the office. She wondered when she would see Obi and what he would say now. He should have been the officer accompanying Madeleine Turner-Jones; it was his case that led to the visit.

"The good news is that we don't think there is a substantive threat to you, I want to say that. We had a meeting this morning on the subject chaired by AC Hunt. We will monitor intelligence networks. It's a priority with our triad unit also, but we don't see any other need at present.

"Tomorrow you will take your mobiles - the Met's and your own - to Services and they will set up 'panic button' software on them. So don't let the batteries go flat or you will be hearing sirens coming to sing to you. If anything untoward does happen, or something just looks amiss, then press the button or call the rapid response number. Your status has been adjusted with them; they will be right there."

Her voice lightened.

"Other than that, we are giving you some well-earned extra leave. That's it."

She smiled and paused, clearly wanting to gauge Catrin's response to the decision.

"Well, that's good news, ma'am. I wasn't sure what to

expect, to be honest. After last time, I thought it could be more complicated."

Worsley said nothing in response; one word of a real threat and it would change in an instant, she knew.

She moved on.

"You will first see Dr. Herrington tomorrow and we need to see how that goes but otherwise, it's your call, in a sense. You are allocated a week's extra leave on the condition that you get away from your usual haunts while we monitor things, just in case. Anyway, you have had assignments in Norfolk, Scotland, Cornwall then KL, one case after another. You need a break, I think. Just keep me informed as to your whereabouts.

"Now, we are seeing Hunt briefly; her office. She's still in here, working."

She looked at her watch and stood up.

As the entered the assistant commissioner's suite they encountered a younger police officer just leaving. He was locking a weapon's safe near his desk in the outer office.

Jane Worsley said, "Sergeant Egar, you are in on Sunday, too?

"Yes ma'am, I have just been catching up, sorting out some things for next week's schedule; the AC has a busy week, as usual."

He looked at Catrin, who recognized the face, but she didn't know the man. She had seen him several times at a distance; once with Hunt leaving the building, another time standing behind her at a formal reception line at the Yard for some visiting dignitaries. She knew he was an aide and security officer.

His expression showed he knew who she was and what had happened.

He smiled. "Welcome home, DS Sayer."

"Thank you," said Catrin, 'It's good to be back."

He nodded and looked at Worsley again.

"AC Hunt is expecting you both, ma'am. Go straight in."

He led them across to the inner office and pushed open wide the partly-closed door, announcing them both.

Assistant Commissioner Hunt said, "DS Sayer, welcome back. I have had discussions with Superintendent Baksh, as you know. I am sorry this happened to you but wanted to thank you personally for your conduct in Malaysia. You represented the service well. The FCO has been on to the Commissioner, all are pleased, as am I. Not something we would have wished for you to be involved in, of course, but… well done."

Catrin murmured, "Thank you, ma'am."

Hunt paused, becoming more relaxed, informal. "Catrin, as a junior officer, you have come across my radar more often than most others, leaving aside those people within my immediate team structure in this office. Do you know that?"

Catrin looked a little apprehensive.

"No, ma'am; you have a lot of responsibility, I realise, and I just know about Brixton policing and the ACU, really. But, I want to say, I really thank you for taking the interest, both now and after the Glasgow incident."

That had been the last time she had spoken to the assistant commissioner directly.

Hunt nodded. "We are looking at how to deal with any potential threat to you, if it arises, but we don't see anything at present, I am pleased to say. But be assured, it will continue to be monitored."

She paused. "DCI Worsley says you are going to take some leave."

"Yes, ma'am, that's what I understand. Thank you."

"Well, don't waste it; enjoy it. That's my advice."

She stood, indicating the meeting was over.

"I suggest that we all get out of here; it is still Sunday, after all."

Privately she planned to go to the organ recital at the cathedral and stay on for the Eucharist. The meeting with Sayer had worked out nicely for that, in terms of timing.

On the way back to the ACU area Catrin asked Worsley about her current other files, casework on hold as she left for Malaysia.

"They are covered, Catrin, don't worry; it's off your plate. And, in a week, you will find yourself rather busy, I assure you."

She looked at her.

"It's a big one, but it can wait; in fact, it has to, and that has nothing to do with you. But when it starts; it's yours to lead, understand?"

Catrin saw the meaning. She would not be assisting Marshall or Worsley; she would be leading a case, and an important one at that.

"Thank you, ma'am. I will do my best."

"I'm sure you will," said Worsley, dryly.

She was thinking of the discussion with Neville Coltrane on Friday and Hunt's admonition to give Sayer some interesting work on her return. Jane had decided that Sayer would be going to Rome with Coltrane, not her.

In any event, Worsley had her own issues. She was recovering well from recent surgery but had little appetite for being away overseas at present. She had thought of Keith Marshall for the Houghton Bank case briefly, but he was busy, too and she had no illusions about putting him on a case with Caldwell. They wouldn't get along; there was too much history between them, she knew. When Hunt had said, 'give her something meaty to work on', the Houghton Bank robbery seemed just the assignment to fit the bill.

~~

Li went to the Cwmbran Kiln and sat talking with Jean and Melanie, enjoying their company. Jean Hughes and Melanie Farrar had met at college, fallen for each other and eventually decided to set up the little 'art pottery' business in the Spitalfields Arts Market complex around the time Catrin, a friend of Jean's from their childhood in Pontypridd, had moved to London. It was through her friendship with Catrin that Li had met them.

Whenever customers came in or looked around, Melanie would move to the front of the shop, looking after things.

Jean said, "Frankly, I am worried. I haven't talked properly with Catrin yet, just a quick call. Compared with the Glasgow thing, she seems fine, but this is just one more blow. Thank God she found Chris and has some happiness from that in her life."

Li said, "Has she said anything to you about what happened in Kuala Lumpur?"

Jean said, "No, we have not had a chance yet, so we know nothing other than what we found on the internet once we started looking, and Catrin wasn't mentioned by name, we saw. You say that you can't tell us anything, though, but I didn't ask why?"

"No," said Li, "I can't. I sat in on the meetings with her in KL, as a lawyer. I have professional confidentiality obligations to respect. But she will be talking to you about it, I am sure."

There was a short silence.

Li said, "What I came round for, really, other than to see you both, my hidden motive… is for you to watch her closely over the coming months. I know you do that anyway but it is easier for you than for me, at a distance. And I want to know how she is, by your estimation."

Melanie started to assure her that they would do so but Jean, looking up from the potter's wheel she working at said, "Why?"

Li smiled at her. "I can't answer that either. I just want to know how she is coping, dealing with events. Killing a man, even for good reason, has hit her hard; you will see that. And for me, monitoring her on Skype or over the phone is not easy; she always puts on her best face. Is that OK?"

"OK, sure," said Jean.

"You are starting to worry me, too," said Melanie, staring at their visitor.

Good, thought Jian Li. Progress.

Afterwards, she walked round to Catrin's flat, to spend some time getting to know Chris once Catrin headed into the office. They both were waiting for her return from Scotland Yard; their plan was to go out and eat together quietly, just the three of them. Tomorrow, once she was more 'back to normal', Catrin had said, they would eat out with Jean and Melanie at an Italian restaurant they all liked.

Chris didn't, of course, mention to Li his conversation with Catrin about moving to London; he thought they should announce that to family and friends together. But somehow Li read it clearly; how, he wasn't sure.

"So will you move here then, rather than have a long-distance relationship?"

"We are talking about it," said Chris, trying to be enigmatic and failing with this woman.

She just nodded.

"Catrin is really in love with you and she is my very good friend, so I hope it all works out well for you both."

Chris said, "She hasn't told me how you two became friends, other than it was through a case."

"It was in the newspapers, and you are my new friend so I will fill you in on most of it, but not all of the gory detail. And you work as a police computer technician, I gather. So will you tell me about that?"

He smiled, "Other than the gory detail, yes."

"So what type of technician are you, then, saying that?"

Chris said, "Computers, cybercrime. At present I support the vice and sexual assault teams in Devon and Cornwall; cases involving cyber-bullying, violent internet imagery tied to blackmail or physical assaults, on-line entrapment, sometimes of kids or teenagers; not very pleasant stuff, really."

Li nodded and replied, "I chose maritime law partly because I was interested in it, partly because I didn't want to become a trial lawyer dealing with the human tragedies. You must see a lot of that."

He responded, "Only at a distance and generally I see it on a screen. Officers like Catrin are the ones who have to face it on the front line."

Chris was thinking back to the case in which they met.

He continued, "If I am lucky, I will get transferred back to fraud and system security issues; numbers and codes, not images. That's what I used to work on."

Li looked at him, reading him.

"So," she said, "How I met Catrin; how she became my friend …"

Chris sat back and sipped his coffee. He felt, for some unaccountable reason, as if he had passed some sort of test.

8 THE HOUGHTON BANK

Des Hewitt arrived at the Houghton Bank in good time for his shift on Monday morning, as he always did, barring train delays. As Wendy had said, each workday he was on the road by 6.30 a.m., parked by 6.50 at Brookman's Park station and then on the 6.58 to King's Cross.

Despite the loss of the paintings and his role in it, he had received only support, not criticism. He had worried at first that he would lose his job; a security guard at a bank co-operating with the criminals. His supervisor had visited him at home, had told him more than once that he would not be penalized; he had been a victim, not the perpetrator.

His mind was only truly at rest on that point when, on his first day back, he was sent up see Sir Kenneth Lowell, the chairman of the Board of Directors, who even invited him to sit down while they talked. For Des, used to military ways in the past, it was a little uncomfortable; he would have preferred to stand.

Lowell said, "Our standing instructions are for employees to co-operate when threatened with violence, which you did, Desmond. Our primary concern is always the safety of our customers, the public and our own personnel."

He was solicitous about the family situation. Mrs. Cresswell from Human Resources was also sitting in on the little meeting. She made it clear that any special needs for Wendy or Emma would be covered under a BUPA medical plan that the bank carried.

"Priority treatment by the best, Desmond, and as much time as you need to look after things at home until they get back to normal," Sir Ken had said.

Des was very thankful; it was a weight off his mind. He hadn't expected senior officers at the bank to take such a personal interest in him or his family.

That was two years ago. Other than Emma, they were as now as normal as they could be.

On his return to work Des had a meeting with the new Head of Security, a Welshman called Blinney. He had been brought in directly after the dust settled on the robbery. Blinney had not been with the bank sector previously; his background was employment at a London security firm, so he was an unknown entity to bank staff. He didn't say much; his security team were still finding their feet with him, they had told Des. Blinney seemed to divide most of his time between security contractors installing new equipment and in reviewing old files.

"Mr. Hewitt, I see that you and two other colleagues had suggested seven months ago to install a dual code entry for the executive door, part of the employee incentive programme."

Des replied, "Yes we did, ironically enough. John, Kumar and I were talking over a lunch break and the idea came up so we decided to make it a joint proposal. But nothing happened."

Blinney nodded. "With the new system, we don't need it now, but it was a good proposal at the time."

A dual entry code would allow for the usual alarm cancellation within thirty seconds after entering the building, but it would also give a person a second code which could be used. It would allow the same access while silently alerting central security to a problem without any alarms or other audible or visible warnings. A situation similar to the robbery would have at least given Des a chance to warn someone, if he had chosen to do so.

He had thought about it afterwards, ironically, in his musings at home about the whole traumatic night. He wouldn't have used the silent alarm code he realised, even if it had been in place, not with his family still with those men, given their threats.

Blinney said, "The three of you are getting the employee incentive bonus for it, belatedly; it wasn't your fault that it was not acted on."

Des and Kumar talked later. They agreed that Blinney may not be very talkative or friendly, but he was sharp - and seemed fair.

~~

The financial loss to the Houghton Bank of few million pounds associated with the theft of the Stubbs' paintings was trivial, by their scale; most of the loss was covered by insurance. That was not the issue. The loss of art that had been in the building for more than a century was one aspect, a mix of sentiment and history. The damage to their reputation was the more significant blow.

A merchant bank in London since the early nineteenth century, Houghton was not especially large, neither was it controversial or newsworthy. It prided itself that it was solid and reliable. They didn't need the marketing and sales visibility with their clients that so occupied the major high street banks. Their clientele, however, didn't want to see the sort of media coverage that ensued following the robbery.

Their state-of-the-art security at the time of the robbery covered the bank; well, almost. By tradition, a door on the side of the building with its own security guard did not require the pass-card swipes and routine personalized security codes that protected the bank's assets elsewhere in the building. After all, the door only led up a plush staircase to a higher floor; the

'Executive Floor', as it was referred to. It was a suite of rooms where only the board of directors and senior bank executives met. There they could talk and strategize in an atmosphere that was more akin to a private club than a business centre.

Access into the main bank from the Executive Floor was via an upstairs doorway protected by the normal security system, so bank assets and documents were protected, they believed. In retrospect, it was true - other than the art work acquired over the lifetime of the bank that was located on the Executive Floor. And among these, the two Stubbs paintings.

Security measures in place for the artwork, they had argued afterwards with the insurers, were as good as at any top-notch gallery; they were just not good enough. It became clear to all, however, that the weak point for the theft was the elite aspect of the VIP structure. Important men and women did not want during daytime and evening to swipe cards, stop for fingerprint scans or enter security codes; they wanted to walk in with a member of the security staff saying, 'Good morning, Sir Kenneth or Mrs. Courtney-Smith', someone touching their forelock, metaphorically, then hurrying to open doors or help with bags or coats. It had been that way since… well, since the bank started.

The Executive Floor and its access hallways had held about twelve valuable paintings and sculptures at the time of the robbery. Of these, three specific works had been stolen; a selection which still puzzled all involved in the effort to recover the artwork, particularly the insurance investigators.

The two paintings by Stubbs and a painting by the artist Hamlet Winstanley were taken. The small Constable painting was untouched as was the Roubiliac bust located at the top of the stairs. These latter items were the most valuable assets in the collection alongside the paintings by Stubbs, according to the most recent appraisals and both the Constable and the Roubiliac were as transportable as the Winstanley work.

Des, of course, had let the thieves in. He had no choice. Even then, his co-operation didn't protect his family enough, he found out afterwards.

~~

After the break-in at their home that night, after the shock and realisation why these men were there, Des had dressed and left with the others. He recalled Wendy looking terrified, holding their daughter, who was sobbing intermittently.

After they left, Wendy tried to get a hold of her emotions and calm down. Of the two men, intimidating in their black balaclava-type masks, one was clearly in charge, the way he had talked to them, his threats. His voice sent chills through her.

"Stop crying, give it up, girl," he ordered, after a while.

This brought another sobbing bout from Emma.

He yelled at Wendy. "Shut your bloody daughter up, will you!"

Wendy replied, "If you just calm down yourself I will try; she is frightened, with you lot bursting in, her dad being taken away. In fact, I'm frightened; she is terrified."

The anger grew in her voice as she spoke while in her mind she realised that it was the last thing she should have done, show her own frustration and fear; it would be taken the wrong way. She should have spoken calmly or not at all.

The blow was a slap, a heavy-handed, full-strength slap by a powerful man that sent Wendy's head crashing into her daughter's. Then the return strike, back-handed, caught the other cheek and eyebrow, sending Wendy to the floor. The man let out a cry of annoyance or frustration and gave her a heavy kick on the thigh. She screamed with the pain. Her head had caught the side of the dresser on the way down and there was blood now running into her eye.

The other man came in when he heard the noise. He had been in the front room, in the dark, keeping watch on the road through the front window after the others left.

"What the hell - ," he said.

He looked at the situation.

"Perhaps you should keep watch for a while; go out and

have a smoke if you need to. But calm down. It is going to be hours yet, you know that."

His tone was suggestive, not commanding. Rather, it was conciliatory, with a tinge of fear; it was clear who was in charge here and it wasn't him; he wasn't armed.

The man who hit her left the room without another word and the younger one, from his voice, helped Wendy up.

He said, "You are going to have a black eye; it will puff up. And we need to clean and tape that gash above it." His voice was calm. It helped.

Wendy said, voice trembling, "I can feel it swelling already."

She was trying to control herself because of Emma, stifling her own sobbing. Her daughter, ironically, was now quiet but white as a sheet.

He said, "Do you have a First Aid kit?"

Emma answered. "It's in the bathroom, in the cupboard. Can I get it?"

He could see that the girl was now focused on helping her mother so he said gently, "Emma, yes. No monkey business; get it and a cold damp towel for your mum's eye. And then get some ice from the fridge. It will help. While you are there, put the kettle on, we can have some tea - do you drink tea?"

Emma nodded, but said nothing.

"Let's have some tea. It will help calm us all down to deal with the wait - and then it will be over with. We will get a call and leave. You will do nothing, Mrs. Hewitt, as he said earlier, until you hear afterwards from your husband."

He looked at Emma, about to leave the room, "And put sugar in his, it will help calm him down, perhaps."

As Emma opened the room door, she said, "Sorry Mum, I just couldn't stop..."

Wendy just said, "It's not your fault, Emma. It's not your fault."

~~

After the robbery, the wrap-around glasses went back on in

the BMW and Des was driven away. Eventually they led him into a building, into a room and he prepared himself for the worst, as best as he could.

But they made him repeat his instructions and he heard a door lock. He spoke a couple of times without getting an answer, so he then took the glasses off. He was alone. They had locked him in a lavatory, of all places. There was no working light switch, he found out. The room was dark, but some light from a street lamp came through the window higher in the wall. On the wash basin stand was his mobile phone; fully charged, he realized later. They had even thought of that.

The family had been extensively interviewed, Des several times, including an interview by an Inspector Caldwell of the Art and Antiques Unit at New Scotland Yard. Des told the police and his therapist that it was his main fear after the event, sitting there on the toilet seat, wondering if sending the text he had been instructed to send was either to activate or deactivate an explosive device at his home or behind the locked door of the room he was in. Nevertheless, he followed the instructions given to the letter; he was too scared to do anything else, he admitted.

There were checks on the telephone number for the text Des had to send at 4.55 a.m. They told him during his interview that it was an international number for a mobile phone located in Arica, a coastal town in Chile near the border with Peru and Bolivia. All Des sent was a code; three letters. The Chilean police said that the number wasn't traceable.

Des told them that he had not put the telephone number in the phone; it was added by a member of the gang. If it was an error, it would be with the gang member.

"It went through, I think," he added.

He was asked about this strange text a number of times. Des just had to remember the three-letter code, he repeatedly told them. He had no idea what it meant.

After he called Wendy at 5.00 a.m. as ordered, she had said that the men who stayed behind left at 4.30 a.m. precisely, repeating their warning. She, too, had done nothing; just comforted Emma and waited for his call. It was his daughter who told him breathlessly about her Mum's beating.

Des then realised that, in fact, they had survived the ordeal; the gang had simply wanted the breathing space to make their escape. He called 999. When the police came for him, he found that he was in a petrol station on the Mandeville Road near Northolt. It closed at 11.00 p.m. and opened at 6.00 a.m. The officers said that the perpetrators must have had or made a key to the washroom and altered the lock on the toilet door and disconnected the light switch.

He knew there would be checks to see if he had been given money, whether he knew any likely suspects or was receiving any kickbacks by other means, that sort of thing. But he wasn't too worried about that; he was just wanted to keep his job. Lose a security position for trust issues and you need a different line of work; there wouldn't be any more security work. Word gets around.

Wendy was the strong one through the early days, despite the physical injuries and the emotional upset.

"People will do the right thing, Des, I believe that. And we have nothing to fear from the police."

On the latter score she was on firmer ground to know, he thought, but he still worried about his job. It was the meeting with Sir Kenneth that took away his anxiety and started his own recovery

~~

On the Monday morning as the bank opened and settled into its routine, Blinney passed Des in the corridor, stopping suddenly and turned to him.

"Des, do we know a firm called Hodson Securities, someone from before my time, by any chance?"

Des thought for a moment.

"Not that I recall, sir."

Blinney nodded. "Kumar said the same. Mrs. Woodley had

two calls from the company last week trying to reach Mr. Cronin, but there weren't any meetings of the directors here last week. I just wondered."

Blinney follows up on everything, Des thought. He said nothing else, just stood, waiting to be released by his boss. A call to a member of the Board of Directors here seemed a trivial item to him.

Blinney turned. "She referred him to Cronin's office," speaking to himself, it appeared, as he walked off.

9 HODSON

Alice called out, "Trevor, she is leaving again."

Her husband came through from the kitchen to the lounge and joined his wife. She was standing close to the window with the blinds partly tilted, but the scene in front of the entrance to the flats across the road was quite clear. Not much that went on there missed Alice's eyes when she was sitting in the lounge sewing.

They lived in Rainham, in Essex, in a terrace house overlooking the marshes. He always regretted the decision not to buy a house in the block further along the road. They had been built in an earlier development phase; there the front of the homes faced the marshes. Their own home faced the other way, more conventionally, on to the road - and across from the four story block of flats they were now looking at.

He said, absorbing the scene, "It looks as if she is leaving for good this time; she has the cat in a carrier. And there are more than suitcases in her little car."

As they watched, an Avis rental van arrived and parked next to the Fiat. The woman putting her possessions into the car approached the two men who stepped out of it. Clearly she knew them. They must be helping with the move.

Alice said, "Hodson is on the balcony at the back, I think;

probably staying out of the way."

Her husband looked at her. "How do you know?"

Alice smiled. "I can see puffs of cigarette smoke blowing from there around the side of the building - and that is their balcony, on the first floor."

They watched as the woman and the two men went in, re-emerging a few minutes later carrying boxes and a floor lamp. She hugged one of the men, shook hands with the other and went over to her car. The men went back inside.

"I'm right," said Trevor, "All her belongings this time. It's not just a temporary thing like last time."

He and his wife watched as the men emerged, one carrying a rocking chair, the other a bicycle.

"How many is that then; women in his place, I mean?" he asked.

Alice replied, "She is the third. We have been here five years. There was one that left we never met, just after we moved in. Then Carla, who works at the Forum; I see her there from time to time; and now Sammie. She is nice. We talk to each other in the street as we pass."

Trevor said, "He goes through them, then. And he seems so quiet. Remember running into them at that bistro in Upminster? They seemed happy enough then."

Alice said, "I don't know. I have never felt easy around him, to be honest. There is something… the eyes, the look. It gives me a chill at times. Carla had a bruise on her cheek as she left, remember? Sammie seems OK, though."

As she spoke, the woman climbed into her Fiat 500 and visibly winced as she reached to close the door.

"Perhaps not," said Trevor.

Tony Hodson stood on his balcony, smoking, just waiting for it to be over, for these two men to finish collecting her things. Sammie had made it clear it was final this time.

"Thank God I never married you. It makes it simpler," she said at one point. She had already said if he came within an arm's length of her, she would call the police.

"This time I will file a complaint, I swear… and see it through. And I have the bruises developing to prove it."

Later, when it was clear he couldn't talk his way past it, he said, "The rent is due in three days."

She looked at him, incredulous.

"I have paid it myself the last two months, the full amount."

He said quietly, holding back his frustration, "I haven't any work, and when I was working, I paid for more than six months before you coughed up a penny."

She wasn't buying it.

"Not my problem; it's your place, remember? You have had more than the rent from me, in money and in… putting up with you and with this now."

She pointed at her side.

Then she smiled. "As I said, it's not my problem. The flat is in your name, not mine. And if they evict you, try taking it out on the bailiffs; they can probably handle a man like you easily enough."

There was no goodbye. She picked up the bags, her face in a grimace, and went out to her car.

Next thing he knew there were two men she knew, co-workers, who had offered to help, no doubt. He only glanced at them briefly, trying to see which one was her next target. In fact, neither of them was, he thought; they both wore wedding rings. He knew she had a thing about not starting anything with a married man. It was one of her first questions to him.

"No," he had said at the time, flashing his smile. "I never have been married, either. I need to meet the right person."

Neither man would have worried him, if it got physical, but he also saw one keep his mobile in his hand, a finger near a speed dial key. She must have said something to them. The cavalry came as a pair and were wary enough to be ready to call the police if anything happened.

Standing smoking, thinking about it, the fact that she was another woman who was leaving him, he thought at least he would never end up shackled in marriage. But he had more important issues on his mind. He needed money.

He could pull out his service record easily enough; it was good and would be useful, to a point. But he wouldn't be getting any references from his last two employers and he knew that the gap in his employment would stick out a mile in any regular job interview. He needed a way into a job that didn't require a regular interview or he had to find money from other sources.

And he needed Ryland Cronin to return his call.

He was still on the balcony long after Sammie and her helpers had gone.

10 HERRINGTON

It was 11.30 a.m. the same day, Monday, at a medical office block near University College Hospital; the same location Catrin had visited after the Glasgow incident. She was shown into Dr. Herrington's office and invited to sit across from him, both doctor and patient in easy chairs rather than separated by a desk.

Herrington began, "Catrin, I don't need to give you the preamble again, do I?"

He meant that he was contracted by the Metropolitan Police to assess her following a violent incident; her fitness for work. Whatever she told him would be kept confidential but his call on her suitability for duty was unlikely to be second-guessed.

She shook her head.

He smiled, continued. "You seemed happy with the call to see me this time, I was told. I can understand that - leaving ego on one side - as you told me previously how therapy had helped after the encounter with Cheney. So I want to get right into it. What is it that you think discussion with me will help you with now?"

Catrin nodded, she had clearly thought about that point herself.

"I turned twenty-eight on the day I flew to Kuala Lumpur, Dr. Herrington, so I think of myself as young still. I killed a man there, a young man even to me. I am having flashbacks during daytime and I am waking at night when the sleeping pill wears off. I see the bullets hitting his chest and I recall the decision to put two more into him because his arm holding the gun was still raised. I remember that second set vividly, as I fired again. I consciously chose to kill a young man."

She paused.

"Remember last time?"

He said, "What about last time?"

"You told me everyone was telling me I was right to arrest Colin Cheney the way I did and you said, despite all that positive reinforcement, I needed to get to the bottom of my own feelings, my reasons. I need to do that again.

"I know I had no choice. The man, Loh Ghee, had shot and was still shooting at another officer and he was turning on me. But he was still a human being."

She stopped. Herrington was reading her face and body language as well as her words and voice.

"Is the feeling of guilt overwhelming?" he asked.

Catrin said, "No, it's not 'in my face'. I think about the incident a lot. I know I had no option but something is… lurking, somewhere, I feel. I don't know how to describe it. And now I am told I am probably not in danger, but there is the possibility that the person who ordered Ghee to kill Sergeant Farra could have someone try to kill me.

"There is the fear of that; for me, for those around me. I am so angry about that, this triad boss acting like an emperor, choosing who should live and die. I suddenly find a wave of anger sweeping over me coming out of nowhere. It's more about him than the man I shot, to be honest, I think."

She paused. Herrington could see she was vacillating a little, deciding what to say next. Patients often want to share part of their feelings and fears, not the whole thing at the beginning.

"And I have another dream that wakes me at night. I take Sergeant Farra's weapon and turn to fire, but I am too late. It's me lying on the floor. I am looking at everything through, strangely enough, the eyes of the dead man."

Herrington closed his file and stood up, which surprised her. In previous sessions he had always sat across from her, file open on his lap, appearing relaxed. He walked over to his desk and pressed the intercom button on his phone.

"Cynthia, I will be working through lunch with this patient. Can you get me a sandwich before my 2.00 p.m. appointment? Thanks."

He came back to his chair.

"Catrin, we have no time constraint. Forget about that. Now you know how I work. I ask you to relax, think of something. Last time it was a place on the Welsh coast, I see, or sitting in St. Paul's Cathedral. These were the starting points that you chose at different visits last time."

He was looking at her file notes.

"Choose somewhere now. Close your eyes and tell me where it is. Think of that place for a minute and then you will tell me in sequence exactly what happened from leaving the Hilton Doubletree Hotel that morning."

How did he know that was the hotel she stayed at? He must have already had a background briefing from the Yard, Catrin realised. Then her mind went to the rows of chairs in St. Paul's Cathedral, sitting there. For some reason, it always worked. It's why she still went back there, would be going again soon, for the sense of peace it brought.

She closed her eyes.

Later he summarized.

"You need to come back but I don't see anything like last time; no denial. You have had a traumatic event and elements of that are playing back, as we would expect. I think you are actually handling it quite well so there is nothing telling me you need to be on leave of absence for medical reasons.

"I would encourage you to stay in touch with the Farra family, at the right level of engagement. You mentioned that his wife had expressed that wish and, whether or not you want to personally - after all, you hardly know the man - it could help you. You dismiss too quickly the fact 'you had to do it' and need to absorb that you saved a man's life, kept a family intact. That is the only additional specific action I would recommend at present, other than take it easy for a while.

"The most difficult part to deal with is the anger at the older man, the person who started the incident. That, I think, is the more serious concern and will be our focus next time and probably for a few sessions to come. Take some days off; go to the pottery and make some of your art."

His eyes strayed to a bookcase, to a small vase that Catrin had decorated and given to him on her final visit two years ago.

Catrin said, "DCI Worsley has given me a week's leave anyway, above my allowance, but not at home - just in case. No choice, but I am glad to have it."

He smiled. "That sounds well-deserved. Now go and enjoy it. Talk to Cynthia and book a regular appointment for shortly after you return."

~~

Li had been shopping in the Bond Street area but timing things to enable her to take a short taxi ride east to Holborn, to fit in a visit she had organized with a friend from Bangor University days, Lyn Phillips. They had studied law together for the year. Phillips was now working at Lincoln's Inn, part of a legal team of one of the barrister's there. Later Li was to have dinner with Catrin and Chris, Jean and Melanie. Her flight back to Hong Kong was the following morning.

After catching up with Lyn and meeting some of the more senior members of chambers, she asked, "Do you have a really good student here, Lyn; someone who can do research well and wants to earn a little more?"

Her friend laughed.

"What do you think, Li? It's the way we work, articling

people."

She went out and returned with a young man. After introductions and a quiet chat for five minutes, he left beaming. The student needed the money and this was a windfall. Within a week Jian Li was going to have an up-to-date background paper on triad activity in the UK; key names, operating practices and trial summaries of triad prosecutions involving violence. It would be a briefing document that any barrister at the Old Bailey would be pleased to read as they prepared for a new case.

Later, the dinner of the five friends together at Carluccio's Restaurant in Spitalfields was going well. They stayed off the topic of Malaysia mostly. At one point it came up and Li interjected very seriously, "It was awful in Kuala Lumpur, simply awful."

Melanie looked at her, concerned.

"How do you mean?"

Li said, deadpan, "I didn't get to see the sights and I couldn't go shopping in Bukit Bintang; they have nice shopping there. I suffered a lot, you know."

They all laughed, especially Catrin.

Melanie said, "Well, hopefully you got some shopping in today."

Li said something non-committal and the conversation picked up, moved on.

A few minutes later Catrin said to Li, as an aside, "Penny for them; what are you thinking about?"

Her friend seemed to have switched off.

Li responded without thinking it through.

She said, "Funnily enough, about our walk down Glanrafon Hill three years ago."

The hill close to the university in Bangor was the point when Li told Catrin about her family history. On the walk down it she had talked about her grandparent's arrival in Hong Kong and disclosed in confidence the strange connections between her father and two men; Enlai Lin, now her boss, and

Michael Yau, a member of a triad.

It had been a big step for Li, to share such information, knowing Catrin was a police officer and both men in Hong Kong had interfered during the investigation into the disappearance of her brother. She knew she must tell her, but was anxious that it could lead to trouble for Lin and Yau.

It turned out to be a step across a bridge of trust between her and her new friend. Catrin had honoured that confidentiality, she knew.

Now, at the restaurant, Catrin gave her a strange look, not sure how to interpret Li's remark.

Li covered it quickly. "We have always been good friends from that time."

The conversation turned to how long they had known each other and soon moved to Jean and Catrin denying each other's memories of events from their childhood in Pontypridd.

Li felt she had handled the recovery quite well.

11 PRALLA

Lucia Moyano put down the phone, annoyed. This was the second time this man Hodson had reached her this week, asking to speak to Mr. Cronin. The first time he had been businesslike but a little abrupt. That wasn't so unusual these days in her work in London. It was something she missed from her life in Spain, the elegance of the communication, the usual courtesies. This time he had not said anything different really. It was the tone of voice, the insistence that she put him through to Ryland; it had an almost threatening undertone.

Eventually she said, "Sir, he is not even in the office today, he is on a business trip. But I will pass on your message yet again. He is terribly busy, you see."

She looked at Ryland's door now closed, his office empty. When her boss returned from this trip, after the major items had been dealt with and she did her usual review of actions with him, she would make a point about her discomfort with the calls from Mr. Hodson.

~~

Three days later it was raining gently in Falmouth, with a prospect of the weather clearing in the afternoon. Catrin Sayer and her boyfriend were inside his sister Jenifer's home near the city centre, having travelled down first to Pontypridd for a day to see Catrin's parents then on to Exeter, to the flat that Chris still lived in. After a couple of days there they went on to Falmouth to stay with Jenifer.

It was a short walk from the shop 'Treneer Handmade Paper' to Jenifer's home. Chris had said that as much as it was social, he needed to meet with his sister, to discuss some plans for the business.

"Cornwall; it makes more sense, with Chris working there still," Catrin had said to Worsley when asked about where she would spend her extra leave.

Worsley nodded. "We will flag it anyway to Devon & Cornwall Police. So if anyone looks a problem, anything happens, call their tactical response unit direct. I will sort it out with Superintendent Pender."

Catrin looked at her boss. "I thought you said, ma'am, there was no credible threat; that we didn't need to take special measures?"

Worsley looked a little uncomfortable.

"That's what we agreed, yes. But put it down to me working too long in DPB, or that I am getting older, whatever; we should take all reasonable measures we can."

She looked at Catrin, defensively.

"An extra telephone number in your speed dial is just a precaution, that's all."

Catrin said, "Yes, ma'am," trying to decide which excuse best fitted her boss's explanation of her concern.

Inside Jenifer Treneer's home, Catrin was trying to get through to Mason Carrington, Jen's partner, and failing miserably to interrupt his phone call.

She was saying, "Mason, you shouldn't have. It was a commitment you made."

Carrington, a watercolour artist, and Jenifer Treneer were not married nor lived together, but they had a long-standing relationship. The arrival of Chris and Catrin and the discussion of her reason for returning to Cornwall so soon had hit him hard.

Impulsively he had said, "Catrin, if these two are discussing business, let's you and I go and paint."

Jenifer had said, simply, "When and where? Antibes, remember?"

Mason had picked up his mobile, called his agent and said he couldn't turn up for the watercolour class he was teaching in Antibes on time; he would have to cancel part of it, at least. Something had come up. The phone was still tucked into his shoulder, half-buried in his shock of curly hair. He was listening, making the occasional apologetic noise, holding his other hand up, warding off Catrin's interjections to dissuade him.

Eventually he said, "That would work; thanks Eva, yes, I am an absolute pain in the rear, I know. Send me the details."

Jenifer said, "What did you do?"

She was all smiles.

Mason said, "They are fixing a place in an air taxi; a Citation jet coming into Newquay Airport will collect me at 2.30 tomorrow afternoon. One stop on the way and I will be in Cote d'Azur airport and on to the villa in time for dinner and some fulsome apologies with the class about the cancellation of the first afternoon session. That gives us, Catrin, the rest of today and tomorrow morning to paint together, if you want, and if I can steal you for a few hours each time from this lovelorn nerd."

He looked at Jenifer. "Eva said she will pacify the class with a free signed giclée of one of my paintings for each participant."

Giclées were high definition prints, carefully produced copies.

Jen laughed. "Rotten businessman you are; that's the equivalent of nearly half the course fee returned to each participant."

"It's like printing money," he beamed.

She hugged her man. It was a good idea.

He said, "It's very selfish of me actually. Now I don't have to fly with the hoi polloi through Heathrow."

Catrin just shook her head. The man was a character.

She said, "I brought my old watercolour paint box and also the new Roberson box you gave me, though it is still empty. See, I was actually thinking of painting while I am on leave down here, using some Treneer paper, no less. I am destined to be carrying two paint boxes around now, I think."

"Great!" said Mason, "Let's fill the Roberson with my paints; we can even squeeze them in nice and neat, the way you like them, not like mine."

Chris was laughing. He said, "You two get out of here; my sister and I have a paper-making business to talk about."

Catrin Sayer, a part-time ceramic decorator, was going *plein air* watercolour painting with a world-class artist in the medium at short notice, with his guarantee that the weather was going to pick up.

Mason was driving his Range Rover, talking about the plan for the session, a coastal scene he loved to paint again and again.

"You seem OK, but are you, Catrin?"

She smiled, recalling how he had taken the news about the reason for the sudden holiday. Like some of the news during the Greaves case when she had first encountered Mason, there was a very soft, emotional side to the big man that was generally masked by his hale and hearty public persona.

"We saw nothing on the news here," he said.

"There isn't much coverage outside Malaysia," Catrin responded, "and most of that locally is about the Malaysian officer, Sergeant Farra. He is recovering slowly I hear, but there was a lot of damage."

She smiled at the man.

"I am OK; in myself and with Chris and... with you and Jen and my friends. I am lucky to be alive, lucky to be painting with you today. It's wonderful."

Mason was now quite subdued as they drove, lost in thought until they turned into Porthallow Cove and he saw the view he had planned for them to paint, when his voice returned.

"Here we are; a beach, a village with some fishing boats and a hillside for us to paint, Catrin. The place is called 'Pralla' locally."

They parked and started pulling equipment from the back of the car when an older woman came strolling over.

"One of your students, Mason?" she bellowed into the wind.

"Nessa, my dear," he said, "No, my friend is Catrin, Catrin Sayer. She's Welsh. She going out with Chris, Jenifer's brother. We are going to paint a bit."

"Then if it rains, or anyway later, please come over for a cup of tea, the two of you. Take that as an order, not an invitation, Mason."

She shook hands with Catrin.

"Good job you are a friend. This man gets away with robbing people blind for squiggling paint around. Daylight robbery, it is. Don't give him any money, now."

She planted a hearty kiss on Mason's cheek. He looked injured by the comment.

It was later, as they were finishing up the outside work, that Catrin said, "It was fun, but a little intimidating, to be honest; you are such a brilliant artist."

She was looking forward to doing the finishing touches to her own painting later; it had turned out well, but nowhere near as balanced and elegant as Carrington's own work.

Mason looked at her, astonished.

"Me... intimidating you? Now that is rich, Catrin Sayer. You saved people's lives just days ago and it's only weeks since you were working here as a detective - on a case that is still in the news. Not to mention you and Jean are hot-shot ceramic artists. I thought it was the English who were known for their sense of understatement, not the Welsh."

His facial expression made her burst out laughing. She went up and put her arms around the big man.

"Thanks for today. It has been just what I need, honestly. Paint and a view; it takes away the world."

"It does that, Catrin, it does that. Tomorrow morning early I have decided we are going to be painting rough water at the Lizard. If this takes you out of things, doing that will take you out of this universe, believe me. After that I will leave you to the tender mercies of Treneer."

She looked at him. "And I will enjoy that too. And I will enjoy Cornwall this week, while you are playing Lord High and Mighty with your watercolour students in the south of France. Now that's what I call intimidation."

He smiled then said, "Let's pop in on Nessa. If we don't she will give me hell next time."

Catrin was enjoying the easy conversation in Nessa's kitchen, hearing about Mason's family and friends and fending off a second piece of homemade cake. It had emerged that the woman was a friend of Mason's mother. Suddenly Nessa said, "Come see, in the lounge."

She led Catrin through to see the Carrington painting on the wall, one of her home and the cove in evening light, an original.

"It's lovely, Nessa. He squiggled quite well that day," said Catrin, with a smile.

The twinkle in the older woman's eyes belied the response.

"He says it is worth a bit, you know; claims that people would pay good money for it. I just told him he was lucky I would give it house room."

It was clearly Nessa's pride and joy.

PART 2

SET-UP

12 MRS. ROSALIND HEATON

Carnforth, Lancashire, 1744.

"Winstanley caught the radiance in you, Rosalind," said Edna Kingsley, looking more closely at the portrait.

She had been studying it intently for a minute as Rosalind Heaton poured more tea for the two of them, now they were alone.

In the company of others, including their husbands, they retained the more formal address; 'Mrs. Heaton, Mrs. Kingsley' and so on. In their last meeting, during the afternoon walk together of the two families in Arnside, Edna had said, "Mrs. Heaton; you must call me Edna and I hope I may do likewise and call you Rosalind, if it is not too presumptuous. After all, we could well be meeting more often in the future."

Her eyes were on the young couple ahead, Sarah Heaton and her son Geoffrey, chattering away, happy in each other's company.

"It would be a delight for us to be so intimate, Edna," said Rosalind.

Inwardly she was overjoyed; yet another milestone in the pleasure of her social engagements. The Kingsley family had lands near Grange-over-Sands, ten times the area of Longfield Farm. Tenant farmers managed the properties as Mr. Kingsley was a professional man, a lawyer who had recently been elevated to the position of magistrate.

Today at Longfield Farm, Sarah and Geoffrey had been allowed some time together under the less-than-watchful eye of Aunt Hilda. Somehow, Rosalind knew that Mrs. Kingsley was attuned to that aspect of John's sister and appeared not to be that concerned, which perhaps spoke well of the boy or of the Kingsley's perception of their own daughter.

John and Mr. Kingsley had just gone out to see the new-fangled seed drill made in Rotherham that her husband had enthused over, leaving the house with pipes lit, puffing away agreeably together.

Rosalind said without artifice, "Why thank you, Edna; but I am no beauty, let us be honest; not like your good self. The portrait he did of you and Mr. Kingsley catches your beauty wonderfully."

Edna Kingsley turned and looked at the woman, assessing her still. Geoffrey had fallen for the Heaton girl and they were a good family, prosperous, honest, her husband had said. She thought it true, but was checking nevertheless.

"I said 'radiance', Rosalind."

She sat down, accepting her teacup and saucer with a nod.

"Beauty, physical beauty is God-given. While I am grateful, it will not last much longer; time is passing and taking its due. Fortunately my husband and I have always been soulmates. He saw more in me at the first meeting than most men, who see the face and body but not the woman as they beam at you and make your acquaintance. I saw that same look too in Geoffrey, in his first meeting with your daughter.

"No, I meant what I said. You are a capable woman, clear in your path in life and in your self-worth, hard as it is for our sex at the best of times. Not vain, I might add; I did not mean that, but… you know yourself. That shines out from the portrait. Mr. Winstanley caught it exactly."

She paused.

"Why, in that sense, I think it might be among the best I

have seen from him of the society he has painted in these parts."

Rosalind looked directly at Edna Kingsley, deciding if this was pleasant conversation or if she was being tested in some way.

13 ASSIGNMENTS

It was Ryland Cronin's first day back in his office in the City. A senior executive of Medway Analytics, he was going through plans and task assignments with his personal assistant, Lucia. When he was in the office, it was a daily ritual, both morning and before closing up for the day.

They had a lot to cover arising from his business trip to India; the investment business was white hot there.

On Lucia's list for him were numerous calls received in his absence that weren't important enough to pass on earlier. For all of them except one caller he fired back a quick answer; the next step. With that one he hesitated.

All she had said was, "We had two calls from Hodson Securities, a Tony Hodson. He said he had worked for you previously and wanted to touch base. I looked for a file to refer to, but there isn't one."

Ryland Cronin took a moment to decide what to say.

"No, there isn't," he said slowly, "I engaged him on a private matter several years ago."

Lucia said, "The second time he called, he wasn't rude, as such, but it was not a comfortable call. Not like some people, you know, angry or anxious about the market, more… threatening, to be honest, I felt."

Ryland said, "Give me the number and I will deal with it myself."

She did so, relieved. She hid her immediate conclusion; that her boss had hired a private detective to check on his wife. She knew they were separated and understood him well enough to bet that any extra-marital shenanigans were likely to be on his side, not his wife's. Which led her to wonder further; why did he really need a private detective?

After she left his office, Ryland checked the number on the paper, saw it was Hodson's mobile number and threw it in the waste bin. He had no intention of talking to the man again.

~~

When Catrin reported for duty the same Monday, she was well tanned and looked relaxed. She took a deep breath and removed her jacket at her desk as she settled herself in. DC John Obi was looking at her.

There was a handwritten note on her desk from DI Steadman in PCeU, which both pleased and amused her. Pen and ink from a computer guy. It said, 'I came to see you after I heard. Will see what can be done about Chris; we talked. Charles.'

John came over, looking awkward.

"Catrin, I am sorry, I really am. I had no idea when I dropped you in it..."

"Oh," said Catrin mock-seriously, "things have happened here, then?"

He looked perplexed.

She said, "I mean, you being promoted to God; being able to take responsibility for everything. As if you should have foreseen in the seconds you thought about not wanting to leave Kaila and your daughter to go to KL that I would go through this."

She saw the pain in his eyes and her dry humour, something he normally was good at responding to, was not getting through.

She took one of his big hands in both of hers and squeezed it. "John, it's OK; it's life. It happened. The fault is with a Chinese gangster in Kuala Lumpur, no-one else. I am seeing Herrington and it's really helping. I had a great week in Cornwall, not even part of my annual leave, either, so you have absolutely nothing to feel bad about. You apologised for dropping me in it earlier. It's done, let it go."

He nodded, appreciative and relieved.

She knew she had to do that, even though there had been moments in the past week when she could have happily blackened his eyes for passing the buck to her for the Malaysian visit. He should have gone to Kuala Lumpur; the recovery of the missing ceremonial knife and painting had been his case. His worry about leaving his family with his wife pregnant with their second child had been the reason Catrin drew the assignment.

Each time it crossed her mind, she had the follow-on thought, 'At least I went to Milton for firearms training; John didn't. What would have happened at the Twin Towers if he had gone?'

At the morning briefing, DCI Worsley was acting as if she had been spring-cleaning. Several older cases in which there had been no progress were off their books formally, returned to regional authorities or other departments. Some active files were placed on a 'watch and monitor' status, including one that had recently had DC Obi shuttling to Southend-On-Sea, working with the Essex Police. He sighed with relief when she announced it.

"Catrin, you are to see Neville Coltrane later today, Aina will tell you when. After a trip to Rome on Friday with him, you and John will be working on a new case together, you leading it. And it is local, London, I think. Come see me after the briefing and before you trundle along to Coltrane."

"Rome!" said John Obi. "Do I get to go, too?"

"Do you actually have a passport, John?" said Jane.

He caught the tone, and the message. Worsley, too, was

remembering his reluctance to go to Kuala Lumpur.

"Yes, ma'am, it's somewhere, gathering dust."

Towards the end of the briefing, when Catrin hadn't been given more to cover, she looked at Keith Marshall, raising an eyebrow. 'What else' was her silent question? Keith had drawn a lot of work during the briefing.

Jane Worsley caught the exchange.

"Don't worry, Catrin, you will be very busy in the next couple of days."

The final item of the briefing was administrative, but important, Worsley said. The Art Crime Unit had been established with a three-year mandate before review and that time was up; in fact, it had officially passed by eight months earlier. Worsley and Aina had recently been involved in the preparations for the Structural Review Committee meeting where the unit's future would be re-assessed and hopefully endorsed.

"We are in good shape, we think. Assistant Commissioner Hunt is no longer chair, she rotated off last year. Assistant Commissioner Thoms is chairing and as you may or may not know, he is a 'statistics, spreadsheet and numbers' man. Our weakness is that we have too much 'indirect contribution' rather than direct ownership of either financial recovery or convictions. But that is consistent with our mandate."

She sounded as if she was trying to convince herself as well as her staff.

Marshall, ever suspicious of his old unit, asked, "Is the Art and Antiques Unit pressing for amalgamation, ma'am? After all, with the Degas they recovered and the case officially closed now, they have sizeable financial and conviction contributions to their credit at present."

Worsley said, "I don't think so. Neither Neville nor Bob Matheson is sending any signal to Jack Taylor that they are pushing that approach. In fact, given our recent help to PCeU on the Greaves case and the capture of the German hacker, Chief Superintendent Matheson is positively fulsome about us."

She glanced over at Catrin; it had been her assignment, her success.

In her office later Jane Worsley said she was going to take Catrin through what she knew about the Rome assignment.

"I've never been there, ma'am."

Worsley said, "Well, this visit will be short and sweet, an overnight trip. Try not to shoot anyone there, will you?"

She had been checking her out carefully during the briefing, assessing her recovery.

Catrin said, "No, ma'am, I will do my level best not to do so; even DCI Coltrane."

Worsley looked at her and smiled.

"I am doing you a big favour. Madeleine Turner-Jones is back, visiting us tomorrow with her boss to 'debrief' on the Malaysian situation now that she has 'decompressed'. They will meet Jack Taylor and me. There is also the issue of the gifts from the Datuk Allam to be presented at the Malaysian High Commission to Obi and the young constable from the West Midlands who first spotted the kris, in recognition of their roles; yes, those are still active. She expects you to be in the meeting and attend the lunch being organized for DC Obi and Constable Ryerson.

"We will bring John in at some point tomorrow, I think. Madeleine can brief him on protocol for the High Commission ceremony. I will allow plenty of time for her to do that so I can watch his expression. She will bore him to tears and he is frightened stiff of all the formality associated with diplomacy."

Catrin laughed.

"Well, Kaila will be thrilled by it, the lunch I mean; to see John get the recognition."

Worsley continued. "But you will not be on a picnic during the next few days, or on Friday. After all, Neville is taking you to the 'Queen of Heaven'.

Catrin looked blank.

She continued, "The Regina Coeli Prison, Catrin. It's not a

tourist trap, for sure. You will accompany him to an interview with an Aussie there. That's where I was off to with Neville, not sightseeing at the Trevi Fountain."

Catrin said, "It's not the Trevi I would go to, ma'am. It would be the Vatican gallery or the Gallery Borghese. There are paintings there I have only seen in…"

She stopped. Worsley's expression said, 'Spare me the details, we have to get on.'

Catrin forgot from time to time that Worsley had no particular interest in art.

As she talked more about Coltrane's request for ACU assistance, Worsley made a note to herself, writing, 'Borghese'. Later she would send a quick email to Neville Coltrane.

"After you meet DCI Coltrane you are to go to this address and ask in reception for Jim Norman. When did you do your last surveillance course, do you recall?"

She handed over a slip of paper with an address south of the Thames. Worsley knew the answer to her question; she, after all, had Catrin's personnel file. She was testing Catrin's memory.

"My second course was here, in my first year, ma'am. February, I recall; it was cold weather. I did my first course after basic training while I was stationed at Brixton."

Worsley nodded.

"Our surveillance training is about keeping tabs on people without being detected. Jim will be training you how to be the person under surveillance; how to spot people, counter-surveillance. It is, was, his background. He was in undercover work."

"Was, ma'am?"

"He was shot. He walks with a limp."

She looked as Catrin absorbed it all.

Catrin said, "I thought that the threat level is very low, ma'am?"

"It is Catrin, but we don't know exactly, do we? This is about as much as I can do on my own remit. And Jim is doing it as a favour to me to fit you in, rather than wait for a regular course. Safety sometimes means spotting things early and finding a suitable bolt-hole. You will learn about that."

As they wrapped up, Catrin said, "You sounded worried, a little earlier, ma'am, about the Structural Review, if I may say so."

Worsley nodded. "A little, Catrin, I must admit. Perhaps it is just me. Sandra Hunt is fully behind us, so there would be no reason to close us down or amalgamate us. But there are some sizeable changes in the Met taking place, yet again. It's easy for a goldfish to be swept along in the tides of change when they are dealing with bigger sharks.

"To be honest, it is the 'death by a thousand cuts' I worry more about; budget reduction. I didn't want to say that in front of John."

Obi had been brought in after a modest budget increase, one that could be cut back, she was inferring.

~~

After a walk of about 200 metres from Waterloo station Catrin found the nondescript building Worsley had indicated. It looked nothing special.

As she entered, she saw the porter, a smart young man. The entry hall had a door behind his desk and an elevator. Clearly no-one got anywhere without his approval.

"I have a meeting with a Mr. James Norman," she said, pulling out her warrant card as identification.

Unlike most people confronted with a police identification card he didn't nod and say yes, he examined it carefully and then her also, in the same manner as any immigration officer. Then he checked a list, picked up a phone and dialled an extension.

"Your visitor is here, Mr. Norman."

He paused, listening, then he said to Catrin, "Please wait; he will be down."

Catrin looked around. There was no waiting area to sit, so

she just moved closer to the wall in the open foyer space. She pulled out her mobile to check and respond to messages. A little while later she felt that someone was also waiting near her. She looked up.

In fact, two people were there, one only a metre or so away, a man about her age and directly across from her was an older woman.

"Eleven seconds," the woman said.

"I'm sorry?" asked Catrin.

The man said, "I am Jim Norman, this is Lauren. She is saying that we were watching you, close to you for eleven seconds before you looked up or realised. How many people are in front of the building at present? Any idea?"

He was looking at her reaction.

Lauren spoke, breaking the pause, "Seven."

She was looking directly at Catrin, not at the door and window.

The woman continued, "Four to the left, a group standing; one walking, approaching the door and two in a car near the curb."

Catrin nodded, seeing it.

"I guess we have started whatever DCI Worsley wanted me over here for?"

The man said, "You could say that, at least as an illustration. Let's go inside and talk a bit before we hit the road. Most of this is practical work once the principles are established. And concentration; that's the hard part."

Catrin suddenly realised that she was with people who looked at the world a little differently than herself, in a way Worsley wanted her to absorb. Her boss was far more worried about the security situation after Malaysia than she was acknowledging, publicly or privately.

Jim Norman was soft spoken.

"Catrin, you live in zones. Get used to the concept. It's not you in the street, in a room or an entrance; there are defined areas around you all the time. Within, say, 10 feet, is the strike zone. Anyone competent could get close to you very fast, with hand or weapon. You have had basic police training about what to do in this situation, but I take it you are not specialized, don't have Seventh Dan ranking in a martial art or the like?"

Catrin shook her head. "Nothing like that. Two and a half years of working the beat in Brixton was as rough as it got, plus refresher training. But it was mainly pub assault scenarios, crowd control issues, that sort of thing. Not many of those either, thank God. And I wasn't alone."

He nodded. "We know about the Glasgow assault, read about your action there and have seen the report of the KL shooting from DCI Worsley."

Lauren said, "You don't, at least, lose your head in these situations."

She produced from her bag a lipstick case and a fob for a key-ring. "Incapacitant sprays; the larger one is for your purse and the fob one-shot version attaches to your key-ring."

Catrin looked at them.

"Not standard issue?"

Both were smaller than the standard self-defence spray issued with her police service equipment, in her desk at the Yard.

Jim said, "Not with the Met, no."

He didn't elaborate.

They took her through the routine; the self-defence zone, the weapon check, the sniper lines, the unattended package scan.

"In routine situations, alone, particularly in a complex landscape like the city, you must work the permutation of checks until it becomes intuitive, almost a sensing thing. But at the beginning there are a lot of elements to cover - horizon lines, corners, open windows. Above all, for close encounter risks, it is about where people are and where they are heading. Look for anyone vectoring on you, moving deliberately parallel with you or behind you.

"It will become habitual and faster but at first it will seem as if you are moving at a snail's pace through life. And in a couple of days, we can do no more than take you through the principles, get you started."

Lauren said, "Outside the close contact zone, it's an issue of escape routes and bolt holes, leaving the scene. Remember that always; escape not defence. It is about constant awareness of opportunities in front, behind and around your movement path. And being a woman, places that a man would not enter or would stand out like a sore thumb, given that most assailants are men.

"Ladies washrooms are a 'no go' generally, whether they are empty or busy; they are usually single entry/exit and you don't want to be trapped. Department stores are great, as are pubs and fashion shops, places where other women and people known to be 'safe' are located. A place you can scream if needed and get a lot of attention, particularly from security staff hired by the location."

Catrin thought of the two security officers that she knew quite well; Jim Halliwell and Henry Walsh. They had looked after her, both during her trip south from Glasgow on release from the hospital and on her court appearance trip up there more recently. The moment's hesitation in a doorway; the way their heads moved, what they were doing other than talking to her. It now started to make more sense, the job they did.

She hoped it really was a case of Worsley's 'mother hen' paranoia.

~~

Each evening over the next couple of days she was exhausted by the process and the constant concentration needed to stay aware of her surroundings and people around her. On the second afternoon a complete stranger had come up to her unnoticed, got within five feet before she saw him. Catrin looked at him, certain that he was one of Jim Norman's team - but he wasn't.

She had Wednesday afternoon off to see Herrington again, so Jim had her doing street surveillance for two hours from 10.00 p.m. until midnight around Westminster.

On Thursday, in the morning rush hour, she was practicing the process of losing a tail on an underground train - getting off through the crowd at a stop, pausing to adjust her purse shoulder strap then re-entering the train as the doors closed. In the rush hour it wasn't easy, Jim had said, trains are busy. She re-entered forcefully to the annoyance of the already crowded entry area and grabbed hold of a bar. She knew she had three stops before she had to exit at Borough Tube station.

Her office mobile rang. It was Worsley.

"Enjoying it, Catrin?"

"It's a killer, ma'am, I am being worn out by Jim and Lauren; but it is good training, thank you."

Worsley laughed. "Well, you are done for today, at least with this level of work. I just talked with Neville; head on back and review the Houghton Bank file again, please, then go home and pack. You both are on the evening flight to Rome; it's confirmed.

"Neville booked the hotel rooms, so expect your bathroom to be decorated with cherubs and make sure you have a credit card with plenty of room on it for when you check out."

Coltrane was independently wealthy; his family had established decades ago the Coltrane Foundation for the Arts, a philanthropic charitable organization. Neville had good taste, it was known, and little reason not to indulge it.

In fact, Catrin found later, Coltrane had chosen a reasonably-priced four star hotel near the Vatican gardens with an old, almost austere exterior and a tasteful, ultramodern interior. By the way he was greeted at the check-in Catrin saw he was clearly well known there. And his Italian police contact had arranged a driver and car for their visit. There weren't even taxi charges on her expenses when she got back.

14 THE QUEEN OF HEAVEN

The Denmur Riding School was nicely located near Great Bookham, Surrey. It was not too far from London but far enough into the Green Belt to make its clients feel as if they were well away from the city and suburbia. After her split from her husband, Ryland, Muriel Cronin spent all her time there. The settlement had been adequate.

He had his yacht, the family home in London and a new, younger woman; generally not the same one each time on the rare social or family occasions when they had to meet. She had the Surrey house and land which now housed the riding school. She had named it carefully, using elements of her maiden name, Muriel Elizabeth Dennison, in part to make the point with Ryland. This time the split was permanent.

It was her passion for all things equestrian that had been a deciding factor in the break-up, she knew, but she felt no real guilt about that; there was nothing she could do about it. It was not just an enthusiasm; it was a way of life that Ryland had barely tolerated. In the last bout of attempted reconciliation they had made an effort to fit into each other's interests; for a while at least. She was still sea-sick while sailing and he was still slipping away at the stables to call his current woman. They called it a day, too tired to fight about it anymore.

He was based in the City; his life was in luxury offices and clubs, a number of boards and committees, his sailing world and the business travel. And it gave them the wealth, as some would say, 'to which she had become accustomed'.

They never actually divorced, they just separated permanently, each accepted. Their lawyers had drawn up wills that protected each of them and both felt to be fair. It was a civilised change of life. Apart from one time near the end when he, somewhat drunk, had exploded about her mania for horses ruining his life, the breakup had been without rancour. She hadn't bothered to remark about his mania for other women.

Now, of course, it was an ideal arrangement.

The new prospective clients wanted their daughter trained properly and the Denmur Stables had been recommended. It was evident to Muriel's sharp eye that they may not quite be in for any long-term commitment, but she never let that stop her in the past. If the daughter showed a true love of horses and an aptitude for advanced riding, jumping or dressage skills, she would accommodate them. If it was a transient hot passion that wilted in the reality of the work and effort, it would show quickly and the girl would be gone soon.

The mother's eyes were roving the conservatory and living room after they had signed the forms. Muriel was explaining the next steps and setting appointments with the father.

"The painting is beautiful," the mother said.

"Yes," said Muriel, "Thank you. I love them; there is a second in the dining room. They were bought by my husband; nice copies of two works by George Stubbs, which I like, and also that painting over there, the portrait of a woman, which I am not too partial to. I must really look up where the originals are hung; then I can tell people. I always forget to ask him."

The husband turned and gave the painting behind him a glance, then looked again.

"Who is it by, d' you know?" he asked.

"The original is by an artist called Hamlet Winstanley, that's all he said," Muriel answered, "they are copies painted by the same artist, part of a fund-raiser by the Houghton Bank. I don't know who the copier was, though."

The father took it in; a woman, pre-Victorian dress and hairstyle, he thought, but what? Regency or Georgian; one of those, he decided. She wasn't particularly pretty, though, but shrewd, judging by the eyes.

He said, "I like the horse better. The originals are probably in America now. Everything of value ends up being bought by them."

The wife tried to cover the husband's critical comment, saying, "Yes; George Stubbs. He is famous for his horses."

"Of course; he is the horse artist without equal, dear," said the husband, as if he alone was the arbiter of such decisions.

Muriel thought, he is a categorizer; Stubbs, horses; Monet, lily ponds. But she just smiled, showing her agreement.

The daughter had been staring at the Stubbs painting during the exchange.

"I like it; he is so… real. He is a lovely stallion; so powerful and such a nice coat."

Muriel said, "That's what I think too, Tania."

~~

The British Airways Airbus was on its descent into Rome's Fuimicino Airport, the lights of the city clearly visible from the aircraft window. Catrin's conversation on the flight with DCI Neville Coltrane had been very enjoyable. She got on with him, she realised, better than many in the Met who saw him as a wealthy art lover who had gone into 'soft' police work, dealing with art theft and forgery. Not a 'copper's copper', as they say. Some of the critics missed entirely that he was also a good policeman, dedicated and effective in his field.

They had started on the flight from Heathrow talking about the dining table centrepieces that Catrin and Jean had designed and made recently; three platters that his partner, Sylvia McNair, had commissioned. They had been commented on very favourably at several fund-raising functions. Catrin, in turn, had remarked how pleasant McNair had been to work with as a client, despite her busy life running a large charitable trust.

He said, "You have a boyfriend now yourself, I heard, Catrin."

She smiled. The news was getting around, it seemed.

"Yes, sir, someone I met on the case in Cornwall, the one I started soon after we went to see Peter De Marr together in Weston-Super-Mare. You dropped me at the station in Bristol; he met the train in Falmouth to take me to the hotel.

"Chris, Chris Treneer, is a computer specialist with Devon & Cornwall Police. He is hoping now to move to London, perhaps to the Met, to make it work for us, so we can be together. We will have to see if a vacancy comes up and if he gets an interview that is successful."

Coltrane said nothing. He had heard about it in a briefing, a comment by Chief Superintendent Matheson to DI Steadman on exactly that subject. Matheson had been grateful for the help on the Greaves case and he made that clear to Steadman.

She hesitated, not sure how much more to say.

"Although, given the Malaysian thing, I may need to make changes anyway, so it is all up in the air, really. There's nothing really to go on at present, but… Chris is currently assigned to vice and assault case support; hence we met on the Greaves case. His background is financial work; fraud analysis. There may be opportunities in London for him."

Coltrane said, "Is he an artist too, or has he an interest?"

Catrin said, "Not an artist, but he and his sister also have a small handmade paper business in Falmouth. She runs it. They make art papers in their range, too, including watercolour paper. Mason Carrington uses it exclusively, among others. He is in a relationship with Chris's sister, so I know him quite well now. Mason is an interesting man; he had Jean and I join him on a session he was doing for a training video, painting in London before I left for Malaysia. And he let me paint with him last week, too, when I was on leave. He really has an eye for what works in the medium."

Coltrane smiled, "Ah, Carrington… yes, I have met him. It was a year or so ago, at a Royal Academy event, I recall. He has certainly brought a fresh visibility to English watercolour painting in the last while."

He paused, took a breath. Catrin expected a lecture on the limits of loose, expressive watercolour versus other painting media but Coltrane's just asked, "What do you like about his work?"

The rest of the flight was taken with discussion of watercolours and paintings in general. Coltrane, it turned out, had in his own collection several Thomas Girtin tinted etchings and an original watercolour by Girtin, all eighteenth century works. When she was with Neville Coltrane, they always got back to art.

~~

Coltrane had explained in his office on the previous Monday the reason for the trip.

"We are going to see an Australian about two stolen paintings by George Stubbs; at least that is one of the objectives. I am also going to meet with Major Vittorio Cuoco of the Italian Art Squad, the 'Comando Carabinieri per la Tutela del Patrimonio Culturale', to be precise."

It rolled off his tongue in accented Italian without effort, Catrin noted. It was, she knew, the Italian art crime specialist unit equivalent to A&A.

'That's on A&A business, but it doesn't involve you. So Vittorio and I will meet and talk at the Borghese, walk around the gardens while you can while away time in the museum. How does that sound?"

He had set it up with the Italian after the email from Worsley came in; Vittorio was more than happy to get out of the office to meet Coltrane there.

Catrin beamed, "Thank you, sir. That sounds very nice indeed. I have always wanted to see the art in the Galleria Borghese."

The museum was a masterpiece, with art works she had only seen in books and on computer screens.

Coltrane continued, "The Australian is Edmond Cox, now in trouble in Italy. He is a long-time UK resident, with a criminal record associated with theft and break-ins, mostly art-related. We had an unexpected email from his Italian lawyer passing on a message from Cox; he wants to talk about the Houghton Bank theft."

"I read the file, sir, at least I caught up with the background."

He nodded.

"I want the art, but I want the man who terrorized the Hewitt family and beat up the mother. That, frankly, is the main reason for involving DCI Worsley and, in turn, you, now that the case has a new lead. Reading the file, it seems that the events at the house are behind them; the mother is recovered, the husband is back at work at the bank. It simply says that one of the men hit the mother, frightening the daughter severely."

"But it is not like that, Catrin."

The problem, Coltrane knew, was that Emma didn't believe her mother when she said it was not her fault. Nor did she accept it during the period when the bruises to her mother's face and body were healing or afterwards.

The doctor had said to Wendy, "It's a mainstay of her problem, the assumed guilt. Her fear of his return is not only for herself, it's for you."

They hadn't been able to shift that.

Within two months of the robbery, with little progress, the investigation team had largely focused on the paintings, seeing if they were in the black market system somewhere now. Sure, a woman had been hit and kicked but it wasn't 'major'; not a permanent injury, a sexual assault or a particularly cruel attack. Compared with many assaults that Met officers have to deal with, this one was nothing exceptional; two slaps and a kick and a daughter frightened, having a hard time dealing with it.

That was the context for everyone other than Neville

Coltrane and the family itself.

Coltrane continued, "To me it is a violent assault by a dangerous man who should be put away; that should be the priority for you. We will chase the art; you chase the people who did this. Cox wants to talk about it; he was a 'possible' at the time but had a solid alibi. I think that he knows a lot more about it and wants something in return.

"And Catrin, as we will be going first to the Regina Coeli Prison, please dress accordingly. I don't normally comment on clothing choices of other officers but…"

The Regina Coeli Prison dated from the seventeenth century. The building was first a monastery, she knew, and it became a prison in the nineteenth century. It was old, had a fearsome reputation and was overcrowded.

"I understand, Sir."

~~

They were sitting at an old, well-used table in an interview room. On their escorted walk through from the entrance Catrin took it all in. She thought whimsically that she could see places where the rack for torturing heretics would not be out of context. She was looking at one such place now; an alcove where a coffee machine stood, one side-panel light illuminated; the other side broken.

The man brought in and seated opposite her and Coltrane was balding, big-framed and in his early forties. His criminal record had been part of the briefing package.

Edmond Cox said, "As you can tell, it's not very nice here, Mr. Coltrane."

He was from Brisbane.

"Nonsense," said Coltrane, "you are in the cradle of civilisation here in Rome, Edmond."

Cox looked at him.

"I am in Dante's circles, Chief Inspector. I thought I was in four and found myself in seven."

Coltrane said to Catrin, "Edmond is an art thief, but really he is a book man at heart; he thought he was with the thieves, DS Sayer, but found himself in with the violent crowd."

He added, looking directly at Cox, 'But I think that was also the case on the Houghton job, was it not?"

The smile dropped from the prisoner's face.

"Mr. Coltrane, here's what I want; simple really. I know I won't get off the charge here with the Italian system, so I want to serve my sentence in Norwich Prison with earliest transfer to a category D if I behave myself. And I want written agreement from the Crown to that, plus no opposition to early release on parole, if my solicitor can wangle it."

He wanted a transfer home, an open prison environment and early release.

"You can't serve your time for a robbery in Rome in a British prison, Edmond. The villains in Pentonville will want to switch to one on Majorca, to have a holiday in the sun," said Coltrane, lightly. Then his voice turned serious.

"What do I get from this proposal?"

"You get me for the Houghton Bank job, if you agree to a common sentencing with these people here; no extension to my time served. And you get a really good lead on the three paintings that we took, the two Stubbs and the Winstanley. And that's all I can give; a lead. I don't know where they are now and I have nothing that would constitute evidence to tie in the name of the organizer, the only person I will give you. You will have to do the spade work yourself."

Neville Coltrane said nothing for a few seconds; he just stared at Cox. Then he said, "I want the names of all the others involved and particularly the man who terrified the Hewitt family. Then I will talk to people, but no promises."

Cox shook his head immediately.

"I can't give him to you. It can't come from my lips."

Coltrane said, "Do you know why I want him, Ed? Hewitt's daughter is still in counselling two years on; still seeing a therapist, still having nightmares. I talked with her mother last month. She can't get through three consecutive nights without waking up screaming at least once, unless she is medicated. Her mother doesn't want her medicated all the time and she doesn't want her screaming, but the doctors are saying it is still a matter of time.

"I may budge on the fact you are really aren't giving me the paintings, if you don't know where they are now. But the names of the other gang members and their roles I won't move on. Otherwise we are done here. You talk about Dante; which circle do you think that girl is in because of your robbery? I want the men who stayed at the Hewitt home during the robbery in gaol or we have no basis for a deal."

His voice had become more forceful, with a tinge of anger, as he spoke.

Catrin looked at the two men. This was a different Coltrane than his reputation conveyed, the man who agreed a sentencing deal with Peter De Marr, an art dealer who should have gone down for a major stretch – and didn't. The Chief Inspector was uncompromising and hostile.

She thought Coltrane knows this or he is missing it, so she asked anyway.

"Why did you say Norwich Prison?"

Cox looked at her. "My daughter lives there, in Norwich, with my ex-wife. She will turn fourteen in two months, so she will be old enough to visit the prison then. I will get to see her, talk to her."

He was trying to stay calm but was beginning to lose it, his own emotions rising.

Catrin looked at Coltrane, essentially for permission to continue. He nodded gently, backing off.

"So if you have a daughter, why hold back on this man with us? You know there was no reason to terrorize Emma Hewitt; her father had gone with you and was compliant."

He looked undecided, hesitant. If there had been a window, she thought, he would have stared out of it, deciding what to say, but there wasn't, so he looked down at the table. After a moment he looked up at Coltrane. Disappointment seemed to be the emotion on his face, not anger. He spoke calmly.

"Mr. Coltrane, with all due respect, the Art & Antiques team know their paintings and the people who steal them. But this man, he is different. You know me; I can get in and take a painting from almost anywhere but the… person who put the bank team together chose him to handle the access through the guard. I am sorry he did what he did with the Hewitts but, frankly, he puts the fear of God into me, too.

"Don't take me wrong, but your lot are too soft to get him, keep him and put him away. And if you miss and he knows I turned and gave you his name, I am worried it will be my ex and my daughter he will go after before he goes after me, I think. He is that sort of bastard."

He paused.

"I know that from his own mouth, something he said about a thing he did overseas once when someone crossed him."

Then he started to get angry, too, sensing that his hope for a transfer back to England was fading.

"You know what the threats were to the Hewitt family. If either Hewitt didn't co-operate or if his family didn't, the other would be killed. This man didn't come with Hewitt and us to the bank; he chose to stay with the woman and child because he knew none of us had the stomach for seeing it through, he said, if it was needed. It was as if shooting the woman and girl would be no more difficult than buttering toast or swatting a fly.

"I was in too deep by then, but that wasn't me, my style at all; you know that. That's my problem, that's why I can't turn him over. I asked you to bring someone from the Serious Crimes Squad, people who deal with that sort of person. I knew it would come up."

Coltrane looked at him.

He said, "But it won't be the Art & Antiques Unit going after the man. It will be this officer and her unit, the Art Crime Unit. They aren't interested in the art - they want the criminals; it's their reason for existing."

Cox looked at Catrin afresh and said candidly, "You look too young for it, frankly. Where did you get that scar?"

Before she could answer, Neville Coltrane said, "DS Sayer got it taking out Colin Cheney, an enforcer for Dominic Connolly in Glasgow."

Cox nodded slowly, his understanding evident. He seemed to know about Connolly, a drug baron on the East Coast of Scotland who was now in prison.

Coltrane continued, "DS Sayer works with DI Marshall, the ex-army officer who used to be with A&A; and they both work for Superintendent Jack Taylor in Serious Crime Command, the group you asked for. I did what you asked me to do."

Edmond Cox eyed Catrin, studying her, thinking it through. Catrin was hoping Coltrane didn't bring up the Malaysia thing with him.

Coltrane spoke again, his tone a little softer. "And the Art Crime Unit head, my counterpart, used to be a senior officer with the Diplomatic Protection Branch. She knows about keeping people safe, so I will talk to her about your ex and her daughter. We will do what we can to minimize any risks while we bring the others in. The investigation won't be tied to you; we will do our best on that."

The two officers then sat quietly. It was now all up to Cox.

"I can't stay here," Edmond said, after a minute. "Mr. Coltrane, I am going to give you the names and the details of the robbery that I know, once I have the deal in writing, with lawyers. I can't guarantee the paintings but I know who had them after the job, all three of them."

He looked at the two officers and took a deep breath.

Coltrane looked at him. "Tell me now; not the name, but if you know. Someone had inside information; they knew that Des Hewitt had the access codes. Will we find out who that was directly from you?"

Cox said, "Yes. I am the B&E guy, remember? My skills weren't even needed at the bank, in the end. I was there to try to cover that aspect and make sure Hewitt did things properly. At the Hewitt house, I made the key for the front door to allow access; I went round when it was empty and that was a doddle. As was the lock-up for Hewitt afterwards, in the toilet at the garage. But at the bank, Hewitt did everything we needed.

"You will get all the details, Chief Inspector."

It was now his turn to wait on these police officers.

Coltrane said, "We'll do it, Edmond, in principle. I will agree to the deal when I have an agreement also from the Italian authorities. And I will go back and talk it through with the right people at home. You probably want your lawyer present when we confirm all the commitments."

Cox nodded. "Yes; I don't just want this Italian guy I have here, I want my man back in England to come over. Bring him with you, will you? Gregory Hathaway, in Romford; he is in the book."

Coltrane sighed. "Mr. Hathaway has no standing here, Edmond. It's your Italian lawyer Rimini that counts."

"I know," said Edmond, "but I want someone I trust to pin Rimini down. So I know where I stand."

Coltrane shrugged then agreed. "We will bring him over. Flight will be on us, the rest on you. We aren't paying your legal fees."

Cox looked first at Coltrane, then at Catrin. "Fair enough, Mr. Coltrane. Do this right, sergeant, I am counting on it for my daughter's safety and my own."

Catrin said, "We will act on whatever you provide, Mr. Cox, but it needs to be good to lock someone away on remand without a chance of bail. It doesn't sound as if you have a lot of direct evidence we can use."

Cox said, "I know that. But what I have to give you is gold, really genuine. You need to find the way to bring them in.

"I will give you this now. I don't know why, but it was made clear to me that the Hamlet Winstanley painting was as important to the top man as the Stubbs. Figure that one out and it may help you. It wasn't taken as a stupid error, it was targeted specifically and we left behind much better paintings. You know what paintings and sculptures were there at the time, Mr. Coltrane. You and I know that a Winstanley is worth peanuts compared with a Stubbs or a Constable. Fix the deal and you will have the names and who did what. And I can tell you where the paintings were the last time I saw them."

They stood up. Coltrane became more his usual self.

"Edmond, you were a little foolish to steal from the home of a wealthy 'Magistratura ordinaria'. His buddies will put you away for sure. This is Italy."

"I know, Mr. Coltrane, but I don't speak Italian so I didn't know it was a judge's house. The others didn't tell me."

15 HONG KONG

Jian Li Yeung had been home from her trip to Kuala Lumpur and London a little more than a week now and her internal clock was just about back to normal. It had taken several days on her return to Hong Kong just to feel that life was normal again. Her mind was on the disturbing events in Malaysia, the time with Catrin there and the memories of her visit to London.

Being at her family's church in Kowloon was certainly part of 'normal', even though her visits here were infrequent these days. She had grown up spending part of most weeks in her childhood visiting the building either for services or church community events.

She stood with her parents and the three visitors in front of the columbarium attached to the old Methodist church. It was a neat and private sanctuary with its own small courtyard, a place of peace for both the dead and the living, she thought. Every cemetery and memorial garden in Hong Kong now had long waiting lists for places for the deceased and they were hugely expensive. Compounding the space limitations of Hong Kong itself was the refusal of communities on the island to accept new crematoria or cemeteries. The dead and the living did not mix; it was bad *feng shui*.

With the early death of Jian Li's grandmother, An Li, and their family's devout and active participation in this church, her grandfather Shen Yeung had secured this precious space for cremated remains at the time the columbarium had been built, long before the current crisis. Which was just as well, Jian Li thought, morbidly. Without this space, it would be easier and cheaper these days to have her own ashes flown to Wales and interred there, the only other place outside Hong Kong that she had ever lived.

The small door with its plaque marking the resting place of her grandparents and her brother, Han, was just in front of them. With her parents and herself, this was it; the Yeung family in Hong Kong.

Her father, Daniel Yeung, spoke; it was his place to do so, as the head of the small family. He alternated between Mandarin for the visitors and Cantonese for special comments to his own family. His role in this anniversary ritual was to recount the story of their arrival from China into Hong Kong, then a British colony.

It was a sudden decision, he said, taken by others. In 1949 his father and mother had boarded a Lutheran cargo plane to escape a threat leveled against Shen Yeung by a member of the local militia. Daniel was then a baby, but he talked of Shen and An Li's arrival, with its initial strangeness and the shock of upheaval, as if he experienced it directly. He had grown up with the story and the related feelings shared by his parents. The upheaval was tempered, fortunately, by their adoption into this church community, in which Daniel and Eu-Meh, Jian Li's mother, were still very active.

Driven by his more entrepreneurial wife, Shen had done well; a village tailor had grown to own a bespoke shirt-making business located in one of the premier gentleman's tailors in Hong Kong. His son faired even better; Daniel was now the co-owner of that business, still named after its English founders, Coulter & Yarrow. He talked about these aspects as matter-of-factly as he could, trying to keep pride from his voice as he expressed gratitude for good fortune and also regret without bitterness for the parts of the family story that were less welcome. An Li's early death was one sad element and, only three years ago, the tragic death of Li's older brother, Han, a cruise ship officer, murdered in Wales.

The visitors were from Guizhou, the region that was the Yeung ancestral home. The extended family felt privileged to be here today and they would talk about it frequently with other family members when they returned home. The opening of the geopolitical boundary between Hong Kong and mainland China that had closed firmly after Shen, An Li and Daniel flew south now allowed them to be re-united.

Twenty months ago Jian Li's parents had made the big step of visiting Daniel's birthplace. The small village near Tongzi was no more; it had become part of the new urban development in the area. Not having any memory of the old village, they were there to meet family members for the first time. This was the first reciprocal trip that relatives had made to Hong Kong. They were staying in the Yeung family home, sleeping in the rooms that Jian Li and Han had once considered their domain.

For the two older visitors, there with their own daughter, they were hearing again the story of Shen and An Li's life journey from this successful businessman, the baby that they, as young children, had seen driven away in an ox-cart. Shen and his family had left in the company of the strange red-headed pastor, Harold Eckersley, the Englishman who had then led the small community of the China Inland Mission in their village.

Shortly afterwards, with great sadness, Eckersley too had left China with others as the Cultural Revolution hit; the last of a line of missionaries that had embedded Christianity there, that as a 'house church community' somehow had continued and survived over the decades. The visitors were active Christians, very happy to be in the Methodist church and to attend its services and activities during their visit.

Jian Li found this anniversary visit each year to be moving, somehow strangely fulfilling. She had missed it on only two occasions; the year she was studying in Bangor, the year that Han had gone missing, and last year, when she had been away from Hong Kong on business. Her role as a lawyer specializing in maritime law issues at LinTan Shipping, a mercantile fleet operation based in Hong Kong, was the reason this last time. Being on a team unravelling a situation for her employer in the port of Manila had taken precedence. On her return she had re-coded the day in her work calendar. In future she would not be available for work on this date, she had decided.

Daniel's voice was soft, it didn't weaken or hurry; there was no rush. Knowing the story so well, Jian Li found her mind wandering a little, looking at the plaque, now with her brother's name added. She thought back to the beginning of her year in Bangor, to her relocation there after Han went missing, about the awful truth of his death and her time in Wales after his body had been found.

Inevitably and naturally, it moved on to think of her friend Catrin Sayer, whom she had met there, a police officer then new to her role as a plain-clothes detective. It had been the beginning of a friendship that had grown stronger over the years.

A little later, as they finished the small ceremony and left the church, Daniel pulled out his new Huawei smartphone from his inside pocket and turned the silent mode off, smiling at Li, both in the appreciation of the gift and showing her his competence in the use of the new mobile. Her parents had liked the new phones, her father particularly. He remarked about how slim it was, not disturbing the line of his suit as much as the old one. He would be mentioning this to some of his customers, he added; they should think of this aspect also.

Her mother was just happy with the camera in the new phone.

"I get such beautiful pictures now, Jian Li," she had said.

Her mother seemed to photograph every child in the church congregation these days, a prescient sign of her expectations for me, Li thought.

She had made the set-up of the phones as close an approximation to their old units as possible. During the transfer and update process she noted the telephone numbers 'Michael Y' and Shep Kip private' on her father's phone. She wasn't sure which one would reach Michael Yau. The last time she had spoken to him had been at her brother's memorial service. A practising maritime lawyer in her twenties and a triad boss in his seventies had no common ground, despite the strange relationship between her father, her CEO and this man.

Tomorrow she would try to reach Yau. She hoped he would help her understand better Catrin's predicament and what could be done about it.

Auntie Koe, really her great-aunt, said something to her in Mandarin. Jian Li bowed her head slightly and looked at her parents, smiling. She had just been told that the future of the Yeung family branch in Hong Kong now lay with her.

Daniel said, "Jian Li is doing very well in her career and will, no doubt, meet someone and make a fine marriage."

The confidence in his voice was not feigned; he believed it. For Jian Li it was a goal that she wanted to fulfil, but on her terms; a man of her choice, a good man, but not necessarily one her parents would choose. Yet her mind went back to Catrin again, for some reason. She, too, was an only child, with the same parental hopes for her future now she had fallen in love with a man she had met recently in Cornwall.

One difference between them was that Catrin had a relationship that, she hoped, she had confided to Jian Li, would lead perhaps to marriage. Li currently did not. She had started seeing someone, but it was far too early to have such thoughts or say anything, or even to mention it to her parents.

The other difference, she thought, was that Catrin may have a threat against her life. And Li really wanted to help her if she could.

16 BORGHESE

As promised, Coltrane asked the driver to take them to the Borghese Gardens. On the way he phoned 'Vittorio' and Catrin listened to the mellifluous dialogue as Coltrane took about twice as long in Italian as he would in English to sort out the rendezvous.

After being dropped on Viale dell' Uccelliera, a man smartly dressed in a light grey suit came towards them on the short path to the former villa. He looked to be about Coltrane's age. Coltrane did the introductions.

"Maggiore Vittorio Cuoco, my colleague from the Art Crime Unit, Sergeant Catrin Sayer."

The Italian policeman smiled warmly. "Sergeant Sayer, your fame comes ahead of you. Welcome to Rome."

Catrin thanked him then said, "I hate to ask, but fame, sir…?"

She looked at Coltrane with the expression, 'What have you said?'

Vittorio smiled. "A double first in fine arts and art history - and stopping this man in his tracks with your comments on the Garin painting the first time he met you; he was truly impressed. He hadn't expected such a fine eye and artistic understanding, he said."

Now Coltrane was looking a little uncomfortable and Catrin suddenly felt happy. Not about Glasgow, nor KL, just about art. For some irrational reason it felt wonderful.

They were climbing the stone steps leading to the entrance. Vittorio looked at his watch and then glanced at the people in the vicinity.

"The crowd is waiting for the next session for visitors to enter, at 13.00 hours. One has to book days in advance for the museum, longer at times. Numbers are very strictly controlled, you know. It is impossible these days to just turn up."

He smiled at the two staff members at the door as he led his visitors through the portico entrance at the top, apparently oblivious to the contradictory nature of their own gatecrashing. He led them through to the room with the Bernini statue of Apollo and Daphne.

"DS Sayer, we will leave you here and come and find you later. Unfortunately, this man wants to talk business, can you believe it, in the middle of this beauty? But please enjoy, as I would doubly enjoy if I was spending my time far more usefully to escort you myself."

He gave Neville Coltrane a look of despair and Catrin laughed.

"You two really do know each other well, I think."

The Italian laughed also and nodded as he led Coltrane back outside.

Catrin caught the reflection of the Chinese man behind her in the marble tiles on the wall, the shape and features blurred in the imperfect mirror it made. She had been absorbing Giuseppe Cesari's painting 'Rape of Europa' positioned higher up the wall when the light changes made her aware of his presence.

The art she had seen in the past forty-five minutes had overwhelmed her in its beauty, quantity and importance; so completely that she had simply become immersed in it. In doing so, she had forgotten the basic mantra taught to her only days ago; know who is around you, who may be focusing on you, all the time.

He was at least six feet away and she was, she saw, only about the same distance from the Borghese security guard, but the guard was in a suit and wasn't armed; he was there to protect the art.

The man behind her wasn't moving closer so she slowly turned round. She found that he wasn't looking at her, after all; he, too, was lost in the same painting. Across the room she saw two Chinese women, one his age, the other a generation younger, closer to her own. They were walking towards him.

The Chinese family stopped talking in whispers and the younger woman stepped closer to Catrin and smiled at her, as the older couple looked on enquiringly.

"Do you speak English?" she asked gently.

Catrin nodded and said, "Yes."

"My mother wants to know… do you know why the women in many of the paintings here are so plump... is that the polite word? Yet the men aren't; they are mainly fit and muscular. We are from China and it is all very beautiful but, it is too much, in a sense, so much art in the same place."

Catrin smiled at both the question and the irony of the same sense of surfeit that she too was feeling. With her training it was something she could happily answer; the perspective of particular artists and the cultural norms of different eras. But she was happier still that these Chinese people were not there to kill her.

Later, they chose not to call Catrin's mobile to coordinate the departure. Vittorio Cuoco led Coltrane on a bet instead, walking from the gardens into the villa.

"One of two places," he said. "If it's her first visit, she has not had too long in there. I will be right, Neville."

Catrin Sayer was standing in front of Titian's 'Sacred & Profane Love', Vittorio's second guess.

"We need to be going, Sayer," said Coltrane. He was feeling famished, but knew that a late Italian lunch would have them scrambling to make it back for the return flight; better to snack in the business lounge at the airport and get home. He had a busy weekend of social arrangements ahead.

"Detective Sergeant Sayer, it has been a very brief pleasure to meet you; too brief. You must come back," Vittorio said elegantly, shaking her hand formally. He then smiled, cocked his head towards the painting and said, "So what do you think?"

Before she could answer Coltrane said, "Oh, no!" and then came a stream of Italian which had Vittorio laughing.

"Another time, perhaps, Signorina," he said.

In the car to the airport she complimented Coltrane on his Italian, to which he answered, "I have lived in Italy and France at times, so I try to keep brushed up on the languages."

Catrin had needed mainly a written understanding of Italian, French and some Latin for art purposes at university, but had no real oral competence in the language.

She said, "I didn't follow what you said to Inspector Cuoco at the Titian as we left."

Coltrane looked irked then he smiled. "I told him that if he started his discussion of the interpretation of the Titian painting with you, we would never get home; that you probably knew all the theories and debate. Then I reminded him of the last time he and I had talked about it. It was nearly one in the morning at a restaurant on Piazza Navona when we finished that time."

Sayer smiled. "I am sure we wouldn't discuss it that long, sir. After all, it's best to let experts just talk on – and he does sound extremely knowledgeable. I could learn a lot."

"He is, Catrin, but I think we need to get back. I can't have your boyfriend thinking I will aid and abet you gallivanting around Rome with an Italian policeman, can I?"

"No sir; not now he is planning to move to London. But it is tempting."

17 PERSUASION

"Mr. Yau, good morning, it is Jian Li Yeung," she said into the phone.

Li was at her workstation in the corporate offices of LinTan Shipping. Her colleague with whom she shared a workspace area was in a meeting, she knew, and the doors of the offices of the senior legal staff were closed; both were at a formal lunch with an important client.

She noted that Michael Yau hesitated slightly before responding.

"Jian Li, good morning, how are you?"

Li worked her way through the ritual pleasantries.

Each week, generally on a Thursday, her father, Enlai Lin and Michael Yau met at a bathhouse on Shep Kip Mei Street in Kowloon to talk 'just as men, about families, about life, not business'.

That is the way her mother had explained it to her.

It had started many years ago, not long after her father joined Coulter & Yarrow. Now he managed the high-end tailor's business but at that time he was just finding his feet there. His first career choice had been a fireman. Before she was born he had been injured at a response to a fire in an apartment block in Kowloon while trying to save the lives of two boys; the sons of Lin and Yau.

It was that event which led to her grandfather Shen meeting Enlai Lin. Enlai, despite his grief over the loss of his son, wanted to help Daniel now his injury would end his role as an active fireman. He had insisted on buying into Coulter & Yarrow for Daniel where Shen had already established his niche as a shirt maker.

Several years later Daniel had started going to the Shep Kip Mei Street bathhouse, as he had discovered how much it helped with the pain in his leg. A friend, a fireman he knew with a shoulder injury, had encouraged him to try it. Unbeknown to him at the time, it was also the meeting place for Enlai and Michael Yau each week, a meeting that had arisen out of their common pain of losing sons. They became aware of his visits and invited Daniel to join them in their weekly meeting.

When Han and Jian Li found out about their father, a pillar of the church, enjoying privileges in a luxurious private room at a bathhouse and meeting with both Mr. Lin and this known triad member, they were somewhere between being shocked and amused. Eu-Meh was quite unperturbed.

"It's God's will," she said.

There were some biblical quotes added, inferring an almost evangelical outreach context for the meetings was on her mind. While he said little, it became clear to the siblings over time that it was simply that her father enjoyed the discussions with the men as much as the therapeutic benefits of the bathhouse. It was a social contact of three people from the most unlikely backgrounds; a shipping magnate, an organized crime figure and a devout Methodist tailor which went on week after week.

Later, after her brother's death in Wales, Li could tell from the odd comment by her father that the common pain of three men each losing a son had cemented the relationship still further.

"I am calling to ask you for your help, Mr. Yau. My friend

Catrin Sayer is a British police officer. You may recall her name, I think, from my time spent in Bangor."

She had decided to make no reference other than that, at this point; she would tread gently to begin.

"Recently, during a visit to Kuala Lumpur for work, she shot and killed a triad member. It was self-defence; he had shot a policeman she was accompanying at the time. I want to understand the implications for her from someone who can give me an accurate insight."

As the silence developed, she could tell he was vacillating about what to say. Her line of attack would depend on his response.

"Jian Li, I did hear of this incident. And I know of the enterprise. There is nothing I can say really. It is no-one I know personally, I don't know the circumstances and it is another country."

Enterprise, Li reminded herself. Triads saw themselves as business enterprises; they were societies, not criminal organizations. At least he had not commented on her calling him, asking her how she obtained his number. He would have worked that out.

She responded, "Is it possible, do you think, for you to find out?"

'Stroke, stroke' before everything else, she had decided. He hesitated in answering again, being careful.

"I am retired now. I have no personal contacts there, no… history. So, not really, I am afraid."

She persisted. "Then, could we meet, perhaps, so that I could hear your personal perspective on this incident?"

Yau said, "I am not sure how I can help, to be honest. What good is my speculation, really?"

Li realised she would need to be more forthright. The background document she had received from the student in Lincoln's Inn was proving useful after all.

"Mr. Yau, I will be frank. I understand that although the death of this triad member occurred during an attack on a police car, triad rules of response could be either to ignore it or make it an 'enterprise' response against the person who killed their member. Failing that, they could leave it to the person most affected to make it a private matter of revenge, if they so choose. Is that correct?"

She knew that putting it in such bald terms would not go down well with the older man. Her father had said little about him over the years but she had always got the impression that he was a very polite person, private about his professional life. She waited.

He answered after a moment. Yau could see that she had been looking into the issue.

"Roughly speaking, Jian Li, you have it summarised; but I don't think I can help."

His voice sounded as if he was at the end of his thought process, end of the conversation. Li decided it was time to play 'hard ball' before he closed the call.

"Mr. Yau, Catrin Sayer is not just a police officer or my friend, but the woman who saved my life. You know that, I am sure. And you know the real reason why my life was at risk. I hold to the same values of friendship and loyalty as you and your 'enterprise' members profess to, I assure you."

Michael Yau sighed.

"I am not sure what you are leading towards, Jian Li."

His voice now had an edge to it. He knew well enough. She didn't care.

"I would prefer to invoke your help in family friendship, in the memory of my brother. You tried hard to help clear Han's name, I know, for my father, despite unforeseen consequences in Bangor. I was almost shot and Catrin saved me. It would be better that way, would it not; in friendship?"

She had hoped that she would not need to go the final step, one from which she would have no road back; to threaten him. She was now right on the brink of doing so. Her threat was that she would talk to Enlai Lin and her father, separately. Both had met Catrin during a holiday visit she made to Hong Kong two years ago.

In Bangor, Li had been close to being shot until Catrin

intervened. How could they continue to meet Yau, she would ask, given he was from the same world that was now threatening her friend? She would become an uncomfortable, ever-present thorn in the side of a relationship between these men.

She expected a sharp response or another sigh and silence, or the phone link to be closed. What she got was a chuckle.

"Jian Li, you will be a good lawyer, I think. You build your case carefully and drive it hard. We will meet and discuss this. Let us say tomorrow, at lunch time, one o'clock at The White Moon, a restaurant on the top floor of the building with the bathhouse your father attends. Can you find it? I will reserve a table."

He gave the address.

"Thank you Mr. Yau, for being most understanding. I will be there."

"I will look forward to seeing you then," he said.

Michael Yau closed the call. He had not wanted to get into this matter at all. But Jian Li was determined and he admired her loyalty to her friend and her persistence with him. It could not have been easy for her to do this. He worked out the next steps and made a call of his own.

18 PROPOSAL

On Monday morning Catrin met with Worsley, Obi and Coltrane to review the interview with Edmond Cox and discuss the path forward. She had been giving it a lot of thought over the weekend, feeling the weight of responsibility on her now. As a detective sergeant she was well aware that Worsley and Coltrane would be watching her closely, not letting this investigation develop along lines with which they were not themselves comfortable. But they had indicated they trusted her to take the initiative, to propose a plan for the approach to making the arrests.

At the meeting she put forward her proposal, not sure if it was going to meet their styles of work or their joint approval. The plan was meant to flesh out the paintings and the criminals logically, without giving away that they had access to the names of the robbery team - or would have, if Cox went through with the deal.

She had even thought of alternatives, if elements of the trap didn't work, because that is what it was; a trap. If Cox gave them the names, it was a process to lead to an arrest of these people by a totally separate investigative route. And key to it was the Hamlet Winstanley painting of Rosalind Heaton.

After some discussion, Jane Worsley said, "I can go along with this, Catrin. It's a little less direct than I would normally think of, but that's me. But are you happy with ACU handling the case in this way, Neville; honestly? We are talking about two Stubbs' works here. Hundreds of thousands, if not millions, right?"

She was giving Coltrane an easy way to say no; set the priority on the works by George Stubbs, not the Winstanley painting. After all, she thought, he is the 'Goya chaser', known for citing the cumulative value of recovered big-ticket art by his Art and Antique Unit.

He paused a moment, considering, looking at Sayer's face. Then he said, "The value is in the millions for sure; and yes, Jane, I think it is in good hands."

Catrin saw that he meant it; he clearly he liked the proposal.

Coltrane continued, "And if we can help, provide any resources, we will. As you say, paintings by George Stubbs are big league, by any measure."

Jane and Neville Coltrane exchanged looks. Catrin saw that there was something off-record also on this case, something that would make Coltrane accept the transfer of part of this investigation to the ACU so easily. Worsley knew why, she gathered, but she wasn't saying more.

John Obi said, "And a Winstanley that is only worth thousands at best; a strange mix."

Coltrane nodded.

He said, "The only thing we could think of at the time was that Stubbs apprenticed with Winstanley briefly, as a young artist. We thought that might lead somewhere, but it didn't help us at all. It wasn't, for example, a copy made by Stubbs as student exercise subsequently misattributed; there is no evidence of a second painting of Heaton and its provenance is solid, well documented. Both the signature and key brush marks are undoubtedly Winstanley's own work, according to prior appraisals. Caldwell's team spent some time on that aspect.

"But they are in different leagues, to be sure, in terms of

market value."

He changed the subject.

"We have to wait on the Italians, of course. They have to agree to the proposal to transfer Cox and that won't happen until he is found guilty there. But we also need to prepare the ground. I will have people handle that side, do some work with the Foreign & Commonwealth Office people, too, to work it diplomatically.

"And while I think we need some time to reflect on Catrin's proposal, perhaps think about alternative approaches or 'what if's' once we have Cox's information, I think it is worth the cost of the preparatory stage. I recommend we get Sophie Cartwright on it. My unit will pick up the cost of that, right now."

Catrin was not surprised that Coltrane would look after the FCO link and the deal with the Italians; it was logical. But funding Sophie Cartwright now took her unawares; Cartwright was a top-line copyist. She hadn't even considered the person who would do the first stage she had suggested; faking a Winstanley painting.

The plan was based on the comment at the prison that the Winstanley had been a specific hit with the Stubbs; they were to take no other paintings at the bank. Edmond had said as they were preparing to leave, "There are people out there who would pay double a Sotheby's best auction price for some of the paintings we left alone, Mr. Coltrane. Why was the Winstanley so important?"

Coltrane said, "I will organize a meeting between Caldwell and you two when he returns from Philadelphia; he is meeting with the FBI Art Crime Team there this week. He handled the original investigation. He knows the material and will still be on the case regarding the recovery of the works by Stubbs.

"But we will get the insurance photographs of the Winstanley painting from the evidence locker today. They are the best that Sophie will have to work with and I will contact her; start it rolling. Sayer, we need to talk about her sometime, but not now. She can be difficult to work with."

Great, thought Catrin, just what I need.

After they finalized the details and Coltrane had departed, Jane Worsley said to both her team members, "This is a big one. Focus on it and don't get distracted. It will be in stages, given what we have discussed and you each have other things to do; but when this develops, keep it on top.

"And Catrin, you once told me you felt that you 'owed' Coltrane for helping you with the Kinnington Church thing."

Catrin said, "Yes ma'am, and I still feel that. He went to bat for me in Scotland."

"Well, make this one work and you will have batted one back for him, I assure you."

She let the enigmatic comment rest there. Neither Obi nor Sayer asked why; the look on their boss's face made it clear that she wouldn't say more on that point.

~~

"How are you feeling?"

Dr. Herrington posed the question almost as soon as the session started. By now, knowing the man, Catrin knew the psychologist wasn't just being polite.

"Well, I am glad that I don't need security coverage, but I also feel a bit 'exposed' in a sense. It's the additional surveillance training that DCI Worsley sent me on, in part. The sense of, if something actually happens, I could be gone, just like that. I will need to come to grips with it. Above all, I resent all this; that there is a potential threat."

He nodded. "Like the need for all the heightened security everywhere because of terrorist threats at airports and stations; nothing substantive but ever-present."

"Yes," she said, "Like that, but personal, focused at me."

He paused.

"So how are you dealing with it currently?"

"Like my mum does," Catrin answered. "She says that

resentments are a killer and you have to be grateful. But it's not easy."

Herrington nodded. He knew Sayer's mother was a recovered alcoholic; it had come up in the sessions after her injury in Glasgow. It was one of the standard elements of recovery, he knew, telling people to make a gratitude list.

Catrin continued. "So I am grateful it has brought my boyfriend and me closer; for him to want now to move to London; for the way my friends won't let it make any difference in the way we relate and live; for the Met and its support; for your help. It's just an adjustment, that's all."

Herrington asked, "And the man in Kuala Lumpur that you killed?"

"I am still waking in the night, seeing the eyes. But I go back to sleep now. I remind myself he is dead, he can't hurt me and that I'm sorry I had to kill him. I can't do more. I turn over and next thing the alarm is ringing."

"It's getting easier then, at least that part, it sounds; as it should if you continue to deal with the sense of guilt, recognizing it has no foundation."

Catrin paused. "The hardest part continues to be the thought that there is a man out there that probably wants me dead, may even be planning it."

Herrington said, "You are going to have to deal with that in the same way as I told you to think of Cheney; I am sure he wouldn't be too upset if you were killed either."

Colin Cheney was in Barlinnie prison in Glasgow. He was now serving a cumulative sixteen year sentence. He had been convicted only weeks ago of manslaughter following an attack on a fellow inmate a year earlier. Catrin had been surprised to be called as a 'last minute' defence witness at that trial, a move to show that Cheney being injured by Catrin during the earlier Kinnington arrest was a contributory factor to the later crime. It was a defence move that back-fired. Colin Cheney certainly had no goodwill towards Catrin Sayer.

Herrington's strategy with Cheney had been for Catrin to recognize how sociopathically alienated the man had become through his upbringing; a dangerous but damaged individual.

She looked at the psychologist.

"I don't think I am ready for that yet, to be honest. In Cheney's case, I could see it as soon as you mentioned it. In this case, I don't know what is driving this man in Kuala Lumpur. I don't understand this triad mentality or a man who would send a young man on a whim to kill a police officer, or me."

"We are going to have to work on that together," Herrington said. "You don't have to understand his motives to help him, Catrin, only to help you."

19 THE WHITE MOON

Li walked into the White Moon restaurant on time and mentioned Mr. Yau's name at the reception. The hostess led her through to a private dining room with a table set for three. Standing at the window were Michael Yau and a woman she had seen only once before. Her recognition was instantaneous.

Yau smiled and said, "Jian Li, welcome. You have met Emily Yang before."

Li said, "Yes, in Bangor, at the Old Library. Although I recall you introduced yourself as Professor Iris Huang. I think that was the name you gave me then."

She looked the woman over as she shook hands. She was still strikingly beautiful, wearing the same sort of business attire she wore at their 'chance encounter'. It took place in the entrance to Bangor University Old Library during the time Jian Li was a student there.

Their meeting had been brief, but with a purpose. Emily Yang had presented herself as a visiting professor but had actually arrived in Bangor hours earlier to ferret out a missing Russian painting. Events overtook her and she ended up with the simple assignment to select some expensive earrings for Jian Li to use in an interview. She had arranged the encounter at the Old Library simply to see Yeung face-to-face, to better prepare for the selection of the jewellry.

Emily smiled and simply said, “Hello again.”

Jian Li said, “It never occurred to me that you were working with Mr. Yau. So you were in Geneva and Dubai, too, back then?”

Emily replied, “Let’s just say I am here now.”

Yang had been Yau’s emissary during the Han Yeung investigation. All Li realised now was that this woman worked for the triad, not the Australian National University, as she had claimed on the library steps.

Michael Yau said, “So why don’t we start lunch, order and then discuss the problem.”

Jian Li sensed the tone of the remark.

“So there is a problem, then?”

“Possibly, possibly,” said Yau moving to the table. He was hungry.

Yau started the discussion after they had ordered and the serving staff had left.

“Jian Li, you made an implied threat to me yesterday. In your anxiety for your friend I understood your meaning well. As you know, I value very strongly the good relationship with your father and Enlai Lin.”

Jian Li looked down briefly to acknowledge the point, but made no apology. She wasn’t backing off.

He continued, “So we can only deal with this matter objectively, analytically, which is why Emily is now here. She is a representative of the enterprise from which I am now retired. I mentioned that to you yesterday. She is a business executive here at my request to talk with you, a lawyer. You must fulfil for her the obligations of a lawyer regarding secrecy if we are to proceed; is that clear?”

Li thought. “I cannot enter into a contract. First, I am contracted to LinTan Shipping. Also, by law I cannot engage in activities with a triad - with your society. I just wanted insight, on a personal basis, not details of triad business.”

He nodded.

"There is no contract of work or representation; only the protection of privileged information provided by an individual to you, as a lawyer."

Li said, "That I can do; I give my undertaking on that; after all, I asked for this meeting."

Yau nodded at Emily.

Yang began, "Our society is known as Folding Square. I think you know that. Our business interests are in information, primarily in industrial and commercial information. In the distant past we had interests that overlapped with those of another society known as Ten Dragons, which has a branch in Malaysia, one of many they have in other countries. All this is known to police around the world; it is no secret. You can read it in books or on the internet.

"A man called Nam Wu is with Ten Dragons in Malaysia; a mid-level position. It was a member of Wu's team that the police officer killed. Your friend acted in self-defence, we understand."

She paused. The door had just opened to bring in the dishes for their lunch. They waited in silence until it closed again and they were alone. It gave Li a chance to absorb this information, tally it with that provided by the Malaysian police while she was with Catrin.

"I understand from Mr. Yau that you have a rudimentary understanding of our code of conduct. It is governed by old traditions and set commitments known as the thirty-six oaths of membership, requiring honesty among members, support for each other and, what you have latched on to, aid to members and response to harm done to them by others.

"So I can say that the Ten Dragons is not engaged in any action against your friend. If it had been a matter of betrayal or wilful killing of a society member for a purpose other than self-defence, it could be another matter. In this case, they see it as a private matter, quite unrelated to their business."

Li was finding it hard to concentrate on this issue in such disembodied, impersonal terms but something told her to stay quiet and wait.

"So, to use your term mentioned to Mr. Yau, it was not a business issue or a society vendetta."

Li nodded.

"However, we understand that it is a private matter of Nam Wu that is active. How active we don't know, but it was not denied by my contact when I asked. That means a lot. Wu will seek revenge, we believe, because he saw the opportunity for revenge with Sergeant Farra, for one reason. The Malaysian officer had killed a member of his team some years earlier during a raid.

"We understand from our sources that the sighting of Farra was opportunistic; an instant decision by Nam Wu. Sending his man to kill Farra was a very bad decision."

'A bad decision' Li thought; like a poor stock transaction. A sergeant in a police force is nearly killed, badly injured. This really is a different world she had entered.

"I think it is something that will not be left to 'opportunity' this time. The reason why it will be more active is that the man killed was not just a member of Wu's team; he was a nephew of his first wife. She died in a car accident several years ago and Wu had promised her to look after Loh Ghee when he entered Ten Dragons. It is more personal, you see."

Suddenly Li didn't feel hungry at all.

Yang continued. "With Sayer being half-way around the world and probably not returning to Malaysia any time soon, if ever, he can't leave it to happenstance; he has to plan it. So we now have to consider the options. We should do that from two perspectives."

Emily Yang paused, assessing the young woman.

"Jian Li, you should eat. The food is excellent and you are going to need to deal with this analytically if you are going to help your friend rather than simply sympathize with her situation. I arrived in Bangor, remember, as the incident at Craig-Y-Don Road occurred. I know this means a lot for you, for your guanxi with her. No-one here wishes you or her any harm; you are among friends here, honestly."

Li looked at her directly, looking up from her food. This woman had her pegged precisely.

Yang smiled. "Be strong - and eat."

Li returned the smile, suddenly feeling she should try to eat after all, whether she wanted to or not.

Yang continued. "As I said, there are two perspectives; the efforts by the police and what we can do, or at least, what we are prepared to do. You may, in due course, learn more about the police actions from news provided by Catrin Sayer herself to you."

"She would not share police information with me," said Li, suspiciously.

"No," said Emily, "but she may tell you of security measures that are in place for her, or that she has to be relocated and change her name, or that she simply has to use new contact information; things that would indicate that they are taking specific measures."

Jian Li nodded, understanding.

"They will also look out for Nam Wu and try to arrest him, either in Malaysia or if he foolishly tries to enter the UK. We don't think he will; he will probably hire an agent to do the hit and send a family member to observe. That, at least, is what Mr. Yau and I think."

Yang looked at her mentor and former boss. Clearly it was his turn.

Yau said, "He is much younger than me, but no spring chicken. He will not want to be in a foreign cold country waiting, or take the risk of a clandestine flight with the airports alerted. That is a young person's approach. He will be satisfied to have a representative there.

"So the police need to be on the lookout for any of Wu's relations travelling to the UK. They will be aware of that, I am sure, but I am not convinced that the UK authorities will be on top of it. So I have asked Folding Square to help in that respect, a favour to an old man."

He smiled at Li.

Emily continued, "So we undertake to have our people check and keep track of Wu's family and people - not a small job I should add. It's not foolproof either, but it is a second line of defence, in a sense. If we find anything we will anonymously let the British authorities know. That is as much as I can agree to do. We do not want to become embroiled in a fight with Ten Dragons; it would be counter-productive for both enterprises."

Jian Li immediately asked, "Will you inform me also?"

"No," Yang said, emphatically. "In fact, we will have no contact with you directly whatsoever. It's for your benefit and ours, frankly. We respect Mr. Yau's special relationship with Mr. Lin and your father and we hold Mr. Yau in very high esteem. But you are not part of us. We are doing this for Mr. Yau, Jian Li, not for you."

She looked at Michael Yau. Li could see the business part of the discussion was at an end. He bowed deeply, seated next to Yang; it was in gratitude for her help, obviously. Li could see that it was well-received by the woman; her former boss treating her with such respect.

Emily Yang rose in a fluid movement, bowed to Mr. Yau after placing her napkin on the table.

"Goodbye, Jian Li, I must now leave."

She made a move towards the door and Li stood up impulsively, reached out and took her hand, stopping her.

"Thank you; for Bangor and for now, I truly appreciate it."

The triad operative nodded, smiled, shook her hand and then left the room.

Michael Yau indicated that Li should be re-seated. She thanked him again then said, "Mr. Yau, I am sorry for the way I did this."

He looked at her, waited a moment and then smiled.

"Jian Li, never apologize for being a true friend. Now, let's continue our lunch and you can bring me up to speed on your life. I hear about it from Enlai and also from your dad on Thursdays as we talk, but now I get to hear it first-hand."

He sounded like a jovial great-uncle, she thought, and then the image of her straight-laced dad, her elderly boss and this man naked together in the bathhouse, in deep conversation about life came to mind. She burst out laughing.

"Did they talk about my sailing?" she said.

He nodded, "Oh yes, they cover that, at least your dad does. I think Enlai wants to start a LinTan Shipping racing team and make you skipper."

She laughed, "That's the first I have heard of that idea! I am not that competent; but I could crew. I suspect LinTan has a lot of sailors who would vie for the role of skipper on a racing yacht for the company, if he ever made that happen."

Probably it was one of Enlai's daydreams shared with his friends at the bathhouse, she realised. Her face turned a little mischievous.

"But they didn't say I like sailing with James Hoi, Clark Hoi's son, and I think we might just be interested in each other…"

Now he laughed.

"No, they didn't mention that."

She said, eyes smiling, "That's because neither of them know yet; only you. Tell them one Thursday at the bathhouse, then they will ask how you know. You can have some fun with it, a small token of my appreciation for your help.

"And please, Mr. Yau, call me Li; my friends do."

20 SOPHIE

It was later the same week. Catrin and John had spent two days on detailed planning of the operation when the message came through from Art & Antiques; Sophie had agreed to the proposal but she wanted to meet the people she would be working with, at her studio.

As Catrin and John Obi crossed the River Orwell south of Ipswich, her personal mobile rang. The two detectives were on their way to Aldeburgh in Suffolk. John had agreed that he would drive the pool car there as he knew the area better; Catrin would bring them back.

It was Chris Treneer calling her.

She said, "It's my fella; close your ears."

Obi smiled and said nothing, eyes on the road. He could see her listening for a while, then she said, "That's… that's perfect, Chris. The last time I saw Mitchell he was so formal, but he was grateful for the help, I know.

"I will call you later. I am with John in a car and he blushes easily. It's great news. Love you."

She closed the call. Obi smiled at her.

"I blush easily; me?"

John's skin was as dark as his parents; he was the son of

Kenyan first-generation immigrants. Everyone in the ACU team knew Catrin blushed easily.

She sounded excited.

"He is coming up to London. We knew that Steadman put in a good word for him; people are looking for a place in one of the e-crime units in the Met but he is a Level 3. There is more turnover at Levels 1 and 2 among junior staff, but not so much in the mid-level and higher up. It's a matter of time and a good interview.

"Then he gets a call to see his boss this morning, who tells him he is being seconded to City of London Police for two months, to work with them on a big e-crime fraud case; to learn the latest… whatever technologies or techniques they use; to bring it back to the Devon & Cornwall team. His boss said Superintendent Mitchell and Bob Matheson fixed it with a crony of theirs with the City people."

The City of London Police, not the Metropolitan Police, deal with all policing matters in the city centre including the Stock Exchange. Chief Superintendent Matheson at the Met, she knew, was grateful for her help in the Greaves case. It was his PCeU team that had been part of a successful international effort to track down a German hacker.

"Chris was about to phone me when he took a call from Superintendent Mitchell, the father of the victim in Falmouth. He said he had heard the news and asked Chris to pass on his regards to Sergeant Sayer when he visited London. Chris said that he hadn't spoken to the man since the case; not even a one-on-one conversation with Mitchell then, yet the man called him now. He was in this fix up to his eyebrows, he could tell."

Obi said, "Well, you knew Mitchell appreciated your efforts; and it was his daughter at the sharp end."

Catrin was thinking. She said, "Chris is coming up and moving some stuff at the end of next week, staying over the weekend. I am going to buy new sheets and pillow-cases for the bed… and some new towels."

John Obi let out a laugh. "Women!" he said.

The modest bungalow in Linden Road, Aldeburgh was set behind some trees and bushes with open fields behind. John pulled into the driveway, parking next to a small Opel with a sticker in the window calling for improvements in art education funding.

He said, "We are in the right place, I see."

As they got out, the front door opened and a middle-aged woman, slim build, wearing jeans and a shirt opened the door. She was intrinsically attractive, Catrin saw, but had that aura of being a solitary person. This must be Sophie, she thought.

"So what do you think?" asked Sophie Cartwright as they stood in the living room. She hadn't offered to take their coats nor had she invited them into her studio; none of the social or business norms.

Cartwright had just said, "Come on in."

She had led them across to the wall of the living room and posed the question to John.

In front of them were two paintings, oils; one of the Maltings, nearby at Snape; the concert hall founded by Benjamin Britten and Peter Pears. The other was a portrait of an unknown person.

John said, "They are yours; originals?" He kept his voice steady but the sense of disappointment tinged it. Catrin was watching the woman; she had expected a test for both of them and had told John to pull no punches if she did this to him.

"Yes, they are mine, and …?"

John took a deep breath.

"Professional workmanship but… they lack a lot. Sorry."

She smiled at him and looked at Catrin.

"I am not asking you. Neville told me about you."

Catrin thought, he told me about you, too. But she said nothing.

"Come here," Sophie said, leading them into another room at the rear; her studio this time, clearly.

"This is my best painting of the lake scene at Wivenoe Park, from as close to the spot where John Constable painted his masterpiece as I could get. I left out the modern stuff. It is University of Essex property now and I have painted it a few times. And this is my copy of the Constable painting, the most recent. Do you see?"

John said immediately, "You can copy other paintings perfectly, but you lack the spark for great original art. That's it, isn't it?"

"Right, young man, now you have it. I think you can stay after all. I will make some tea or coffee while we talk."

Catrin had moved a few steps to get closer to another painting, a male nude standing with one arm raised, leaning slightly off-balance against a room wall. It was over her desk in the corner of the studio. Painted from behind, the model was lit from the window in front, the partly open shutters casting shadows and a spectrum of colours. The window was French, she thought, perhaps Paris or another French city. It was unsigned.

She said candidly, "I think this is yours too, and it belies everything you just said, Sophie; it's exceptional."

The older woman stopped, stood still, the bristling energy of her exchange with John leaving her.

She answered, "Neville was right, you are good. Yes, it's mine; it's my Andrew, as he was. It was the last painting that moved me that much."

She didn't elaborate.

"I will put the kettle on and we can get to work."

Catrin thought that they were on a level playing field now. Coltrane had briefed her alone about Sophie Cartwright. She could be extremely cantankerous, he had said; she had once sent a DC from A&A back to London empty-handed after he had 'disappointed' her. She refused to work with anyone French and guardedly accepted only certain Americans she knew by reputation.

Coltrane had told her, "She won't work with anyone who doesn't have a solid appreciation for art. She can be rude and confrontational but her work is worth it. You and John need to set it straight with her right from the outset, that's all."

He chuckled. "When I called her to set it up, she told me that she wanted both a fee and a grant from the Coltrane Foundation for a month's painting in Sedona, Arizona. I told her she had more money than she deserved from the fee, she could go to Arizona on that and I wouldn't want to see her Sedona art anyway. She enjoyed that."

They took Cartwright through the project. They were looking together at the insurance photographs and some other illustrations of Hamlet Winstanley's paintings.

Catrin said, watching Cartwright's responses carefully, "Mrs. Rosalind Heaton, wife of a freehold farmer, John Heaton of Carnforth, Lancashire, painted in 1742. She was not a member of the aristocracy, which will have skin and complexion implications.

"Some of the developments in the agricultural and industrial revolutions were starting to hit the area. The family adapted; did well, so probably the Heaton family were enterprising. You can see it in the painting; she looks sharp; a no-nonsense sort of woman."

Sophie said, "So you want this exact likeness?"

Catrin said, "Not quite. I want it to look as if you couldn't tell whether it was Rosalind Heaton or a twin sister; that close, but just off being identical. You know, only mothers and artists painting twins can tell the difference; like that."

Sophie nodded. She said, "I will need to see his paintings, originals; for his brush work."

Catrin replied, understanding, "We have a list of them and their locations and we will pick up the travel expenses. Just be careful; Winstanley did some sub-contracting at the peak of his output; he did faces, another artist did clothing, folds in fabric, the tedious stuff."

Sophie said, "I look out for that sort of thing anyway in my own background research. And I check for any pigment preferences."

Catrin went on, "Bertie Wells is finding an original canvas

for you, the right period, right size; the right frame with original stretchers, of course, and he will prepare it. And if there are any special pigment issues, talk to him."

Bertie was an art technician working with A&A.

Sophie nodded, taking in Catrin's thoroughness. No matter how well she painted the copy, the frame and canvas had to be from the right period also.

She said, "I like Bertie; he knows his work. You are on top of things, I see. Now, these other differences… the alternates to the Dorset button set, for example; let's get some paint and see if we can get exactly what you want while we are together. You want the second set of Dorsets underneath, as pedimento, you say. Do you want them in the same positions or in a different spacing?

"Right, directly underneath," said Catrin. "Make it as if he changed his mind about the button size, for artistic balance, perhaps. Or he may have worked a different sitting with the model when she was wearing a similar dress and preferred the buttons he saw then. Make it as confusing as possible."

Sophie would be expected to produce a second set of the period handmade buttons painted over the first, only detectable by forensic analysis. Discovery of such under-drawings or paintings, called 'pedimenti', were important clues in identification of older art works, where a canvas might go through such changes before the artist declared it a finished work.

They worked away on finalizing the detail required, oblivious to the time passing. Finally, they were done; through the list of items Catrin had noted and Sophie's own questions.

Sophie said, "Catrin, I think I have it now, what I need to do, the preparations I need to make. Is there anything else?"

"Just one more thing. Lighting and tone, let's talk about those…"

Sophie arched one eyebrow. Normally that was left to her to work out. If Neville hadn't told her about Sayer and the woman had raised this at the outset, she would have sent her packing

On the journey back John suddenly asked Catrin, "What was that thing about 'her Andrew'; was she married?"

Catrin was driving. She smiled. "If you google Andrew Helmsley, artist, see what happens. That's what I did."

A few minutes later John said, "I assume it was this Andrew who died in Paris. I saw the window in the painting by her desk, too."

"Yes, that's him. He was an art teacher, but if you dig a bit more, you will see some rumour, conspiracy theory stuff, that he was involved in some activist movement over there and fell afoul of someone, that his death was not accidental.

"Whether or not that's true, Neville told me, when Sophie was arrested for forgery three years later in London, the preliminary hearing was 'in camera' and a man from somewhere in Whitehall made sure the charges went away. It was before Neville's appointment and she has been legit ever since, a copyist. All her works are now fraud-proof, a complex stamping process on the back to prevent them being misrepresented."

John smiled, "Except of course, for the second Mrs. Heaton of Carnforth, in preparation."

She nodded, "Yes, except that one and some others she prepared for A&A or other police services in the past. And she has a letter from Neville on the Winstanley to keep her out of trouble. It was her first request, before the Sedona gambit. He gave her that one."

"She will be busy on that for a while, I think," said John. "I need to get on with the Canterbury theft tomorrow that DCI Worsley wants to see more progress on."

Catrin said, "We still haven't heard anything about Cox's situation, so it goes nowhere for the time being anyway; that was the deal. He still has more to tell."

21 COVENT GARDEN

In the weeks following, there was a flurry of activity domestically and artistically for Catrin, but her police work was 'normal'. She was mainly assisting Keith Marshall on a drawn-out case in Kent, waiting for developments outside her control on the one she was going to lead. John Obi was busy too, assisting Worsley who had an incredible knack of keeping his nose to the grindstone in doing most of the leg work for her.

The Structural Review Committee had met and reviewed organizational and resource changes within the Metropolitan Police Service. The feedback from Taylor that filtered down was that Trident, the gang crime command, had been a big winner. The Air Support Group had taken a loss and ACU, in a rag-tag mix of Specialist Crime Command and Serious Crime Command units, had been deferred until the next SRC meeting, next quarter.

Worsley told her team, "Apparently, talking about helicopters took them well into the evening. Our file is in there, we have presented our best face, so all we can do is wait, forget about it and get on with the job."

Catrin, with Worsley and Taylor, attended the formal lunch at the Malaysian High Commission where John Obi and a young constable called Ryerson, with the West Midlands Police, were presented with pewter vases similar to the one given to Catrin back in Kuala Lumpur. They were gifts from the aristocrat in Malaysia for their roles in the recovery of the family belongings.

The High Commissioner and other staff were particularly attentive to Catrin, the HC taking her on one side privately at one point hinting that she would be back soon for a further recognition in her own right.

Catrin enjoyed the pleasure of seeing the pride in Kaila, John Obi's wife, on her husband's recognition. It more than compensated, she thought, for Obi's own discomfort at the formal event.

But the visit to the Malaysians seemed to make her own recovery stutter. For several nights afterwards her sleep was disturbed and she had flash-backs to the Twin Towers, something she had thought she was through.

Dr. Herrington said, "Revisiting places associated with the case can do that, Catrin. I am not at all surprised. But it will ease again."

It did.

In the same period, Chris Treneer partly re-located from Devon. Not yet having a permanent position in London, he kept his flat in Exeter and just brought what he needed for work and play. For the next two months he had a travel allowance from Devon & Cornwall Police. He could use some of that to pay towards Catrin's rent and share other living expenses.

They had to decide what to do about his car in London. Catrin got by without a personal vehicle and, given their work similarities, so could he. Although her flat was just outside the geographical boundary for the astronomical London Congestion Fee, a daily surcharge, parking in the area was a perennial problem even for residents. In the end he loaned it to Melanie and Jean to share the use of; they had a parking spot paid for as part of the Cwmbran Kiln lease.

So the couple adjusted to a new-found domesticity.

For Catrin, she hadn't lived with a man since her boyfriend, David Jameson, back in Aberystwyth. But that was as a university student in a college environment. This was different again.

Chris just seemed to take it all in his stride, adjusting to the new world of London, his job assignment and, within a short time, taking up with a five-a-side team in Hackney. He seemed content and, within days, Catrin wondered why she had held some apprehensions about the change; it seemed natural that he was there and they were together. It helped to have someone to share the costs of her flat and, even more important, for her not to feel alone at times when the worst of the fear of her situation regarding Nam Wu hit her.

It was so good, she felt, her art should have flourished. But initially she found she just hit a road block each time she went to the Cwmbran Kiln.

"Catrin, stop where you are, right now, before you ruin it."

Jean's comment cut across the silence in the workshop area at the Kiln. She was looking at the vase that was half-finished, tilted in Catrin's hand.

Melanie's voice came from the front area, the shop, where the doorbell had just signaled that a customer she had been serving had left.

"It's domestic bliss, Jean; it must have destroyed her artistic streak. She needs to be single, alone and yearning again."

Catrin said, in her defence, "I am just working out where…"

To be cut off by Jean, firmly. "No, you are struggling to finish something you have lost the vision of, I can tell. I know you."

Catrin looked at her friend, with whom she had spent many hours over the years in companiable silence in this pottery, knowing the truth of the statement. Melanie came back to the workshop and picked up exactly the situation, the concern on her own partner's face for their friend. This time there was no quip.

Catrin said, "Professional artists turn up, day in, day out, do the work. Sometimes it's adequate, less frequently it's wonderful. It's just one of those days…"

It was Melanie who responded.

"That's what Jean and I do to keep this business going, to produce the goods. What you and Jean do is different. Jean may make the pieces and she contributes to the design, but it is almost all based on your inspiration for the decorative elements; that's the hallmark. Don't fool yourself."

Catrin sat back and took a deep breath then wiped her brush, starting the process of cleaning it.

"Do you want to call it a day?" asked Jean.

Catrin thought for a moment. Then a look came into her eyes that her friend recognized.

"No, I want to do something quite different and get it out of my system. I need a different shape of bisque; a flat surface like a platter perhaps, so it will have to wait."

The bisque was the clay after its first firing, porous and unadorned.

"No it won't," said Melanie, opening a cupboard door. "Take your pick; Jean made a whole mix of bisques for you, both platters and vases, while you were in Cornwall. We were thinking… well, we know how you were after the Kinnington incident. What you produced then was quite different from everything else."

Catrin looked, reached over, pulling out from the set of blank pottery a slightly beveled rectangular platter, raw, unfinished but with a smooth, perfect surface. It had asymmetrical ends, a style Jean had designed. Catrin enjoyed working on these at other times. She looked at her friend, who was smiling encouragingly at her.

"You," Catrin said, "and you, too," she added, looking at Melanie, "are something else. Thank you."

"With you around, we have to be," Melanie retorted.

"They must be based on his eyes, the man in Kuala

Lumpur," said Jean later. She was preparing the kiln for several pieces, including the platter Catrin had finished.

"Yes," said Catrin quietly, "You see that. In the overglaze enamel there will be a single tear from the left eye, silver with a marine blue centre line."

"For him? Or you?" asked Jean.

She and Melanie had heard it all from Catrin, about how she felt.

"For both of us and also for Jared Farra; we are all victims," said Catrin.

After a slight pause, she gave a sigh.

"I am glad I did it, though. We will see what Liz says about this one."

Liz Marshall had exclusive distribution in London of the pieces produced by Catrin and Jean, selling works from her art gallery off the Fulham Road. She handled only works by British artists and had a real eye for what would sell.

Catrin's personal mobile rang. As she answered it and talked to her boyfriend her face clouded over, bringing the full attention of Jean and Melanie on her.

"It's Chris,' she said, "he sprained his ankle playing five-a-side; he is on crutches and another team member is driving him home instead of him taking the Tube. I'd better head out."

Melanie said, "See if he wants to eat with us, well, both of you. If you want. I am making my mum's quiche."

Melanie had made it for a meal for the four of them a couple of weeks earlier; Chris had raved over it.

Catrin nodded and talked into the phone.

When she closed the call she said, "He would be delighted to; he will be dropped off here. Then, he says, he can hobble the walk home to our flat like a hero."

As Melanie headed upstairs to the living area she made a comment about heroes that would be unrepeatable to others.

~~

It was a week later and Chris's ankle was back to full

strength, he said. Catrin had taken him to Covent Garden market, the tourist market area as it now was, part of the list of things that she wanted him to see in London. He was looking at items on a market stall when he suddenly realised that Catrin wasn't there, wasn't near him at all.

He looked around and couldn't see her. Then he re-surveyed the area slowly, spotting her in an archway about twenty yards away, her gaze in a different direction. He walked slowly towards her then noticed the object of her gaze, a Chinese man actively seeking someone.

He moved more rapidly towards Catrin, then saw a Chinese woman come out of a shop and wave at the man, who gave a characteristic shrug; he too had lost sight of his partner, it seemed. As they walked off Catrin came over to Chris and gave him a smile.

Chris said, "You didn't say anything, Catrin!"

He knew about the surveillance training; she had talked about it. He knew also it would be her call whether to fade out of sight and leave him or grab him to leave with her. It would depend on how she perceived the threat and whether he was also at risk.

She saw his worry and anger intermingled. But she couldn't help that; these decisions were on the instant and she had been told not to second-guess herself.

She said nothing at first then, after a moment, said quietly, "It's OK now."

The look that passed across her face made something in Chris Treneer twist up with anguish; that his girlfriend was constantly living in 'surveillance' mode when out and about. And he could do nothing about it, he knew.

He just pulled her forward and gave her a big hug.

"Sorry," he said.

She smiled. "Lunch, then we should go back. I am going to the Kiln. I promised Jean we would do something there this afternoon, OK?"

He nodded. The Cwmbran Kiln was for Catrin, for whatever reason, a safe place, not that there was any logic to that. He knew she was scheduled to see Dr. Herrington again tomorrow and thought that, given the fright just now, she would probably take one of her pills tonight; sleeping pills prescribed for just such nights.

As much as they enjoyed being together, as beneficial as the sessions with Herrington or visits to St. Paul's Cathedral were, as she claimed, Chris felt that Catrin had a spring inside her that only tightened, increasing its tension click by click, and it never released. He had no idea what to do about it.

~~

"What I don't understand," said Daniel, "is why Jian Li chose this convoluted route to tell me she is going out with a young man called James Hoi? She knows we would like her to find someone in our community, but what matters is that whoever it is should be a person of good character."

The three men were in the bathhouse on Shep Kip Mei Street.

Enlai Lin thought he knew what Daniel meant by 'our community'; a member of their faith, perhaps even from their Methodist church.

He said, "Because it will be me telling you about the Hoi family. I know the parents. And while they are not in your 'community' Daniel, they are a fine family. James is a good young man, hard-working and intelligent, a pleasant person and -"

His eyes twinkled.

"They are prosperous. If they marry it will be a good match, I think."

Enlai Lin was extremely wealthy. Daniel wondered what 'prosperous' meant when Enlai used that term. Now he thought it, he wondered if this suitor was related to a Hoi who was one of his clients, an older man.

Enlai looked at Michael, who had been silent after the announcement; the look to Yau saying clearly that he should say more.

Michael said, "She also wants you to know she came to see me, of course."

Daniel looked surprised by the fact he had missed that point. His relationship with this retired triad leader had developed over the years and their unwritten rule that business issues stayed outside the doors of the bathhouse had made him forget the significance of the original remark.

Yau went on, "As you know, her friend Catrin Sayer, the police officer, shot a triad member in Kuala Lumpur, a young man ordered to kill the police officer she was with at the time. She was worried about whether there would be any retribution against her friend."

Enlai looked at Daniel, suddenly serious and concerned as this aspect of Yau's life came into the room and it now being associated with his daughter.

Daniel said, "I didn't know she knew you. Do you and Jian Li have any contact, Michael?"

"No," said the older man, untroubled by the question and the inference. "The only other time I saw Jian Li to talk to was at the memorial service for Han. She called me out of concern. There is guanxi between the two women, so she is very worried."

"I hope -." Daniel's voice had risen a little, as Enlai gently cut him off.

"All is well, Michael?"

"Yes, Enlai, it is. I met with Jian Li only once. I told her not to worry about it. She wanted to know if I would keep her informed. The answer was 'no'. All she knows is that I will help."

Enlai saw in Michael Yau's eyes a sense that it was more complex than his explanation but heard Daniel's relief in his voice as he responded.

"Thank you, Michael," he said. What he meant, Enlai knew, was he was glad that Michael was not developing further any relationship with Jian Li. Our little world in the Shep Kip Mei Street bathhouse each week is a strange one, he mused.

PART 3

TRAP

22 CRONIN

Catrin, Neville Coltrane, Jane Worsley and Bertie Wells were examining the painting again.

"Sophie did a good job, she really did," said Bertie. "Mind you, we gave her some original pigments and the canvas; she had a good start."

They were looking at a framed portrait of a woman bearing a very close resemblance to Rosalind Heaton. It was signed by Hamlet Winstanley.

Catrin picked up the photographs that Bertie had prepared, added them to a file folder that she then put it into her brief-case.

She said, "I had better head over to see the people at the Houghton Bank."

Stage one.

Five days ago the Italians had agreed to the deal regarding Cox's transfer. Coltrane had sent Detective Inspector Caldwell over to see Edmond Cox with the lawyer from Romford, Hathaway, to get the names and the additional information; he was still the person who knew most intimately the details obtained during the investigation of the Houghton Bank robbery.

Now they knew the people involved. Catrin and John had spent two days doing background checks and organizing preparations for phone taps, surveillance tracking and media intercepts.

There had been five people directly involved during the robbery. The two that stayed at the Hewitt home were a Tony Hodson and a Noel Johnson; the others, including Cox, accompanied Hewitt to the bank and removed the art works. Hodson was the planner, the man who had decided on the Hewitt hostage strategy.

The most important name provided was that of a sixth person, the one who had commissioned the robbery. He was a member of the board of directors of the bank, a Ryland Cronin, a senior executive in the City at an investment firm called Medway Analytics. After locking up Hewitt, the final task of the men in the BMW had been to deliver the three paintings to Cronin's flat in London. That was the last time Cox had seen them.

Philip Caldwell had joined them in a conference call from Rome after his meeting with Cox, during which John did a quick on-line check on Ryland Cronin.

He said, "But Cronin is rich; why does he need to do this?"

Worsley said wryly, "It's not about wealth, it's about ownership, I suspect. Probably the items that are bought and owned by the bank are not for sale. Or perhaps the reason he had to have them is linked to the selection of the Winstanley with the Stubbs; we need to look into that."

Coltrane nodded. "In any event, we will need to locate the paintings or secure a confession from one of the robbery team about Cronin's involvement."

They had already established that Cronin was in New York at a finance meeting on the days around the robbery; it was part of the original investigation file; the whereabouts of bank staff and associated personnel at the time of the robbery. His alibi was good unless they found other linking evidence.

"It's a pity that Cronin wasn't in that place in Chile at the time, the one Hewitt send a text to - although you would have picked that up earlier, no doubt, sir," said John.

Coltrane smiled. "Yes, a director of the bank that had been robbed being in Arica, Chile would have had us asking questions. In fact, Philip probed the issue of Arica with Cox. He had no idea what that text was about. They knew about it but weren't briefed as to the reason by Hodson."

The final item of discussion of the meeting was the path forward for the A&A and ACU teams involved. Worsley and Coltrane had confirmed that Catrin's plan would go forward. They wanted all of the gang as well as Cronin. But particularly they wanted Anthony Arnold Hodson, no prior record. He was the man now identified as the perpetrator of the attack on Wendy Hewitt.

John came back to Catrin later that day.

"I was checking on Hodson. He was a petty officer in the Royal Navy. Cronin was also in the navy for six years; he left with the rank of lieutenant. It's in his bio. Looking at their two careers they could have overlapped. But we need the military records to check."

Catrin groaned. They both knew that co-operation between military and civilian police went well only when the focus was a civilian issue; if it involved a serving or former military person then either the military got protective of their turf or of their people.

There was a 'worry bead' element, also. Start talking to the military and you never knew who started to hear more, leaks to give senior people a 'heads up'. Given the need to protect Cox, this was a significant issue.

Catrin said, "Let's talk to Keith; see what he thinks."

Inspector Keith Marshall had military experience, at least, and more importantly he still had plenty of contacts in the services.

"No criminal record for this man Hodson; nothing?" asked Keith.

"No. A fine upstanding citizen, apparently," said John.

"Then you will get nothing out of the Navy, not even official records unless you can provide a basis. And I wouldn't do that, obviously, given the nature of your little gambit here, Catrin."

She nodded her head, agreeing with him.

He asked, "Also, this overlap period you mentioned. When was it?"

John looked at his notes.

"It was between the years 1996 and 2001. Hodson was at Dartmouth when they first overlapped, a two year period. Then a break, then Hodson served on a ship at the time Cronin was there, it appears. Hodson was in the navy twelve years, overall, it seems, Cronin around six. Then Cronin left the service, joined the investment business in which he is now a senior partner. So there are at least two periods when they overlapped during Cronin's military service.

Keith asked, "And Hodson's rank?"

Obi replied, "Petty Officer at Dartmouth; PO afterwards, no promotion we know about. All this is ferreted out from tax returns, Vehicle Licensing and Customs & Immigration records, that sort of thing. It's all we have."

"I bet Hodson was a trainer when Cronin was an officer cadet," said Keith. "It could be important to find that out. During training, what went on… well, I doubt you will find out much through official channels, though. In the army at Sandhurst, it was, well still is, a very closed shop indeed. It's the same at Dartmouth."

Obi said, "So how far would we have to push this up the chain to get co-operation, then?"

Marshall said, "A long way. Don't try. How old are you John?"

Obi, surprised, said, "Twenty-five."

Marshall replied, "You would be thinking about retirement when this was processed. There is only one easy way. I should say 'not easy', but it works. I have used it with the army."

He looked across at Worsley, who was watching this

discussion from the sidelines. She said nothing.

Catrin said, "And what is that, although I am almost scared to ask?"

Keith smiled. "Bribery, corruption and the 'old boys' network'; the first two will get you gaol time though."

"I am too young to be an 'old boy', sir," said Obi.

Catrin was looking at Keith looking at Worsley; it meant something. But their boss said nothing and they left it at that.

~~

You are not an expert, you just have a fixation about the case, they had agreed as an approach strategy. Catrin thought about that as she was shown into a meeting room at the Houghton Bank. She had noted the security cameras and keypad access panels as well as the guards. The bank had upgraded its security throughout, she saw, after the embarrassment of the loss of the paintings.

The door opened and a woman, Mrs. Iris Woodley, came in. She was the bank employee responsible for the Executive Floor, its assets and its smooth functioning, she said. With her was a Douglas Blinney. He introduced himself as the head of security, appointed after the robbery. He was Welsh, too, but Catrin made no light conversation about that; nor did Blinney.

Introductions over, they got down to the point of the visit.

Woodley said, "You said on the phone, sergeant, that you have a painting similar to one of ours; one belonging to the bank that was stolen, I gather. What you mean by 'similar'?"

"Yes, Mrs. Woodley, I did. It's by Hamlet Winstanley, the portrait artist from Warrington."

She looked at her notebook.

"Your painting was called, I gather, 'Mrs. Rosalind Heaton'. Ours has no name, just an annotation in black ink on one stretcher bar, at the back. It says, 'Longfield Farm'. The Metropolitan Police Art & Antiques Unit told me that the farm where Mrs. Heaton lived had that name, so I suspect the people in the portraits are related. I am hoping, without saying anything more about my own investigation here, I must add, to find out about this painting from people who may know about these works."

Woodley and Blinney looked at her in silence, waiting for more.

Catrin continued. "They seemed similar to me, so I thought I would check with you. There aren't that many Hamlet Winstanley paintings around, you see? That's what the Art & Antiques Unit told me. They handled the investigation of the bank robbery, as you know."

She placed the photograph of Sophie's masterpiece on the desk, moving it towards them to invite their comments.

Blinney said, as he stared at the image, "Yes, that's the group that Inspector Caldwell is part of. He led the enquiries, I recall, but nothing has come of it so far, we understand."

He was looking closely at the photo.

Mrs. Woodley said, "Well, I look after the Executive Floor but I am no art expert, so I am not sure how we can help, really. Half of the bank's board of directors are interested in art, in one form or another. You are more likely to do better with them than us."

Her final comment had been an attempt at humour, Catrin thought, but it was a 'plus'; it meant she didn't have to open that subject herself now. Woodley was seeing the irony of a police officer coming to the bank because a painting appeared 'similar' to one they once owned.

Blinney was more serious in his evaluation, Catrin saw.

He said, "It does look similar to the one we had, from my recollection of the photographs of the missing items. I wasn't on staff at the time of the robbery. I came in afterwards but I have met several times, obviously, with Inspector Caldwell. I would say, though, there is something different in this photograph. I can't place it without getting our file photograph to compare."

It's the buttons; they are the most obvious difference, thought Catrin. We chose different buttons for the front of the dress. She continued to look at him, saying nothing.

He added, "Do you mind if I keep this? I can send it over to Mr. Cronin. He is one of the directors. As I recall from my predecessor, he was a member of the board who actually liked the Winstanley and he is probably the person who is most knowledgeable, knowing something of his tastes in art now. You may also want to contact the art dealer from whom the bank bought the painting; I can check the record; but Mr. Cronin would know that person too, right Iris?"

Woodley nodded, "I think Mr. Cronin saw the painting there and mentioned it. That's when the bank took an interest."

Catrin said, "In what way?"

Woodley said, "Well, it was the chairman's idea, Sir Kenneth Lowell. I was told to buy it for our general collection, but place it in the boardroom for a while so that Mr. Cronin could get to see it regularly. His work on the board is highly valued and it was thought of as a nice token of appreciation, I guess. But it disappeared anyway, unfortunately. Inspector Caldwell will have all this on file, I am sure."

Catrin responded, "The Art & Antiques Unit is very busy, Mrs. Woodley, and I know their primary focus is on the recovery of the Stubbs; they are the valuable ones, really."

She paused.

"To be honest, this case of mine - the Winstanley painting - is not quite on their radar. They would be very interested of course if it was to shed any light on the paintings you had lost. So, I would certainly appreciate the name of the dealer, if you could dig it out, Mr. Blinney. Also, if you could consult with Mr. Cronin and any other directors knowledgeable about the bank's paintings, that would be most helpful. I expect that directors of banks like this are not too accessible, being busy people."

"You can say that again," said Iris Woodley. "But Miss Moyano, Mr. Cronin's executive assistant at Medway Analytics, is highly efficient. She will certainly follow through and get back to me. I will let you know."

"Thank you," said Catrin, "I'll leave additional copies of the photograph and my card as well, in case anyone has any ideas or suggestions. Any help at this stage would be appreciated."

Woodley stood, indicating she thought they were done.

Catrin stood also. "It was just an idea to run it by you. If nothing comes of it, that's the way it goes. But I will wait, if I could, Mr. Blinney, for you to locate the details of the dealer who sold the Winstanley portrait to the bank."

"Ah, yes," said Blinney.

He was back in three minutes with a handwritten note. Catrin knew the answer already; she just wanted to establish a bona fide source for the knowledge.

~~

It was two days later in the early evening. Catrin looked at the number that had just appeared on her work mobile as it rang. She was running, on a route that took her into and across Weavers Field, a park area near her home. As a result of her surveillance training, she now deliberately varied the times and routes for her exercise, but wasn't going to stop running because of Nam Wu; she enjoyed it too much.

She moved a little further into the park. The mobile had been by her side continuously since the visit to the Houghton Bank.

"Detective Sergeant Sayer," she said, trying to control her breathing.

"Good evening, Sergeant Sayer, this is Ryland Cronin, a director at the Houghton Bank. Mrs. Woodley passed on to me a photograph and a query to assist, if I could. You went to see her, I gather. I am sorry to bother you in the evening but I have been rather busy and this has only just surfaced. Is it convenient now? I don't know the hours you work but mine are all over the place, these days.

"But you sound a little breathless. Are you able to talk now?"

Catrin said, with enthusiasm, "Certainly Mr. Cronin. I appreciate you getting back to me. I am out for a run at present but would be happy to talk now, take a breather. It was something of a stab in the dark to approach the bank, but it seemed so similar, the painting we now hold and the one that was stolen."

His voice came over the line. "I quite understand and I am glad that you did, but it creates a puzzle for me. I can confirm it is not our painting; that is clear. But I hate to leave it there, to be honest. I know I can't really pry about any case you are on, however there are some very interesting questions raised by your painting."

Catrin said, "Well, we did ask for help, so I would be happy to be as open as I can; not about the investigation, of course, but about the painting, what we know - which is not a lot, to be honest. What questions?"

Cronin said, "It's hard to be specific without seeing the painting myself, although I am no art expert, you understand. I was just quite taken with the Hamlet Winstanley work. It seemed strange to me that there are two paintings of the same woman by him."

Catrin smiled to herself.

All she said was, "Would you like to see the painting, perhaps, if you think it might help us? If you have time, that is. Life must be busy as a bank director."

He laughed, "The Houghton Bank directorship is not a big time consumer compared with my main role at Medway Analytics. Actually, your offer is much appreciated; that is exactly what I would like to do. And I could then tell you about the problem, as I see it."

Catrin said, "It would need to be at New Scotland Yard, though; I can't let it out, you see."

"I quite understand. Let's make an appointment."

"Yes, sir; I am just looking at my schedule on my mobile as we speak."

Anytime day or night, twenty-four/seven, she thought; but she wasn't going to convey that, of course.

23 HAMLET

Bertie Wells, the art forensic technician in Art and Antiques, said, "Both the frame and first glance at the pigment colours seem consistent with the period, and the canvas and craquelure looks to be about the right age. But we haven't undertaken any more detailed technical work on it, Mr. Cronin. It's not actually a priority item for us in Art & Antiques, you see."

Catrin thought that Bertie had conveyed nicely to Cronin so far that he was fitting this in for the ACU, that the 'priorities' were cases of much greater importance to the Art & Antiques Unit. Cronin could tell that this Welsh police officer had been bothering the expert about this particular painting before.

Catrin watched Cronin absorb it all; he occasionally glanced around the laboratory looking at instruments and works of art there. Catrin had a feeling that a marble bust of an eighteenth century nobleman with some rather vulgar graffiti across the forehead had been placed next to the Winstanley for effect, but doubted that the lab staff would ever admit it.

Cronin said, "Well, I do understand. Winstanley's works are hardly in the same league as big name artists. But looking at it, being familiar with the man's work and from what you say, it may well be real," he said. 'However, it's peculiar, very peculiar."

Bertie said, "I am sorry, but I really need to get on…"

Catrin interjected, "Mr. Cronin, perhaps we could go to one of our meeting rooms to talk further? We need to leave Mr. Wells to his work."

As Cronin turned towards the exit before her, Catrin squinted at the bust and then at Bertie, who gave her a quizzical, innocent look.

Later, once they were seated in the meeting room with coffee brought in by Aina, he said, "It's this concern I have; the idea of Hamlet Winstanley painting the same woman twice in different dresses doesn't seem right. I don't believe that it is a sister or a relative; although the facial features are almost identical, as I recall, with those in the painting I saw at the bank."

He looked at her as if this revelation would explain everything. From Catrin's expression, it clearly conveyed nothing at all.

She gave the impression that she was taking a stab at a reason, trying to help.

"I thought portrait painters back then did that, visit a house, sometimes they stayed with people for a period; undertake paintings of some members of the household, some on more than one occasion, that sort of thing. So…"

Cronin could see, despite the business card that this detective had provided referring to her being part of an art crime unit he had never heard of, she needed more background in art history.

He explained patiently.

"The man was a high output portrait artist in the eighteenth century. Generally he did your portrait and moved on. Now, if you were aristocracy or wealthy landed gentry, what you suggest might well be the case. He would enjoy a particularly pleasant summer season as a guest on a great estate that threw elegant parties and provided fine wine and good food. It also provided multiple subjects for his sittings. That was also good business, as these guests were probably people who would want him back at their own estates in the future if they liked his work; eighteenth century networking, so to speak.

"Hamlet Winstanley was particularly attached to Knowsley Hall and the Stanley family; that is, the Lord Derby of the period, in the way I have just described. He even went abroad at his Lordship's request and painted in Rome and other places for him."

"Well, you do seem to know a lot about the artist, Mr. Cronin," said Catrin. "This is very useful."

Ryland Cronin nodded his acknowledgement but didn't lose stride in his explanation.

"But, to have this artist paint a wife of a local farmer in Carnforth twice… I really can't see it. You know, he even had a system; he would paint the faces then send the finished linen off to an artist called Vaneken in London, who would glue it on to a canvas and finish the work, do the clothing, the background. It was just so Winstanley could keep up with the number of commissions. Why paint the details when he could be lining up another commission? He was a businessman as much as an artist."

Catrin looked intent. "Well, if what you say is true… and there are unlikely to be two paintings of Mrs. Heaton, or it is not one of a relative, it raises the issue that ours may be a forgery, I suppose. Not necessarily a recent forgery, I mean. It is a possibility. It could have been made in the period that Winstanley was more popular, or afterwards. Forgery doesn't necessarily mean a copy made now, as you know."

Cronin nodded. He had reached the same conclusion earlier. This detective was starting to see the situation.

She paused. "But if our painting here is real, then…"

"Exactly," Cronin said, letting out a breath, as this plodder finally clued in. "I am now wondering about the one the bank purchased that was stolen. Despite the provenance, it could have been a forgery. I sincerely hope not. After all, I drew it to the attention of some people at the bank."

Catrin looked at him. "So you really like this artist, I gather, sir? You are very knowledgeable about him."

Cronin paused, becoming a little more guarded in his response, she thought. "It's not that, sergeant. I mean, I was well aware of the artist - I have an interest in British art of the period. It was simply that I had mentioned to the Sir Kenneth Lowell, the bank chairman, at lunch that I had just seen this painting in a gallery in Bloomsbury. I was leaving for the USA that afternoon."

Catrin said, as casually as she could, "So, are you on the committee that selects art acquisitions for the bank, sir?"

He shook his head, "No, not now. I used to be. They have one director on the committee at a time, the rest are staff who volunteer. The Houghton Bank prides itself on having artworks throughout the bank.

"The turnover of pieces is quite small but it does take place. We occasionally donate art for charity purposes. It provides tax incentives for buyers and helps relationship-building with clients and others. The board position on the selection committee rotates and I had finished my stint sometime previously. I could be asked again in the future, of course.

"No," he added, almost musing. "I came back from the USA trip, and when I next went to a meeting at the bank Sir Kenneth showed me the Winstanley acquisition. He thought I would be pleased that they had acted on my comment… which, of course, I was, naturally.

"It's part of my concern now, of course, with this new information you provided. I hope the bank did not buy a painting that was a forgery on my account."

Catrin looked at him. The last remark seemed to convey that he had closed the loop on the reason for his interest, but earlier she sensed that perhaps he had a tone of regret that the bank had acquired it. He wanted it for himself, she thought, and had missed the boat buying the painting from the gallery.

But why did he want it so much; to the extent that he would organize a robbery?

She said, "Well, Mr. Cronin, we would need to find it first;

or I should say, the Art and Antiques Unit would need to find it; the bank robbery is still their case… even, though, to be frank, I think they have somewhat run out of lines of enquiry."

Her voice trailed off, then she added, "They will continue the investigation, of course, and if it is found, then this line of discussion we have had could be checked out further but at present, it is a theoretical exercise."

"Indeed, Sergeant. Well, thank you."

He stood up and looked at his watch. "I really must be going…"

His voice sounded as if he still had questions.

He said, "Look, can I ask, in broad terms, how did you find that painting?"

She answered as she stood herself.

"The Art Crime Unit's job is to assist regional police services on art-related crimes, to provide support for issues often below the radar of the Art & Antiques Unit. Information from different crimes in two regions happened to line up; we assisted the Essex Police in a follow-up at the premises of a former employee of a museum and this painting was in his possession. We don't know more, he is not talking about it at present and… I can't really say more than that to you, I am sorry."

She paused then added, almost as an afterthought, "I can say we have obviously checked the movements of this individual against the timing of the Houghton Bank robbery - we had already thought of that - and there is no link whatsoever; he couldn't have been there. We had hopes that he might turn out to be a suspect that we could share with Art & Antiques. But it is quite separate."

He nodded, "Well, thank you for that."

"And thank you for coming in today," she said. "If nothing else, it is good to have the formal confirmation that the Winstanley is not the item taken from your bank, for the record. You have been very helpful."

She escorted him to the front door of the building making it clear that their meeting had been interesting but was obviously a one-off; their investigation would go down different avenues to the Houghton Bank enquiry and she didn't expect any further contact.

He had already called his chauffeur and the car had pulled up outside. As he walked over to the vehicle, she thought about the next meeting with the man.

~~

Two mornings later, Superintendent Jack Taylor came into the Art Crime Unit area unannounced, heading rapidly for Jane Worsley's office and beckoning Catrin to join him as he walked through.

Obi looked at her. "Something's up."

Catrin stood up and said, "I'll let you know."

Taylor wasted no time.

"I was at a 'do' last night," he said, in his broad Yorkshire tones, "when one of our little slimy friends whispered that a plodding sergeant in my area, they thought, had been bothering a very important person in the financial sector about an irrelevant little painting. He was looking across the room at a group of financial people, none that I knew. He didn't say more than that, so it was just a warning shot across the bows.

"So your plan is working, it seems, Sayer, but stick to the white line and tread carefully. I don't want you getting a pudding in your face from our friends, like your boss did."

Jane Worsley said somewhat pointedly, "Thank you, Jack, for putting it so eloquently. But, as you say, we are on the right path if Cronin is sending noises out."

Taylor replied, "He may not be, other than perhaps mentioning the painting to someone else. Cronin wasn't there last night. What worries me is why our brothers in the intelligence services are even aware or interested."

Worsley looked at him, getting the drift.

"Are we somehow treading into deeper water? Is Cronin involved in something else, I wonder? If he is, I doubt we will be told."

Catrin watched the two more senior officers lost in thought. Taylor looked at her and changed the subject quickly, something he was noted for.

"Sayer, are you holding up OK? Still seeing Doctor Herrington?"

"Yes sir," she said, "On both counts. He helps and… it's good to be busy, actually, I don't think much about the Malaysian thing with this case now."

He looked at Worsley, nodding. He was just checking that Sandra Hunt was right about giving Sayer something 'meaty' to work on. To him, though, despite her claim, he thought she was looking strained; he had seen it often enough in other officers over the years.

After he had gone Jane let out a sigh. "You know, when he is in one of his 'do's', as he calls them, he is eloquent as hell; even speaks the Queen's English. 'Pudding in the face', indeed! But we are on the right track, Catrin."

Catrin laughed, knowing the pudding reference was to Worsley's appointment following the arrest fiasco during her time with the Diplomatic Protection Branch.

"And 'slimy friends', ma'am? MI5?"

"No," said Jane, "SIS, formerly MI6, Catrin. MI5 are our 'slippery friends', to use Jack's colourful terms; MI5 may do things in different ways but they are generally on the same page as us. SIS, well…"

She stopped, suddenly looking serious.

"No, we don't want a pudding in your face."

~~

Catrin's next meeting with Herrington, coincidentally, was early the following morning.

She came right out with it.

"I'm struggling, Doctor, to be perfectly frank. It's far worse than the Cheney thing for me. I'm frightened of Nam Wu, frightened of what I might need to do to escape him. But the thing which bothers me the most is the thought that I may need to start again, a new identity. No-one has said anything but it's on the cards potentially, I know it.

"I am OK when I am working; alright for a while after seeing you or after going to St. Paul's. But as soon as I start my surveillance routine, or I see a Chinese person approaching me that I don't know, it starts again."

He nodded, understanding. They talked through again the elements of her fears.

"And your sleep patterns, Catrin? How are they now?"

"Funnily enough, they are fine when Chris is there. By bedtime I am exhausted, nervous exhaustion as much as anything, I guess. When I am alone, it's broken. He went back to Exeter last week for three days, for meeting at the Devon & Cornwall Police headquarters. I took a sleeping tablet before going to bed each night but still woke up around three a.m."

He said, "Well, I don't want to increase your dosage, to be frank."

He paused, thinking. "What is it, I wonder, about St. Paul's Cathedral that works for you? You said previously that you are not a practising Anglican, but I know this sense of finding peace there started with the Cheney case."

He was leafing through the pages going back through her file notes.

Catrin said, "Yes, with AC Hunt taking me there while I was on mandatory leave during the PIRC investigation."

She reminded him of the event. A sudden appearance of the Assistant Commissioner at the Cwmbran Kiln, a pep talk about staying with the Met while riding with her between appointments and, at the end, a visit to Hunt's beloved St. Paul's.

"I just sat down like she did on one of the chairs. She likes to pop in to pray, she told me. She prayed, I closed my eyes and suddenly twenty minutes had gone by and I was at peace. She was gone. That still happens for me when I go there; but I can't live in the place, Doctor Herrington."

"No, I agree." He smiled at the thought.

"Catrin, you should go talk to someone there, I suggest, and find out what it is they think that is working for you. You need to bottle it and have it with you, in a sense."

Then he added, "And I don't mean at all the sort of bottle your mother used to like!"

It was Catrin's turn to smile.

"No, alcohol is not the solution for me; I know that. I think I would be permanently blotto if I did, the way I feel most days. But I will go and find someone to talk to at St. Paul's."

He leaned forward, glancing at the clock behind her, she saw. Her session time was nearly up, she knew.

He said, "And Sergeant Sayer, it's not a criminal investigation you are doing there. Forget your role, switch off the logic and park your analytical mind outside the door. Open yourself up a bit there. Let me know how it goes next time."

24 PENTIMENTO

They waited for another three days, monitoring the communications traffic around Cronin and watching his movements. Then Catrin called him. His assistant took her call, telling Catrin that he was in meetings all day but she would pass on her message. Her tone of voice did not convey hope of a response today. But the return call was only twenty minutes later.

"Mr. Cronin, thank you for returning my call. I just wanted to update you. It seemed only fair."

"Yes, Sergeant Sayer?"

Catrin continued, "We discussed our case with the Art and Antiques Unit, based on the additional information you provided. However, Inspector Caldwell doesn't see how it helps and, frankly, I don't think it is going to bring the investigation into the robbery at your bank any further forward, unfortunately."

He responded very politely but she could tell by his voice he felt his time was being wasted. So she added, "But we did find pentimento, Mr. Cronin, in our painting, around the buttons. Your information helped persuade A&A to do some further investigation for us."

His voice was now more alert. He asked, "Pentimento, you

found pentimento; of what?"

"Other buttons, sir," Catrin said.

There was silence at the end of the line for a moment.

She went on. "Mr. Wells was instructed to do the X-ray fluorescence examination of the painting for us once I explained the conundrum to Inspector Caldwell that you mentioned to me. The ACU doesn't really have the facilities or budget, to be frank, but it was really helpful for me to hear about it from you and… they agreed. So thank you for coming in to assist us. Good day, sir."

His voice leapt down the phone. "Sergeant Sayer, can I see it, I mean, is it possible to see the pentimento? I really would like to see the images."

She said, "Well, unfortunately it's not related to your burglary, so no, at least, officially, no. But you have been helpful, though I can't provide copies to you."

He said, "And I am tied up all day then I head to Paris this evening for meetings tomorrow."

We know that, thought Catrin, which is why we called now.

"Well sir, let me see if I can help. Where is your office? I should have it to hand on your card but I put that somewhere on my desk just now and can't lay … "

He told her the address, which she knew, a building on Watling Street, a stone's throw from St. Paul's, ironically.

She said, "What if I bring a copy of the pentimento image on my iPhone? Let you see it but not keep it, though? You see, a colleague and I have to be at a police station in Wapping later this afternoon and it could fit from a routing perspective for us."

They had worked this out days ago, if the case developed this far.

Cronin said, "I would be extremely, extremely grateful, Sergeant Sayer. I will let Lucia, my assistant, know. Please contact Lucia Moyano when you get to reception."

It was 4.00 p.m. when Catrin and John arrived and were taken to the fourth floor, the top floor of the old building. As an office area it was sumptuous, with furniture and art work that caught Catrin's eye in every direction she looked. If she wasn't working, she would have enjoyed looking around.

Lucia looked as if she could command an army. She was probably descended from a Spanish general who did, Catrin thought. As an executive assistant to Cronin, she had to man the barricades daily, organize appointments and handle a lot of people with big egos. Two mild-mannered younger police officers looking uncomfortable in these surroundings were no problem for her.

Twenty minutes later, while they sat in the waiting area, the door to the office behind her opened and Cronin came out.

"Sergeant Sayer, I am so sorry for the delay. A conference call in preparation for tomorrow in Paris took much longer than I expected."

Catrin looked stoic; John looked annoyed. They had also prepared this response in the event of such a beneficial delay. As they were ushered into his office John's mobile rang; he had pressed the dial button to send a text to Aina as the door opened and she had called him back.

He said, "If you don't mind, I should take this. Please go on, I will join you."

Cronin led Catrin inside as John moved closer to the window, still well within earshot of Lucia but giving the impression of seeking privacy. Aina said nothing, she didn't have to; John knew his lines.

"We have been delayed."

Pause.

"Not sure. Say twenty, no half an hour at tops. Then it will take us fifteen to you."

Pause.

Ok, it will be longer, the traffic, sorry."

Pause.

"It's my sergeant, she insisted on this detour, I'm sorry, sir; it's not my fault. You know how she is about the Essex case, this painting."

Pause.

"I keep saying that. Look, I think DCI Worsley is going to close this one, pass it on; even she is seeing that it is going nowhere."

Pause.

"OK, as soon as we can."

He closed the call and put his phone away, turned and forced a smile on his face for Lucia.

She said, "You can go straight in."

She stood by the open door, ready to close it. He knew as he passed that she had heard every word; she was apparently working at her keyboard but he hadn't heard the sound of her fingers typing. It would get back to Cronin, he was pretty sure.

Catrin was showing Ryland Cronin the image on her phone as the door opened and John entered. Cronin was in the middle of a comment.

"It looks as if there is another button shape beneath the final painting, I agree. It is similar in size and type to the one in our painting, the one that was stolen. The larger button is the one on your painting, I recall. Am I reading this right, do you think?"

"Well," said Catrin, "You are reading it the same as Mr. Wells and he is an expert, so yes. That seems to be the case to me also. This is quite extraordinary, given what you said about Hamlet Winstanley."

She looked a little lost; unable to explain it further.

As John walked up he said, "I said to the sergeant, sir, it could be sisters. Perhaps he painted sisters in Carnforth; but the truth is, it is not really part of our enquiry to unravel that aspect, Mr. Cronin and, Sergeant Sayer, Inspector Whittaker called and …"

He looked at his wristwatch.

Ryland Cronin was shaking his head.

"Not sisters, no…" he said, quite emphatically. Then he added, "At least I don't think so," in a voice that was less certain.

Catrin nodded. "We must be going sir, we are running late

ourselves."

Cronin said, "Well, thank you for dropping by. To see that your painting had two button styles is really interesting for me, given the bank's loss of a Winstanley. I wonder, is it possible to get a good quality photograph of the painting in your possession, do you think, something larger than the small one you passed on to Mr. Blinney earlier? I would really like to look at it more closely, if I could."

"I am not sure I can release that, sir," said Catrin, cautiously. She looked at John.

He said, "It's not evidence, Sarge. The X-ray image is, so no to that, obviously. The photo, well we had copies made from the gallery's own file. I can't see a problem."

He added, "You don't plan to sell or copy the photo yourself, sir, by any chance; we don't want to breach copyright too much, do we?"

Then he smiled, to show it was his sense of humour. He reached into his briefcase and pulled out a thick file, opened it, flicking to several archive quality large photographs of the painting. He passed the top copy over to Cronin.

Catrin's face looked as if she wasn't on board with this largesse by her colleague but the cat was out of the bag. She wasn't going to address it in front of a member of the public.

In fact she was glad Cronin had asked; they had developed several strategies to get a copy into his hands today and his own request had been the preferred 'dream' option.

She just said, "We need to go. But thank you again for your help, Mr. Cronin."

She shook hands and led John out as Ryland followed them, thanking them again for the information and the photograph.

As he went back into his office he thought, not sisters. Rosalind Heaton hadn't a sister living in Carnforth; she had two brothers in Bolton, but no sister. He knew the family history well.

After all, it was also his family history, in part.

They talked outside the building.

"What did you make of that?" asked John.

Catrin said, "You mean, the emphatic bit about there being no sister, that the painting could only be Rosalind Heaton? He has done a lot of research on the painting."

John said, "Or the family. Anyway, we will have to see what he does next. If he doesn't pull in Hodson, we are going to need to move to the back-up approach and pressure him, Sarge."

He was walking on as Catrin suddenly stopped and stood there. She said, "What did you say?"

John stopped. "We may need a new way…"

"No. The family thing; I get it, I think, but what specifically did you mean?"

"Nothing specific, just being logical," said John. "The only way for him to know whether Rosalind Heaton had a sister or not is to look into the family history of the subject of the portrait. He doesn't know we forged it to be confusing."

Catrin's eyes lit up.

"Yes, and he was so sure about it, then he deliberately moderated his position, backing off. John, you are going back to the office to check on Cronin's family history and what we know about the Heaton family - on her side and her husband's side also, please; see if there is any linkage. Phone Aina, get her started on it."

"Go back now; tonight? It will take all evening at least. We should give it to one of the researchers tomorrow…"

"No," said Catrin forcefully, "us; now. Well, you now. I will be in later in the evening if you get nothing - or I won't if it turns out to be a dead end."

He looked at her, unhappy with the turn of events. She knew John liked regular hours whenever possible, but that was tough. Handing it to a support technician to check genealogy databases tomorrow would take time and they didn't have time. It was the operational phase, not background research.

"And you?" he asked.

"I am having dinner with someone. I can't get out of it and

don't want to. Let me know how you get on."

As John entered the ACU area in New Scotland Yard he found Aina wrapping up to leave and only Worsley left there, working away in her office.

Aina said, "The searches I started are on your desktop in a folder; the Cronin family has links to Lancashire starting two generations ago but I haven't got further than that - and I have to go."

"Thanks," said John. "Catrin said it couldn't wait, so I will keep looking into it," loud enough for Worsley to hear. "I will be here half the night. She has gone to a dinner."

In her office Worsley paid no attention, it appeared, but smiled inwardly. She knew that Catrin worked all hours and John, with a family, generally didn't unless it was critical. Fair enough, she thought; he has young children and too many police marriages break up over absentee fathers or mothers lost in their work. On occasion, though, it was needed and she was pleased that Catrin had both made the decision and delegated the work. It showed she was developing.

She also knew why Catrin was at dinner.

~~

"It's about goodwill, Catrin and it is not as if you need to return to Malaysia, given the circumstances. The ceremony will be at the High Commission in Belgrave Square," said Madeleine Turner-Jones.

For a larger woman, she appeared to eat relatively little, Catrin noted. And she had been doing most of the talking. They were in a restaurant on Regent Street that Turner-Jones had picked, one Catrin didn't know, a contemporary atmosphere where the plates were large and the portions small but immaculately plated.

Turner-Jones had thanked her for the opportunity for an informal discussion, 'before this gets elevated between the Met and FCO'. She had kicked off by saying she was doing this because she owed Catrin and wanted the best possible outcome for her and for the country.

Madeleine said, "The commendation for bravery from the Royal Malaysian Police is quite consistent with their record; it is not in any way 'fixed' for political purposes, by them or us."

Catrin reiterated the position she had taken when the initial information had come down to her through higher management.

"I will be pleased to accept it when Sergeant Farra is awarded a decoration for bravery also. He was the person who got out of the car to defend us both, Madeleine. And if, despite the wounds, he hadn't made the effort to pass over his weapon, who knows? He deserves it."

She left the rest unsaid.

Turner-Jones responded, a little irritated, as if Catrin didn't see the 'big picture'. "Well, we can't exactly tell another country how to issue their bravery awards, can we? Really, it is beyond our control. You were the one who brought the gunman down, after all, not Farra."

Turner-Jones didn't dwell on it. She moved on to other things but, Catrin noticed, she circled back to the issue later, trying once again to convince her to change her mind.

Finally Turner-Jones said, "I will do what I can to hold all of this off. It has been nearly three months now since the incident and the Malaysians have made their decision and want to get on with it.

"I will tell people you are busy with new cases. But my people in the South-East Asia section want it to happen soon and the issue has already been raised with the Director General once. DG's talk to the head honchos at your place, so you could be squeezed on this, I regret to say."

The 'regret' didn't sound too heartfelt, Catrin thought.

"I will have to deal with that when it arises, Madeleine."

That was where they left it.

On the walk to the Tube station after the meeting, Catrin thought about the printout of the email sent by Hunt to her;

the one in which FCO had formalised the request. The paper copy had come through internal mail to her, annotated in Hunt's handwriting at the bottom.

"Stick to your guns on this unless I say otherwise. And I have spoken to Baksh; he is in the loop."

She didn't expect any trouble from 'her head honcho', as Madeleine put it.

Once she boarded the train and sat down she checked her phone. She saw the text from John and called him. He was on the District line, heading home.

"You were right, Catrin; there is a family link between Cronin and the woman in the Carnforth portrait. That's why he wants the painting, I think. I will show you in the morning. But it all ties in."

Catrin said happily, "Thanks John, for tracking it down - and it was your suggestion, so well done."

John said, "Something to cheer you up even further; Communications told me just as I was leaving that Cronin telephoned Hodson. He made contact at last."

They were monitoring the mobiles of Tony Hodson and Ryland Cronin.

Catrin said, "Thank God for that… it could be the break we need after all."

John said, "See you tomorrow, Catrin."

25 TRACKING

Tony Hodson was surprised to receive the brief call from Ryland Cronin setting a time for a follow-up call, after which he rang off. He knew from the phrase 'catching up' that Cronin would be calling from another phone to his unregistered phone; it was the alert phrase they had used in the past.

Ryland had told him after the Houghton Bank affair that he would have no further contact with him, so he had not heard from the man in over two years. Cronin had been angry about the report of the treatment of the Hewitt woman; it had garnered as much attention as the robbery itself in the media.

"Whatever I owe you is paid; no more, Tony, do you hear? Or all this will come back on you," Cronin had said angrily at the time.

Hodson said softly, "Are you threatening me, sir?"

He didn't sound particularly concerned. He had always called him 'sir' even at the most difficult times of their relationship. Sometimes it had the edge of a sneer, an insult, not a sign of respect, but it was always 'sir', never 'Ryland'.

Cronin surprised him with the answer.

"Yes I am, in spades. We now have something on each other. If I go down, you go down deeper."

Tony thought that Cronin had the depth issue wrong. Ryland Cronin, after all, had called him to work on the Houghton job and had been in overall charge. But he stayed silent. Cronin wasn't, for once, eating humble pie.

His calls to Cronin in the last few weeks had not been returned and when he had followed up, the assistant made it clear that the message had been passed on; she knew it was not a company matter. Mr. Cronin would return his call in due course but he was a very busy man. He knew he would get nowhere with her.

And now he was calling him with something, not simply returning Hodson's call, it appeared.

Ryland Cronin had begun this time with a straight clarification and in a far more placatory tone of voice.

"Tony, the situation as of our last conversation stands; I want no more pressure from you. But I have news that we both need to consider. The Winstanley taken at the bank may not be genuine. I have seen a second one, painted at the same time it appears, that is part of a police investigation in an unrelated case."

"And how does that concern me, Mr. Cronin?"

He sensed that it was best to keep his original plan to press for money on hold.

"I want you to get to the bottom of it with McNeil, the art dealer that sold it to the bank and also I want you to retrieve the Winstanley for me. With McNeil, no violence, understand. But you have always had an intimidating effect, not just with me, but with others, too. You will get more from him than I would, if there is a cover-up of some sort.

"I will call Muriel and you can pick up the Winstanley at the Denmur Stables. Then I want you find someone who is a real art expert and is not too bothered by legalities; I don't know who nor do I want to. But I need the issue resolved; is my Winstanley genuine or not?"

'My Winstanley', noted Hodson. Cronin had wanted that as much as the horse pictures, despite the value difference.

He had finished by saying, "And I will pay you well. Money

should concern you, I think; I just checked your bank status and credit rating."

That Hodson needed money was clear - and Cronin had the means to find that out easily enough. Tony would need to play along; the routine work, the risk, the role of cut-out from the people involved.

"Quite a lot of work, Mr. Cronin, but I can do it for the right price. You are correct; I do need funds, so some up front would be appreciated. How do you want me to approach McNeil to begin with?"

Cronin said, "Well, in the past you have been a private investigator in my employ, right? That was the title we used to justify your past 'earnings'. You can be that."

"No I can't, now," said Hodson. "There is a licensing system for PI's now."

Cronin snapped, "Then call yourself a security consultant; that's what your card used to say anyway, didn't it? Just don't link it to me. You have a client, that's all.

"I am couriering over to you two images; a photo of another Winstanley painting that the police now hold and a sketch that I did of buttons hidden in it, determined by x-ray techniques. The larger button is the finished button in this second painting; the smaller one shown on X-ray looks to be the same buttons that are on my Winstanley. With the photo records McNeil must have on file that should give you a start.

"If you sense anything was wrong with the painting the bank bought, well, you have the ability to inspire people to co-operate. Get to the bottom of it with him then find me an expert to look again at the painting."

Tony Hodson said, "OK, Mr. Cronin, I will do it. Now you need to tell me how much I am going to get for doing all this; I don't expect to have to haggle with a man like you."

When they had completed the call Ryland Cronin crushed up the simcard and threw the cheap mobile in a waste bin.

~~

At New Scotland Yard the following morning they reviewed the new information. The technician assigned to the monitoring of phone and internet communications gave the first update.

"Cronin left a message on Hodson's mobile that he would call him, then he called his wife in Surrey on his own mobile saying that he was arranging for Hodson to stop by for something in the next day or so. What, he didn't say.

"He was seen later, though, in a shop in Blackfriars buying a pack of cheap mobile phones and several simcards with cash, to make contact with others now, including Hodson.

"There is nothing additional on Hodson's home line or registered mobile. Hodson has another unregistered phone, it turns out. We traced that during the second call from Cronin to him, so we have that identified now. We can track it now, too."

"Not exactly the behaviour of people whose lives are above board?" said Obi.

"No, indeed," said Catrin. "We will have to ask him about it sometime - in a way that doesn't show we are monitoring him, though."

The technician continued. "So far Cronin has made no worrisome travel plans that would send a flag he is bolting."

Catrin asked, "And the wife?"

He responded, "Much the same. Everything she does is local, tied to the stables business or her friends. Muriel Cronin had a call a little later from Hodson's regular mobile. They talked for about ninety seconds to arrange a time for his visit later today… that was it."

Catrin looked at the technician. Somewhere in London Chris was working, perhaps doing exactly the same sort of thing with a team of City of London police officers.

The technician's mobile rang and he quickly answered it, causing a grimace to appear on Worsley's face.

'Sorry," he said, "I left instructions to phone me only if anything developed on this case. Hodson's mobile is now on the move. It's near Dartford Tunnel. Clearly it is in a car, from the speed and location. He is on his way to see Cronin's wife."

Worsley nodded. "Let's follow him on CCTV as well."

She looked at the technician. "We can do that, right?"

He replied,. "They have already got his vehicle details in the system, so, yes. And CCTV will show him at the tunnel entrance also."

Thirty minutes later they were sure where he was going; the Denmur Stables in Surrey.

Catrin said, "John; does your daughter like horses?"

He looked at her, suspiciously, though he knew where this was going.

"Why, Sarge?"

"Well, it's never too early to think of her taking riding lessons. I have just the place we think would be suitable."

He nodded but looked at Worsley, verifying she was on board.

Worsley said, "Check the place for paintings, discreetly, but only after Hodson's visit and don't be a policeman. Head on down there, we will tell you when to go knocking."

~~

They waited until Hodson had left Brookfield and was well away, heading back to London then John Obi stopped by the place. He had worked out his story.

"I was just passing, well actually, I came off the Leatherhead road just to look around the area a bit and saw the sign. Your riding school looks exactly the sort of place we would want for my daughter to learn to ride. My wife has been on to me about it. You know."

Muriel Cronin smiled indulgently at the young man's open enthusiasm. "I am really pleased to hear that you want your daughter to learn to ride; it is a wonderful sport that truly develops character. Do either you or your wife ride?"

She thought she knew the answer to that, but checked

anyway.

"Not me," said John, "My wife did ride as a girl, near Birmingham, but gave it up. Her grandfather used to train horses for show jumping. One went to the Olympics in the sixties."

"Really," said Muriel, "Where? I might know of him, if he was a trainer."

"Kenya," said John, "I am second generation here; my parents are from Kenya; my wife's are the same."

The ID he was using was fictitious; the last thing they needed was for Muriel and Ryland Cronin to compare names. And John's wife's family was from Pakistan, not Kenya.

Muriel laughed. "You know, I may not know your grandfather but if one of his horses did well, I could have heard of it; it's my passion."

A short time later she concluded. "Well Mr. Kaneki, as I said, probably a stable closer to home working with young beginners would be an ideal start; then perhaps in a few years if she shows interest and promise, we can talk again. The two stables I mentioned are very good; they are much closer to you and have very solid reputations."

John had told her they were from a little further east and south, in Crawley. He stood up, taking in the Stubbs painting on the wall of the living room through the doors.

"Nice horse," he said, smiling. "Mrs. Cronin, thank you very much for your time and advice."

She turned, looking at the painting. "Yes, people admire them. My husband commissioned them, two copies of George Stubbs originals, that and another I have. They belong to him though. But when he decides how he wants his home remodelled they will go there, I think."

The phrase 'his home' conveyed a lot, Obi thought, mainly about separation and failure.

His eyes drifted to a space on the wall of the conservatory nearer to the desk, where another painting had been hung, he thought.

"I had better be going; thank you again," said John.

From the car he reported in. "The office is the former conservatory. It has a set of double doors leading through to the house. There is a Stubbs in plain view in the living room, a copy she says, and a space on a wall in the conservatory; it looks about the size to have hung the Winstanley. There is a hanger there and it looks as if a painting has just been removed - a bare spot, out of balance."

He continued, "She made a comment that the Stubbs belonged to her husband, not her. I think it sounded genuine; so we will need to be careful; she may or may not be involved."

Catrin acknowledged the information.

"And the second Stubbs, John, did you see that one also?"

"I only saw the one at a distance; it is certainly looks to be one of the Houghton pair. She was open about having another in the house, in another room. I said it was a nice painting and left it at that. I didn't dwell on it; after all, I was not meant to be that interested in paintings."

"Thank you; head on back."

She closed the call. She thought, now we wait on Hodson's next move. They knew what that was. The unregistered phone they had been tracking had called Peter McNeil, the art dealer who had sold the Winstanley portrait to the Houghton Bank. He planned to visit the art dealer the following morning.

26 BLOOMSBURY

The Ainsley Gallery was located near Golden Square, not far from New Bond Street and Regent Street, in the same area as a cluster of other art dealers and Sotheby's. In an old four-story block, the ground floor had been modernized with large plate glass windows rather than traditional Georgian small panes. It was as much a security measure as a means of making the art inside visible to passers-by, Catrin thought.

They waited until Hodson had been inside ten minutes. Then Catrin went in. John Obi listened to her speak to the receptionist as she entered the gallery; Catrin was wearing a hidden microphone.

They had watched Hodson arrive.

"He troubles me, Catrin. I wish I was doing this, not you," John said. "It's the look, the mood; he is constantly pent-up or brooding. You will need to watch him like a hawk. If he loses it..."

John Obi had been a uniformed officer in Tower Hamlets in East London prior to joining the ACU; no easy area to police. And he was a big man. John was thinking of the photos of Wendy Hewitt in the file. That was when he had lost his temper, let fly. He could easily do the same thing here; this time with a purpose, to get away.

She said, "I will be careful. Anything goes wrong I will scream and run like hell - honest!"

Obi raised one eyebrow in disbelief.

"Just like you did with Colin Cheney, right?"

As she left the car he said to her, "Anything, anything, just yell, I will be listening. I'm less than ten seconds away."

He was now wearing a 'police' tactical vest and his baton was in his lap. He was serious about taking Hodson down if he needed to. Parked around the corner, thirty seconds away, was a marked police car waiting for Catrin's call if all went well.

Catrin said, "It will be fine, John."

She reminded him that she had built the image of herself as the plodding detective obsessed with the painting, not him.

The young woman who approached her said, "Can I help you?"

Catrin replied, "I need to see Mr. McNeil, please," as she showed her warrant card to the receptionist. She put on her 'no nonsense' expression, perfected during her time in Brixton.

The assistant said, "He is with a client but… shall I call him out or what?"

Catrin sighed, "Well, do you know how long he is going to be with this client?"

"Not really."

Catrin said, "You had better ask him to step out, then. I would rather not interrupt him myself."

Implying she was quite prepared to do that.

The woman frowned at the remark but moved to the closed door of the office, tapped gently and went in. Catrin was careful to get close enough behind her but not place herself directly in the doorway. She heard the assistant's soft voice as she approached the desk.

"I am sorry to interrupt but there is a police officer here. She needs to see you. She's a little pushy to be honest… and she wonders how long you will be tied up?

She looked at Hodson.

"My apologies, sir, for interrupting your meeting."

Through the crack in the partially-closed door Catrin saw Hodson sit upright; he looked tense as he did so, but he didn't get up.

McNeil said to Hodson, "If you will excuse me a moment, I will be back as soon as I can."

He glanced at Catrin as he came out, annoyed, as he pulled the door closed. The assistant came out a moment or so behind him and left it slightly ajar as she returned to her reception desk. That would do nicely, Catrin thought.

She introduced herself and said, "We are pursuing enquiries regarding a painting by an artist, Hamlet Winstanley. I spoke with a Mr. Cronin and people at the Houghton Bank recently. Have any of them been in contact with you?"

"No," said Peter McNeil, "not recently."

"It's about a painting we came across in the course of our enquiries. It appears to be similar to one you sold to the Houghton Bank, we understand; one which was subsequently stolen."

She pulled out the photograph and showed it to him.

"We wonder whether you know anything about this portrait."

He looked at her, surprised.

"Nothing, except that the gentleman in my office also just showed me the same photograph, would you believe? That's extraordinary!"

"Really?" she said, stepping forward, peering into the doorway. "One moment; wait there, sir; if you would, please."

She could see that Hodson had now stood up, clearly uncertain what to do. She pulled out her mobile and pressed the speed dial. It was the mobile number of one of the officers in the police car around the corner. She said, "I would like backup now at the Ainsley Gallery on Lower John Street; nearest car please." She closed the call, knowing that the sound would have travelled into the office.

She said to McNeil and his assistant, "Please wait here. Other officers will be here shortly."

Then she walked over and opened the door but remained in the doorway, blocking it. Hodson looked at her and she eyed him up, as if for the first time.

"Sir, I am a police officer. May I know your name?"

"Tony Hodson," he said coolly. He hadn't moved, he was still standing there.

"Mr. Hodson, Mr. McNeil has just surprised me by saying you have a photograph of a painting with you; the same one, it appears, that I also brought along related to a current criminal investigation, I might add. Not believing in coincidences, I am a little interested in the reason for your visit here and where you got that photograph."

She pointed to the print on the desk.

He said nothing in direct response, clearly thinking. After a moment he said, "It's a private matter."

The flashing lights of the patrol car, arriving as if in response to Catrin's call, came past the window and stopped outside the entrance.

"I think, Mr. Hodson, if you are not going to say more than that, I am going to ask you to accompany us to Scotland Yard, if you would, please."

She could hear the two uniformed officers now crossing the gallery from the door, as could Hodson. He just stood there looking somewhere between stupefied and angry at his bad luck.

She waited. After Hodson had been taken away, she sat down with Mr. McNeil. He was agitated, upset with the events. In their plan there were details to cover before the art dealer spoke to Cronin or vice versa.

For the next half hour she went through the gallery's role in the acquisition of the Winstanley painting for the bank, making it clear at times that she was suspicious of his possible involvement in the theft, which he duly wailed about.

"It is of some concern to me, Mr. McNeil, that you are involved in a transaction of one Hamlet Winstanley painting that subsequently was stolen from your client and now you are being consulted, you say, about another Winstanley that was stolen, at a different time. I am asking myself what the link is…"

He also almost exploded in his indignation.

"Link! Really, Sergeant Sayer, you stretch things too far, indeed. I met this man, Hodson, for the first time only minutes before you arrived and, apart from hearing he was acting on behalf of Mr. Cronin, whom I have done business with, I have had no contact with this individual before.

"Other than one or two gallery events where Mr. Cronin and I have been together, I haven't talked about specific paintings with him since he popped in to ask about the Winstanley painting, the one that the bank bought. My links to the Houghton Bank are simply the transaction details of the sale. That's all.

"I am quite affronted by the inference you are making."

Catrin responded, "Mr. McNeil, I am just pursuing enquiries, as considerately as I can. Would you prefer to be interviewed at Scotland Yard with your solicitor present?"

"No!" he said, backing off, "I have nothing to hide."

She took him through the details of the discussion with Hodson regarding the second Winstanley, making notes as she went along. Then she led McNeil to make a comment on the photograph of Sophie's copy of Rosalind Heaton.

He said, "It looks a forgery to me, to be honest. I didn't have time to tell Mr. Hodson that, but I was going to. He was concerned that this," - he pointed at the photo - "was real and the one I sold to the bank was a forgery, I gather."

"That was the purpose of his visit then?"

"As far as I could tell; we had hardly got started when you arrived, so I don't really know."

Catrin paused.

"This painting came to us through quite different enquiries; but I wish I had talked to you earlier, sir. What makes you think it is a forgery? You haven't even seen the original. Mr. Cronin did; we have it at Scotland Yard. He seemed satisfied with it."

The dealer gave Catrin a look that said Cronin's satisfaction was irrelevant. Then he went to a filing cabinet and took out a folder, pulling from it his own photograph of the painting sold to the Houghton Bank. He laid them side by side.

"I know this painting intimately and its provenance. As I know most of the paintings that pass through our hands here. Look at the two photographs; not the buttons issue that you mentioned, but the lighting. Even the photograph is enough to reveal it, frankly, I would have thought, to anyone."

Catrin hid the pleasure of the man's revelation as much as she could.

"It looks similar to me, sir."

He looked at her as if she was an idiot.

He said, "Similar! It is exactly the same. Exactly! They have the same lighting, the same shadows and the same tonal range. There is even the same placement of the subject. I bet you I could line them up and they would probably overlap. Sergeant Sayer, you may be with …"

He looked again at her business card.

"the Art Crime Unit, but you should talk to some of the experts in Art & Antiques at Scotland Yard, I suggest. Ask them how an artist in the seventeen forties in England painting by natural light or candlelight is going to get exactly the same lighting, tones and seating postures at entirely different sittings on two different paintings. It didn't happen. It's a forgery, I tell you."

She looked at him, apparently crestfallen. "Well, sir, we will look into this further."

She stood up.

"Thank you for your time. It was very useful and, I think, your information may deal with the concern that Mr. Cronin had raised with me, if it proves to be the case."

From his expression she could see that his irritation wasn't abating. Catrin was pretty sure that Cronin would be hearing about this not only from Hodson but directly from McNeil, as well.

He said, as he escorted her to the door, "And, sergeant, if

you want a professional opinion from me on this painting of yours to support what I just told you, the Met will have to pay my appraisal fee accordingly. Good day."

She left and went over to the car where John Obi was now sitting at the wheel wearing his suit jacket. As she got in she saw him chuckle.

"Perfect," she said, "I like the man; he's good. I may buy from him myself if he ever had something I wanted and I could afford it. Fat chance of that happening though, with the price of stuff I see in galleries around here."

She looked at John then smiled.

"It did work out. I am glad we sorted this out with Sophie; the mimicry aspect. She would get a real kick if we told her - which of course, we can't."

John said, "You were suitably contrite at the end. Well done. But you bated him mercilessly earlier, Catrin. You have an evil streak, I think."

"Thank you, John, for those kind words. Now let's hope that his anger is sufficient to get him to give Cronin a call and unload on him the story of an oaf of a police officer arriving on his doorstep today."

27 INTERVIEW

Catrin and DCI Worsley entered the interview room and sat down.

Jane Worsley began.

"Mr. Hodson, I am Detective Chief Inspector Worsley. You have met my colleague already, Detective Sergeant Sayer. Now, we are not on record here, at least as yet. But if you want to formalize things and bring in a solicitor then we can do that; we can wait. At this stage we just have some questions and perhaps this would best be handled informally. Then we can all move on, perhaps. But it is your choice."

"I am fine with that, Chief Inspector," Hodson said.

He now sounded more confident. He must have his story straight, Catrin thought.

Worsley said, "Well then, perhaps you could explain how you had in your possession a photograph of this painting by Hamlet Winstanley. The painting is involved in an investigation and Sergeant Sayer was diligently trying to track down more information about this work of art. Then she came across you with the photograph."

She emphasized 'diligently', making it clear that Catrin was, if anything, being over-zealous.

Hodson nodded, appearing as if he wanted to be cooperative.

He said, "It's simple. I was asked by a client, Ryland Cronin, to look into it. As the sergeant knows, I gather, it puzzled Mr. Cronin that this painting was so similar to the one bought by the Houghton Bank.

"I got the impression he is fretting about the concern that the painting purchased by the bank might be a forgery when they have received insurance compensation for its loss. His worry, I think, was a little excessive but he asked me to look into it. That is why I was talking to Mr. McNeil."

Hodson had thought it through. There was no way he could get out of this without giving Cronin's name. If he didn't like that, it was tough.

Worsley said, "The painting that was stolen from the bank, you mean, the same time as the two paintings by the artist George Stubbs?"

Hodson said, "Yes, I understand from Mr. Cronin it was part of an art theft but I don't work in that area."

"And how do you know Mr. Cronin?" asked Worsley.

"I have worked for him from time to time in a private security role. That's my background, you see."

Worsley said, "Not art-related security, then?"

"No. I am involved in other security work. I can't really say more without client permission, you understand, but I have a military background."

"Oh," said Worsley, "I see; army?"

"No, I served with the Royal Navy."

He pulled out a business card from the top pocket of his jacket. 'Hodson Security Services' was the business name. It looked freshly printed.

Jane said, "And how long have you known Mr. Cronin may I ask?"

"You may not. It's private, as is the nature of his business with me, as I said."

He smiled.

Worsley gave the impression that she was satisfied, apparently; that the man's story held together and he knew what he was doing.

"Are you able to account for your whereabouts on February 18 of this year, please?" she asked him.

"Why?"

"That was when the event took place that brought this painting - the one in the photograph, not the one owned by the bank - to our attention. I want to eliminate you from the enquiry, if we can."

Worsley was sounding reasonable, helpful.

'Fair enough," he answered.

He pulled out a pocket diary. A man who still worked with paper, she saw.

"Good job it is this year," he joked. "I was in Ibiza."

"Did you visit for work?" Worsley asked again.

He responded, smiling, "No, I was on holiday - I don't like cold weather. I was there for two weeks. I have a time-share."

We know, thought Catrin, which is why we gave you that date, to make you over-confident, perhaps.

Worsley gave Catrin a look which said, 'I think we are at the end of the road on this one'. It was her pre-agreed sign for her sergeant to take over.

She said, "It seems that Mr. Hodson can go about his business. We will arrange a car to take you back. Sergeant Sayer, anything else?"

Catrin said, "Did you work for Mr. Cronin at the time of the robbery from the bank?"

Hodson responded, "When was that precisely? I know it was about two or three years ago, but not exactly."

She told him and Hodson appeared to give it some thought.

"No," he said, "not then."

"And where were you on or around the dates that the painting was stolen from the bank. Here or in Ibiza?"

He stared at Catrin. The look said he was co-operating with the tiresome blind shots in the dark from this junior officer.

"I don't know off-hand; I would need to check my diary from two years ago when I get home. I only carry the current one with me. I think I was in the UK, not doing any work abroad at that time… and it isn't my time-share period."

Catrin said, "We would like to take your fingerprints and a DNA sample, to eliminate you from our enquiries."

"Go ahead," he said smoothly, "I have no problem with that."

His eyes are smiling, thought Worsley, but his mouth isn't. She sensed the tension in the man - and it was focused on Sayer.

"Thank you," said Catrin. "Then you will be free to go, but I want you to call me with the information on your whereabouts at the time of the Houghton Bank robbery when you get home and check; just for our records."

He looked at Catrin, trying to appear slightly amused.

"I would be happy to do that, sergeant."

He looked at Worsley. "Will that be all, then?"

Worsley said, "Once we have taken your prints and a swab, yes. We appreciate your assistance."

She appeared to hesitate.

"You might want to pass on to your client that Mr. McNeil told us that he is sure our painting is a forgery; seeing as we interrupted you finding that out yourself -"

She looked at Catrin then smiled at Hodson.

"- we may as well save you the trouble of going back to ask."

Hodson nodded, expressing his appreciation. "Thank you, Chief Inspector Worsley."

He liked this senior officer more than the bureaucratic little sergeant with no humour and a scar on her face. Despite the unwelcome interruption, he was going to get some additional payment from Cronin after all. But, he was thinking, the issue of a confirmatory evaluation of the Winstanley from the bank may not be necessary now, so he would need to pump Cronin for as much of the original fee as he could get.

It wasn't his fault that the police turned up when they did, he concluded. And if he ever caught this Welsh woman alone on a dark night, she wouldn't be so pushy with him then.

As he stood up he caught the senior officer looking at him,

her own face blank, before she left the room.

They gathered afterwards to review the interview, agreeing that it went according to plan. Now, they hoped, forensics would find something in the retained samples from the Hewett household to nail Hodson. This was the weakest part of the strategy, they knew; they didn't have a lot to work with.

The alternative was to engineer a 'discovery' of the Rosalind Heaton portrait in Hodson's possession, but no-one was truly comfortable with that.

As they wrapped up, Worsley said to John and Catrin, "When we get to arrest this man, John, you are going to do it with a really big officer beside you to thump him if he resists. Catrin, I didn't like the way he was looking at you at the end."

Catrin said nothing. She knew what her boss meant; she had just hoped it would be glossed over. It wasn't.

28 BETTER LATE THAN…

The email arrived into the inbox of Inspector Terry Entwistle marked urgent. He had set up his smartphone to play a sound clip loudly for urgent emails, so the noise came at a time when he was taking a particularly tight shot at the snooker table in the game after work. He missed and cursed, then took out the phone. On checking the email he cursed again and said, "Sorry Roger, but duty calls."

He waved the mobile at him as he headed away from the table.

Inspector Roger Crabtree, a friend and fellow officer, just nodded. It came with the job. Over the years they had been playing together, one evening a week, and interruptions were a regular occurrence with work calls to one or other of them.

Entwistle forwarded the message to Sergeant Hua then called him.

"We are too late, it seems, if the date is right. I am hoping that wherever this email came from, it made a departure date error and we can have the woman met at Heathrow tomorrow morning."

"I will check passenger lists and get back," Hua said.

Entwistle said, "And I will alert Sayer and her boss. See you back at the Yard. We have to move fast on this one."

Catrin had only been home half an hour after the wrap-up with Worsley and Obi when the call came. She was sitting down, shoes off with her feet up on the coffee table listening to Chris talking about when he would next need to go back to Exeter. She put down the phone. Chris could tell there was a problem.

She said, "A niece of Nam Wu, a woman, is either on her way to London or arrived this morning. They are checking passenger lists."

As soon as she finished speaking her phone rang again. Again Chris sat through the discussion hearing 'yes, ma'am' twice and finally, 'we will be ready.'

She looked at Chris. "That was Worsley; she is sending a car. We need to pack for overnight or a couple of nights. A hotel is being arranged. Once they work out what's happening we will know too."

He nodded and got up, heading to the bedroom to sort out clothes and his case. Her voice followed him. "It's probably unrelated; she is just here to shop at Harrods."

Catrin didn't sound very convincing. He could hear her following him into the bedroom, facing up to the reality that they were going into protection at an undisclosed location. Part of her mind was on that point, but she was also thinking that this could development could foul up the Houghton Bank investigation for her.

~~

Rhona Ng had arrived in the UK that morning, Sergeant Hua discovered quickly. Discussions later with their liaison in the KL Police showed why she hadn't been flagged by normal routes. Ng was a student in Thailand, at Chulalongkorn University in Bangkok. Her ticket had been booked in Bangkok direct to London.

The Royal Malaysian Police liaison said, "Bangkok is a hub, we aren't. People travelling to the UK would fly direct from

Bangkok if they were there already."

Entwistle suddenly remembered Superintendent Taylor's sarcastic quip about the size of Nam Wu's family; it was coming back to haunt them now. In the back of his mind was the issue that they still had to find out who sent the email, if it wasn't the Royal Malaysian Police. His worry was that it was a red herring; getting them looking in one corner, missing what was happening in another.

At least they had Sayer on the way to safe accommodation.

Later they were patched into Heathrow Airport Police, reviewing a clip from a security tapes at the airport. The Airport Police had identified the young woman quickly from the immigration check and were sharing the relevant CCTV footage from the Arrivals Hall. Ng had a pull-along bag and also had checked luggage. She had been met by an older woman.

Sergeant Hua was doubtful. He said to Entwistle, "It doesn't look like a triad operative meeting a colleague, does it?"

"Find out her declared UK residence address during the visit. If she is there, we will find out. If not…" Entwistle replied.

An older woman had met Ng in the Arrivals waiting area after she cleared customs. They had hugged and were talking energetically, in no rush to leave or act in a clandestine manner. The CCTV subsequently showed them taking the cases down to the Underground where they took the Piccadilly Line train into London.

~~

In fact, Rhona had been delighted to see her aunt at Heathrow and looked forward to the visit. Her checked suitcase was largely filled with clothes that her cousin Mo and her aunt had asked for, brand name items bought at the Platinum Mall area in Bangkok at prices that Londoners would be wide-eyed about.

Back in Stratford, East London they caught up on family developments, both good and bad. While the birth of a son to Rhona's sister was a wonderful development, the latest news of another uncle, Nam Wu, and her more distant relative, Loh Ghee, was one that led to sadness and a silence.

"This is what happens to that side of the family. I have become used to it," said her aunt. "It is why your mother and I have always made you keep clear of them, even at family marriages and gatherings. They talk of the strength and history of their ways, they flash money around and always drive new cars, but what they call business is always someone else's misery and sometimes it is their own."

Rhona pressed her lips together. She was only nineteen but while she would occasionally lead her mother and father astray about staying away from Nam Wu's family, this aunt in London was one of her favorite family members. She felt bad about the deceit.

She had visited her London family five times since childhood and enjoyed the sights and experiences of the city with them. On recent visits she had gone out to dances with their daughter, Monica, always known as 'Mo', who was a year older than herself. She would be home from work soon and they planned to go out together that evening.

Her aunt shook her head. "I don't know where you and Mo get the energy from. You are eight hours from home time. I am tired just thinking of my last trip there a year ago."

Rhona laughed. "We are young, aunt… all energy. And I sleep on planes. Perhaps I will crash tomorrow but I feel fine at present. And we won't be too late."

Later Rhona put in her bag the envelope that her other aunt in Kuala Lumpur, Nam Wu's wife, had sent her. She had sent Rhona money to pay for the trip and included in the courier package with the envelope a voucher for a restaurant. Then Nam Wu's wife had called her. She wanted Rhona to have a good time but also asked for a favour; the envelope needed to be hand-delivered. It could be dropped off at a flat close by the restaurant and would be a birthday surprise for someone.

Rhona was so happy with the gift of the flight she was happy to oblige, even meet her aunt's request that it should be done on the evening of arrival. How could she say no?

It was the mention of this woman and Nam Wu earlier that had caused Rhona's queasiness. Now she just wanted to get rid of the letter and forget about it; she would have met her obligations.

As she and Mo headed out for the evening she said, "Can we make one stop not too far away? It's on the way, I checked. I have to drop off an envelope to someone. And I have a place to eat near there, we can use a voucher."

Mo said, "Where did you get a meal voucher for a London restaurant?"

Rhona had passed it over and Mo looked at it; a voucher valid for Las Iguanas, a restaurant in the Art Market in Spitalfields. It should more than cover the cost of a meal for two, Mo thought, and remarked on it.

Rhona said, "It's from a friend at Chula; she came back from seeing people here and gave it to me. She didn't use it and she is made of money."

Chula; Chulalongkorn University. Mo knew the nickname.

Now Rhona was feeling even more uneasy. She had lied to her parents about the ticket, sat through her aunt reminding her of what was right and wrong and now she had lied to her cousin. This great idea for a visit was not turning out the way she had hoped - and the only thing she could think of was to move on and put this part behind her.

Mo said, "It has good food there, I hear. We can go out after and look at the shops around there, see if you are up to dancing afterwards or not."

"I haven't eaten Latin American food before, Mo," Rhona responded. "I want to try it, though."

"Can't you put it in the post?" said Mo, pointing at the letter. "I have some stamps."

Rhona said, "No, I have to deliver it myself. I promised."

Mo replied, "No problem. We have plenty of time - unless

you crash and fall asleep."

It was only two stops to Liverpool Street on the Central Line and then they headed east on foot, Rhona following the map on her phone.

"It's along here, number 122, a flat upstairs," said Rhona, as Mo just walked along beside her.

As Rhona saw the numbers and knew they were only three buildings away approximately, she thought of getting this chore over with. She hoped this Latin American food was good and the voucher wasn't turned down, for some reason.

Her thoughts were interrupted first by the squeal of brakes as two cars mounted the curb, hemming them in, then they were wiped from her mind by the appearance of armed police officers pointing weapons, shouting at them repeatedly to stand still, not to move. Rhona lost any thought of doing anything other than exactly what they said; the weapons and voices were frightening, so close to her.

Within seconds they were handcuffed, being searched, separated and taken into different vehicles. Mo was in tears, asking what it was about. Then she asked for her parents to be contacted.

A car had taken Sayer and her boyfriend from the flat past this exact spot only twenty minutes earlier.

~~

They had moved Catrin and Chris into the Marriott Hotel at West India Quay, part of the Canary Wharf complex.

"Wow," said Chris, "a great view of the Thames."

He was looking out the window after they dropped their bags, trying to be positive. He knew the choice of room would, in part, have been to ensure they were not overlooked. You would need to be in a helicopter to see into the room and a stray helicopter on the flight path into London City Airport would be spotted in seconds.

"This," said Catrin, putting down her phone after a

discussion with John Obi about next steps, "is a royal pain. Not just the disruption, but where we are in the case I am on, I mean."

She knew she couldn't leave, there was a security team in the hotel monitoring the hotel CCTV cameras, including the hallways on their floor.

"This," said Chris, partly mocking her, "is a chance for a romantic dinner for two and a night with my girlfriend in a room with a beautiful view. We can't do anything about it, Catrin, so we may as well make the most of it."

Catrin looked at him, the expression saying clearly, 'Don't humour me'.

He completely ignored it, heading to the door and saying "I will be back in a while."

She looked up; she had been about to call Aina.

"Where are you going?"

He smiled, looking back at her. "Where I want to; I am not under protection, you are. I'll be back in a while."

With that he left the room, leaving her looking bemused.

29 DENIAL

"The envelope contained only photographs; they are an implied threat," said Inspector Entwistle to Worsley and Sayer.

It was the following morning. Entwistle and Hua had joined them in Worsley's office to brief them on the new developments following the interception of Rhona Ng.

He produced copies of the contents of the envelope Ng had been carrying. There were several pages, mainly of photographs of Catrin. One had her smiling at someone as she exited the Broadway Post Office, across the road from Scotland Yard. Another showed her running near her home and a third caught her with Chris coming out of a supermarket, both carrying grocery bags. The final photograph in the set was of the dead man from Kuala Lumpur, laughing and smiling at something Nam Wu had said.

There was no message, other than the implicit one that Nam Wu had her in his sights and was still thinking about Loh Ghee.

Entwistle added, "The shots of you were taken with a long lens, from about fifty metres."

He left unsaid the implication that it could easily have been a rifle instead of a camera. Catrin mused that, despite her training and regular application of it, she had seen nothing at any of these locations to worry her.

"Sergeant Sayer, there is more, I am sorry to say; not here, in Kuala Lumpur. RMP are reporting today that several people within the lower ranks of Ten Dragons have heard that Wu intends to eliminate you and Sergeant Farra before the first anniversary of Loh Ghee's death; he has taken a vow to do so. If lower ranks are hearing it, then it certainly has been shared at higher levels. And without some countermand from someone more senior, he will have no choice but to carry it through, or attempt to do so.

"We think he timed the message to coincide with the delivery of the photographs, leaving the images as innocuous as possible, given it was his niece acting as the messenger.

"I will leave it to you and DCI Worsley to consider your next steps, but I now have to retract my earlier position given to AC Hunt. I think you will need to consider other security measures, perhaps quite radical ones. That is what I would recommend."

Worsley just sat looking at Catrin, who said nothing for a while. Then she said to her, "He is toying with you, Catrin, letting you know that he will be having a go at you sometime in the next nine months - a long time span, I know. We need to revisit the protection plans, look at longer term arrangements, I think."

"No," said Catrin suddenly, "I need to go home. It's my call, ma'am."

You can't talk about my life, my identity in this abstract way, she was feeling, her anger mounting. You mean well but it is such a big thing; losing all this, starting again somewhere else; to do what? Be what? I have just found Chris; what about us? It is not going to happen. My life is not going to be shredded up, re-woven to be a new person in another place.

It must have shown all over her face. Worsley looked as if she was about to argue, or try to reason with her, but in the end she said nothing, just sat looking at her junior officer, then glanced at the two triad team officers, who remained silent.

She said quietly, wanting to calm her team member's clear

agitation, "If you insist, but please think it through, Catrin, as must Jack and I."

Catrin looked across at Entwistle and Hua. "Why did they use this woman Rhona Ng, sending her all the way here rather than just mail or courier the letter to me or have someone local drop it off?"

Entwistle looked as if he was trying to answer in as diplomatic manner as possible but Sergeant Hua just came out with it.

"To make sure you got the message, whether the letter reached you or not, so that you know, not simply suspect. He has invested family effort in this, sending her and he will do so again, at the time. A member of his family will be here to report back to him in person when they make the attack. He is leaving you to sweat about it."

Entwistle added, "And to flush out whether we are being vigilant in our coverage of you, watching his relatives, seeing how well we understand the situation. Ng was also a sacrificial lamb, so to speak."

Catrin nodded. "I am too close to it; I should have been able to answer my own questions, shouldn't I?"

"Not all of them, Sergeant Sayer," said Inspector Entwistle. "For example, we don't know where the email alerting me to Ng's arrival originated. It's been tracked back to a service provider in Malaysia so far, but technicians believe it probably originated somewhere else in Asia."

"Well," said Worsley, "the young woman may be just a sacrificial lamb and may be bleating, but she will soon be talking to Superintendent Baksh's team in Malaysia. She is being deported right now."

~~

Rhona said disbelievingly, "I can't come back? Never? But I did nothing wrong. It's so unfair!"

She was feeling bad; for herself; for Mo and also for Mo's parents. She had been told about the other police cars arriving in Stratford at the family home; the disruption and distress she had caused by her actions.

The immigration officer with the police team had just stamped her passport prior to her being placed aboard the flight to Kuala Lumpur.

He said, "You are fortunate, Miss Ng. The coding is UK domestic only. It won't flag you to Interpol or place you on any no-fly list, so you shouldn't have difficulty travelling to other countries in the future; even to Singapore, where you study. It could have been a lot more severe."

He was an older man and had a daughter about her age.

"About you doing nothing; that is untrue. You brought an envelope not belonging to you into this country in breach of your customs declaration. You know it was linked to a member of your family with gang connections, yet you still did that. Fortunately it contained papers, nothing more dangerous. If it had, I don't think these people would be letting you go home so quickly."

He nodded to the two officers with the Heathrow Airport Police.

One of the police officers, an older woman, said, "You are also lucky, I think, that you are not facing a charge of being an accessory to an attempt to kill a police officer."

The young woman looked dumbfounded.

The officer continued, "The person you were delivering this letter to is a British police officer. She was visiting your country and happened to be in the way as your uncle sent one of your cousins to his death. She shot Loh Ghee in self-defence. And this is part of her reward, a warning that your uncle wants her dead also."

Rhona said, "I had no idea. I was told it was just a letter to a friend," she whispered.

Her lower lip was trembling and she was on the verge of tears. They knew that was the extent of it. From her interview and from discussions with her aunt and cousin in Stratford, they had pieced it all together.

The officer continued, "That was the message inside. Nam

Wu wants to let a young woman not that much older than you know that he intends to kill her. Delivering that message was your role. One which, in about fifteen hours' time, you will be discussing with the Royal Malaysian Police."

Rhona was still wrestling with the fact she would never see London, her aunt or Mo again, unless they visited Asia.

The female security officer from the Malaysian High Commission standing with the group said to her in Malay, "They want us to go now. We are boarding the flight early, before the regular passengers."

The officer wasn't looking forward to the trip. She thought there would be a lot of tears on the journey.

~~

Jian Li saw the incoming Skype phone call from Catrin and answered it; she knew it was about 11.00 p.m. in London.

"Hi Catrin, I am getting ready for work."

"Yes, it's why I called now, so early. I have a question, Li."

Li stopped what she was doing, anticipating the subject, hoping she was misreading Catrin's tone of voice.

"Yes?"

"Remember our dinner before you left? You mentioned Glanrafon Hill, you may recall. Do we need, figuratively speaking, to take another walk down it?"

Catrin's last comment was said lightly but Li could sense the seriousness of the question. All Catrin could hear was her friend's breathing.

Then she heard Li say, "It probably would be a good idea, yes, seeing as you ask."

"When?" asked Catrin.

Li thought through her schedule and the time zone differences. She said, "You know my regular day today. After work; call me there."

Jian Li visited her parents for dinner every Wednesday if she wasn't travelling, Catrin knew.

She said, "OK, that will work. Li, a big hug for you, but we need to talk."

She closed the call.

Li thought, I should have realised Catrin would work it out. But something has happened, clearly.

The following morning Catrin phoned Aina first thing saying she would be in a little late but would be available by phone, if needed; she was stopping by the Kiln for something.

So when Eu-Meh, Li's mother, saw the call from the UK number, she said, "Jian Li, I think the call from Catrin you were expecting has come through on our line."

She took the handset after Eu-Meh had exchanged pleasantries with Catrin, then said, "I will take it in the living room."

She had worked out what to say.

"Catrin, the phrase I think is, 'tit for tat'. You tell me how you knew and I will tell you what I did."

"Li, I know what you must have done; you spoke with Michael Yau and asked for his help. Why I am calling is my concern that you can't do this and get involved in this way. You are my friend but you are also a lawyer; you have professional standards to abide by. You know what happened last time this sort of meddling occurred. But tell me exactly, please?"

Jian Li explained her meeting with Yau, but didn't mention Emily Yang at all.

"It was one meeting, Catrin and they won't talk with me further, but if they see from their networks that a person linked to Nam Wu is going to the UK, they will flag it to the police there. Is that what happened?"

Catrin said, "I can't tell you any details, but yes, a person came to deliver something to frighten me; not kill me. Just let me know I was on Wu's radar. She was intercepted and didn't get close to me."

Li said, "So Mr. Yau did what he said he would do."

"You shouldn't be involved, Li. And it's not just professional liability I am concerned about; it's your safety too.

The woman who delivered the message to me is now banned from the UK; she is being questioned by the Malaysian Police. I don't want you caught up in a fight between two triad societies over this."

"This isn't a triad issue; I know that. Mr. Yau clarified that point. It's a personal thing with Nam Wu. And now I can't do anything anyway; Yau's people will not tell me anything, they said.

Catrin said, "You can at least tell them to pull the plug on this surveillance system they have to spot Wu's relatives coming to the UK."

Li said, "Did Scotland Yard already know about this person, then, the one they have sent back?"

There was no response from Catrin to that, just a repeat of the request.

"No," said Jian Li, "I won't go back to speak to Mr. Yau. Whatever is in place, it stays. I won't interfere further unless... the colleague of Mr. Yau's dealing with this asks me to; which she won't. But you are the target, not me. I doubt Nam Wu would do anything against me; it would be a blow against Mr. Yau. So forget about it. Besides…"

She stopped.

"Besides, what… Li?"

Li's voice lightened, losing the argumentative tone. "It actually feels good to be helping you on this one, in a sense. Do you know what I mean?'

Catrin sighed. "That is exactly what I didn't want… but, thank you. I should have said that at the outset, I think."

"Yes, you should. And my mom is waiting to serve dinner. So you take care and I will take care, too. I love you, Catrin; you are very special to me."

Melanie had popped her head around the door to the little office at the back of the Kiln to see if Catrin wanted coffee before going on to work. She saw Catrin crying and saying, "And I love you too. Say hello to your parents from me."

"Chris?" asked Melanie, as Catrin put the receiver down.

She was concerned.

"No, Jian Li. She is an idiot."

Melanie looked at her.

"She's your friend, Catrin. We are all idiots to be friends with someone who keeps getting into the sort of trouble you fall into. Do you want coffee or tea?"

Then she went over and put her arms round her, hugging her until Catrin regained her composure.

"Yes,' said Catrin, as she stood up, wiping her eyes and blowing her nose, "You all are, and Chris is the biggest one of the lot."

"Why?" said Melanie, antenna up.

"Two nights ago at the hotel where we were, I was looking at the in-room dining menu. He had gone out earlier. He comes back in with a waiter pushing a trolley. Flowers, a selection of food he knows I love. None of it was off the room menu. It must have cost …"

She trailed off.

"He's a hopeless romantic. We were hiding away, not out on the town."

Melanie smiled. "He's in love with you. Enjoy it wherever you can. And, do you…"

"Coffee, please… and thank you. I am forgetting to say that to people these days, it seems."

30 DARTMOUTH

The fingerprint check was competed well before the DNA tests. Nothing showed up against the evidence set from the Houghton Bank or initially from the Hewitt household. Four days after the interviews with Hodson and McNeil, the lab came back to Catrin.

"We may have a 'possible' on the DNA. The sample from the subject is clear, no problem. It's one of the samples from the evidence set at Essendon which is the 'possible'. It's taking some time, but we will continue working on it. It could take another week."

Catrin said, "How good is it?"

"I can't say for sure, DS Sayer. In a few days we will either rule it right out or… given what I see so far, make it a match. Everything is expedited; it is simply the nature of the testing time now. Not much more we can do about that."

Catrin thanked her and said, "I should have sent the samples to 'CSI Miami'."

The scientist snorted with laughter. "Yes; on television shows DNA testing takes about three minutes and it is always the answer that the investigator wants."

She briefed Obi and Worsley.

"We may have to break Cronin by charging Hodson for possession of the painting; use the 'suspicion' angle and go after the Winstanley that he is holding at home now, before he transfers it. But it will be much cleaner if we have something solid on Hodson from the robbery itself. He won't crumble but Cronin would do so more easily if we had Hodson on a platter."

John had earlier pushed for taking Hodson in for possession of the Winstanley; it would link him to the robbery and the cards could start to fall.

Catrin was not supportive of that.

"I don't think Hodson would break. He would say nothing and probably blackmail the others, make them pay for him to maintain his silence. In any event, we don't really have grounds for a search; we would be acting simply on a suspicion, we could claim. But he could pick up easily, I think, that we actually know more and that could lead back to Cox."

"Let's wait on the test results," said Worsley.

Catrin looked at her boss. "In the meantime, I would like to go to Dartmouth, ma'am, and try Keith's earlier suggestion, even if it is a closed shop."

John said, "He also said we would get nowhere with the Navy."

"We have to try," said Catrin.

Worsley looked at Sayer, seeing the intensity of her focus on the case. It was a good thing, but she also thought that it might be something she was doing to get her mind off the Malaysia issue. They still had to sort out the relocation decision and she knew Jack Taylor was working on that as she spoke.

Worsley let out a sigh.

"Well, it could be time to call in some favours," she said, explaining nothing further, just sitting with her arms folded, thinking hard.

Obi said, "You weren't in the Navy, ma'am, or have an uncle who is a rear-admiral, that sort of thing?"

Worsley smiled. "Even better than that; I went out with a navy pilot once."

Worsley was an amateur pilot. Her love life was known to have been one pilot after another, relationships that never lasted - until the current one, an RAF transport aircraft captain now assigned to diplomatic support work in Whitehall. She had met him several years ago, ironically, at a reception at the Russian Embassy during the formal transfer of the Garin paintings, Sayer's first case. He had attended in recognition of one of the Komarov sisters, the subject of one of the three paintings recovered. The woman had been a World War II Russian Air Force navigator, killed in action.

"I don't see how a pilot can help much, ma'am," said Obi, pessimistically.

Worsley said, "That was back then, a good while ago, John. Roy keeps getting promoted. He is up there now…"

She hadn't wanted to talk to Roy Fanshawe again, but it seemed as if she needed to do so after all.

~~

It was the following day, in Dartmouth. Worsley and Sayer were in the office of Captain Eric Fallon, the number two at the Royal Navy Training Establishment, known to be the service's primary officer cadet training facility.

They had left London early that morning. Catrin had driven the second half of the long journey in Worsley's car; she knew this part of the world better than her boss, who anyway wanted to work on a file and participate in a conference call while they travelled.

"Commodore Fanshawe says that you are reliable, Chief Inspector. That if you say it's off the record, you mean it."

Captain Fallon was eyeing Catrin as he spoke.

Worsley said, "Quite so, Captain Fallon. That applies also to my detective sergeant."

He looked at Worsley, as if she would need to understand.

"Younger people don't necessarily see, 'off the record' in the same way that Roy, you and I …

Worsley smiled, understanding.

"DS Sayer has a commendation for bravery and is likely to get another from the Royal Malaysian Police Service soon; she is both experienced and reliable. Nothing we hear from you will be used with anyone… of course, unless people volunteer it themselves or it arises naturally during the course of our investigation."

Fallon was looking at Catrin's scar, sizing her up. Catrin was looking him in the eyes. The message was, DCI Worsley is right, and I don't expect to be sent out of the room while the grown-ups talk.

After a moment's silence, he nodded.

"Petty Officers can be bloody intimidating. Let me say that from experience. They know more than the trainee and they may call you 'Mr.' but there is no doubt about who rules the roost. Their dominance is part of character building, if you will. An officer cadet has to learn to take it, eventually rise above it and, in the best of circumstances, learn to command such men. The bond between a PO and an officer serving in the field becomes one of trust and support that is hard to match. I would say it can't be matched outside the military services."

He stopped. He looked at the two women sitting across from him, not sure if they would understand.

Worsley said, "Please continue."

"Sometimes, though, it goes wrong. The cadet never rises or the PO doesn't let go… others have to intervene. Some people are moved, reassigned perhaps, but it all works out."

Again he stopped, assessing them.

"I take it," Worsley said gently, "you are hinting that it didn't work out between Cadet Cronin and PO Hodson? I assume Hodson was in that capacity."

Fallon nodded.

He added, "It didn't work out and it wasn't addressed because neither Hodson nor Cronin made it visible."

Worsley said, "I see. Was there something specific in this… relationship that was different, that needed to be hidden away?"

"Sexual?" said Fallon, candidly, "No, not in that sense, no, not between them, nothing like that. It was all about power and control, I gather."

Catrin was getting a little exasperated. Would this man just come out with it, whatever it was, or would Worsley pull it out of him? No, she thought, Worsley will go along with the guessing and inference games for a while.

Fallon said, "There is nothing on record, for either person, by the way."

Worsley started to say something, stopped and started again. "May I ask the nature of the hold that Mr. Hodson, then Petty Officer Hodson, has or had on Cronin?"

Fallon looked at Catrin, then at his desk. "There was a rumour, just a rumour, that Mr. Cronin had a relationship with a local girl back then. She became pregnant and had an abortion."

Worsley said, "I see. OK, but this was the nineteen nineties not the nineteen thirties. It sounds like blackmail. Would revelation of that situation have truly blighted his career then or… is there more?"

He focused on Worsley. "That was the rumour and it's all I am able to share. I believe it to be the basis for the dominance that PO Hodson had over Cronin at the time. But I don't know anything factually.

"I will add this… I graduated two years after Ryland Cronin, the year before Hodson was transferred and they served together on the same ship. PO Hodson was transferred dockside again a year later to another training role, but not here. I don't think he is the sort of man to fit into a crew, a team; he is too much for himself, too dominant and a loner."

Worsley asked, "And can you summarize Lieutenant Cronin's career?"

"Unblemished, unremarkable; did his stint; then he joined a City firm. He had a relative there, I gather, and seemed to find his feet in that world. He has done very well by what I read."

There was more, but Worsley wasn't going to probe, she decided. Still, they had enough to do their own searches of databases now.

Catrin said, "What year did you graduate, sir?"

"1999."

"So Ryland Cronin graduated in 1997?"

"Yes he did."

"So this affair between Cadet Cronin and a local woman would have been in the period 1996-1997."

"Yes, sergeant; it was around that time."

Catrin said, "It must be the uniform, sir, dazzling the local girls."

It was said evenly, neutrally, Worsley saw, but knowing Sayer well, she could see the distaste in her eyes. She was from Pontypridd and could identify with the concept of a 'local girl' being treated in this way. Normally Sayer wouldn't have commented, though.

She is wound up tighter than a Swiss watch, Worsley realised.

Fallon had kindly invited them to lunch, which they accepted. Over the meal the man relaxed and talked about his career and how he knew Roy Fanshawe, Worsley's former partner.

Later, in the car heading back to London, Worsley was driving and musing about the meeting.

"So what do you make of it all, Catrin?"

Catrin said, "There is something more, ma'am, than simply knowing about the man getting a girl pregnant."

"Agreed, but what?"

Captain Fallon said 'girl'. When he talked later at lunch about other people he and Commodore Fanshawe knew, even early in their careers, he used the term 'woman' or 'ladies' at times, I noticed. Some men would describe any female as a 'girl' but not Fallon, I think. I wonder if, consciously or sub-consciously, he was being literal. Did Cronin get an underage girl pregnant?"

"I see where you are going … a possibility."

"Ma'am, I am thinking back to my time in Brixton. We saw some underage pregnancies, as you would expect. But girls generally have the final choice on abortion, or not. But it wasn't that way for a long time after the Abortion Act was passed. For years they needed the parent's permission and..."

Worsley nodded as she drove, butting in. "Perhaps the girl's parent's needed some persuasion."

Catrin said, "Yes, something like that."

After a minute she said, "Or, ma'am, it could simply be that this relative, the one who got Ryland Cronin into Medway Analytics, was someone who would have rejected him utterly if this incident had ever surfaced, a moral principle sort of thing. Cronin may have already expected to go there after his military service and not wanted his chances ruined. Perhaps he wanted someone to handle payoffs to keep everything quiet."

Worsley said, "All good reasons, Catrin, but we don't know. And if this DNA sample on Hodson doesn't turn up trumps we will probably have a lot of work to do to find anything to leverage Cronin into talking. Let's get John started on tracking down the woman in Dartmouth. Give him a call."

~~

As they drove back along the motorway Worsley took a call on her speakerphone, looking at the number on the dashboard display and saying just, "It's Jack," as she connected.

Her boss, Superintendent Taylor, she meant.

"Jane, where are you?"

"With DS Sayer, on the M3, Jack; we are about an hour from the office, allowing for traffic."

"Right, when you get back, both of you come on up to see me."

The line disconnected.

Catrin looked at Jane. Whatever it was, her boss knew, she realised. It was also clear that she wasn't going to talk about it while driving.

They were seated around the table in Taylor's office.

Superintendent Taylor said, "Catrin, we have been looking

into options for you. Not to push them on you but to give you something to think about, given the crystallization of the threat against you from Nam Wu."

His face was serious and Catrin intuitively saw where this was going. It had been on her mind. She knew her current case was the relief valve for her; an escape from the issue of the threat against her. When she concentrated on her work, she was fine. Even at the Kiln, she couldn't concentrate on her art at all at present.

Taylor continued. "I have talked with both the Welsh police and the Devon and Cornwall police. Both are prepared to offer you positions with a new identity. The Met will fund the transition costs. You could work as a police officer under a new name, new background; simply disappear from any radar as Catrin Sayer but remain a detective sergeant. And you would be in parts of the country you know and, we think, that you like."

He leaned forward, focusing on her intently. "Don't dismiss it out of hand. There are ways of staying close to family and friends undetected. And the offer extends to your boyfriend, should you both wish; although, to be fair, we think that can only be decided based on your intentions, so to speak. I know it's not that long since you met."

Catrin said, "We are in love, so I will have to discuss it with him anyway."

She looked at the two senior officers but said nothing. She was clearly thinking it through.

Worsley said, "We don't want to lose you, Catrin. But we don't want you living under this threat either."

Catrin asked, "Superintendent Baksh is no further forward with the information from Rhona Ng?"

"No, to be honest," said Taylor. "Entwistle says that the RMP are also convinced she was just a pawn, set up to do the delivery. There is street noise in KL about rifts within the family because she was treated this way. They are trying to exploit these but have had no luck so far; it has just driven Nam Wu deeper underground, it appears. People who normally have some communication with him aren't hearing anything, the RMP says.

"But they are going full tilt against Ten Dragons, pulling in anyone they can and making it clear why. And so are we."

Worsley said, "I hadn't mentioned any of that, Jack."

"You need to know, Catrin," Taylor said. "We have made four triad-related arrests in the London area, one a more senior member, none from Ten Dragons, though, although we are all over them, too. Three of the arrests are cutting short existing surveillance operations in place, pulling them in with whatever we have. They are all hearing on the street that we will be squeezing their lemons at every opportunity.

"Assistant Commissioner Hunt is dealing with the flack coming back about police harassment of the Chinese community here; it's coming through the politicians, of course. And she is giving instructions within the Met to up the pressure still further on the triads, all of them, as much as we can."

Catrin nodded, understanding. She had not given any thought to this aspect.

She said, "Please thank everyone for the effort being put into this, sir. I will talk with Chris."

On her mind now was the thought that all this would stop if she simply disappeared under a new identity.

After Sayer and Worsley left, Superintendent Taylor phoned Assistant Commissioner Hunt.

"The seed is planted, ma'am, but she is not quite ready yet, I believe. I think Sayer assumes that as Nam Wu has declared a 'window' up to the anniversary of the KL incident, she hopes she has some breathing space. We know better; it could be any time.

"But I think she is now seriously considering our proposal, not rejecting a new identity out of hand. Her boyfriend will be part of the equation, I think. They are obviously serious about each other."

Hunt asked, "Can you think of anything else, Jack?"

"Nothing legal, ma'am; no I can't. I have half a mind to talk to SIS and ask them to send their people over to KL and deal with the man; take it to him rather than wait. But we don't do that sort of thing, do we?"

There was a silence for a moment. He wondered if Hunt was thinking of something similarly illegal; it would be a shock if she was.

"No we don't, Jack, but what you said brought back something Baksh said. I need to think on it, but I may have another line to throw out. Give me a few days, even if Sayer shows herself to be more willing to relocate."

The phone went dead.

Jack Taylor wondered what it was he had said that caused Hunt's response.

31 THE LIGHT OF THE WORLD

Enlai Lin met Michael Yau at The Felix, the restaurant in the Peninsula Hotel in Hong Kong harbour, an invitation to lunch at a prized window table with a spectacular view. It was at Michael's request; a rare one to meet outside their usual time at the bathhouse each week with Daniel Yeung, Enlai thought.

On the drive over, Enlai tried to remember when the last time such a meeting had occurred and asked his long-time chauffeur, Oliver, who had a memory better than a computer for this sort of thing. It was faster, anyway.

Oliver replied, "We drove to see Mr. Yau twice after the memorial service for Mr. Yeung's son, Enlai. Both times were within a month of that service, but you have not met with Mr. Yau alone since, unless you went without me driving you or he came to see you."

Enlai recalled those meetings. They had met to discuss the consequences of the Bangor affair and the discovery of Han Yeung's body. It had been a disturbing time for Enlai; he had been called by Jian Li only days earlier while she was being held during a botched blackmail attempt, the one in which Catrin Sayer had intervened. Then he went to see Michael a month later, to tell him of his decision to give shares in LinTan Shipping to Jian Li, along with an offer of a job. It was not an alternate to hard work and a career, he said, but he would feel more at peace knowing her to have financial security, having been part of the reason she had been placed at risk.

"What do you think?" he had asked Yau.

Michael shrugged his shoulders, uncertain.

"It's a pay-off, Enlai. Not to her, to you. She hasn't asked for anything. But if you feel better by doing it, it's a good pay-off to do."

"How do I tell Daniel?" Enlai asked. "Should I ask him first?"

Yau grinned. "That's the real question, right? You tell him; no, you don't ask first. Do what you did with his father when Daniel was injured. Just tell him it is very important for you to do this. He will accept that."

But, Enlai realised, both of these meetings had been at his instigation. This was the first time he could recall that Michael requested a meeting without Daniel.

Once they were eating, alone, Michael Yau asked, "What are your plans for Jian Li, Enlai?"

Enlai looked across at his strange friend.

"Well, she will develop in the company, if she wishes. She seems to like the legal side and isn't showing any real interest in the commercial aspects. But she has a good handle on those too, really; she was on the team that closed the deal in Yokohama last year, a mix of legal and business elements.

"If you were to pin it down, I hope she would eventually become senior legal counsel for the firm, but I will retire soon, as you know. It will be up to my son and to senior management. I have taken care of her financial security already, assuming she is prudent in managing money. But what's this about?"

Yau smiled. "I wasn't thinking that far out, so I didn't phrase it well. I should have said, 'in the near future' really. I would like her to be away from Hong Kong, from Asia if possible, for around a month, starting in about a week. Short notice, I know but it would be good for her to be totally out of the way. Can you arrange that?"

Yau could see the alarm growing in Enlai Lin's eyes.

"She is not at risk, Enlai, and isn't likely to be, assuming nothing goes wrong."

"Wrong; with what, can I ask?" Lin came straight back at him.

"It is something involving her friend in the UK, the police officer."

Enlai said, "Catrin Sayer? I know why Jian Li went to the UK, Michael, instead of a short holiday in Kuala Lumpur; she explained it to me. Is there going to be an attack on Sayer?"

Michael replied, "Nothing specific that I am aware of at present, but the threat is there, made more visible now. You have met her, right?"

Enlai Lin nodded. Catrin Sayer had visited Jian Li on holiday. She had brought a piece of pottery, a small jar and matching lid quite intricately decorated, as a gift for the Lin family. She was grateful for a first class airfare that Enlai had given her through Jian Li to make the visit; in fact, she had been overwhelmed by it.

"I liked her. But she and her art made a big impression on Yolande, who gave her a piece of pottery from our own collection in return."

Yau laughed, remembering the story. Daniel had blushed when he found out during their regular meeting.

"I recall."

It hadn't bothered Enlai to lose the expensive piece of 18th century Qing dynasty porcelain; it was a piece that his wife, Yolande, particularly liked. Sayer and her pottery friends had been overjoyed when it was delivered to them in London, import duties paid. They had loaned it to a museum, he recalled, as the shop insurance coverage would have been a problem. Now Sayer's potter friends made copies in the design to sell.

"Well," said Michael, getting serious, "the business of our triad is about information flows, as you know. An overt threat has now been made against Sayer. I want to take some steps to make sure that neither this woman nor Jian Li will have any further concern in this regard. It's when I do that I need Jian Li to be well out of the way."

"To start in about a week, you say?"

"Yes, and I need a window of about a month, perhaps a little less, from the start date."

Enlai Lin nodded, looking at Yau, realising it would not be productive to ask for further clarification.

~~

Catrin had gone to St. Paul's Cathedral after finishing work. It had been a long day with an early start; Dartmouth, then the meeting with Taylor. It had given her a lot to think about. The Wu threat was coming to a head, she knew, both for the Met and for her.

Normally, on arrival at St. Paul's she would sit on one of the wooden chairs in the nave or sometimes she would walk through the north aisle into St. Dunstan's Chapel. It was always open for private prayer. This time she went for some reason to the north transept and her eyes came to rest on William Holman Hunt's painting, 'The Light of the World', a work she had looked at, or to be more honest, had studied, on previous occasions.

She knew it was much-loved by visitors, clergy and locals, the figure of Jesus about to knock on an unopened door, but she had no particular liking for the works of the Pre-Raphaelites, Holman Hunt included. But Herrington had told her to stop being analytical and somehow, she found herself absorbed in the painting, particularly the image of a door with no handle; it could only be opened from within.

She was just thinking about the need to find someone to talk to, a member of the clergy, when she heard a familiar voice from behind her.

"Taking in my namesake's work, Sayer?"

It was Sandra Hunt's voice. She had walked over behind her, seeing Catrin there, lost in the painting.

Catrin's first thought was, 'I was switched off yet again', referring to her surveillance training.

She asked as she turned round, "Is he a relation, ma'am?"

The Assistant Commissioner was in street clothes, not in uniform.

"No," Hunt smiled. "I have been asked that before. You come here from time to time, I know. I've seen you and also Dennis mentions it. Your scar was quite fresh the first time you came with me, as I recall; quite a marker for him, although he does have an extraordinary memory for people and faces."

Catrin remembered walking in with Hunt after the pep talk in her limousine during their first meeting over two years ago. The AC stopped off here a lot, she knew.

"I find peace here, Sayer," she had said at the time.

They had encountered 'Dennis' as she put it, the Dean of St. Paul's, in the entrance.

"You need to go in,' was all he had said to Catrin at the time, looking at her face with the scar and stitches, still so angry and fresh, as Hunt remarked.

I did, she thought, and I find peace here, too. I just need to bottle it, take it with me and have a few sips from time to time.

"Coming here helps, ma'am, as you once said to me," she responded.

Hunt nodded, understanding the need, particularly for this young officer now.

Catrin thought Hunt looked as if she wanted to say something more, but didn't. She wanted to get away from her; she couldn't talk to Hunt openly, she knew. Their interactions were so formal, prescribed by their roles. She now wanted to find someone, a member of the clergy. She smiled and started to move, to indicate she was leaving.

Then Hunt said softly, "Catrin, hang on until next week. I know the Houghton Bank investigation is going full speed now and Jack has spoken to you today about relocation, but hang on, please. I will see you sometime next week, I promise, and I will try to have a solution for the KL issue by then, I very much hope."

Hunt stopped herself, looking as if she had said too much, Catrin thought.

Then Hunt added, "No promises; just my level best for you."

"Yes, ma'am, thank you," said Catrin, as the Assistant Commissioner whispered, 'next week' again, and turned away.

Catrin walked towards the choir area wondering where to go next when suddenly she had the feeling that she had found someone to talk to, after all. She went back into the nave and sat down, waiting for Evensong to begin and closed her eyes.

32 MALTA

"Jian Li, we have to think strategically."

After his opening pleasantries, it was Mr. Lin's first remark to her and her direct boss, Mr. Soh. She rarely saw Enlai Lin on a business basis at the office. He was the CEO and she was well down the totem pole of the management hierarchy.

"What do you mean, Mr. Lin?" she asked.

She knew the man. To nod in agreement when she didn't know what she was agreeing to would not impress him.

"We operate a mercantile fleet and know well the legal issues of our business. Yet the seas and the ports are highly regulated by governments. Our managers and captains, with the help of our legal department, know how to ensure our business complies with laws and deal with issues if something goes wrong."

Jian Li nodded. It was self-evident, obviously a prequel to his main point.

"What we don't know, Jian Li, is the mindset of the people who make those regulations and deal with us in governments. Sure, we know some of the people over the years, but it is incidental, haphazard. We need the future management of LinTan Shipping to understand the world we move our ships in from the perspective of the bureaucrats who set the rules.

This will tell us how things may change in the future, to help us plan ahead. And where do we learn that, Jian Li?"

She thought a moment then spoke. "From people in government we have good contact with over the years; from our experiences; from our trade associations?"

"Yes, from those. But what about the future, rules that are not yet in place?"

Again he posed the question and waited.

Li thought, this is getting heavy. She looked at her own boss, hoping for inspiration but getting only an encouraging smile. He knew what Enlai was thinking, she thought.

Suddenly she had it, from his opening remark. "We need to talk to the strategists, the people who are developing the future regulations, not the people applying the rules in each port. People in national capitals developing marine legal strategy or the International Maritime Organisation, IMO, people like that."

Enlai nodded, his face revealing she had progressed far enough.

He said, "One of the biggest centres for such learning is IMO's Law Institute in Malta. You know it, I think, they call it IMLI. It's there that we can learn a lot about the people who are or who will become these strategists. Mr. Soh came up with the suggestion to send you there to explore it; to do one of their short courses. You will get a sense of whether, if we send our local people for such training in the future there, it can be of strategic advantage for relationship building."

"Me?" said Jian Li.

"Yes," said Enlai, "A special project; a very good idea by him and an opportunity for you. The course begins very soon."

"It starts in just over a week, Jian Li. It will last three weeks," said Mr. Soh.

She looked at her boss. At her last performance review he had suggested future training in the form of an advanced course in contract law for the Gulf States but, with the current workload, he had said it should be postponed at least for three months.

Then two days ago, with the allegations of a ballast regulation breach by the LinTan Crown II near the Cairns coastline, he was telling his law team that they were overloaded; he would see Mr. Lin about increasing the contract legal assistance budget with outside suppliers, expensive as they were.

Now her boss was beaming at her, looking as if he was fully in line with Enlai on this one.

She said, "But what about the Crown II file. I am to prepare …"

"It's covered," said her boss. "Porter & Harrison will handle it locally; a good firm, highly reliable."

And terribly expensive for preparatory work that was normally the role of in-house legal staff, Li thought.

Enlai Lin said, "Jian Li, you are young, you have been a student only a few years ago, so you can mix well with these graduate students at IMLI more easily. Who knows, perhaps you will be asking us to do a masters or a doctorate degree there based on this experience sometime in the future? Malta is a very nice place, I hear."

By the time she had thought it through, Enlai Lin was complimenting Mr. Soh on his good suggestion and making it clear that it should go ahead. He had already given Mr. Soh the course slot he wanted Jian Li to attend before they invited Li to the meeting. Mrs. Chung, Enlai's ever-capable assistant, had secured a place on the IMLI course within minutes of the request, somehow, earlier that morning.

Mrs. Chung came into the office with a new folder, the brief for Enlai's next appointment and a signal that their meeting was over. Jian Li found herself thinking that there was far more to this assignment than meets the eye. She had been 'stitched up on this one good and proper', as Melanie would say, when she was imitating her London friends in an accent part-Cockney, part-Somerset.

The strength of Melanie's humour was her rapier sharp wit, not her capacity for mimicry, Li recalled, but the phrase, well imitated or not, certainly applied today, she thought.

33 ARRESTS

It was the following week.

After the Monday morning briefing of the team, Worsley called Catrin to her office.

"Have you had any further thoughts on Jack Taylor's proposal?"

She didn't elaborate further; she meant, of course, about the identity change. It had obviously not been discussed with others at the morning briefing.

"Yes, ma'am, Chris and I talked it through. We don't want to rule it out but we don't want to say 'yes' at present, either. But, the good thing is it would be 'we' not just me, if it happened."

"It comes down to how well I can handle the pressure, the… keeping my surveillance up, living with the thought it could happen. It could get too much, I realise; it's not easy this. But I want to see this case through, at least, if you agree. After that, we will see. It would be Wales, we think, if we did it."

Worsley said nothing, just listened. She was assessing her team member, seeing the considerable movement by Sayer away from total denial.

Catrin had decided that she wouldn't mention her encounter with Hunt to anyone. They were both off-duty at the time and she was still at a loss to interpret the senior officer's comments made the previous Friday.

Catrin said, "So for now we say let's keep things as they are; for the time of this case, I hope, at least."

They were interrupted by Aina popping her head in.

"Sorry to interrupt but, Catrin, the lab called about the DNA test results."

She had a smile on her face.

~~

Trevor was in the back garden in his home in Rainham, thinking about lunch as he watched the birds over the marshes. Alice came running down the garden path, still wearing her slippers.

"Police, lots of them, Trev; they are across the road."

The couple rushed through to the lounge. Indeed there were, thought Trevor, several in plain clothes and a number of officers in uniform, armed. Most of them were already leaving, it seemed, walking to a van parked down the close.

"They are one of those response units that break down doors," said Alice.

"Well, whatever the excitement was, it appears to be over," said Trevor.

Then they saw a tall uniformed officer lead Tony Hodson out, handcuffed. A big, black plainclothes officer in a suit was with him. They placed Hodson carefully into a police car and took off.

"He must have hit someone else," remarked Trevor.

"It's more than that," said Alice, pointing.

Two people, a man and a woman were walking up to the entrance carrying cases. They were wearing white coveralls and held white overshoes, which they put on as they entered the building.

"Sockeyes," said Alice, triumphantly. She loved detective series on television.

"SOCOs, you mean," said Trevor, "scene of crime people,

getting evidence. Do you think he killed one of his women this time?"

Then there was a rat-a-tat-tat on the kitchen window at the back. Lorna, their next door neighbour, was knocking. She must be in her garden leaning over the wall between the two terrace houses, Alice knew.

She said, "I am going to talk to Lorna, see what she knows. She may have seen more. Keep an eye out."

Trevor sighed. The women would be talking about this for ages.

~~

Around the same time, Catrin and Worsley went round to the offices of Ryland Cronin unannounced. Worsley said she would handle the interview. If it went wrong, given the influence of the man, her boss thought it only right to take the flack herself.

Worsley demolished Lucia without even showing her warrant card as she made it clear that she was going into see Mr. Cronin and they were not to be interrupted.

"But he has - ," Lucia started to say.

Worsley stopped, looking back at her dismissively as she and Catrin walked into the astonished executive's office, then she just closed the door.

He was very pleasant at the outset, thinking it was a somewhat overbearing continuation of the last set of discussions.

"Any progress on your Winstanley, Sergeant Sayer?" he said cheerfully.

"Yes, sir," said Catrin, looking at DCI Worsley.

Worsley said, "Our investigation has actually changed direction, to a Mr. Hodson and, I have to say, to you. That's why we are here; to give you a chance to talk with us off the record before I caution you."

Catrin had seen it happen previously during arrests; both officers watched the colour literally drain from his face.

"Are you alright, Mr. Cronin?" said DCI Worsley, softly.

"Yes, thank you. Just a shock, what you said, I mean. Why 'caution me'? Do you mean arrest me? For what reason, can I ask?"

Jane continued. "Sergeant Sayer continued our enquiries into the case in Essex, the one with the Winstanley painting. She went to see the art dealer who sold the other Winstanley painting to the Houghton Bank, Mr. McNeil. It was just on the off-chance he might know something. She found your Mr. Hodson there, asking about the same painting.

"You do know him, I take it? He says he was working for you, that he was actually there on your behalf, in fact. I expect one or both of these gentlemen may have talked with you about it by now."

Cronin responded, "Yes, frankly, he was and both of them did. I asked Mr. Hodson to find out more. Part of my concern was the point we discussed, sergeant. The idea of a second 'Mrs. Heaton' and whether the one the bank bought was a forgery, that they had possibly been defrauded. It played on my mind. After all, insurance payouts were made. You do see, don't you?"

His tone indicated that he really did want them to see.

After a moment, he said, "I also wondered; if it was genuine, if both were genuine, what would be the process to perhaps buy the work, the one you had. I know it is tied up in some case but… I thought it might be nice to acquire it, to give it to the bank."

He finished lamely, as if he himself didn't believe his last statement.

Worsley let the silence go on a little.

Then she said, "Is there anything else you want to tell us before you accompany us to Scotland Yard? You see, we asked Mr. Hodson when we interviewed him informally if he would provide a set of fingerprints and a DNA swab voluntarily, which he did. Just to rule him out of our enquiries regarding this other painting, we thought; being thorough."

She looked at Catrin, the meaning obvious; the dogged

plodding of Sergeant Sayer.

"We were about to rule this little investigative episode over when forensics found a match, tying him to the robbery at the Houghton Bank. Very seriously tying him into that robbery and an assault, I will add. And as he works for you from time to time we really have to reconsider your role, given it is clear that you have a strong interest in at least the Winstanley painting. So that is why we are taking you in."

"I like it, true -"

"So you should," said Jane, "Rosalind Heaton being a distant ancestor of yours. We just checked that too."

Even more colour left Cronin's cheeks; he was positively grey.

She continued softly. "Art and Antiques have, as of this morning, brought the Houghton Bank robbery to the top of their priority list and Inspector Caldwell will want to re-interview you, in some detail. We are now searching premises; Mr. Hodson's home; your home and any other property that you reasonably have access to; your wife's place, even your yacht."

She opened her shoulder bag, pulled out the relevant search warrants and served them.

"Oh, and Tony Hodson was taken into custody in Rainham just now. A preliminary search of his home found a painting which may well be a Winstanley, we understand; it is being brought in as we speak."

Catrin thought the man across the desk may well collapse and looked anxiously at her boss. Worsley just kept her eyes on Cronin, relentlessly pressing on.

"The Art Crime Unit is focused on the people who committed the Houghton Bank robbery and in particular, the assault on Mrs. Hewitt, the wife of the security guard, not the paintings. Somehow, I don't think that was part of your plan and perhaps you are regretting that happening. We are here because it may well prove beneficial for you to talk about that aspect before being charged and interviewed by the Art and Antiques Unit. Theft of paintings is one thing; criminal assault of a woman and her daughter, kidnapping the father and terrifying the family is quite another.

"We are giving you a chance to clear the air."

She stopped talking; just sat there waiting for a response. He just bowed his head and his shoulders dropped.

He said, "You seem to know all about it, then. I will say something, but I want my lawyer with me."

"That's a very good idea," said Worsley, standing. "Now, if you would come with us quietly, there will be no need to make a fuss here… otherwise I will insist that my sergeant handcuffs you and I will arrest you formally. If you co-operate, we will handcuff you once we leave building. There are uniformed officers outside, I should add. Do you understand?"

He nodded, standing up; he was looking a shadow of the confident man Catrin had seen previously. He pressed the intercom to his assistant. "Lucia, I am going with these officers to Scotland Yard again."

His voice sounded firmer, more in control; one last act for the office.

"Yes, Mr. Cronin," she said. "You have developed a real interest in that painting, I know."

"Yes I have," he responded, flipping the switch then walking with them to the door.

Catrin was thinking as they left how well Worsley had handled it, to get Cronin to co-operate so quickly.

~~

His solicitor took more than an hour and a half with him before saying that she was ready for the interview. Worsley had co-operated, wanting at this stage the maximum information they could get voluntarily.

When Catrin and Worsley went in, they saw that Cronin was showing all the signs of co-operating; he looked beaten, not defensive. A dishevelled collar and tie, hair a mess and tear-stained eyes all contributed to the image.

They began with the Winstanley, something they were

nearly to regret later. Why select that with the Stubbs?

"Because it is a Stubbs, and Rosalind Heaton is a member of my ancestors painted by Stubbs, despite the signature," he said softly.

For some reason, Catrin felt, as hard as that was to believe, it was the truth.

"During the period Stubbs was apprenticed to Winstanley, I take it," said Catrin, suddenly catching on.

Cronin looked at her. "Yes, that's right. So you aren't the art simpleton you pretended to be."

Catrin ignored the inference and said, "Art & Antiques told us that Stubbs had studied with Winstanley. How did you know?"

Cronin said, listlessly, "I found a family letter in the possession of my grandmother; a pack rat. Years ago after she died I helped my parents deal with the belongings. We took away vanloads, but I found some really old letters… including one from Rosalind Heaton to a friend, Winifred Castell. It was in a box of Castell's letters from Rosalind, returned at some point to the family."

He stopped, rubbing one side of his forehead.

"I kept the box. Stored it away over the years but forgot about it, to be honest - it was just 'family stuff' and ended up at the Surrey house, now Muriel's home. When I saw the painting in the gallery in Bloomsbury, the name Winstanley came back but the title meant nothing; it was too long buried and my mind was on other things."

He paused, reflecting for a moment what to say.

"You know how you get those 'cold water shock' moments sometimes, as a memory comes back? I was in the meeting in New York, two days later. There was a painting on a wall, nothing like the Heaton portrait, but it made me think of the one that I had seen in Bloomsbury and the name Rosalind Heaton hit me. I had seen it in the box of correspondence, I recalled. But I couldn't be sure. I needed to get back to Muriel's place, but …"

He closed his eyes. Catrin thought that he was starting to

look unwell.

"I emailed Lucia to call the gallery; find out the price and put a hold on it until I could confirm things when I got home. She came back to me on it the following day, said it had sold. I emailed Muriel, asked her to dig out the box and courier it to the London flat: she did that for me.

"When I did get home from New York I looked at the box of letters and realised that I had been looking at an unknown Stubbs - and a painting by him of one of my ancestors, to boot. I hadn't bought it. I was overwhelmed at my stupidity and the missed opportunity.

"I should have said nothing about it at the bank before I left, I realised later, but I did. You know the rest. I went to the bank for a meeting the following week and it was on the wall, with Mrs. Woodley smiling at me, telling me that Sir Kenneth had sent her to acquire it and had cleared it with the selection committee.

"He wanted to surprise me. He certainly did that."

~~

1742, Carnforth, Lancashire

My dearest Winifred,

I write a short note, my dear friend, to let you know that the issue of our portraits is now fully resolved, thank God. A solution always comes if we pray hard enough, does it not?

The painting was delivered this week and is gaining much admiration by family and friends. Even John smiled and was full of bonhomie, saying it was the right thing to do. I must say, it does resemble me well, makes me look… competent, I would say. I like it.

Though signed by Mr. Winstanley, most of the work was done by his apprentice, a George Stubbs. When we arrived at the Crossed Keys for the sitting Mr. Winstanley was clearly over-committed and he was becoming a little exasperated, I think. The agent and his assistants were in a flap.

Mr. Winstanley sized up our situation clearly, as by our arrival it was agreed between my husband and me that only my portrait would be painted. John could then use the sum saved towards the farm. He raised it with Mr. Winstanley directly, wanting it clear so the man had no expectations of a second painting or fee.

The artist is a shrewd businessman, Winifred. He hinted at a solution and asked for a quiet word with John alone, of course, it being a business matter, but I said to him, "Will it have your signature, sir; without it…"

"Of course, ma'am," he said. "I will do the finishing touches to make it mine, to my satisfaction. But Stubbs is good, very talented and knows my style. It will help me considerably to divide the work this way… and reflect of course, in a still lower price again to your good husband."

I must have shown my discomfort with the situation, as Mr. Winstanley added, "Mrs. Heaton, in truth I am at the top of my work, my profession; I think you know that. But young George is tremendously talented and I doubt will be with me long, he learns so quickly and has such an independent fire for the work. One day he will surpass me greatly, God willing. Your portrait will lack neither in quality, ma'am, nor in my signature."

Somehow, Winifred, I saw the truth in Mr. Winstanley's eyes; he was not simply trying to fob us off, I realised, so I looked at John and he knew that I was in agreement. The men went and talked and it became a happy compromise.

Mr. George Stubbs was so young, but he had great self-assurance and skill. Mr. Winstanley was in and out with him, of course, but interfered little. Having seen the portrait of the young Moore girl only yesterday at their home and comparing it in my mind with my own I must say that I am as pleased with the outcome as much as John was pleased with the price. I rely on you, my good friend, to reveal this to no-one else, of course, but I treasure our intimacy in the sharing of secrets of this nature….

~~

Catrin said, "A previously unknown portrait by George Stubbs… that was the reason for the robbery?"

Cronin nodded. He looked at the end of his rope.

"For me, yes. Once the two other Stubbs' paintings were transferred…"

He sighed. "At first it was simply that; how much would the Winstanley be truly worth? There are collectors who would pay well given the provenance, despite its recent history; people who take a long-term view. But I was undecided, given that it was my own family. In the end, I made the decision not to be rushed."

Catrin had exchanged glances with Worsley. They had both caught it. What did he mean by the phrase, 'Once the two Stubbs' paintings were transferred'?

"Which brings us to the Stubbs - where are they?" asked Catrin, for due process.

As she spoke, the blood started pouring out of his left nostril and his head hit the table with a thump.

34 MRS. ROSALIND HEATON

Carnforth, Lancashire, 1744. "Stubbs, the apprentice did it?!" said Edna Kingsley.

"Yes," nodded Rosalind. "And, Edna, I think you saw something when studying the painting that gave you a clue. You were seeing, if I am right, whether I would be open with you or not. So I am.

"And if I offend you, that such capricious thoughts are mine only, not yours, I do humbly apologise. But it is better you have the truth now, with which I will trust you and, in doing so, our good name. So many of our neighbours and friends have seen the portrait, during which we have remained silent on this point of its creator; the signature was enough.

"Mr. Winstanley approved it; he supervised Stubbs, gave it his finishing touches and signed it; that is enough for most people, I think. But you…"

Edna placed her saucer and cup on the table and reached over, touching Rosalind on the arm, to calm her agitation. She smiled at her.

"I thought it was another hand on the brush, to be honest and… I admit, I was testing you, in a sense; but not through capriciousness. My son is taken with Sarah and, obviously, she is with him and …"

She hesitated, looking for words.

Rosalind looked at her. "And Longfield Farm may be freehold and doing well but we are hardly of your station…"

Edna shot straight back, firmly.

"For which neither my husband nor I give a fig, if truth be told, providing you are not criminal or destitute, which clearly you are neither. I was assessing character; of the girl, of the family. That is what matters to us."

"And so what do you think of me? Now I have told you?"

Edna looked at her.

"That you are a shrewd woman, Mrs. Heaton, and can spot another one. And you are a mother who wants to do well for her daughter, as I do for my son. On which note…"

She stood and picked up her bonnet and shawl.

"Perhaps we should walk a little? Encounter your relative who is chaperoning the two of them - or not - at present and make sufficient noise to alert them to our coming?"

She had well understood the capacity of the aunt to be a less than vigilant chaperone. Rosalind stood up also, happy with the outcome.

"That's a good suggestion, Mrs. Kingsley. After all, we do not want youthful ardor to go overboard and get in the way of a fine marriage."

She went to the coat rack in the vestibule and picked her own new bonnet and matching shawl, bought only last week in Carnforth market with today in mind.

As they walked out into the yard and down past the pond, Edna Kingsley said, "The young man Stubbs is now in Wigan painting portraits, I hear, and studying anatomy. He believes it paramount for the accurate portrayal of the figure and he is becoming such an authority on the subject that the man is being asked to do medical illustrations, would you believe? Hamlet told us Stubbs already had more than enough knowledge in that area, having completed the standard life class drawings. But George Stubbs is his own man, not to be an apprentice to anyone, Hamlet said; he must be off and do it his way. The young artist is doing well, I hear."

"You know Mr. Winstanley, then?" asked Rosalind.

"Not well, but we have been together at a number of social functions over the years. It was a dinner in Bolton two months ago where I heard the news I just passed on to you. And Rosalind, I suggest we study together this fine view across the pasture directly ahead of us for a moment."

Rosalind Heaton was caught for a second by the sudden change in subject, but then she understood.

"Our children?"

"Indeed. I saw your daughter poke her head out of the barn and withdraw quickly. It might be prudent to allow them to approach us rather than vice versa."

Rosalind said, "I will act surprised. And not ask them where and when they slipped away from John's sister."

35 DECISION

Cronin had been taken by ambulance to the Royal Hospital. Although he regained consciousness within a minute, long before the ambulance arrived at Scotland Yard, it was obvious that no further questioning was possible. Worsley had started to say something when his eyes opened but his solicitor said, "Don't even ask."

"I only wanted to know how he was feeling," said Jane, sounding injured.

They watched the duty emergency response people dealing with him and then organized officers to accompany him to the hospital.

'Stress,' they were told later.

His solicitor said, "It could have been anything; an aneurysm, embolism, something fatal. Once he is stable he should be cleared for questioning. In part, he needs to accept the psychological dimension; he is facing serious criminal charges. It will be tomorrow at the earliest but probably the day after when he can be interviewed further, I think."

"But now for Mr. Hodson," sighed Worsley, now back in the ACU.

As Catrin started to get ready Jane Worsley took a deep breath.

"I doubt he will faint," said John, seeing Worsley suddenly touch Sayer's arm, urging her to sit still. He knew what was about to happen.

Worsley said, "Catrin, you will watch from outside. John and I will be interviewing Hodson."

Catrin looked upset but she saw that Worsley had made her decision, it was clear.

"He focused on you last time at the end of the interview and I didn't like what I saw. Clearly he sees you currently as the reason he was caught. Hodson is a dangerous man. You have had enough of dangerous men for a while, I think."

She smiled at her.

"We will do it; I will make sure he vents his anger on John."

"Thank you, ma'am, I am sure," said Obi, also trying also to lighten the moment, looking at Catrin's face. Worsley had spoken to him earlier, setting him up for this.

Catrin was still looking really upset.

Jane Worsley said more softly, "We want him locked away without bail. But we don't control the courts and if he is put back on the streets I don't want him thinking of you as his downfall."

She added, almost defensively supporting her decision, "After all, it's not as if we are going to get much out of him, is it? Let's be honest."

Catrin looked at her, not sure what to say, suddenly realising the logic, the senior officer's concern for her, despite her feeling that her ownership of the case was being overridden.

All she said was, "Yes, ma'am; thank you."

This time it was a formal interview. They all identified themselves for the record. Hodson's solicitor was a man called Knowles.

Just before the police officers entered the interview room, once they knew who the solicitor was, John said to Catrin and

Worsley, "Knowles knows me; he represented a car thief in Tower Hamlets, one that I was part of the arrest team on. It got a little rough."

"Even better," beamed Worsley, "Knowles will tell Tony Hodson how nice you are, then. Probably Hodson didn't get the chance to find that out when you arrested him, with all the wonderful people from the Tactical Unit there with you."

But John couldn't read his sergeant on that exchange; she certainly wasn't joining in with the joke.

Worsley posed the first question.

"Let us begin with your relationship with Mr. Ryland Cronin, shall we? How do you know him? You have described him as your occasional client or employer and that you are in security work. Correct?"

Hodson said, "Yes."

His answers were again going to be minimal or non-existent, Catrin saw, as she watched on a screen.

Worsley continued, "Would you care to tell us more about that? The times you worked for him, the nature of the work and so on. How you first met?"

Hodson said, "Not really."

Knowles said, "Specific questions please, Chief Inspector. You have made serious allegations against my client."

Worsley seemed unperturbed. She went on with her questions.

"Did you meet Mr. Cronin, then an officer cadet at the Royal Navy training establishment in Dartmouth while you were a Petty Officer there?"

Hodson took a moment, then said, "Yes, he was one of the cadets in Dartmouth and I was a Petty Officer training cadets there at the time. It's all on record."

Worsley nodded, looking down at the file as if she was corroborating what he said.

"On 14 April 1996, did you assault a Mr. Derek Frazer in Dartmouth and threaten his wife?"

Hodson blinked, surprised by the question.

But all he said was, "No comment."

Worsley continued, matter-of-factly. "Their daughter Trisha had told Cronin she was seventeen, but she was actually two years younger when she became pregnant. That happened almost immediately they started their relationship, she said; 'naïve, no precautions, just passion' were her words. She was fifteen and her parents were refusing to let her have an abortion."

Hodson thought about it. He was in no hurry to answer, Catrin thought.

Eventually he said, "So he told you that, then?"

Worsley ignored the response and said, "Please answer the question; questions, actually."

Hodson said contemptuously, "I met the Frazer family at that time. I helped Mr. Cronin deal with an issue. He was gullible. I just encouraged them to make the right decision. And they never filed any complaints, did they? Check the records."

"We have," said Worsley, "and we have had a word with the lady in question. Her parents are both dead now, as it turns out. She used the term, 'beat up', not assault."

"I have nothing more to say on that," said Hodson.

He knew it was years ago; no charges could be laid.

John Obi leaned forward, opening a file.

"You like hurting people, don't you, Mr. Hodson?"

Knowles put his hand on his client's arm. "Don't answer that."

Obi pulled out some file photographs.

"Mrs. Hewitt, the wife of a security officer at the Houghton Bank. It was taken at the hospital. Did you do this to her?"

There were lacerations to her face and the bruising was developing. Her left eye was closed and swollen.

Hodson said, "I don't know what you are talking about."

The lawyer spoke up, glaring at Obi. He did remember him, after all, it appeared.

"DC Obi, you are fishing. How do you tie my client to this matter? Please be more specific or move on."

He glanced at Worsley, conveying that he would appreciate it if she would keep her colleague in line.

John continued. "We have evidence of your presence at the scene, Mr. Hodson. We hadn't identified it until a day or so ago, after we took your prints and DNA samples. Just for completeness, we ran them against the evidence set for the Houghton Bank robbery."

Clearly Hodson didn't believe John Obi. His face showed it, but he said nothing. Catrin, watching the video feed, knew he was thinking it wasn't possible; both of the men had worn gloves.

John said, "The daughter couldn't stop crying so you hit and kicked her mother. Your accomplice told you to go out, have a smoke; he needed to calm it down before anyone passing the property heard. So you did.

"You walked down the path and took off your mask but kept the gloves on while you smoked. You were careful. You didn't drop the match or perhaps you used a lighter. You put the cigarette butt back in your pack and didn't drop that, either, I suspect."

He paused.

"But the cellophane wrapping, the bottom part, the part that stays on after you peel the top open; that came off the pack. You probably used your teeth to pull the sealing strip and top part off and had, I suspect, kept that too. Perhaps you didn't notice the bottom piece blowing away; an insignificant piece of flimsy cellophane. But your tongue or lip caught it, Mr. Hodson. We have a good DNA match on it. The cellophane was found trapped in a bush on the path the following morning."

The solicitor looked at his client, who said nothing.

John continued, "So, Mr. Hodson, to be specific, as your solicitor asked, can you explain that finding? Or can you tell us precisely where you were you on the night of the Houghton Bank robbery? Do you wish to change your statement given previously in this regard?"

"I have nothing more to say," he said.

"Really?" said Worsley, jumping in. "We are going to do a voice identification parade for which you will need to read a text. You will say something then or a charge of failing to co-operate with the police during the course of our enquiries will be added to the file sent to the Prosecution Service. You have a very characteristic voice, by the way, Mr. Hodson; did you know that?"

The two officers stood up. Worsley said, "We will be back. We will give you some time alone with your solicitor to talk further. DCI Worsley and DC Obi are exiting the room at 15.20."

She switched off the recorder.

Catrin met them outside.

"What do you think, Catrin?" said Worsley.

Sayer said, "I think we are going to go after him for a long time and he will say nothing. I doubt his lawyer will tell him to plead, not on a case of violent assault, death threats and kidnapping. And you were right, ma'am. It's clear that John is not exactly his best friend at present."

Worsley nodded, listening. She was also checking her smartphone emails while they were talking.

"We will give the two of them ten minutes then go back in. John, move on to ask him about the Winstanley found in his flat. Place the robbery entirely on him; make Cronin an exploited 'white knight' and infer that Hodson blackmailed him to reveal information on the location of the paintings, their value and the name of the security guard who could provide access. Place the whole thing on him.

"If we can get him worked up over that and hold back on Cronin's confession, then he may react and things could come out.

"Catrin, you had better go and see Mrs. Cronin. Bring her in anyway. I don't think she is involved but we need to know. Neville is on to me about it."

She waved her phone to indicate the source of the last comment.

"They have the stables under surveillance and Caldwell will send in a recovery team for the Stubbs paintings but only after you pick the wife up. I insisted that the ACU do that. Neville is getting anxious about leaving the Stubbs out there now."

Catrin said, "Yes ma'am."

John Obi was looking at Sayer. He couldn't tell from her face how she was feeling, both about being excluded from the interview and now being sent off on another task instead. She was unreadable.

Every difficult decision has a tipping point. Worsley's well-meaning action to deflect Hodson's focus on her had been Catrin's; it had been rolling around in her mind as she watched the interview. She couldn't work with this sort of 'special consideration', she concluded. She had no problem with John doing the interview if Worsley had said that she simply wanted to give him the experience or to use him to provoke more effectively a response from Hodson. She, too, had been given that sort of chance early on in her time in the ACU. But the reasoning around protecting her was wrong; for her and for the team, she felt.

She decided to leave it until either Taylor or Hunt called her in, as they clearly planned to do. Chris had said it was her decision; but he would go with her; he just preferred it to be Wales, not Devon & Cornwall.

He said, "I don't know how I could do it in Cornwall, Catrin, knowing so many people in the area. It wouldn't work there unless we staged a break-up and got together later without me changing identity. I don't know even whether the relocation people allow a person with a new ID to go back to a partner in such a way, or whether it ruins things from a security perspective. A new start for both of us may be the only safe way."

They had been talking about the possibilities and implications for days now. She made her decision; she was going to start again in Wales.

~~

Muriel Cronin sat down with a thump when she heard the news; just dropped on to the nearby stool. They were in the stable building itself. Her reaction didn't seem faked, Catrin thought, which tied in with Worsley's assessment.

"They are real? I have had original paintings by George Stubbs in my home for two years and I thought they were good copies? No wonder I was entranced by them."

She paused.

"Mrs. Harland just used to swipe away at them with the duster every Tuesday…"

Then she realised.

"Ryland has been arrested, hasn't he?"

"Yes," said Catrin, "He fainted during questioning and had a bad nosebleed. He is currently in the Royal Hospital but will be taken directly back into custody once he is released."

She nodded. "It has happened before, the nosebleeds; the Hungary deal when he lost the best part of a million through a stupid mistake. He is either on top of the world or it hits him in the face and his nosebleeds start.

"He had a nosebleed too when I told him I was leaving him; I wanted the country house for my stables business; that was all. The rest was his."

Inspector Caldwell was outside talking with the surveillance team. They had expert movers with them to transport the paintings properly. All were waiting for Catrin to finish with Cronin's wife and give the go-ahead.

Muriel Cronin looked at Catrin, "But you aren't sure, are you? He will tell the truth about me, I know, but you are going to question me, right?"

"We are asking you at this point to come into Scotland Yard and be interviewed, yes. We are not taking you into custody, just asking for your co-operation."

"And then?"

"If your story checks out, we will bring you home. You can have your solicitor present during the interview."

Muriel laughed. "My solicitor is local, an older man who

knows about conveyancing, horses and contracts. I doubt he has seen a courtroom in years. But I will come. How long will I be?"

Catrin said, "I can't say, Mrs. Cronin."

It depends on whether you knew anything, she thought.

Muriel said, "Give me a moment to set up with people to cover for me, please? The horses still need looking after, the clients as well."

"No rush," said Catrin, "Please take your time."

She realised that she was actually enjoying the break away from centre stage on the case.

Muriel Cronin said, "It's not as if I will make a run for it and head for France or anything, so do you need to keep me in your sights? I would like to talk to my staff alone, if I could."

"It's no problem, really," Catrin said. "Officers and staff from the Art and Antiques Unit are waiting; they will take the paintings away now and I will drive you to Scotland Yard when you are ready. Besides, you can't run to France, your passport expired last year, we checked."

Muriel stopped short.

"Did it really? I have been so busy here; I haven't even thought about a holiday."

She changed the direction she was walking, towards the house.

"I am going back to the house to see the paintings first, one more time, before they go. Is that OK? Next time I see them they will probably be in a museum."

Then she looked crestfallen. "Or back in the bank. I can't exactly go to see them there now, can I?"

Catrin said, "You will have to see paintings by George Stubbs in the National Gallery, like the rest of us."

Muriel replied, as she walked with this Welsh police officer into the conservatory, "I will, won't I?"

Catrin entered alongside Mrs. Cronin and they stopped at the first painting. The woman was looking at it earnestly. Catrin looked more closely then called out to Philip Caldwell to join her.

Caldwell came in, looked at her expression, then at Mrs. Cronin, then finally at the painting.

He said, "Oh, hell; where is the second, Mrs. Cronin?"

She said, "In the dining room, through there."

He moved through, switching on the light to give some refection off the surface. "Same thing, Catrin," he said, dejectedly.

Catrin pulled out her mobile and dialed Aina back at the Yard.

"You are going to need to pull John out of the Hodson interview; it's really urgent; I'll wait."

A couple of minutes later his voice came on the line.

"Catrin?"

"How close did you get to the Stubbs?" she murmured into the phone, moving away from Mrs. Cronin, who was looking now at Inspector Caldwell.

Obi said, "Why?"

Then he realised.

"I just saw one from the seat by the business desk, if you are in there. I didn't want to make an issue of it."

Catrin looked at the line of sight from the desk in the conservatory office into the lounge.

"I am… and I understand."

He said, "They are not the originals, are they?"

"No," said Catrin, just as Mrs. Cronin said to her, "I thought they were such nice copies."

"They are, Mrs. Cronin, they are," said Catrin.

She could hear Caldwell on his mobile in the other room; he was probably on to Coltrane right now.

Obi said, "What now?"

Catrin said, crestfallen, "Tell Worsley; pull her out to brief her, don't do it by giving her a note in front of Hodson and his lawyer."

She closed the call.

"Mrs. Cronin, you won't need to come in just yet, after all."

Muriel said, "So where are the originals, then, if you

thought these were them?"

Catrin looked at the woman.

"We are searching all his premises, Mrs. Cronin. We saw this painting as we arrived and looked for you at the office, then I came out to the barn. I think my boss will soon be putting that question to Mr. Cronin.

"I am sorry, I need to go now."

36 BRIXTON

"I didn't know that you didn't know, crazy as that sounds," said Cronin, in explanation. "In my office, you gave the impression you knew everything anyway, I thought. After that, I could hardly think straight."

His voice sounded tired. He was still pale and seemed worn out as he lay back on the pillow. He had suffered two more heavy nosebleeds in hospital and the doctor had talked about cauterizing his nose once his blood pressure had stabilized.

His solicitor looked at him, obviously wanting Cronin either to say nothing or to explain himself more clearly.

It was nearly 8.00 p.m. They were in a private room at the Royal Hospital and Cronin was lying on the bed, under guard. He hadn't been discharged, but given the findings at Denmur Stables, his solicitor had agreed to questions on that specific issue as a matter of urgency providing he was under medical supervision throughout.

But he didn't need to explain the statement. Catrin, Worsley and Neville Coltrane stood there, knowing that they should have posed the question before sending in the team to the stables.

Worsley had said to Neville before entering the room,

"Thank God the time stamps on the search warrants for all Cronin's residences are identical."

A search team had been sent to Cronin's flat, in part for show purposes, but also for evidence collection in general. At least it would not appear as if the stables had been singled out because they had advance information from a source, she meant.

"We told you in your office we were searching your various premises, so when we saw the copies at the stables, our team's first thought was they were the originals. So now we are asking specifically, Mr. Cronin."

Cronin said, "The Winstanley was there, the Stubbs never were; they are the copies I bought for the charity fundraiser. Talk to the bank about that. Muriel didn't know anything about it, by the way."

Cronin's solicitor interjected. "My client will tell you the rest under certain conditions regarding his personal protection. And he wants a deal; he will plead and co-operate, but wants sentencing leniency also. When you hear what he has, I think you will see that is reasonable. We were going to tell you that in the interview earlier, once you asked about the Stubbs' paintings. He collapsed before we got to it."

Jane looked at Neville Coltrane to take the lead. He was chasing the paintings, after all.

"Spit it out," said Coltrane. "The basis of the deal and why we should want to go for it. You will hold back the good stuff, no doubt."

"No I won't," said Cronin, matter-of-factly.

He was showing some spirit after all, Catrin thought, as he added, "And it's not Tony Hodson I will need protection from, either, if that is what you are thinking."

Later, outside the hospital entrance in the light cast from the doorways behind them, Coltrane and Worsley stood together apparently lost in thought. They were deciding on the next steps based on the bombshell they had just heard.

John Obi, who had not been in the room during Cronin's interview, was standing with Catrin a few feet away, watching and waiting for instructions. Both junior officers knew they had no role in this decision now, given the revelations.

Jane said, "We have started the ball rolling with Ryland Cronin's arrest, Neville; we can't go back. And we have to be quick before…" she left the rest unsaid.

"Yes," said Coltrane, "We will need everyone on this, on duty until we are done. I will call Philip Caldwell's team in, and Inspector Tyrell has people who can help. I can also wangle some document specialists on overtime, no doubt. Jane, will you buy time…"

She nodded, "I will go directly back to the Yard and call Jack Taylor and Bob Matheson. I suspect we will all end up trooping along to Sandra, to see what can be done; particularly to keep Jack's 'slimy friends' at bay."

Both senior officers were looking miserable as they separated a small distance to make calls on their mobiles.

John said softly to Catrin, "I didn't ask, as I didn't want to look stupid, but… this is really big now! Why the long faces?"

She looked at him, realising this was a new arena for her colleague.

"It is big; and much bigger money is involved now than the value of the paintings. We have about a day maximum, I predict, before A&A and ACU lose control of this case entirely. That's why."

She wasn't feeling too happy about it herself. But she was also thinking it was nearly over for her, anyway; she had new personal challenges she needed to face. She had to start the process of detaching from this case as she would soon put all this behind her.

~~

They had worked late into the evening back at Scotland Yard, sorting out a path forward. Catrin had called Chris, explaining only that she didn't know when she would be home;

she may be working into or through the night. He understood.

Thank God my man is in this business, she thought. And I can't talk to him about my decision on the relocation over the phone; it's too hard; it will have to wait.

Officers from the City of London Police came over to Scotland Yard led by a DCI Canning; all were people that Catrin didn't know. Superintendent Jack Taylor addressed the assembled officers at the end of the briefing session. When Taylor spoke, he was plain-spoken, right to the point.

"Several of you are assigned to the collection of bank people. Others have search roles and some are on the arrest preparations. No one on this Task Force will email anyone, on the team or elsewhere as of now. You will call no-one outside this group, speak only among the team and seek decisions from DCI Coltrane, DCI Worsley or DCI Canning only; no-one else. Communications must be watertight until tomorrow morning.

"This is not a request, it's an order; remember that."

Several team members looked a little surprised or perplexed. As they broke up Catrin looked at Worsley and mouthed 'S' then 'F' so that only her boss could see. Jane Worsley just nodded; the measures were a direct outcome of Superintendent Taylor's concern about the SIS comment at the function he had attended as this case started to roll out.

Around 11 p.m., a team went over to the Houghton Bank after picking up the head of security, Douglas Blinney, at his home. He, in turn, had identified two other employees to join him; they were all asked to remain under police supervision until preliminary questioning had been completed.

"It is for your own good, really," they were told.

They needed no explanation; they were bank people. They understood secrecy.

About one in the morning at the bank, Blinney came over to Catrin.

"Knowing where this is going now, even though you have told us nothing, I want you to look at a document that has been nagging at me since I first saw it."

He led her to the file and opened it up. She read it and said, "Mr. Blinney, where are you from, before this job?"

He said, "I was with Holbey Trantor, the security people, for eleven years. Before that, well, I was with your lot. Not here I mean, with Heddlu Gogledd Cymru. You are south Welsh, I can tell."

Heddlu Gogledd Cymru; the North Wales Police, he meant.

Blinney added, "I wasn't going far career-wise; I was tired of living in the same area, so I packed it in and joined Holbey Trantor."

She nodded, finishing the document, understanding the significance.

"Diolch, Mr. Blinney."

If she wasn't in the middle of a formal investigation she would have liked to talk with him further, to see if he knew people in the North Wales Police she had worked with on her first case with the ACU. But a 'thank you' in Welsh was as much as she should do while this was in progress. No-one knew how big this thing really was yet.

At the end, near four a.m., Jane Worsley said, "It's compensation, Catrin, for taking away your interview with Hodson, if you like; it was your case then. We are being given the first interview after all, it has been agreed.

"Neville wants you and him to do that one. He went back into the Yard about half an hour ago to talk with people overseas. It was his request, just as he left. And he suggested we use a really hard police station, not the Yard, so I thought of Brixton, your old 'manor'. It should be 'real world' enough for him.

Catrin smiled to herself at the thought; the irony of the situation. She recalled a discussion with Inspector Anderson, her old boss when she was attached to the Drug Squad in Brixton; how a girl from the Welsh valleys would never end up in a job in the ivory tower of New Scotland Yard. Now she would be going back.

Worsley said, "Now, take a break; get some rest somewhere for a while; find an armchair or a sofa. The rest of them will wrap it up here. Coltrane says he will collect you and drive over to Brixton. You may need to guide him once you are south of the Thames; he probably hasn't been to your old stamping ground before. And if his Bentley gets graffiti on it while it is parked there, don't smile."

Catrin laughed at her boss's jibe at Neville Coltrane. At one time they were wary of each other, now they got along well, really.

"It will be parked in the Brixton station, ma'am."

"You're right, Catrin; it won't be painted; they will just swipe the Bentley wings off the radiator faring."

Catrin laughed out loud again.

"Thank you, ma'am; but I think they are theft proof. Mind you, coppers have the right tools for everything…"

Worsley could see that Sayer was at ease with her; they were through the issue of the last interview, at least.

For Catrin, somehow there was more to it, this selection of her to do the interview with Coltrane. She realised, intuitively rather than for any logical reason, that it was meaningful; she would be going full circle, in a sense. It was as if they knew she had made a decision to start again elsewhere without her saying anything yet, she thought.

~~

Members of the Task Force picked up Sir Kenneth Lowell, the chairman of the Board of Directors of the Houghton Bank, at his home just after 6.00 a.m. They took him to Brixton Police Station, putting him in a bare and much used interview room awaiting the arrival of his solicitor.

There was the noise of a working police station, the bustle around the aftermath of night work: drunks complaining; the litany of drug users and dealers arrested, the aftermath of domestic disputes broken up and the banter of officers changing shifts. It would probably not sit well with Sir

Kenneth, they thought. He would also be uncomfortable about not being formally dressed in a suit and tie. His shirt, cardigan and a pair of gardening pants he had dressed in hurriedly were not his normal public attire.

Catrin was watching him on the monitor, Coltrane next to her. She recognized the interview room, even the dent in the wall panel, old as it was, recalling the story of the event that had put it there, even though she wasn't involved. She really was visiting old home ground.

When the solicitor appeared at nearly 7.30 a.m. it was not the person Coltrane thought it would be.

"It's a senior partner; his own solicitor must have called him in knowing that this must be serious. I know this one, Fielding; he is good at his job, but a nice sort."

He headed out to the corridor to intercept the solicitor. He shook hands as if they were about to enter round one in the boxing ring, said a few words and then returned.

"He asked for twenty minutes with Lowell; that's quite reasonable, really."

He paused.

"Catrin, do you remember the interview with Geri Roper?"

She laughed. "How can I forget, sir? I was terrified; my first big interview - and with Geraldine Roper. I couldn't believe it when you said, 'you lead' just before we went in."

Catrin was then a detective constable leading an interview to disconcert a woman who was both a pretentious art critic and a forceful media personality.

He smiled. "You lead the same way. Let's get some more coffee while they talk."

Two hours in limbo in the reality of life in Brixton, as seen by its police station, had certainly worked wonders with Lowell. He was livid, barely containing his anger despite the initial questions from this mild-mannered junior police officer.

He knew Coltrane, of course; had met him at least twice at art events over the last twelve months, despite Coltrane's claim of no memory of doing so. The man was just trying to annoy him; that was obvious. Lowell realised that getting this junior officer to put the questions was part of the same strategy. Well, it wouldn't work on him. Coltrane would hear about it later, in other surroundings than a woebegone police station in Brixton, he decided. He had friends in the art world too, and in other places that could make things awkward for the man.

'Life is so busy, Sir Kenneth, for both us; we meet so many people,' had been Neville's response.

After the preliminaries, Catrin said, "We have arrested Ryland Cronin and four other people for the planning and execution of the Houghton Bank robbery, Sir Kenneth. Another man involved in the robbery is now in Rome, we find. He is in prison there for another theft. We will be requesting his return to stand trial here in due course."

Clearly it had not been leaked; the chairman of the board was struck by the news.

"I can't believe it. Ryland Cronin. A solid man, a good board member; you must have it wrong," he said tersely.

"He has admitted it, sir," she said.

She looked at him, waiting a moment.

"He wanted the Winstanley painting; it is a relative of his, someone in his family tree and he claims that George Stubbs, not Hamlet Winstanley painted it during the period Stubbs was apprenticed to Winstanley. He thinks of it as an unknown Stubbs and it would be worth… a great deal; beside the family connection, that is."

Lowell's face was impassive. The man had spent much of his life in financial negotiations; he wasn't going to react even though that would be news to him, they thought.

She looked down at her notes.

"We see that three months after the robbery the Houghton Bank secured a financial deal with a company in Bolivia owned by a Mr. Hermano Suchar, a communications magnate. It was announced that the contract is worth 1.2 billion US dollars over a four year period. What was the profit realised by the Houghton Bank on the transaction costs of the first phase of the contract, please?"

"That is irrelevant to your enquiries, sergeant," Lowell snapped, his anger rising further. "Such information is highly confidential; a bank cannot break a client's trust just like that."

Catrin asked, "Was Mr. Cronin directly involved in this deal negotiation?"

Sir Kenneth paused, calming a little. "No, it was a bank matter. Other than approval by the board members at a regular meeting, that is. The negotiations were led by the bank president at the time who consulted me of course, as chairman, as and when appropriate."

"The president was then Norman Johnson, now retired, I understand?"

Lowell said, "That is correct."

Catrin pulled out a piece of paper.

"You would recognize Mr. Johnson's handwriting, of course? Is this it?"

She placed the page in front of him and his lawyer.

Lowell scanned the page, a routine annotation on a letter, and said, "It looks to be, yes."

Catrin pulled out a second document.

"This is from the current security director's file. We saw him at the bank earlier, before you were woken by our officers. It is an employee suggestion form, as you can see. Three security staff members proposed a modification to the entry to the Executive Floor, to the alarm system. If you look at this copy you will see an annotation. It says, 'Discussed with KL; no changes to the executive wing at all' in Johnson's handwriting."

Lowell was intently looking at the document.

Catrin said, "We assume KL is you. Why would you say that?"

Sir Kenneth said, "It may not be me. I don't recall such a conversation. But generally we had a very traditional 'don't change things approach' to the area… it could be that."

He sounded reasonable, helpful; he was controlling his earlier anger, it appeared.

Catrin said, "But for Johnson to consult you on something so trivial, it seems strange, doesn't it? Did you involve yourself in such low level decisions regularly?"

"Certainly I did not. I haven't any idea why he did so, if he did. It may have come up in passing… I have no idea."

He looked at his lawyer and raised his eyebrows. The message was, 'why are they bothering me about such trivial stuff?'

Catrin pulled out another page.

"This document, Sir Kenneth, is not a board document at all. It is a note regarding the decision to make copies of the paintings on the Executive Floor. The copies were to be sold to board members and employees in support of a charity fundraiser. Tax receipts all round, no doubt."

Lowell nodded, "You may be cynical, sergeant; but it was for a good cause."

Catrin nodded. "Indeed. Ryland Cronin paid for a copy of each of the Stubbs paintings. Other board members bought items also."

Newell said, "I bought a copy of the Constable myself, Sergeant."

Catrin said, "We know. Now sir, can you tell me about these manuscript annotations, the priority order given to the copyist? The work by the copier on the orders was to take some months, I am led to believe."

Lowell squinted as he pushed his glasses further up his nose, intently staring at the note she had passed over.

"No I can't," he said. "They could be anyone's."

"Well, Sir Kenneth, we believe they are yours; the ink, the formation of the numbers. Not much to go on, but we do have experts ready to look at it, analyse the ink and so on. After all, we can take your fountain pen, search your home and office and work from other documents at the bank you have annotated or signed."

He said, "It could be me, I saw so many documents, you see. I don't remember. And I use ordinary ink refills available to anyone."

Catrin retrieved the document from his hand.

"It's the fact that this wasn't a board document at all that puzzled us. We also wondered why the two Stubbs' works had been marked as numbers 1 and 2 for copying. Can you tell us that?"

"No," he said.

She thought, because you agreed to that point with Cronin; he wanted the copies before the originals disappeared and it was all part of your sweet deal. But her face showed nothing.

She paused a little then continued in the same manner.

"Does the name 'Arica' mean anything to you, Sir Kenneth?"

"No idea, to be honest," he responded.

They were watching his eyes, listening to his voice. The last few questions were showing his increasing discomfort, something to Catrin that went beyond irritation and boredom.

"It's a town in Chile, sir."

Cronin's confession had clarified the reason why the unusual text had been sent from Des Hewitt's phone at 4.55 a.m. after the robbery. He told them that Hermano Suchar wanted confirmation that the Stubbs paintings had been taken from the bank; it was an agreed performance point in the bank deal she had just mentioned; the paintings were the bribe that Suchar had requested.

One of his agents in Arica was to be informed. It had been Hodson's job to send the text to the cell phone number in Arica seeing as Cronin was overseas and wanted nothing tracked to him. Hodson's stupid variant was designed both to frighten Hewitt and achieve that goal simultaneously. It had been the final straw in the split-up between Hodson and Cronin. It was a bad error, giving a link between the robbery and South America, inexplicable as it was.

Cronin claimed that he had concealed the fact from Lowell. Coltrane wanted this question asked to see how Lowell would react, as Arica was an operating base for Suchar's organization.

"Chile?" echoed Lowell, "I am here to answer geography questions? Really?

His voice had risen in volume.

Catrin said, "It's a free port for Bolivia, Sir Kenneth. With the contacts your bank has in Bolivia we wondered. We note that the owner of the communications company in Bolivia, Mr. Suchar, is an extremely wealthy man and that has a passion for both art and horses; he is known for his interests in both areas."

"What are you getting at?" said Lowell, suddenly alert to the change in topic. His lawyer leaned forward, all attention.

"I am asking you -"

The lawyer interjected, "You note and ask a lot, sergeant, of very trivial items. I would point out that Sir Kenneth was taken from his bed, has not had a chance to shower or shave and he is an extremely busy and important man who needs to get on with his day."

He wanted this interview over.

Lowell said, to echo his lawyer, "Why was I brought here, held here?"

Catrin said, "It was convenient for me, Mr. Lowell. I used to work in this police station and we needed an interview room, so…"

"Damn your bloody impertinence!" shouted Lowell.

His anger broke; the use of 'Mr.' and the fact he had been dragged to this backwater of a police station early in the morning for the convenience of this junior officer. The tirade of abusive invective streamed out of Sir Kenneth as his solicitor's voice rose, trying to regain control, seeing the trap.

Catrin struck.

"I cannot believe it," she said loudly, with emotion that was released, unfeigned, after working all yesterday and overnight. "A peer of the realm of England involved in the theft of national treasures, the works of George Stubbs, stealing them and smuggling them out of the country, to be lost from England into the hands of a corrupt South American businessman just to sweeten a business deal…."

She stopped, leaving it open, giving the impression that she was lost for words, as Lowell thundered back.

"You stupid woman, you know nothing of art or history! Virtually all real art is traded for profit, moved between countries, stolen during wars, whatever… it's not just there to sit on bloody walls."

He stopped, suddenly realising that in his anger he had said things he shouldn't have done. The silence that descended on the room contrasted heavily with the last exchange. Catrin just looked at him, her face conveying her distaste for the man.

Lowell looked at his solicitor who was making calming noises to him, trying to stop him speaking again.

He then said, in a near-normal voice. "I deny any involvement in the theft of any paintings. The allegation you have just made is an insult. I will be making a formal complaint at the highest levels of the Metropolitan Police."

He was regaining control. Coltrane could see, however, the concern was still evident on the face of his solicitor, who said, "Neville, I would like some more time with my client, alone; now, please."

Coltrane nodded, taking control of the interview.

He said softly, "Sir Kenneth, this is your opportunity to tell it from your perspective, if you wish. We do have most of the facts, you see. And the Bolivian authorities are assisting us as we speak."

Catrin saw a look pass across Lowell's face, one she read as 'good luck with that.' Meaning, she thought, that Hermano Suchar was an extremely powerful man and they would learn nothing. Coltrane obviously read it the same way.

But what Lowell said was, "I repeat. I deny everything. I have nothing further to say."

Coltrane sat up straight. "Mr. Fielding, you will have that time with your client soon. Sir Kenneth Lowell, you will now be taken to Wood Street, to the City of London Police Headquarters to be interviewed by the team of Commander Saunders, who will decide what charges to lay against you, if any. He, as you know, leads all major investigations into international bribery and corruption cases that involve transactions through the Stock Exchange. The Metropolitan Police will want to question you further about the theft of the paintings discussed here, but the issue is somewhat broader now and financial irregularities of this order regretfully trump our interest in art."

"It is 8.55 a.m. This interview is now suspended."

He waited a moment, as Catrin switched off the recording system.

Coltrane's voice changed; his tone becoming harder, more antagonistic. "And Sir Kenneth, what DS Sayer knows about art and art history leaves you in the dust, I assure you."

Catrin tried not to smile. She knew that Coltrane's final comment was quite unnecessary given the situation, but somehow it pleased her immensely.

Lowell's lawyer was looking extremely tense. The peer of the realm was staring into the distance, lost to all of them, deep in thought.

After Lowell was taken away to the City with Fielding accompanying him, Catrin said to Coltrane, "Thank you, sir for letting me lead, and for your last comment also, although you shouldn't have said it. I am supposed to be the plodder on this case."

Coltrane smiled. "You are right, but I couldn't resist it, particularly after your comment about him. It was right on the ball - a person knighted, doing what he did. Commander Saunders will be very interested in that tirade remark of his as they pick away at him."

Catrin said, "Do you think we will get them back, sir… the paintings?"

Coltrane shrugged his shoulders.

"I am not sure, Catrin. Not long ago the Art Loss Register people worked with the Americans to recover some valuable art that was found in Bolivia. That worked out. ALR and the insurers are involved in the Stubbs investigation, too. It may pan out, despite Señor Suchar being wealthy. Anyway, it is something for Art & Antiques to work on; it's what we do, remember? We track down stolen art."

He smiled at her.

"But I am sure Commander Saunders will be giving Lowell a hard time, checking all transactions, travel, who was sent what, who met with whom and when… and we have a songbird in Cronin, as well."

Catrin's face clouded over.

"Perhaps not, sir; Lowell may have influential friends. Superintendent Taylor said…"

She stopped herself, realising that such news should come from Worsley, not her.

He smiled.

"Jack's dinner conversation with SIS warning us off, you mean? That perhaps it wasn't Cronin they were worried about? You think they were concerned that it could lead us closer to Lowell?

"DCI Worsley mentioned Jack's comment at the time. It was only outside the Royal Hospital when she and I talked it occurred to us that SIS may well have known about the paintings and Lowell's dealings for some time.

"But they aren't going to jump to his defence, Catrin, unless he has something of extraordinary value to offer them. That's why Jack read the Riot Act on secure communications last night; we had to get Lowell into custody before they knew. SIS has no chance to head it off now; they can only try to minimize damages or override us through the political route, if they choose."

"Besides, it will be around the banking community by now that we were in the Houghton Bank half the night and that Lowell won't be showing at his office this morning."

Catrin nodded, "But still, sir, all this work to find the Stubbs and some people in government may have known all along …"

He nodded. "It's the way it works, Catrin. One of the elements in a training course above your level as yet is what to do when the spooks contact us, for some reason. Part of it is always to ask yourself why they are telling us anything or asking for our help; they aren't doing it for chummy behaviour, I assure you."

He stopped, stood up.

Catrin suddenly thought that she could go home to find that Chris had been assigned to the same case, doing computer forensic work for the City of London Police. It would be her now receiving calls from him, saying he wasn't sure when he would be home; or perhaps not, once they talked about her decision.

She stood also. She needed to get home but...

She said, "I had better get back to the Yard. I have to go there before I get to go home."

Coltrane said, "I am off north from here for a while, Catrin, I can't give you a lift back. I know Worsley wants to see you before you get off for some rest, though. She mentioned it."

"That's alright, sir, I will take the Tube from around the corner, like the old days. It seems strange to be back here."

She was looking around her. She meant in Brixton police station, he realised. He started to say something then stopped.

She smiled, put her file in her briefcase and headed out the door, ready to walk to the nearby Tube station, Stockwell. She ran into an old colleague in the corridor, Coltrane saw, as he thought, 'I wonder how Sayer will react?'

Worsley had briefed him in private, yesterday evening.

He went out past her and her colleague to the duty desk and interrupted the desk officer talking to someone.

"Have a car take Sergeant Sayer back to the Yard, would you? Catch her before she heads out for the Tube."

37 THE HEAVENS

The silver Bentley Continental Supersport rolled up to the house in Essendon and Neville Coltrane got out. The car looked out of place in the ordinary surroundings, next to two old wheelbarrows, a Ford Fiesta and a much older Ford van.

Wendy Hewitt, her husband and daughter were at the door as he approached, having seen him arrive and knowing he was coming; he had called ahead. Des shook his hand but Wendy gave him a hug.

Once they were inside and seated, he explained the situation, focusing on Emma. She was in her school uniform, having stayed off school this morning specifically at her parent's request.

Coltrane said softly, "The men who came here and the other men who robbed the bank are now all in custody. The person who hit your mother will stay in gaol awaiting trial and, once the trial is finished, I expect that he will stay there for a very long time indeed. None of these men can harm you or your family any more. You need to know that, Emma; they cannot bother you or your mother again."

The girl nodded.

"You are sure, though, Mr. Coltrane?" she said. He could see in her face the trust decision being made.

"I am sure, Emma. The man who paid for the operation is now in custody, too and he has confessed to organizing the robbery. He has told us everything. We have lots of evidence to present at their trials."

Des looked knowingly at Coltrane. He knew a little already; it was all over the bank that Sir Ken, Ryland Cronin and the last bank president, Johnson, had been taken into custody. Blinney had called him; employees were under strict instructions not to talk to the press or discuss it further.

'Thank you," the girl said and stood, looking at her parents, wanting to leave and get to school, Coltrane realised.

He hoped that she had just made a decision to accept what he said was true. He had heard from the Crown Prosecutor's office on the way up that Hodson had been refused bail that morning. He had been remanded for another week. It was a start.

She looked at her mother.

"Can I go now? I have double maths later. I shouldn't miss it; it's hard enough as it is. But thank you again, Mr. Coltrane."

"I'll drop you off," her father said. He shook hands with Coltrane, thanking him also.

With Wendy afterwards Coltrane gave more details; not a lot, but enough.

"Will Emma have to be a witness at the trial?" she asked.

Coltrane shook his head.

"Des and yourself, yes; Emma, possibly, but I think it is highly unlikely. Once the prosecution team knows more about her medical history they wouldn't want to put her in front of Hodson. DCI Worsley is talking also about a voice identification parade of the people involved, which would involve you and Des listening to recordings.

"You two may also want to give a victim impact statement when the jury comes back. Barring idiocy in court, there is no reason why Hodson shouldn't be convicted and put in prison for ten years."

"Too right," she said, with feeling. "For what Emma has

been through, that's what I mean."

As Coltrane stood to leave, Wendy said, "Neville, your father and your uncle would be proud of you, sticking with this, seeing it through, if you told them. So would my dad, if he were alive also."

There were tears in her eyes.

Neville nodded, said nothing, suddenly overcome himself. Wendy's father had been the head gardener at the Coltrane family estate in Buckinghamshire where Neville, a city boy, had spent long periods during boyhood summers in the home of his uncle.

He had been attracted to Wendy in his early teens; she was two years older than him and had turned from a girl into a young woman as he was still a boy dealing with the emotions of early puberty. But they were divided by a class structure that was very evident and a realisation soon afterwards that it was simply adolescent infatuation.

The Hewitt home in Essendon was rural; it was a small holding. Wendy had inherited her father's love of horticulture and gardens and had a small business herself, growing and selling vegetables for sale at the local farmer's market.

Coltrane broke the silence.

"It was a Welsh detective sergeant at the Yard who came up with the plan to arrest Hodson. It worked well."

And, he thought, it worked well to protect Cox and his family; the Met had held to their part in the deal. Everything traced back to Sayer's plodding zeal with a painting from another unnamed case.

Wendy said, "One of your team, Neville?"

"No. I wish she was a part of it, though," he said. "She is someone I work with from time to time and is very good at her job."

But we won't be working together for much longer, regretfully, he thought.

After Coltrane drove away and with Des still out delivering Emma to school, Wendy retrieved the little jar she had put behind the flower pot. When she handed it and the old strychnine pack stored in the shed to the hazardous waste people, she would talk about still finding her dad's gardening stuff squirreled away after all this time.

~~

Catrin had just got back to the ACU and settled in at her desk when Aina came over.

"DCI Worsley wants to see you now, Catrin. And then you can go home, she said. You look worn out and so does she."

Catrin's eyes swivelled to Worsley's office.

"No," said Aina. "She wants you up in the heavens, in the Assistant Commissioner's office. I just told them you were back."

Aina's face revealed nothing, which was significant in itself; she was Worsley's right hand in many issues, including personnel matters, but she only looked this way when something particularly confidential was in play.

Catrin didn't ask, but her eyes said to Aina, 'What now?' Deeper down, she felt as if somehow this had to happen, whatever it was, after the encounter with Sandra Hunt on Friday. She took a deep breath and let it out. At least she had made a decision about her life going forward.

"Best get it over with," she said to Aina, to herself, to the air. And I haven't had time to talk with Chris yet, even, she thought.

After she pulled her jacket back on she headed out to the elevator, checking her shirt was well tucked in. She had to be neat and presentable in the heavens, even in clothes worn for more than a day now.

She was shown from the outer suite directly into Hunt's inner office, where Jane Worsley was already seated. From the file in front of her boss she could see that Worsley had been briefing the AC on the case.

Hunt indicated to her to sit also, both women sitting side-by-side across from the assistant commissioner.

Not a problem issue then, thought Catrin, suddenly worrying on the way upstairs that the interview that morning was already having repercussions. Sir Kenneth Lowell was a heavyweight hitter, with influential friends. She would have been kept standing, probably, if that was the case, she thought.

Hunt said, "Sergeant Sayer, I know you are tired and it has been a tough twenty-four hours for you. Well done on that success but you are back here now because I have an offer for you."

Hunt paused, letting Sayer adjust. She had seen her looking at the case file in front of Worsley and would be thinking of that still, or the relocation.

"I want you to become my aide and personal security officer. When we first met, you may recall Sergeant Ross had that role and you have met Sergeant Egar more recently. I would like you to take up that position for a while."

Catrin looked thunderstruck.

Hunt continued. "Inspector Ross is now with the Pan-London Task Force and Sergeant Egar's promotion was approved two days ago. He will be joining the Barking and Dagenham borough at Inspector rank. It's a position which generally results in promotion, you see, if you have the aptitude and stamina… and I think you do."

By now it had sunk in. Catrin glanced at Worsley who nodded and smiled.

Catrin said, "Thank you, ma'am, for considering me but… it is not logical."

She paused, trying to find the correct words.

"I am targeted, when, where, if ever, we don't know, but… it's not logical. To increase your risk, I mean."

She thought she could have put it better perhaps, but that was the way it came out. She felt more shocked than tired now and realised she should actually mention her decision on Wales, as the relocation choice. After the encounter with Hunt on Friday she expected to be pushed into relocation and a new identity, perhaps with some incentive, at this meeting.

Hunt nodded, as if she knew this would come up. Or it had already done so, with others.

"On the contrary, I think it is very logical, for a couple of reasons. First, you have shown capability in the area of protecting other officers under fire at close range; few of us get that direct experience, fortunately; and it is a position that requires you to be armed.

"Second, and perhaps the most important reason you should accept it, is that it will help to keep you safe. The word about the appointment will go out to Malaysia, China and to triad groups here; we will make sure of that with the help of Superintendent Baksh and others.

"To kill a police officer is bad enough; to be seen to be trying to kill either an Assistant Commissioner of the Metropolitan Police or someone close to her is appalling. No triad would survive it very well; their business linkages would be badly damaged or ruined, for one thing and every police service would be driving them over the cliff for years to come. Nam Wu will be told to keep his private vendetta on ice, at least during your assignment period on my team. That is the expert opinion, from a number of sources, here and abroad. We looked into it quite thoroughly in the last few days."

She stood up and walked to the door of her inner office, closing it fully then turned to face the two women.

"And I will be damned if I let anyone tell me that my role is so important that I can't stand with my officers if the opportunity arises."

Her voice didn't rise in volume but the anger came through; clearly others had voiced the same concern about increasing Hunt's own risk, it wasn't a criticism of Catrin. And the only people she would have had to listen to regarding that aspect would be her fellow Assistant Commissioners and the Commissioner himself, Catrin realised.

She came back to her desk and stood there.

"So what do you say? Want to think about it, at least? It may even be more appealing than changing your identity and moving away. I know you are tired now, so sleeping on it, thinking about it for a day or so would be fine."

Catrin looked at her then at Worsley, then back at Hunt and said carefully, "I enjoy the art crime work, as you know. But I don't need to think about it further. It would be an honour, ma'am, to work with you as part of your team. Thank you for asking me… and going to all this trouble."

In her mind was the thought that several years ago this senior officer had detoured out of her way during a typically busy day to encourage her to stay with the Met after the Kinnington Church incident. How she knew Catrin was thinking about resigning then was still a mystery to her. And now she wanted to stand by her again and, in the process, give her the opportunity to see policing at a level few in any police service get the opportunity to see. And she wouldn't need to move, change identity and… she would be armed even if the Malaysian sent someone after her; a better fighting chance, at least.

Now she understood the meaning of Hunt's words in front of 'The Light of the World' at St. Paul's Cathedral last week.

Hunt looked at her, realising that Sayer had made a considered decision very fast, then said, "Good, we will sort out the paperwork and you will hear more; advanced weapons training and some other courses that you will need, some new uniforms and an overlap period with Inspector Egar. It will be arranged."

She sat down again, smiled at them, clearly satisfied with the outcome being such a prompt decision.

"Right, that was all, I think, Jane. Thank you, both of you. Probably you want to get out of here and get some well-deserved rest. And I will prepare for the calls from people in the City about Ryland Cronin and Sir Kenneth Lowell, including Superintendent Taylor's 'slimy friends', as he so eloquently puts it, if they raise their heads. I am actually quite looking forward to hear what people have to say."

She stood again suddenly, reached out and offered her hand to Catrin, smiling. "I will also look forward, Sergeant Sayer, to having you join my staff."

In the corridor Catrin suddenly stopped, looked at Worsley and said, "Ma'am, it just seemed right, so - ."

Jane Worsley said, "Catrin, it's a good decision, you'll see. You will learn a lot in that job, I tell you, things that will help your future career, I am sure. As she said, everyone in that position so far has left with a promotion. Unless Keith moved on, it wouldn't happen in ACU, not with our strength and budget, so… you would need to think of moving anyway at some time, for your career. We talked about that at your performance review, remember?"

Catrin said, "I am going to miss you, and the team. That's the thing. I hadn't even thought that through, even though I had been thinking about relocation. And I haven't discussed it with Chris. And leaving now, when the ACU is going through the Structural Review Committee… it doesn't sit well. But I had to say yes."

Worsley looked at her and smiled.

"Catrin, think the last point through again, the SRC comment I mean. The ACU now has a direct contribution of a recovery of paintings by George Stubbs probably worth millions and, with A&A, we are unlocking a multi-billion dollar international corruption case. That's what Sandra and I were discussing before you came back; the ACU will be solid as a rock at the SRC meeting next time. Hell, I may even get Jack to push for increasing our budget!"

Catrin realised that she was really tired; it should have been obvious to her. But she was lost in thought about the changes affecting her personally.

As they reached the lift Worsley said, "Now I am going to have to hire a replacement DS who knows about criminal investigation and art..."

They got in and the doors closed. They were the only two occupants. Clearly she was thinking, too.

"Any first ideas come to mind, Catrin?"

Catrin looked at her.

"Not promote - ,"

Worsley said, "Obi? No, not yet. No. He's not ready; pushing him too early will do him no favours in the long run. If he ever becomes ready; I will have to see."

Both women were shaking their heads in agreement. No more needed to be said.

Catrin started to think hard about who would be a suitable replacement for her, assuming they couldn't poach from Art and Antiques. Or perhaps they could…

"Not a word, Catrin, to the others until the papers are through. Understand?"

"Yes, ma'am, of course; that is, if I can look at Aina and not burst into tears before I go home today."

38 TRANSITION

You never hear the shot that hits you, if they are good, it is said. And if they aren't that good, you are going into shock when the sound wave reaches you, so many who survive are already in sensory overload and so don't hear it anyway.

In this case, witnesses heard the window break and a woman scream.

The first person entering the room was Detective Constable Jordan Ellison, a member of a security unit within Crime Investigation, part of the City of London Police. The Economic Crime people had brought them in at the time they took over custody of Ryland Cronin, given his offer to make a deal and his knowledge of far more than the Houghton Bank robbery.

What he found as he entered was a window cracked radially with a hole in the centre and on the floor was his partner, Callie, screaming, blood pouring out of her shoulder, an ugly red hole with some bone showing.

Ryland Cronin was standing near her, transfixed, unable to react or approach the injured woman. Jordon dived on him, knocking him to the floor as another bullet ploughed through the glass and hit the far wall.

Jordan shouted for Cronin to lie still as he confirmed the

attack into his radio, informing them that an officer was down and they were under sniper fire. Then he crawled over to Callie.

Other officers bursting in as back-up found him with his fingers pressed into the female officer's shoulder, closing down the blood flow from an artery. Cronin was lying there with a lot of blood on his face and hands. Initially they thought he had been hit too, but it was only another nosebleed.

Catrin had come home after the meeting with Hunt and slept, exhausted. When she woke, she called Chris and told him the news. Later, when he came home from his own work that evening they talked it through. Both were happy with the outcome and decided to go out to dinner.

Catrin slept fitfully that night, her head filled with the sense of change. As she got up, finally accepting she needed to read or do something, not lie there, Chris came into the living room a minute or so later.

He said, "Will you miss the art crime work? Silly question, I know. But it's nearly four a.m. and you are padding around. So we may as well talk."

Catrin said, "I am going to make some tea. Yes, I am missing it already but it is the right thing to do. I feel that. I am having trouble sleeping, that's all."

He came over and put his arms around her, holding her.

"The big question," he said, "is not will you miss it, or will you like working for Hunt, but will it quieten the fears about Wu, whether we will learn anything from the Malaysian Police networks to say Hunt and the others are correct."

She held him tightly. That's really why I am up at four o'clock, cariad. You are so good at reading me, aren't you?"

"Diolch yn fawr," said Chris; thank you very much. "See, I have been practising my Welsh."

Catrin let out a laugh. "Welsh, you call it, do you? Who's been teaching you?"

Chris looked mischievous.

"Melanie," he lied.

Melanie did not speak the language but loved mangling it to annoy Jean. Catrin looked at him in disbelief, then gave her boyfriend a kiss and took his hand.

"I have to be at Hendon in the morning. Let's get back to bed."

The wheels of change had already started rolling; she had an email from Hunt's office, copied to Worsley, informing her of the meeting. Hendon was the training centre of the Metropolitan Police Service, officially called the 'Peel Centre' but referred to by everyone as Hendon, after its earlier name.

Tea was off the radar, he realised.

Catrin was informed about the attempt on Cronin's life at Hendon that morning. She was in a meeting, ironically, with the person who would be organizing the training courses she needed, there and at Milton, the firearms training centre. They were working together on scheduling them.

Catrin was pulled out of that meeting briefly by a senior officer, an inspector she didn't know, just as the training coordinator was talking about the difficulty of transition periods in careers, the pull of the old role versus planning for the new. The inspector said nothing until they were outside the room.

"My office, please, Sergeant Sayer. Superintendent Taylor wants to see you; but not for long though as he has a cadet class waiting."

It was clear from his face that it wasn't good news.

"What about, sir?" she said automatically.

"He will tell you, no doubt. But there has been a shooting, I know."

Taylor waved Catrin straight into the other chair at the small conference table as the owner of the office said to him, "Let me know when you are done, sir."

Taylor said, "Sayer, I was on my way here to speak to the new cadet intake when Jane called me and asked me to speak to you. There was an attempt on the life of Ryland Cronin yesterday evening; a rifle shot through the window at the safe house they were using. It is still being decided what deal he should get, so he was in protective custody. He still is, in fact; but it is high security coverage now.

"Jane's up to her eyes, both with the case transfer to the City and other work, as you can imagine."

Catrin said, "Do I need to get back, sir? I don't officially start until I have had some of this training…"

"No," Taylor said, "That's not necessary. It's a City of London Police matter, not us, frustrating as that is, I know. Saunders' team and their security people are dealing with it."

Catrin asked, "Is Cronin injured?"

"No, he was in shock, but uninjured. He had more nosebleeds. But now he is mad as hell, not whimpering about it. It was one of the officers with him, behind him who was hit; the bullet deflected and deformed as it went through the window. It landed in the officer's shoulder; it's quite a mess, but she is stable."

He paused. Catrin didn't know what to say. Her first thought was, 'That could be me someday, whether or not I take this job.' Then she felt guilty about thinking of herself.

"Is the officer OK though, otherwise?" she asked.

"She's stable, Sayer, that's all I know at present. But the news is circulating so we thought you should know and also know that, despite the decision on the position with the AC, the relocation offer will not be taken off the table if you ever feel you need it. Not pushing you; in fact, I am actually very pleased with your decision. But if it ever gets too much… let us know. That was the main reason for telling you about this now."

She said, "Thank you, sir. It's really appreciated. I hadn't thought of it that way, to be honest. I have made my decision. And I want this job - and the training. I wasn't just being polite when I said to the AC that it would be a privilege to have it; I meant it."

Taylor nodded. He hadn't expected anything different.

"Good. I'd better not keep the cadets waiting much longer…"

His face changed, less serious, as he stood up.

"You will be at some important events with the AC in your new job, Sayer. Just remember, two things are important."

He paused. She waited for the punchline, starting to smile.

"Go to the washroom before the speeches start and don't get gravy on your uniform; it's sod to get out. Other than that, be yourself."

"That's three things to remember for these events - 'do's', should I say, sir." She parodied his pronunciation of the word.

He laughed. "I can't resist it, saying 'do's' in broad Yorkshire like that; it gets Jane so wound up."

~~

Later, at the Yard, she heard more from Worsley.

"Cronin is talking his head off and his solicitor wants more breaks on the sentencing deal. She seems to forget that Cronin actually handled the organisation of a bank robbery for Lowell and brought in Hodson to lead it. She will want a medal for the man, not a prison sentence. But what Saunders' team is now hearing from Cronin is going to bury Lowell if it gets to court."

"Do we know how the shooter got to Cronin, ma'am?"

She nodded. "He called his assistant Lucia about something, even though he had been instructed to call no-one. When Saunders heard that he hauled Lucia Moyano in. She is Spanish…"

Catrin interjected, "And Hermano Suchar is Bolivian and Spanish-speaking. Is she a 'plant', then?"

Worsley shook her head.

"They don't think so now. They found that her office and home phone had been tampered with, bugged. The IT folks think it gave - whomever - the mobile number Cronin was using. From that through GPS software, it gave his location. They are finding surveillance bugs on Cronin's equipment, too, at the office and at his home. It looks like some technician had been in very recently to install them, fishing for exactly this sort of lead to find Cronin."

Catrin pursed her lips. "That's a pretty professional organization out to get Cronin and protect Lowell, then, ma'am."

Worsley looked at her.

"I know what you are thinking, Catrin but SIS doesn't operate inside the UK and, if they did, they would know what type of round to use for an accurate long shot through plate glass, I assure you. So I don't think it was them."

She paused, reflecting.

"God, I hope not; 'pudding in your face' is one thing; this is organized crime, we believe. There is a lot more than some paintings and a deal sweetener in this."

She smiled. "Architectural glass and ballistics; funnily enough, with my time in DPB I know more about that subject than I do about art. Speaking of which, I think it is about time we told John and Keith your news, before it leaks, don't you?"

"Yes, ma'am, I do."

Catrin stood up and took a deep breath as Worsley exited before her, asking her team outside for their attention. As she did so, she noticed a mark on the sleeve of her jacket. It was not gravy, thank God, but something picked up during the events of the morning. She smiled, remembering her first visit to meet Worsley here, a sudden call for her to appear during a shift in Brixton. She had a mark on her uniform then, too. It was a good omen, perhaps?

She went out to join the team gathering around Worsley feeling already, in a sense, she had moved on to new things.

39 VALETTA

"It's gorgeous; the weather, the view and the food," enthused Melanie to Jian Li, "I am so glad we came after all."

The three women, Melanie, Li and Jean, were in a restaurant called 'Giannini' in Valetta, Malta, dining on a balcony looking over the harbour. It was their second time at the restaurant in three days. What she meant by 'after all' was that they came to Malta anyway after Chris and Catrin had cancelled at the last minute. They were having a good time.

Li had talked to Catrin, Melanie and Jean about her sudden assignment to a three-week course in Malta. As the island was such a short distance from London compared with Hong Kong, they had talked about the four of them getting cheap flights for a long weekend visit, with investigation of the logistics and the inevitable discussion of timings and 'what to do'.

Then Catrin called on the Wednesday night before the weekend.

"Chris and I can't come, I am sorry, Li. I just told Jean and Melanie. Something has come up."

Work; one of her cases, or one of Chris's perhaps, Li assumed.

Then Catrin, seeming to read her thoughts, said in spurts of incompletely thought-out explanation, "It's not a case, it's… I accepted a new position but it is not public knowledge yet. I have to sort out a lot of things. There are some changes taking place and I shouldn't say anything, but I agreed to a transfer within the Met. I have to go on a training course and I just can't get away. Li, I am sorry."

She stopped.

Li said, "A new job; you are still a detective, though?" she asked.

Perhaps this was the sort of news that Emily Yang had suggested, Li wondered; that Catrin was being relocated, for protection. She recalled how important it had been for Catrin to get the job with the Art Crime Unit. They had just started their friendship in Bangor.

Catrin's voice came down the phone line. "No. Look, I can't say more really, but I will still be a police officer with the Met. I have gone through it just now with Jean and Melanie. They will fill you in when they get there. To be honest, it's a whirl for me at present and I just feel so bad about cancelling."

Li said, "Catrin, it's OK, it can't be helped. And I am here for another two weeks so, who knows?"

She added, impulsively, "If you don't get down here I will see about routing back to Hong Kong through Heathrow; try to see you then."

Catrin sounded better when she next spoke; relieved.

"Thanks for being so understanding, Li. I owe you one, I know."

It was only later, Li realised, that her off-the-cuff response to her friend actually provided the solution she needed.

After nearly a week in Valetta, Jian Li was a reasonably competent guide for the visit of her friends to the beautiful old city. There was only so much that could be done in a few days and they went for the highlights.

Li also had an intensive course of study to follow at IMLI. Her short course was called, 'Maritime legislation drafting; consultation approaches with the regulated sectors', a title which made Melanie look at her and playfully go cross-eyed when she told them about it.

Li had already seen that the strange idea that came either from Enlai Lin or her boss actually was potentially valuable to her company; 'strategically', to use Enlai's term. Already she had met two officials from Asia and one from the USA in positions with maritime authorities that were important to LinTan Shipping and she had enjoyed being able to talk to them in a relaxed and academic atmosphere.

Her other challenge was to identify which positions in their large LinTan organisation could benefit from both the contacts made and the potential study areas. Mr. Lin had said she needed to identify the type of person who should attend, who would fit in.

"They have to represent the company well, Jian Li, and study and do well; they are not there simply to meet regulators; that wouldn't work. Think about it."

She was missing James Hoi, her boyfriend now, back in Hong Kong. They talked daily, generally more than once. It was a good sign for their relationship.

Her mother had made a comment to her before she left, clearly indicating that her father had conveyed the news about James, which he must have heard from Mr. Yau. Her mom had suggested inviting him to dinner.

Li said, "In time, mom. I like him and he likes me, but I don't think we are in any rush. He is busy and so am I. It needs to develop naturally, if it does at all. But once I feel it is... serious enough, I will let you know."

Her mother then wanted to know more about his family.

Again, she kept it vague other than to say, "You should talk to dad. James's grandfather has been buying suits and other clothes from Coulter & Yarrow for many years."

She smiled at her mother's expression; clearly her dad had not mentioned it. A family that bought its suits from Coulter & Yarrow had the right economic standing to please her mother.

Inevitably Catrin and Chris were a major topic of discussion between the three women. Li found out more about the new position that Catrin would be taking up and part of the reason for it.

Jean said, "She is under a lot of strain, Li, as we have told you before. We think that she is holding up but the only alternative is, she says, a new identity and a new start. We can't even comprehend that, really, a new name for her. And a new place to live; not seeing her like we do now. It is very upsetting to even think of it, for us; imagine what it must be like for her and Chris?"

Li said, "It seems from what you say that this new position will protect her, perhaps, from this triad threat?

In her mind was whether or not it was something she would raise with Mr. Yau.

Jean nodded, sitting beside Melanie, but her partner just shook her head, saying flatly, "I don't give that much credit myself, but I can't say that to her and Chris. The only thing that will stop this man is an arrest and even then, I don't know. Perhaps it will only be when he gets his comeuppance in that weird world of his. It could happen anytime to the evil sod, with the nature of gangs and their in-fighting."

Li was thinking that the whole reality of Catrin's dilemma was amplified for her by the concern being expressed by Jean and Melanie. She too wondered about how successful a strategy this job change would prove to be.

On Monday afternoon, as they parted at the airport for Jean and Melanie to go through security, the couple had made one more failed attempt to address the issue that Li had pre-paid for their hotel, not just made the reservation. The hotel desk manager had been part of the plot they discovered, as they checked out.

"Your friend said that if I told you when you checked in you would give her trouble all through the weekend. But your balance is zero."

They failed miserably at redressing that. Jian Li would

never say it, but she knew that running the pottery had its up and downs and these two women didn't have a lot of free cash at times.

They waved goodbye as they entered the security area. In two weeks, Li thought, I will be back here at the airport, heading back to Hong Kong.

As she left the building a Chinese limo driver came across to her and she waved him away smiling. They had travelled out in a taxi but she had a weekly bus pass for Valetta and was happy to use the system.

But he came forward anyway, now pulling out a smart-phone and saying softly, "Miss Yang, for you. If you would care to get into the car, I will drive you back to your residence."

She looked at the phone, seeing the face of Emily Yang staring out of the screen.

She nodded and climbed in the back seat as the driver gently shut the door.

Yang said, "Jian Li, I assure you that it is coincidence that the friends of Sergeant Sayer and yourself were in Malta at the time I wanted to talk to you. But not a surprise to me; you are quite close geographically, London and Malta. But once I knew that you had visitors, I waited; it will make it easier."

In the quiet of the vehicle, Li could hear Emily Yang quite clearly from the phone's speaker. She had recovered her composure at this unexpected turn.

Emily said, "Sayer told you, I hope, that she has a new job? Yes, I can see it in your face, so you need say nothing, break no promise."

Jian Li expressed her surprise, "How do you know about -"

Emily cut her off.

"It is our business; quite literally our business, in fact. Confidential information is the business base of my enterprise, Folding Square, as you may recall."

Jian Li nodded.

Emily moved on to the point of the call.

"Prepare yourself. I am going to show you a picture, but only briefly."

Emily's gaze moved down the screen, presumably to a keyboard of whatever system she was using.

Then the image of a dead man slumped in an easy chair came on to the small screen in front of Li. While there were no marks on his body, Jian Li had no doubt that he was truly dead; seeing the eyes, the slackness in the face and limbs.

After a second the screen returned to show Emily's face; she was looking intently at Li.

"Are you OK? It is a shock, I know, but we had to communicate this to you in a way that would leave no doubt at all, believe me. Your driver has a flask with tea and there are bottles of water and soft drinks in the compartment by you; he can pull over if you need some time to recover. I still need to talk to you."

She said something quickly in a dialect Li didn't follow; Hokkien perhaps, she thought, and the driver looked back at her through the rear view mirror. He had an earpiece in, clearly following the events on audio. He said something back into a microphone.

"It's a shock, but I am OK, really," said Li. She added, "But who is…" realising she knew the answer already.

Li's face showed that she understood.

Yang said, "Yes, it is Nam Wu. Two days ago."

She continued, seeing that Jian Li would be able to take it in.

"Did your friend mention also that her new position would place her very close to top-level personnel in the Metropolitan Police?"

Li said, "You seem to know everything. Yes, she had been told it would help reduce the risk of an attack on her by Wu, she mentioned that. No triad wants to be seen as attacking a figurehead of a police force, she said. Is that true?"

Emily said, "Yes. And in our societies we aren't under contract. We take oaths of membership; seemingly quaint and out-of-date oaths to others but, believe me, binding oaths nonetheless."

"I have read about them," said Jian Li. "They seem very old."

Emily smiled. "They are."

Her face turned serious.

"One of the thirty-six oaths is this; 'I must never cause harm or bring trouble to my sworn brothers or Incense Master. If I do so I will be killed by myriads of swords.' Do you know what an Incense Master does?"

Jian Li shook her head.

"He or she looks after ceremonies."

Jian Li looked even more puzzled.

Emily said, "The Incense Master of Ten Dragons went to see Nam Wu after the news of Sayer's appointment was made known.

"Mr. Yau had spoken with a number of enterprises in the UK, in Malaysia and in Hong Kong. Not all - there are too many - but a number of very old, very established, traditional organizations. They agreed that any planned actions against Sayer and Farra, the Malaysian, must be dropped, given the police pressure on all enterprises as a result of this incident. We had heard around that time that Sayer was being offered a 'witness protection' type programme of some sort, a new identity.

"Given Wu's announcement of his vow to kill her, it was clearly going to get messier and more protracted. This would be very bad for business for our enterprises collectively.

"The news of Sayer's new position came in just before Mr. Yau went to see the leader of the Ten Dragons in Hong Kong, the Mountain Master. He is a person Mr. Yau has known for many years. Mr. Yau conveyed the essence of his discussions; that the risk of 'causing harm or bringing trouble to sworn brothers' in the larger sense far outweighed the issue of retribution for the death of two members of Ten Dragons, particularly as the death of one should be seen honestly; it was as the result of a hasty and ill-planned action, not the work of the police.

"The Mountain Master agreed. They were both now concerned by the latest development. No enterprise would attack a senior police officer for no reason, as you say, so it made the decision even clearer. He told Mr. Yau it would be addressed; he gave him his word, in fact."

"On the first visit by a senior member of Ten Dragons to talk with Wu, the request from the Mountain Master was politely refused. It was a request only and Nam Wu reiterated to the messenger that he had sworn revenge."

She paused. It was clear to Li that Yang had a script to follow but that she wasn't totally happy with sharing so much information.

"It was a Ten Dragon's decision alone, of course. During his own visit, the Incense Master gave Wu the option; a syringe or sign a paper renouncing any future action against Sayer and the Malaysian policeman. It was not a request this time. Wu chose the syringe, using it himself; an honorable outcome for a loyal member of Ten Dragons, one that they fully expected. Not death by swords but death, nevertheless. Chosen by him rather than betray either his oaths of revenge made for the two men killed or, worse still, to act against his Dragon brothers' wishes and his triad oaths."

Jian Li was reminded again of the cold, analytical side that Emily Yang presented in these matters.

"I see, I think. Catrin is safe then? In this respect, I mean?"

Emily Yang nodded. "Yes, she is."

Then Li saw a possible complication, perhaps the real reason for the call.

She said, "I assume the authorities will become aware of Wu's death? Nam Wu's funeral will become known and so the Malaysian Police will then inform the police in London?"

Emily said, "No. In fact, that will not happen. A small funeral ceremony with key members of his family within the enterprise is being arranged very privately. It will not be leaked. There are factions who may not agree with the Mountain

Master's decision.

"We understand it will be weeks or months, perhaps longer, before his death becomes widely known, for reasons I can't go into. He will appear to simply remain in hiding and his duties within the society are being re-assigned. Others will just assume this issue of vengeance is his primary focus now.

"You are being placed in an extraordinary position of trust by Mr. Yau in receiving this information, I might add, Jian Li. Can you see that?"

Li nodded. It was now completely evident that Emily Yang was not comfortable with so much internal triad information being revealed.

She continued, "We want this out in the open too. At least, the other enterprises would, if they knew. It would perhaps reduce the heavy-handed dealings by the police with us at present. But we have to respect the wishes of Ten Dragons. As soon as it is possible it will be leaked - but not by us."

Li said, "So what am I supposed to do? Now I know, do I tell Catrin? I can't do that, from what you say, but somehow I need to let her know the threat is removed. The strain is eating away at her..."

Yang said, "That is the principal reason for calling you now. You have a choice to make. You now know she is no longer being threatened and it may only be weeks or months until this becomes visible, anyway, as I said.

"If you choose to tell her before then, we insist that you convey the news only in person, face to face, not by phone or internet. You can provide no detail or explanation, yet you still need to convince her that it is behind her; that she can't go checking for separate verification, inform the police force she works for or talk about it with others, either. Those are the conditions we impose on you, and for you to impose on her. If you do not think she will be able to meet those, you cannot tell her anything.

"But, Jian Li, Mr. Yau has fulfilled your request for help. If you sort it out well, you can remove the burden from your friend. You cannot, of course, mention Folding Square, or Ten

Dragons, Mr. Yau or me; any of this, in fact. All that you have seen and heard today is just to convince you. But you must not betray our trust at all. Understood?"

Jian Li nodded. "Thank you, for all that you and Mr. Yau did and… I will respect it. I am not sure how to explain to Catrin Sayer, but I will do so, when I can, in a manner that meets your stipulations."

She thought, I can't meet all of them; Catrin is already aware of some of this anyway, but I can honor the spirit of the commitment.

Emily nodded, "You are a lawyer, good with words. You will find a way. Goodbye, Jian Li. Now please pass this phone back to the driver."

"Goodbye, Emily," she said, as the call ended.

She passed the phone over to the front seat, looking up and seeing that they were now close to the university complex. The driver pulled over, in front of an office entrance.

"Miss Yeung, it is probably best that you walk from here. Is that OK?" he said.

"Yes," she said. "Thank you."

She picked up her bag off the seat and moved to open the door. He beat her to it, racing round to the passenger side, ever the perfect chauffeur.

She got out then remembered her original plan at the airport had been to call Catrin, let her know that Jean and Melanie were on their way home. She walked across to one of her favorite cafés, bought some tea and started to phone, then stopped, cancelling the call.

'Factions who would not agree…' Emily had said.

Suddenly she realised that as much as Michael Yau had inserted himself into the middle of this as the representative of a broader set of triad interests, he had taken steps to ensure that Li was totally unconnected. That was the reason for the call, using a smartphone belonging to the driver, the specifics of how she was to do the communication with Catrin. All this was to keep her safe. Even having her out of Asia in the

Mediterranean at this time was probably an element of it, she realised.

If so, it meant that Enlai Lin may not know the details but she was sure he was involved, somehow. It explained the trip; the set-up for it at short notice, out of the blue.

As the logic of it came together, she sent a text instead to Catrin. 'Jean and Melanie are on the way home. Melanie's nose is sunburnt, despite our best advice. Can we talk? Let me know when you will be free to do so.'

Catrin owed her, she had said. And she was going to claim that debt. They were going, literally or figuratively, to Glanrafon Hill for another conversation. She hadn't worked through yet how she would do it.

EPILOGUE

Her predecessor, now Inspector Colin Egar, had explained not only her new job, but the 'unspoken' parts of the position during their first meeting to talk about transition.

"You will be busy, Catrin, particularly when Hunt travels, locally in the Met area, around the UK or other places. She is out a lot around here each week, it seems, and is also involved in international activities among police networks. Those are hardly visible at the ground level. Expect two- or three-day trips with her to Europe or North America perhaps, spent almost entirely on planes or in meeting rooms and hotels, that sort of thing.

"Sometimes you will be at her side; other times you will be with your counterparts keeping an eye on all of them as the leaders talk. In some of the events, particularly community police support, you will probably find people talking to you as much as her - but still you will keep her in your sights; you will be trained accordingly. She knows what your job is and respects it.

"And, just so you are clear, this is going to be about two years. Ian Ross, my predecessor, was around three years for some reason. But two is usual. And you were chosen for the same reason all your predecessors were; she thinks you are dedicated to the Met, that you have shown yourself to be so and you have the capacity to go far in its service. That, you will find out, is the unwritten entry criterion for this job.

"I am not complimenting you or me, although I know of the work you have done; it's just a fact you should know and pass on in time to your own successor. You won't find it in any job description, nor will she talk about it.

"But she always has her eyes open, talent-spotting, lining up possible candidates; moving them on when it seems right to her. So plan on two years, see how it goes; you will probably know when she has someone in her sights, as I did with you."

He smiled.

"Now George, her driver, he has been with her since the days of wooden wheels and Hansom cabs. You will work very closely with him. He will tell you to start counting the number of detour visits to St. Paul's Cathedral you will make."

Catrin laughed, "I know about those; it was my first real contact with her. I was in grubby jeans off-duty at the pottery and she whisked me there on the way to somewhere else, so that's no surprise."

He looked pensive for a moment then smiled.

Catrin said, "Is that how she picked you, can I ask?"

Egar said, "Not quite, but not far off. I was in community policing, not investigative work like you, a constable stationed at West Ham. It was an incident that caught Hunt's attention. I talked a young girl out of killing herself. I just happened to be close by when the call came in. I grew up in West Ham so I fit in more than most and somehow it worked with the teenager.

"Some community leaders were complaining around that time to my superintendent about the heavy-handed policing of youth in the area. Then the same people became sweetness and light about me, about what happened with the girl."

His face took on a smirk of pleasure, a conspiratorial look.

"So I am in the station, had just come on shift when I get called to see the AC; she was there in the Jag with George and Ian Ross. It was soon after Ian was in this position, I found out later. They had taken over a meeting room and I get pulled in. She thanked me for the work I did with the teenager, asked me about it then said things that showed she had read my file before she left. I hardly said anything, I think. She was just assessing me, face to face.

"Then she was gone. As I walked back thinking how weird it was, my inspector comes barrelling down the corridor, straightening his tie, looking like he was late for his own wedding.

"He said, 'Where is the AC?'. 'I think she left, sir,' I said, 'at least, she was heading that way.' He looked so disappointed."

Catrin smiled, picturing it all.

"'What did she want?' he asked. I told him what happened. Her last comment, I said, was, 'Am I studying for my sergeant's exams?' So I said to him, 'I think I need to get your approval for the course, sir'."

Catrin let out a peal of laughter.

"She did that with me too, ask about studying for sergeant's exams; in St. Paul's, no less."

Egar smiled. "She loves only two things, I think; the Metropolitan Police Service and St. Paul's Cathedral. God knows what she will do when she retires. It can't be too many years off."

As they wrapped up, Colin Egar said, "What next for you? Milton and more firearms training, I expect?"

Catrin nodded. She said, "But first I have a couple of days off; I am going to see someone in Bangor."

Egar said, "But you are from South Wales."

"Yes, I am off to see friends, not family, this time."

~~

Jane Worsley said, "Australia, it seems, if the DNA ties in. The victim was a woman in the sex trade. She died of asphyxiation, aspirating her own vomit. But she had been badly beaten, with abdominal bruising. She had been punched or kicked in the stomach and must have thrown up and… you know the rest."

She had gone up to Coltrane's office to break the news.

Coltrane asked, "And it ties in with Hodson's ship being in port then?"

Worsley replied, "Yes; Cronin was also serving on it, but was on leave at the time, in the UK, so it doesn't relate to him. He may not have even been aware.

"The victim was known to target sailors for her clients and had, on two occasions, been involved with allegations of fleecing them. The attacker's DNA samples they hold come from skin and blood, probably from the knuckles or hand, skinned on a pendant she was wearing.

"But who knows what will happen? I am not sure that it will merit extradition, unless they have other evidence to tie him into the beating and her time of death. He could argue she was alive and well when he left her, it was someone else. So it really rests with the Aussies now."

John Obi had received, at last, Hodson's career postings and their timings from the Royal Navy. As expected, Hodson had not co-operated at all during questioning. Worsley had recalled reading Cox's comment in the report of the interview in Rome about 'something Hodson had done overseas' so she set John Obi the task of looking into possible incidents that could involve the man.

There were only two extended periods when, for Navy purposes, Hodson was overseas. Worsley filed details with Interpol; it was a long shot and she expected nothing. A policeman in Sydney had contacted Obi about it, seeing as he was the contact person flagged in the file.

It may mean Tony Hodson could be facing more charges and time inside; and not necessarily in a British prison, but it was early days on that one.

Coltrane said, "Thank you, Jane. I missed that one, I do admit, and I was there when Cox mentioned Hodson's claim. I do owe you, and I know that DC Soames is looking at your vacancy. His promotion has been approved and, as much as I would like to keep him, if he applies for Sayer's old position and you want him, there won't be any objections raised by us."

She looked at Coltrane and smiled. "Well, if he applies, we will see. And we both owe Sayer, I think."

She liked to make her own decisions on who was suitable or not for ACU work. Art knowledge wasn't the only factor, but she saw that Neville was trying to be helpful.

"We do, indeed," said Neville Coltrane.

SIS had said nothing about Sir Kenneth Lowell. The case development in preparation for trial was proceeding well, they had heard, and the Bolivians were making positive noises on the potential for the return of the two paintings by George Stubbs. It was in the hands of Caldwell and the diplomats now.

Both senior officers had been receiving plaudits for the work of their teams on the case. And the ACU had sailed through the SRC review intact. When Jane had broached the issue with Superintendent Taylor about a possible budget increase, he had simply shaken his head.

"Let's leave it this time, Jane; sail through on success and quietly exit as they focus on others with their paring knives."

~~

"Idris retired four months ago," said Dafydd. "He wanted no fuss, just worked until the last day and he wouldn't let us do more for him than a farewell drink at the Glan that evening. No party, no cake, nothing. I think he was a bit overwhelmed that it crept up on him."

Detective Chief Inspector Dafydd Powys now worked at the Colwyn Bay headquarters of the North Wales Police. Prior to his promotion he had been the inspector leading the missing person investigation around Han Yeung through to its conclusion; the recovery of the body and the trials of those involved. It had been Catrin's first case with the ACU and she had worked closely with Idris Bowen, Powys' sergeant.

They were working through the updates of people they knew in common.

Dafydd, his wife Marjorie, Li and Catrin were in the Bridge Inn Restaurant in Menai Bridge on the Isle of Anglesey. Instead of routing back through Heathrow, Li had flown to Manchester after insisting that she and Catrin should meet up with the Powys couple.

"I'd love to, if I can get away, Li. I have not seen Dafydd since… the case."

Li said, "Only one night away, Catrin; dinner, a night at the Eryl Môr Hotel and then I will be off back to Hong Kong. I want to take the opportunity in person to thank them for everything; but particularly for the Ceinwen, face to face. You should be there. We four were together then. It would be very special for me, please, for the four of us to be together."

"I'll do it," said Catrin firmly, making the decision.

The sail on the Ceinwen had been her own last day on the case in Bangor. Dafydd and Marjorie owned the sailing boat and had taken Li and Catrin to the spot in the Menai Strait where Han Yeung's body had been dumped, to place flowers and say prayers.

Dafydd said, "Idris and his wife bought a bungalow near Scarborough. His daughter is in the job; at least she was. Now she may as well be. She is married to a Yorkshire Constabulary sergeant. They have two children, so Idris and his wife are enjoying being grandparents, we hear."

Dafydd and Marjorie had been delighted with the news of the visit, albeit a short one, and found Li had already made the restaurant reservation.

She had said, "Dinner is my gift, if you will drive us there and back, Dafydd."

It was only a ten minute drive between the two locations, the restaurant and the hotel. Li had planned it carefully.

Catrin had arrived in Bangor by train and had taken a taxi to the hotel, to find that Li was already there. She had arrived only two hours earlier and they spent the time catching up on their lives. In no time at all, it seemed, the call from Dafydd came in that he and Marjorie were on the way to pick them up.

After they had ordered their meals, Li produced a box from the small bag she had brought along.

"For you two, with my everlasting gratitude," she said formally, passing it to Marjorie, who in turn passed it to Dafydd to open.

It turned out to be a model yacht made in silver wire, intricately woven and soldered together, a delicate filigree of metal. Dafydd held it up, rotating it, his pleasure apparent.

"A '25', like the Ceinwen. It's simply… wonderful! I haven't seen anything like it before. Li, thank you, but where did you get this?"

Marjorie said, "Don't be rude, Dafydd. Thank you, Li, we will treasure it."

She walked around the table and gave her a hug as Dafydd continued to be lost in the detail of the piece.

Li said, "In Malta; there is a tradition to make models of a local boat in this manner, a Dghajsa it is called. I went to a jeweller's shop which hand-makes such boats with a photo of a Beneteau First 25 and they were happy to do it. In fact, the man was quite excited to try. It's local, high purity silver that they use."

Dafydd passed it to Marjorie and then looked at Li.

"It's wonderful. Thank you again."

Li said simply, "It's a token; simply that, of gratitude that will endure in me for all you did. From the time my dad came over after Han disappeared, to the time you and this one…" - she pointed at Catrin - "duped me during my first visit to the police station, to the sail on the Ceinwen itself."

He looked at her, suddenly serious. "You are welcome on that boat, or to visit and use our Ceinwen anytime."

Marjorie reached out and held his hand. She looked at Li, smiling. "Now that is a big one, this man offering you the use of his baby."

Li looked them both and at Catrin who was sitting smiling, taking it all in.

She said, "One day I will take you up on that."

On the drive back Li said suddenly, "Dafydd, can you drop Catrin and me at the Main Arts Building, please? We need to take a walk together. We will get back to the hotel on foot from there."

Catrin's head spun round to look at Li, but she said nothing. The route through Upper Bangor passed the university buildings but it was still a good walk to the hotel from that point. It was also near the top of Glanrafon Hill, she thought.

They said their goodbyes in the car park by the Old Library; hugs, handshakes and promises, well meant at the time, to stay in touch better than they had. As they watched the tail-lights pull away, Catrin said, "You know, I wondered, on the train ride up, well half-wondered…"

Li took her arm. "Catrin, let's take a walk down Penrallt to the top of Glanrafon Hill, for old times' sake. And then we can walk all the way back up again."

She had decided she had to do this in the same place as last time, face to face. She led Catrin down Back Regent Street, down the steps to Lower Penrallt with students and townspeople ahead and behind them.

They stood at the junction with Glanrafon Hill as other people passed by them. Cars were driving up and down the hill, masking any conversation, but Li waited for a good gap in the pedestrian traffic.

"Catrin, I have something to tell you, by the same rules we agreed last time we walked here, when I told you about Enlai Lin and Michael Yau and how they link to my dad."

Catrin said nothing, just waited. Clearly, for Li this was a big moment and she didn't want to spoil it for her.

Jian Li started to speak carefully.

"When we last talked on the phone about Glanrafon Hill, about Nam Wu, about me talking to Michael Yau, I told you they would tell me nothing more. Well, I have heard more, I can't say from whom or how I know, but you are safe, Catrin, you are safe. Nothing more will be coming out of Malaysia to harm you. I was told that and I believe it. So should you."

Catrin looked at her, astonished, taking in the expression on her friend's face, the seriousness of the message. Li really believed it, she saw.

After taking a moment to consider her words, she said, "Nam Wu took a vow to kill me and Sergeant Farra before the anniversary of the death of the man I shot, Li. No-one knows about the deadline, literally a deadline, outside his triad and the police authorities, we believe. But I am telling you now, seeing as we are sharing secrets. He may have to postpone his vengeance now I have my new job, but he isn't going to stop. So whatever you have heard, I believe you mean it in good faith but -"

Li cut across her, hearing the doubt and rejection in Catrin's voice.

"He took bigger oaths than the one to kill you and Sergeant Farra, Catrin. I can't say why but, I know, I truly know, you are safe. You need to believe me because that's all I can really tell you, you see. I love you and you are safe."

So much for the legal eloquence that Emily Yang went on about, Li suddenly thought, as she burst into tears.

Catrin didn't finish her sentence. She stood there, silently looking at her friend and thinking about what this meant. The bigger oath must mean a triad oath and to break those, she knew, the consequences were usually fatal. She had read a lot about triads in the past months. So Hunt's logic was correct; Wu would need to back off…

Then it hit her.

Li had said, 'I know, I truly know you are safe'. Knowing her friend and her manner of speaking, she would only say that if she had proof herself. She suddenly realised that Wu had already refused to back off and had been dealt with somehow.

As it sunk in she felt the weight of her burden leave her; the dread of Asian strangers, the ever-present worry that she could suddenly look at an unknown face and her life would be over; just like that, that fast. She had to lean back against the stone wall, overcome finally by the realisation that it must be true what Li said.

She let out a sob, then another and put her hands to her face, saying, "Oh my God, it's true after all. He must be dead."

Then she, too, was in tears.

The two male students strolling down Lower Penrallt lost in quiet conversation rounded the corner and found two women standing looking at each other, crying.

"What's wrong?" said one, with a Welsh accent.

"Nothing," answered Li.

The student noticed that the Chinese woman was regaining her composure, apparently happy, not sad after all, whereas the taller blonde had lost it completely.

Li added, after a moment, "But thank you for asking. We used to study here. We came back to see the place and visit some people and… it's a little overwhelming."

They nodded, understanding, ready to move on rather than pry or embarrass them but the other man stopped again. Li realised when he spoke that he was from somewhere in northern England.

"What did you study here?"

Li said, "Law for me and fine arts for her."

Catrin was looking away, trying to get it together, wiping her eyes.

"Ah, that explains it," said the Welshman. "Arts types are very emotional, aren't they? Dan and I are 'Eng.' students."

Engineers, of course, are impervious to emotional outbursts, he implied.

"You two don't fancy coming for a drink, perhaps, at the Harp? It's where we are going; it will cheer you up. Do you remember it?"

Catrin started smiling through the tears, listening to the talk, realising that the men were trying to pick them up, both literally and figuratively, and take them to a pub.

She said, half-crying, half-laughing, "No thank you, but thanks for asking. We are heading up the hill, not down."

Li said 'goodbye' and the two women set off re-tracing their steps as the men continued on their way.

After a moment Catrin spoke, her voice still unsteady, "You don't have to tell me more; I have worked it out, Li. I owe you and others you know a great debt of gratitude, the topic of the night, it seems. But can I tell Chris? I can't keep it from him forever; he's wound up about this, too."

Li nodded. "He wants to marry you, Catrin, I think; so yes, no secrets between you two because of me. But please, tell him no more than you know you are safe and believe it. The same conditions apply to him, though; Glanrafon Hill rules, right? No checking with people or databases or using police contacts to find out more. There must be nothing to indicate I have told you."

Catrin said, "Agreed. I will hold him to those. And Jared Farra - he is safe too, isn't he?"

Li looked at her. "I can't say, Catrin."

I'm a police officer, thought Catrin, reading her friend's face and tone of voice. You just have.

Li said, "Guanxi, Catrin, remember? Up the road there - she pointed in the right direction for Craig Y Don road - you saved my life. I feel better now that I have told you. But apart from Chris, nothing gets out, please respect that. I made promises too."

Catrin nodded. "You have my word."

She stopped, pulled Li towards her and hugged her. "Thank you, thank you. You have my promise - and, to use your word from earlier with Dafydd, my enduring friendship."

"Oh!" said Li, happy to have got the whole thing over with, "I know that."

~~

About a month later, at their regular meeting at the Shep Kip Mei Street bathhouse, the three men were talking away when Daniel Yeung said suddenly, "Jian Li told Eu-Meh yesterday that she is bringing James Hoi home for dinner. My wife is very excited and I hope it goes well."

"Tell her not to talk of marriage, or babies or engagements or... say anything; just watch and listen," said Enlai.

"Ah," said Michael, "The kids will know; they will expect it from the mother; the young men always do."

Daniel laughed then said, "I almost forgot."

He stepped and limped out up the steps of the large bath, put on a robe and delved into a bag on a bench. He pulled out two beautifully wrapped boxes, returned to the bath side, leaned down and held them visible for Michael Yau and Enlai Lin to see.

"One for each of you - presents from my daughter."

The two men got out of the bath and donned robes also. Enlai Lin managed to open his present first. It was a filigree miniature of a Maltese dghajsa, made in gold wire, the thin metal bent, folded and joined in complex patterns to form the work. Yau's was the same.

Daniel said, "Eu-Meh looked it up; she received a similar one made of silver. They are a Maltese traditional boat usually made of local silver, but Jian Li must have found a shop which makes them in gold wire also. They are very nice, yes?"

"They are indeed," said Enlai. "Yolande will be pleased. But Jian Li sent them through you?"

He wondered why Li had not presented his gift to him directly, if he was going to be given one. She had been back nearly three weeks from the Malta trip and had produced a useful report of her course at IMLI, one that was positive about the strategic benefits of sending employees for training there.

Daniel and Enlai were talking about the small sculpture when they noticed Michael Yau sitting silently, no longer looking at his boat but at the small note that had been inside the box. Enlai checked his box and opened a similar note.

"What does it say?" smiled Daniel, "is it from Jian Li?"

"No," said Enlai Lin slowly. "It is a note from the maker, a jeweller called Depiro. He hopes we like the dgha - boats - and wants us to know that they are made of Welsh gold, specially provided by the client. He drew the wire from the small bar personally. As he hadn't worked with this gold source before, in the event of any problems he asks that we return the item and it will be repaired seamlessly and sent back to us at no charge."

Enlai looked at Michael. The fact that they had both received identical gifts and the reason for choosing the specific metal was not lost on either man. Daniel was looking on, innocently oblivious, just proud of his daughter and her generosity to his friends.

NOTES

 This is a work of fiction. Some of the places in this novel are real, others are entirely fictitious. Any portrayal of a particular place or organisation as part of this work is fictional. All persons and events are the product of the author's imagination and are used fictitiously. Any resemblance to actual persons living or dead is entirely coincidental.

George Stubbs (1724-1806) was born in Liverpool, the son of a currier, a leather worker, who lived in Ormond Street, several miles and an estuary away from where I grew up. He worked with his father until age 15 or 16 it is believed. For one of England's great painters, there is scant information available about him.

My earliest home as a child was downwind of a leather processing factory, the British Leather Tannery in Tranmere, established in 1824. I can attest to the malodorous nature of the early stages of converting hide to leather. Apart from any artistic drive, it must have been generally a much more pleasant and healthier occupation for Stubbs to become an artist rather than follow in his father's footsteps.

George Stubbs was largely self-taught until his brief apprenticeship with Hamlet Winstanley, arranged by his father as his own health deteriorated. It appears that Stubbs disagreed with Winstanley on routine copying work assignments almost from the outset and left to become a portrait artist in Northern England shortly thereafter. His passion for anatomical accuracy and his artistic skills led to his lesser known role as a medical illustrator and his more famous career as an equine painter.

There is no factual basis for George Stubbs or Hamlet Winstanley ever going to the village of Carnforth or working in the manner described here.

My thanks go to my wife Gill and my friend Jack Soule for pre-reading the drafts and making editing suggestions. Any remaining errors are entirely my own, of course.

ABOUT THE AUTHOR

Allan Jones lives in Ontario, Canada. He was born and grew up in Merseyside, England. By profession an industrial chemist, he worked for many years as a consultant on international chemical regulation. He has lived in or travelled to most of the regions featured in the Catrin Sayer novels.

IF YOU ENJOYED THE CARNFORTH DOUBLE …

Please read the sequel, the fifth novel in the series, THE POWYS DEACON. It is set two years later, as Catrin Sayer completes her assignment as a security officer and returns to art crime investigation, with a promotion.

An excerpt follows.

The B4363 now led down the hill as he headed west between the village of Bagginswood and the town of Kidderminster. The driver knew he was finally on the stretch close to his target.

During the day the fields and hedges showed gently undulating countryside, a mix of greens and browns, but at night they were a dark wall at the limit of the headlights.

In the variable darkness of a half-moon through cloud, the vehicle slowed as he followed the turn at the bottom, looking for the unmarked side road. Afterwards, as he neared the brow of a hill on the narrow lane, he dropped to sidelights; it was, after all, nearly three in the morning. The driver was being careful; he didn't want the headlights to flash over to the golf club. Just in case.

The entrance barrier to the service track was only twenty

yards ahead, just a simple swing bar of galvanized metal hinged at one post, with a padlock on the post at the other side. The lock was no problem for him; he had lock picks and a lot of experience using them. Once his vehicle was through the gap, he closed the barrier and placed an almost identical padlock, one for which he did have a key, on the barrier. Within seconds he was driving into the woods slowly using only the sidelights, unseen from the road.

In the unlikely event that anyone who wanted access to this track in the middle of the night arrived, they would find that their own key didn't allow them to open the barrier. He had things to do and he didn't want to be disturbed.

At the point where he saw the branch he had placed earlier, he switched off everything and waited with his windows lowered. To him, it was the most dangerous part of his plan, in a sense; idle time. But he wanted his eyes and hearing to adjust and he knew that takes time.

When he felt he was ready, he opened the door, got out and went around to the back, taking a deep breath before opening the tailgate door. Balance would be everything at this point. He wanted to do this cleanly and not leave more evidence of entry than necessary. He pulled the cover off the wrapped body and hauled it half-out. A stoop, a 'fireman's lift' and then he re-established his centre of balance… carefully. He stood still, panting from the effort. Rotating his line of sight, he walked slowly into the coppice, counting the paces, as he had earlier in daylight. He saw the log and the small dip just to the left and gladly dropped the load, freeing himself from the weight.

The log pulled free and rolled clear; a seven inch diameter downy birch, rotten at one end and with a number of radial remnants of its broken branches along its length. He pulled out the entrenching tool from its holder on his belt, opened it and started digging methodically. Better than a spade for close work, he struggled only once when he encountered a sizeable stone. He had to work around it to lift it clear.

It was the only hard part of this phase. After the sharpened edge of the tool cut through the thin roots of ground vegetation, the soft humus lifted more easily than the sandy sub-soil. His eyes were on the task but his ears were tuned to the surroundings, listening for the first sign of any intruders.

Half an hour later the body of the man, now unwrapped but still in the clothes he had died in, was laid in the hole and positioned on his back, as he planned it. He added an initial covering of soil and took a breather, walking back to the vehicle to drink some water first, then some of the black coffee from the flask. Idle time again, but necessary; he wasn't the man he once was, he knew.

His final act was to return to the burial scene with the unframed painting, placing it face down above the soil-covered head. While the dead man may have refused to look at it in life, he now had no choice, at least symbolically, in death.

He said in a whisper the short prayer he had memorized; an extract on repentance from Deuteronomy.

After filling the grave he carefully pushed back the layer of vegetation debris that had been peeled away initially. Finally, he rolled the log back in place and stood back. There were several spots of fresh soil showing so he attended to those before concluding it was as good as it was going to get.

He first drove without lights slowly along the service track for about fifty yards, rounding a bend. He was unable to turn around so he reversed to the gate as evenly as possible, not stopping. In the unlikely event that anyone noticed his tyre tracks, his stopping point in the coppice would be away from the body.

His eyesight was good until he was near the side road, when the flash of headlights from a car on the B4363 in the distance ruined his night vision. But it showed clearly that he was nearing the barrier. By then it was no problem. Windows open and listening for traffic, he exited the path and refitted the original lock before taking off his surgical gloves, allowing his damp, sweaty hands to dry out.

As he climbed back into the driver's seat he felt the first

splatter of raindrops, the start of a shower. He hoped it would help to blur the tracks and settle the gravesite.

~~

Read more in the fifth Catrin Sayer mystery, THE POWYS DEACON.

www.ingramcontent.com/pod-product-compliance
Lightning Source LLC
Chambersburg PA
CBHW020402260626
47156CB00007B/2201

* 9 7 8 1 9 9 9 3 8 1 3 1 8 *